Nightingale

Sharon Ervin

CRIMSON
ROMANCE
F+W Media, Inc.

This edition published by
Crimson Romance
an imprint of F+W Media, Inc.
10151 Carver Road, Suite 200
Blue Ash, Ohio 45242
www.crimsonromance.com

Copyright © 2013 by Sharon Ervin

ISBN 10: 1-4405-6809-X
ISBN 13: 978-1-4405-6809-1
eISBN 10: 1-4405-6810-3
eISBN 13: 978-1-4405-6810-7

Cover art © 123RF

To Bill

Acknowledgments

Peggy Fielding, author, friend, mentor, for seeing potential in this one and awarding it first place in the Historical Romance Category of the Oklahoma Federation of Writers competition.

McAlester's McSherry Writers for candor and patient critiquing over the years.

My sister Frannie Claxton and fellow writer Margaret Golla for sharing expertise on the dispositions and behavior of great, spirited horses.

Historians who made researching England in the 1840s terribly distracting.

Jennifer Lawler and Julie Sturgeon and their staffs for understanding the story I intended to write and clarifying.

Chapter One

Great Britain, 1840

The earth trembled and Jessica Blair's bare feet flew over the narrow dirt path, which was still warm at twilight after the first sunny day of spring. The rumbling was too steady to herald artillery or a turn in the weather. It was hooves and they sounded as if the horses were closing rapidly.

Jessica hiked up her skirt, wadded it over an arm and broke into a full, unladylike gallop. She hadn't taken time to put on the oversized lace-up boots, which jostled clumsily under one elbow. Her lungs burned as she pushed her lean young body, desperate to reach the coops and protect the newly emerged chicks. Their lives depended on her. She had vowed to protect and defend them from all enemies, foreign or domestic. Giving her oath before the nine scruffy hens, Jessica had contemplated enemies like foxes or raccoons. Nevertheless, she would defend them, her body of no more value to the world than theirs, if measured by the meager living she eked out for herself and her ailing, widowed mother.

The thunderous pounding grew louder. Foliage snapped and lowering tree limbs cracked as the relentless riders plundered the path behind her. Jessica needed to reach the twin boulders. She had chosen the site for her coops, thinking the promontories would protect the rickety pens. The stone outcroppings loomed side by side, separated only by the width of her narrow shoulders.

In her weeks of coming and going, Jessica inadvertently had worn a path to the place, one clearly visible even in the fading daylight. Her frequent use had widened it; perhaps giving the impression the path was a thoroughfare. It was not.

Jessica sliced between the twins and burst into the clearing. Dropping her boots and wadded skirts, she doubled over, bracing her hands on her knees, gulping air to feed her burning lungs. Her abrupt arrival set the roosting hens squawking in alarm, batting about in the cages she had constructed from scraps of barrels, and hoops from discarded casks.

In spite of her heart's pounding, she heard the relentless thud of hooves, clanging metal and fierce snorting as if the hounds of hell pursued the horses.

Straightening, suddenly aware of the coming darkness, she realized riders galloping headlong over the trail she had cut, probably would not see the stone pillars until they were upon them. She cringed at the image of animals and men injured or killed in the collision, harsh punishment for following her unwitting footpath.

Her breathing steadied, she slid back between the twins and studied the approach with no clear plan, only the hope she could stop the riders before their flight ended in disaster.

A horse exploded out of the night, hurtling toward her, a huge, black beast, his rounded eyes glistening, steam hissing from red, flaring nostrils. She flailed her arms and yelled. "Halt!"

The rider did not slow. He must be a stupid oaf to propel himself and his mount over such a poorly marked course. Still, she did not want the man to die of his stupidity and certainly could not allow such a ghastly end to his horse.

Fanning her skirts to gain attention, she screamed, "Halt! In the name of the Queen!" It was the only command she thought might bring the intemperate soul to his senses. She braced, prepared to jump to either side to avoid being trampled.

The first horse was almost on top of her when he suddenly planted his front feet, sat back on his haunches and skidded. Just before impact, he reared straight up. His hooves fanned the air over her head. Jessica threw her arms up as a shield and leaped to her left, squeezing her eyes closed.

An instant later, when there was no contact, she opened one eye to find the horse's front hooves still high above her head, striking one another and producing sparks which resembled a bevy of fireflies.

"Whoa," she shouted.

With snorting that sounded like a groan, the animal dropped his forefeet to the ground. His massive body quivered as he danced sideways. His eyes rolled and his sides heaved as horse and woman stood facing one another.

In her eighteen years, Jessica had never been that close to a horse and this one seemed particularly large and noisy, snorting and wheezing in turn.

"There, there, love," she crooned, certain she was more frightened than the animal. "It is only I, Sweetness, Jessica Blair." She resisted the impulse to look anywhere but into the horse's bulbous eyes. "Welcome to you and your intemperate master to my humble hatches." She smirked at the purposeful insult directed at the unseen rider.

When the rider didn't respond, she glanced up and leaned around only to find the saddle empty.

The destrier threw his head high and pranced in place. Metal clanked against metal, the noise she had identified before she had been able to see him.

"Where is your master, love?" She regarded him closely. "Is he lying in the road somewhere injured? He's not dead, is he, Sweetness?"

Eying her wildly, the horse lifted his nose then lowered it in a series of nods.

Jessica swallowed and eased closer. Raising an uncertain hand, she started to touch him, and then stopped. She wanted to quiet the magnificent animal, and he did seem to be calming.

"My, but you are huge," she whispered. His restless movements stopped and his ears flicked forward. "Your color is like midnight and you have a look of enchantment, all spirit and size and muscle." She lifted a hand again to touch him. He threw his head high and she gasped to see his neck slathered with thick white foam.

"What is this?" She studied the goo spattered over his chest and stringing from the dangling strap. She wiped a glob off him and cringed as it clung to her curious fingers. "Are you injured?"

The horse tossed his head, keeping his nose well above her reach while his occasional snorts dwindled to a nervous whickering. She flinched when he lowered his nose and bumped the side of her face. "Even if he mistreated you, you would not have thrown the dullard for revenge, would you? Of course you didn't. It is the role of some to serve and of others to be served. Like me, you appear to be the former."

She fingered the horse's bridle trying to think what she should do. He danced back several steps, his agitation reviving, reminding her that her voice quieted him.

"I have never had a private conversation with a horse." Again, her words calmed him. At her quiet stroking, her fingertips on his face, the animal eased closer. Prickling chills limned her arms as the horse nuzzled her hair, his breath warm against her sensitive nape. When he nibbled a strand of hair, she jerked, startling them both.

"Mind your manners, sir."

As if he understood, he steadied, his neck arched, his feet still. He glistened black beneath the globs of white froth that oozed and abandoned him in dollops. His saddle and tack were black to match his body. No wonder she hadn't been able to see him in the twilight or that one horse his size could sound like many.

She knew no better than to walk behind his rump, but he stood unmoving as her hands ran over his sides, swiping away the last remnants of the froth.

His master must be a large man, judging by the size of this animal and the length of the stirrups. An average-sized individual could scarcely throw a leg over such a monster.

Wondering again what had become of the rider; she turned and peered into the night, straining to see if a form lay on the footpath. She had neither seen nor heard anyone in the darkness, which had completely enveloped them. A full moon slipped for a moment from beneath its cloudy sheath to bathe the open area where they stood. The path beyond, however, was cloaked in the shadowy gloom of overhanging trees.

The horse had galloped, wild-eyed, snorting and whinnying as if the devil himself were in pursuit. Had his master mistreated him?

No. She had felt no welts of scarring. No blemishes of any kind. The clattering his hooves created earlier indicated he was shod. He appeared well fed and his coat was sleek, as if it were brushed regularly.

Perhaps his master had overindulged at a tavern and fallen off. Perhaps the man had been set upon by a thief. She considered again the length of the stirrups. It would probably have taken more than one thief to subdue this rider.

Perhaps she should search for him. How could she? A lone woman? Traveling the road at night? Especially if there were brigands about. She had nothing to steal, of course. She slanted her gaze at the horse. Except him. She would need to take him along in case they found his rider, particularly if they found the man incapacitated.

She stood on tiptoe to work the rein off over the horse's ears, then she looped the leather around a branch and ran back to the coops for her boots. As she put them on, she considered. In the dark, she might overlook a man lying in the brush at the side of the road. It would be wiser to wait for daylight.

She cast a guilty glance at the moon that beamed at the moment, denying her use of darkness as an excuse not to try.

If the man were lying in the road, some passerby probably already had rescued him.

What if he lay helpless? Or unconscious? Or dead?

Her imagination erupted with visions of a helpless wretch lying injured, crying out for assistance while help was delayed, wrestling with her own cowardice.

She resented the nudge, the same goading presence that prompted her to rescue abandoned birds and runaway horses. Could she, in good conscience, comfort the man's animal and not expend some effort searching for the master?

If she could ride the horse, the search would be easier. Also, mounted, she would feel less vulnerable to attack by men or animals.

She had never ridden a horse.

The decision would rest with him. If Sweetness would let her climb into the saddle, she would track back along the road, at least a little distance.

Returning to the horse, Jessica freed the rein and slipped her hand beneath the strap between his ear and his mouth. She applied pressure and he rocked into step beside her. She led him in a wide circle to line him up beside a fallen log, and again fitted the rein over his head.

How should she sit? The saddle was not properly cut for her to ride with her legs to one side, as ladies of the gentry rode. Her oversized dress and petticoat, a cousin's castoffs, might be generous enough to allow her to ride astride as a man would.

Speaking those thoughts quietly to the horse, Jessica stepped onto the log.

As large as it was, the saddle would provide ample seating. She fingered the leather strap, stalling. Brushing a hand over the saddle, front to back, she slipped a knot and accidentally released a garment tied behind.

The horse held steady as Jessica unfurled the rolled fabric. When she snapped the garment open, the mount's eyes rolled, but he only turned his head, as if curious to see what she was doing. It was a cloak, black of course, like the horse and his other accessories. It smelled of wool mingled with a distinctly male fragrance that was not altogether unpleasant. The weave was as soft as Mrs. Maxwell's silken stockings.

"This will serve," she whispered. If she could get into the saddle, she could wrap the cloak around her, and conceal her long, dark hair beneath the hood. Travelers would think her a young man. A youth traveling alone at night would be less remarkable than a girl. Hopefully no one would consider accosting him.

First, however, she must get herself into the saddle.

Would the owner of the horse be angry when she appeared in his clothing riding his horse? Would he accuse her of theft?

Perhaps not, if she rescued him. She prayed to find him in desperate need of saving. Incapacitated, maybe. Not dead.

"Oh, Lord, please don't let him be dead."

What would she do if she found him dead?

She would turn the horse around and return to the coops to devise another plan. Now, however, she needed to concentrate on mounting this enormous beast.

Bracing her feet on the fallen log, Jessica raised her skirts to her knees. She took great handfuls of the mane low on his neck, stretched onto her toes, kicked her right leg up and partially over the saddle.

The horse nickered, but did not move. Jessica teetered, her legs spread in a ridiculous, untenable position. Bouncing on the lower foot, she thrust herself up. Straining, pulling, levering her right leg over the saddle, she kicked, lifted and tugged. With one heave, she acquired the seat, and a split second later clawed frantically to keep from hurtling headfirst off the other side.

In another moment, she sat quaking, surprised and pleased to be securely seated, and drew a shuddering breath.

Sitting a horse so far above the ground was at once terrifying and exhilarating. Brazenly she perched there, her skirt wadded high on her thighs, her lone petticoat scarcely covering her knees, and her legs cradling the massive animal. Her mother's words echoed in her head. "A proper lady keeps her knees together."

But her widowed mother was some distance away and that advice, sage as it might normally be, did not anticipate the current situation. Her mother also had bid Jessica to use her own good judgment, not to be swayed from a proper course by circumstances or the opinions or behavior of others, which was, of course, precisely what she was doing.

Squirming, Jessica tugged at her skirt, modesty requiring that she cover as much of her limbs as possible. In the process, she stretched her legs, which were long for a woman, and the reason for most of her height, but, even pointing her toes, she was not able to reach the stirrups.

"All right," she said, addressing the stirrups, "we shall manage quite nicely without you." She smirked at her use of the royal we.

Shivering with dread or excitement, Jessica arranged the heavy cloak around her shoulders and took comfort in the protection even as it swallowed her. Then she raised the rein high, as she had seen men driving plow horses do, giving what she hoped was the signal to go.

Nothing happened.

"All right," she said and bounced a little in her seat. "Go!"

Nothing.

She leaned to put her mouth as close to the horse's ear as possible. "It must be obvious, Sweetness, I have no idea what I am about. Be merciful. Take me by the swiftest path straight to your master." As she straightened from the tête-à-tête, her heels slid along the horse's flanks.

As if he had understood her words, Sweetness moved several paces forward. Jessica rewarded his effort with high praise and series of staccato pats on the neck. As she straightened, her heels again grazed the horse's sides and again he advanced.

"That's good. That is very good indeed." In her enthusiasm, she pulled back on the rein. He stopped.

Experimentally, she rubbed her heels lightly at his flanks. The horse advanced, slowly at first until Jessica adapted to his gait. Gradually he accelerated until, with no leave from his rider, he lengthened his stride to a gentle lope as they emerged from the path onto the commercial roadway. Feeling at one with the horse, her body rocking in sync with his, Jessica smiled, then laughed out loud at her success.

Clutching the rein, she pulled the cloak more tightly about her and felt as if she had died and gone to heaven. Denied the use of the stirrups, she gripped with her feet, cradling the horse's barreled body until her legs quivered with the strain.

The animal moved effortlessly, requiring no guidance, back the way he had come. He seemed to know where they were going. As the distance grew, Jessica began to note landmarks to assist in her eventual return, a trip she anticipated she would make on foot.

The horse's easy lope became a canter as the distance between Jessica and her coops lengthened and the night deepened.

At first she welcomed the bite of the determined little breeze in her face, but after a while it became worrisome and she drew the cloak's hood over her head and down to cover her eyes and nose. She had little need to see since her companion obviously had their destination in mind.

They traveled for what seemed like an hour as the breeze became wind. Clouds, in turn, played hide and seek with the lemony moon.

Her mother would assume the scullery maids had drawn additional duties at the manor house. Also, her mother knew Jessica's lack of interest in keeping to schedules.

Still, she was her mother's last child, subject to the overprotection of that position. She did not trouble her ailing parent without good cause. A man lost, perhaps dying on the road, qualified. But how far had they come? How much farther must they go to find him?

As the wind slapped tree branches overhead, Jessica wrapped the cloak more tightly and found comfort in the musky fragrance of the garment.

There were few travelers on the road, a half-dozen were afoot and not inclined to look up, or address a dark rider as they passed. Other riders were more interested in Sweetness than in the shadowy form in his saddle.

After her initial excitement, the perpetual rhythm of the horse's hooves, her long day of work in the manor house and her wild flight through the woods took their toll. Jessica nodded only to jerk awake when Sweetness slowed his pace, accommodating her each time the rein slipped from her hands or she slid one way or the other in the saddle.

She roused wide-eyed, however, when her mount began high-stepping and sidling. Perhaps they were nearing his home. She had heard that horses often raced out of control when they neared their barns; therefore, she was puzzled when the huge animal slowed instead of charging ahead. He stopped altogether and turned a wide circle in the road.

Fully awake, Jessica gently applied her heels to his sides. He refused to go.

Without a step to aid her dismount, Jessica gripped the front and rear of the saddle, braced her weight on her hands, worked her legs to the same side of the horse, and then let herself drop.

When her feet met the earth, she stumbled and grabbed a stirrup bar to keep herself upright.

Scoring the more-or-less successful dismount as another accomplishment, she looked at the horse, expecting guidance. His eyes rolled as he tossed his head and nickered, dancing sideways, but moving neither forward nor back.

She pulled the rein over his ears and down to lead him, but when she attempted to advance the direction they had been traveling, he balked.

She regarded him with some annoyance as he jerked his nose skyward and blew a loud whinny into the night.

"What is it?" she asked.

The horse bobbed his head up and down, making the hardware on his bridle jangle loudly in the eerie silence.

Cajoling, coaxing, Jessica turned him around and attempted to walk back the way they had come. Again Sweetness set his feet and refused.

Was he daft? She had come this far. She had no intention of simply abandoning this magnificent creature on a commercial road at night.

Tossing his head, he whinnied and pawed the ground.

Trees and brambles lined both sides of the road. Jessica shivered, feeling an ominous presence. Traveling any direction would be safer than standing in the middle of this deserted highway.

The huge horse shook his head and tamped the soft ground.

Jessica stroked his nose. "Come, Sweetness. Please. We need to be away from this place."

Wind rustling nearby trees produced noises that sounded like human groans. Fearful yet curious, Jessica couldn't help peering into the shadows beneath the swaying branches.

"All right," she said, keeping her voice low to mask the panic inside. She swept off the cloak and anchored it behind the saddle, then sucked up her courage and stepped off the road to their left, the direction Sweetness indicated, squirreling in among the trees, tugging the now-docile animal along behind her.

Metal pieces on the horse's bridle jingled as he followed, as obedient as a lamb. She found the familiar sound reassuring. She led him on, adjusting their course toward the moans that came more frequently and more audibly as she and the jingling, willing mount moved deeper into the wood.

The moans could be coming from an injured animal—a wolf or boar or even a bear recently roused from a winter's sleep and hungry. Surely Sweetness would not follow if he sensed a predator. Of course, he was the same animal who had raced headlong down a footpath and might have broken his neck on the boulders if she had not waved him off. She probably shouldn't rely too heavily on his judgment.

Several yards into the underbrush, Jessica came to a barrier of thistled shrubs. The peculiar moaning sounded as if it were just beyond.

Releasing the horse, Jessica dropped onto her hands and knees to push through the prickly undergrowth. Thorns snagged her shoulders and knifed through worn sleeves to puncture her flesh. She bit her lips to keep from crying out, yielding only an occasional whimper that mingled melodiously with the night birds cooing on their roosts, warbling to report her passing.

Wriggling, she burrowed on, listening for the human sound, tuning out the birds' night calls. Pausing, holding her breath for silence, she heard the distinct sound of running water.

It was neither sight nor hearing, finally, but Jessica's sense of smell that urged her forward. The familiar fragrance of the cloak drew her—a scent which had been both shield and ally during the long uncertain moments of her ride—into a small clearing.

In the dappled lighting beneath a willow, lay a bundle roughly the size and shape of a man's head. She scrabbled closer, settling a foot away from the bundle.

"Hello." She nudged the mound with two fingers. "Please tell me you are a human being and that you are alive."

No response.

Her breath caught as she considered, then reworded her plea. "Please, please do not be a man dead."

A groan prefaced movement. One booted foot rustled leaves six feet away as a ruddy face framed by a mop of pale, tousled hair, floated up from the debris at her fingertips. She scrabbled back.

His flesh looked mottled in the intermittent moonlight through the trees. The face mumbled a string of what might have been coarse language, before the man hiked himself onto an elbow. His eyes were open, but didn't appear to focus. His voice emerged as a snarl.

"I can scarcely move my legs, my head is pounding, and my throat is on fire." He paused. "Alive or dead? You pronounce."

Jessica allowed a smile. If he were able to speak so of his situation, he must be better off than he sounded…or looked.

Her questions came rapid-fire. "What happened? Who are you? What would you have me do?"

His eyes rolled and he blinked but appeared confused. The spotty moonlight sporadically peeped from the branches overhead. Clouds swept the restless nighttime sky. A smudge on the man's forehead ebbed and flowed in the shadows. The blemish might be blood seeping from a wound.

Another shadow, one she decided was facial hair, circled his mouth and made him appear at once sinister and provocative. A thin beard followed the line of his jaws from the goatee to sideburns in the fashion of the day. The man looked to be of unusual size, well conformed, and perhaps even comely.

Spurred by the ooze that trickled into his brow, Jessica leaped up, again aware of the sound of running water.

"I'll be right back."

The man flapped his free hand wildly at the emptiness between them, wheezing objections as she rustled beyond his reach.

Ducking, she wriggled through another span of undergrowth, gained her feet and found a brook not fifty feet from the man's position.

The hem of her worn petticoat tore easily. She rinsed and wrung the scrap, let it soak, then squeezed it only a little as she regained her feet and scurried back to the man.

On her knees at his side, she pressed the dripping cloth to his lips. He clamped a huge hand onto her wrist as he sucked enough water from the rag to swallow twice before he spoke.

"Are you an angel?" The words were soft, but his voice sounded stronger. "Your song is a solo in the forest's chorale." He attempted a smile. "It trills, like a nightingale." He sniffed the air. "Your fragrance, too, is cleansing." He frowned. "Are you real?"

She smiled and wiped the cloth gently over his features, working around the beard, cleaning smudges that could be removed from his face. Other shadowy presences appeared to be bruises.

"No, I am not an angel, and this nest where you roost might be fit for a nightingale, but it is not Heaven."

His features relaxed. "Good. The discomfort here is more than I expected of Heaven." He arched an eyebrow. "Not as severe as I imagined Hell."

She rewarded his jocular effort with a little laugh, but continued her ministrations.

As she brushed leaves aside and his person came into full view, Jessica was impressed by the man's size. Nicely made, he had breadth to match his length, which spanned six feet or more from his head to his toes.

"What happened?" she asked, dusting debris from his shoulders.

"I objected to being robbed. I put a ball through one and my blade through another before someone bashed me in the head. My last clear memory is of pulling my feet out of the stirrups. I did not want death to catch me beneath the heels of my temperamental steed. The lack wits beat me some, but it was a halfhearted effort."

"Thank a merciful God for that."

He cleared his throat. "Of course." His eyes didn't follow as she crawled around him, raking away leaves and twigs. Instead, he gazed blankly into the emptiness where she had been. Interrupting her raking, Jessica again used the dampened rag to mop bits of blood from the man's neck. The sticky liquid had saturated his neck cloth. Her touch startled him and he looked momentarily alarmed before he checked that reaction in favor of another.

"Thank you," he said, turning his head in what appeared an attempt to address her face. "Vindicator is an exemplary war horse, but not at all adept as a nursemaid."

The man groaned as he pushed all the way to a sitting position. His supporting arm trembled and Jessica pushed her shoulder closer to steady him and, perhaps, conserve what remained of his strength.

"Later, I roused," he continued, as if eager to recall the happenings for his own hearing. "Men argued. It was full dark by then, the night like pitch, as it is now." He rolled his eyes and waited, apparently giving her time to confirm or refute the darkness.

She glanced at the moon. For the moment, it illuminated their surroundings and gave form to shapes around them.

She didn't speak, instead resumed her work with the cloth. She dabbed a splotch from his full lower lip. My, he seemed a handsome man. His eyes were deep set but squinting, perhaps against the headache he mentioned. The trim beard gave him a look of devil-may-care abandon and, at the same time, of authority.

Her swabbing reopened a wound at his hairline freeing blood to trickle anew down his forehead.

"I crawled into the weeds, thinking to hide until my sight cleared," he said, seemingly oblivious to her ongoing ministrations.

"I wanted my head to stop pounding and the world to cease spinning. I made for the sound of water. I didn't get there, did I?"

"You are very close," she said. Jessica was wiping scratches and scrapes on his hands, but neither those minor abrasions nor the cuts on his forehead were severe enough to be the source of the gummy dampness soaking his shirt collar and neck cloth.

Carefully, she brushed her hands over his face, which he moved with her touch. Her fingers rasped over the narrow beard as she ran them into the thick hair above his ears, searching for the source of the profuse bleeding that had begun again in earnest.

Suddenly her roving fingers slid into a warm moist well and the man shouted a barrage of what sounded like fluent French profanity.

"Be still." Her voice rang with a competence she did not feel.

Changing position, scooting on her knees to get closer, Jessica steeled herself as her fingers cautiously tracked the blood back to a long, deep gash at the base of his skull. She traced the cut, trying to determine its length and depth.

"Have care!" He snapped the words, but remained still as she continued her probe, attempting to see with fingertips that came away dripping blood.

She shook out an unused strip of the dampened petticoat and dabbed at the gouge. When that scrap was soaked and unmanageably sticky, she tore a dry length from the garment.

"Be still," she repeated, again assuming the authority of the one in charge while attempting to hide her own uncertainty.

He stiffened, started to speak, then, apparently reconsidered, and did as he was told. Perhaps he was a soldier, accustomed to taking orders. No, he wore fine clothes and the boots of a gentleman, not a uniform.

She wrapped the new length of cloth twice around his head and tucked the loose end into itself before checking the improvised bandage. The covering crossed one of his eyes then circled his crown giving him the look of a buccaneer. Jessica disregarded his evil appearance, satisfied that the wrapping covered the wound. She had secured it tightly enough to reduce the free flow of blood to an ooze.

Jessica crawled all the way around him, surveying, but found no other gashes, although shadows played tricks, occasionally making it appear there were more splotches, each of which she investigated despite the man's grating objections. The wound on the back of his head looked to be the worst of it.

As she examined him, she attempted to revive their earlier conversation. "Has your head stopped pounding and spinning now?"

He squinted and cautiously tilted his head. "Not yet. Tell me, child, how did you come to be here in the dark? It is not yet morning, is it? We are still well hidden, are we not?"

Just as she had guessed, in spite of his denials, he realized the problem with his eyesight involved more than poor lighting. She would play along, not dispute his references to the darkness.

"Sweetness. Your horse brought me."

"Not my horse. My horse's name is Vindicator."

"I see."

"Are you part of a search party sent from Gull's Way?"

"No, sir. I came alone."

Her statement seemed to annoy him. "What do you mean?"

"I rode Sweet...the horse, sir."

"My mount's name is Vindicator. He comes from a long line of warhorses revered for their courage in battle. He is not fit for a woman to ride. It was not Vindicator who brought you here." He sounded insufferably, unyieldingly certain.

She frowned into the pale face as he sat cross-legged, staring at nothing. His one uncovered eye shifted anxiously. Obviously he could not see and felt threatened by her nearness.

"I see no reason to argue, sir, over your mount's name or lineage." She liked sounding so mature and reasonable. "A large, gentle, black horse carried me to this place and…"

"Are you an experienced rider?"

"No."

"Well then, it's exactly as I said. The animal that brought you here is not Vindicator. He has thrown every man who has attempted to ride him, including me, until we reached an understanding. In seven years in my stables, Vindicator has accepted no other rider. I personally bred his dam to the finest stallion in all of Britain. Vindicator's bloodlines rival those of the nation's finest families."

Jessica fought her vexation at this injured man who insisted on pursuing an inane argument about a horse.

"Please, sir, might we discuss your horse's name, his ancestry, or his philosophy of life another time? We have more pressing concerns."

His lips twitched and she thought he almost smiled, and then appeared to catch himself. "I am merely assuring you that the animal you rode to my rescue here tonight is not my horse." The man suddenly puckered his lips and gave a sharp, clear whistle.

Beyond the foliage, the horse whickered.

The man scowled, bleated a dismissive, "Ahh," and set his sightless eye back on his companion. "What is your name, child?"

She stumbled getting to her feet, but answered curtly. "My name is Jessica Blair, sir, and I am a woman grown, not a child."

Eying him, she puzzled as another smile nearly escaped his constraint. She had real difficulties to overcome at the moment without wasting precious time speculating about this stranger's mercurial smile.

Jessica stepped to her right just as a breeze sorted nearby leaves, masking the sound of her movement. The man's face did not follow. As he continued looking sternly at the place she had been, he lowered his voice to a coaxing tone.

"You sound like an intelligent girl, Jessica Blair. Have you not learned that lies seldom improve one's position?"

He tried to stand, but as he did so, his poor, injured head grazed a low limb. He flinched and bent, looking uncertain and thoroughly vulnerable.

Jessica wanted to be as truthful as possible with this man whom she now felt certain had no sight at all. "I lie, sir, only when I deem it entirely necessary."

Still stooped, he turned abruptly, addressing the place where her words originated. "And stop calling me 'sir.'" He hesitated, then lowered his voice to a kinder tone. "I am properly addressed as 'Your Grace.'"

Again he tried to straighten, presumably to assume the regal stance of someone of importance, and again banged his poor head into the same low-hanging bough.

"A duke? You, sir, are a nobleman?" She took his hand and tugged him a step forward, out from under the abusive bough. As she did so, she tried to see beneath the dirt, the injuries, and his general dishabille. Except for the expensive clothes, he didn't look the part he claimed.

Still, she saw no benefit in arguing. "I fear the blow to your head did more damage than shows, Your Grace," she muttered. He had nerve, chastising her for suspected lies, then feigning lofty position.

The leaves whirled again and he started, obviously uneasy. She hurried her next words to placate him.

"Sweetness—that is, your horse—is strong, Your Grace, and uninjured. He doesn't even seem tired. You, on the other hand, are spent. We will get you mounted and deliver you to an inn. Surely there is one nearby where we can summon a physician."

"No." Fumbling, he flung a hand forward to brush then catch her wrist in a grip so firm she gasped. "You will convey me to my home."

"Tonight?"

He relaxed his grip slightly but maintained his hold on her arm. "Yes. At once."

"But you need a doctor."

"No." His grip on her wrist tightened.

She forced herself to hold silent.

"You must take me to Shiller's Green. My home, Gull's Way, is near there. Do you know the place?"

"No, Your Grace. I live near Welter. This is my first journey beyond the river valley."

"What are you doing here now then, alone, and at night?"

"As I told you…Your Grace," she stammered again over the title, "your horse brought me."

"A horse, like a soldier, goes where he's commanded."

"Your horse does not, Your Grace, to your good fortune." She didn't like seeing this large commanding man at a disadvantage, stooped as if he were cowering in the shadows. "Do you plan for us to cower here among the thistles and weeds debating all night?"

He seemed caught off guard by her brash words, then covered his surprise with bluster. "Of course not. However, I do expect you to provide a believable explanation of your presence here before this night is over. You would do well to come up with a more convincing story."

With that, he turned abruptly, as if leading a charge. Jessica stood glowering at the back of this man who displayed such a vexing lack of regard or appreciation for her considerable effort and inconvenience on his behalf.

After moments of flailing and being slapped this way and that by wayward branches, he finally set a steadying hand on the trunk of a sapling and assumed a mostly upright position.

Again taking his measure, Jessica straightened to her full height. He definitely was of a size to fit the huge horse waiting beyond the briars. How in heaven's name could she manage him through the underbrush and see him onto his immense mount? As she delayed, the man cocked his head as if listening to her thoughts.

Profoundly aware he could not see her, she had a fleeting, unconscionable thought. She could abandon him. Could take his precious horse, for that matter. He could scarcely prevent it.

Where had such an outrageous idea come from? It was more like John Lout than Jessica Blair. It was this man's fault. He annoyed her almost beyond patience. Of course, she could never live with herself if she left him helpless, friendless. Friendless was probably this man's usual condition, and through no fault of hers. Surely he displayed a more civil attitude toward his peers than he showed those less fortunate who were foolish enough to render aid.

As to his horse, the animal probably would refuse to go in any direction without him.

All right. She would see the ingrate to his horse and mounted. Then the four-legged one, which still had its eyesight and what appeared to be an unerring sense of direction, could deliver this duke home.

She regretted having told the man her name or having mentioned Welter. It would be better if she had simply reunited this insufferable soul with his steed then turned her feet toward home.

Chapter Two

Jessica shuffled as she approached the man with new determination, intentionally making noise so as not to startle him. Addressing him in the kindly tones one might use with a recalcitrant child, she fitted his arm around her shoulder.

"I am strong, Your Grace. If you can walk a little, I can be both crutch and guide to the road."

"Damn this black, evil night," he said.

She had little trouble seeing, her eyes having adjusted to nature's night-lights. His obviously hadn't...or couldn't.

Ponderously, they advanced, taking wide berths around gnarled, vine-wrapped trees and bushes. The duke slid his feet over the rough ground, each step accompanied by groans or the pop of his jaw as he clenched his teeth. From time to time, he leaned more heavily on her. If not for those muted sounds and occasional weight, she would not have known he was in pain.

In the half-light of a small clearing, she glanced up as his jaw muscles flexed and he squeezed his unbandaged eye closed. He no longer made any effort to see. Perhaps he had finally accepted what had been apparent to her from the beginning.

He looked determined, in spite of his obvious discomfort, and she regretted having to take him the long way around to avoid the brambles through which she had tunneled to reach him.

His breathing became labored. He was tiring. Just as she decided they must stop and rest, Sweetness nickered soft encouragement. The man gave a low, rumbling response and his arm around her shoulder tightened, rekindling her own resolve.

They circled a thorned hedge and broke onto the open road, mere steps from the horse.

Maintaining a firm hold on Jessica, the duke reached out to Sweetness who nickered. The duke fanned the air with one hand until his fingers found the horse's velvet nose. Sweetness responded with a series of throaty whickers that leached tension from the man's body.

Eager to get beyond reunions and on with this rescue while both man and horse were cooperative, Jessica waited. Tall for a woman, slender, but strong, Jessica knew she would be no match for the pair if they rebelled.

After allowing a moment of privacy between horse and man, she guided them to a stump where she placed the duke's hand on an adjacent tree trunk. "Hold here, Your Grace."

Instead of complying, he grappled to maintain contact with her shoulder. "I forbid you to leave me."

She marveled at the gall of a sightless man giving orders to someone who could see, but she gulped back a terse response and answered him gently.

"I want to position Sweetness beside a stump you may use as a step onto his back."

Again she had forgotten to refer to the horse by his proper name. She hesitated, awaiting the admonishment she knew was coming. She had not known the man long, but she already had gained grudging insights into his disposition.

Instead of the anticipated reminder, however, he released her, squared his shoulders, and spoke confidently. "Sensible. Tell me when Vindicator is in position."

While his voice rang with authority, his hand on the tree trembled. She glanced at the wound on the back of his head, reassured to find it oozing rather than gushing. Her mother considered moderate blood flow from an injury a sign of cleansing.

The man obviously was accustomed to making decisions, giving orders and having them carried out, a practice that should make them compatible, since Jessica was accustomed to taking orders and doing as she was told.

They were an odd pair: he, a pillar of society; she, custodian of society's leavings; he, handsome and expensively maintained;

she, plain in oversized, cast-off clothing. His shoes had been handcrafted to fit his foot. Her worn men's boots were a gift from John Lout who had probably taken them off a dead man. He had done so before.

Grabbing the tree trunk with both hands, the gentleman wavered. Jessica took a step to assist as he righted himself. She watched until he seemed steady before she returned to positioning the horse.

She led Sweetness close to the stump. There the horse stood like a stone, as if he sensed this was no time to challenge human skill.

Jessica turned, ready to help the man, but delayed a moment to appraise him. Once he was on the horse, they would return to their respective lives.

Again she marveled at the width of his shoulders, the breadth of his chest. Ruffles lined the front of his shirt, exposed by his unbuttoned coat and torn vest. She did not see one measure of fat on his frame. He carried himself proudly, his posture almost regal, in spite of the humbling circumstances. She admired his posturing. She prayed pride would see him home and sustain him if the loss of his sight should prove permanent.

In the dappled light, his face looked chiseled of stone, yet there was a comeliness in his high forehead, which now would bear a scar at his hairline. His nose, which might be oversized on an average face, gave his character. His mouth spanned a firm, determined chin, and he bore creases at the corners of his mouth and his eyes. Did they come from frowning, or from laughter? In truth, Jessica thought him the most handsome man she had ever seen.

In spite of her lesser height and slim build, she was probably sturdier than he, her muscles honed from long hours in the scullery and tending her mother and the hens. Still, her frame seemed spindly compared to his.

Dismissing her silly, idle thoughts, Jessica stepped closer.

"Sweetness…that is, Vindicator…understands his role. He will hold steady." She shot a warning look at the horse as he rolled an eye back. Clutching his bridle with one hand, she patted the duke's sleeve with the other to let him know her whereabouts and to prod him.

Quite unexpectedly, the man caught her calloused hand and twined his fingers with hers. In other circumstances, she would not have allowed a man to touch her so intimately, but instead of pulling away, she directed his hand to the saddle, as if he needed guidance.

A frown darkened his expression, and he pressed her hand open to finger the calluses.

Embarrassed, she pulled free and was relieved that he neither commented nor questioned her. His lack of response at first pleased her, but the pleasure soured as she realized he probably was indifferent to her, a nobleman unconcerned about a peasant.

She was pleased that her voice did not reflect her pique. "The tree stump is just right of your right foot, Your Grace. It is substantial." He slid his foot until his shoe bumped the tree. She prompted him again. "If you will step onto it, we can maneuver you into the saddle."

He waved her back.

Sweat beaded his forehead as he gripped the pommel and cantle with those large, capable-looking hands that trembled only a little.

Jessica fisted her own hands, determined not to assist him until he asked, and certain he would not.

He placed his left foot on the stump and hesitated a moment, seemingly gathering strength before he vaulted. Well seated, he slid his feet into the stirrups, the length of which fit his long, trousered legs perfectly. He wavered only a little before he straightened and took up the rein.

Jessica admired the way he sat the horse, as if there were communion between them.

It had been shortsighted of her not to have planned for herself beyond this point. Her first concern, of course, had been to find the missing rider; her second, to see him restored. She had done her duty, reuniting man and horse. Her responsibility was ended. The horse would deliver them safely home.

Sighing, she noticed the vapor of her breath. The temperature had dropped. She gazed back down the road the way she had come. It was a long walk, the way probably safer now, in the silent hours before dawn. If she put a foot into it, she should be warm enough and home in time to see her mum, feed her hens, and still put in half-a-day's work at the manor.

"God's speed," she said, and slapped the horse's rump. The effort depleted her reserve of courage.

"Where is your escort?" the man asked, wheeling the horse and turning his head as if looking for Jessica's companions.

She deemed a lie necessary. "Back the way Sweetness brought me. I need retrace our steps only a little distance to rejoin them."

The man's voice dropped to a growl as if he were annoyed. "Vindicator. My horse's name is Vindicator."

"Yes, of course. I usually learn things quickly. I meant back the way Vindicator brought me."

The duke's expression softened, along with his tone. "This animal will never be Vindicator to you, will he, Nightingale?"

"Perhaps not, Your Grace, but he will always be the finest horse I ever attended." Why should they part with bitter words? "I know that Vindicator, not Sweetness, is his true name, if not his true disposition."

The duke pursed his lips. "My apologies, Jessica Blair. The thieves left me with not a farthing to reward you for your heroism. Added to that, I have been insufferably rude. I am Devlin Miracle, the Twelfth Duke of Fornay, master of Gull's Way, the keep at

30

Shiller's Green, and other lesser estates, at your service." He gave a flourish as if doffing an invisible hat.

Jessica responded with a quiet giggle. His sudden, brilliant smile set her heart aflutter.

"Disregarding my title, of course, you must call me Devlin, for the events of this night have made us the closest of friends."

Jessica ducked her head to hide her embarrassment—forgetting he was unable to see her.

"And I shall call you Jessica, although…" He shook his head as if casting off an unwanted thought, arched his brows, and added, "Jessica seems too feminine a name for a tomboy like yourself, a bird whose cooing in the forest was more welcome than the song of a Nightingale."

While his somber face had been comely before, easy smiles lifted it to enchanting. Scarcely able to speak, Jessica managed a whispered, "Thank you, Your Grace."

"Devlin."

"Your Grace Devlin."

"Just Devlin."

"I must go." She turned and took several long strides down the road, back the way they had come, toward Welter. She needed to hurry but smiled to herself, secretly entertaining an outrageous thought. No one—not John Lout nor her cousin Muffet nor her brother or sister, not even Penny Anderson—would ever know Jessica Blair had spent this night with a nobleman, unchaperoned except for the protection of a war horse whose name was a matter of dispute.

Devlin reined the horse and might have gone, except Vindicator refused.

Ignoring his master's urging, the stallion stood unyielding and rolled his eyes at the dejected moppet as she exaggerated her long-legged stride, an effort to demonstrate a confidence she did not feel.

Even without his sight, Devlin interpreted his mount's reluctance to leave the waif to walk even a short way alone.

"Here, Jessica," Devlin called, "the least Vindicator and I can do is see you safely to your escort. That is little enough pay for your Samaritan efforts."

"Thank you, Your Grace, but there is no need. You are not fit to ride any further than you must."

"Not fit? Why, child, I have reserves as yet untapped. Now, give me your hand."

"Your horse is tired as well, Your Grace."

"Even absent sight, child, my hands have taken your measure. Your little weight will be a trifle. He carries far more than you when we are armed." He leaned forward to stroke his mount's thick neck. "Like me, Vindicator has a well of strength to draw from, and is particularly pleased to offer it to a fair damsel in distress."

A quick, unbelieving glance at his face indicated he was teasing. Of course. Fair damsel in distress, indeed. The haughty nobleman had been the one in distress—and still was, although he was bluffing it through convincingly enough.

"No, thank you, Your Grace."

He flapped a hand at her and his face took on a glacial look. "I command you. Give me your hand."

She disliked the way his mouth thinned to a grim line, making his beard-trimmed jaws appear again to be chiseled of rock.

Since he couldn't see, he couldn't know whether they met an escort or not. When it seemed convenient, she would tell him she could see her party beyond a place where there was no road. There would be no need for him to know the truth.

She yielded. "All right."

"Can you ride astride?" he asked.

"Yes, but my dress…"

"Hike it up, child. There's no one to see you but me and to my weary eyes, this night remains devilishly dark."

In the open, the moon bathed them in almost full light, but saying, "Yes, sir," she tapped his knee with her fingers to indicate her position.

He caught her forearm with one hand and lifted, swinging her across his lap as if her weight were of no consequence.

She scrambled to throw one leg over the saddle, then twisted and pulled, adjusting her garments. Holding herself away from him, Jessica arranged herself and smiled, thinking how well Muffet's oversized dress had served this night. She reminded herself not to complain again about her cousin's castoffs.

Jessica's legs were modestly covered as Devlin's arms came forward, the rein in one hand, the other hand coiling about her waist.

"You are very thin, child. And cold." He pulled her against him, pressing her bottom between his thighs and spooning her into his long, warm torso. He fisted the handful of fabric gathered at her midriff.

"What is this you're wearing? A tent?"

"My wardrobe comes from a cousin. It is clothing she has outgrown."

"And which you, God willing, will never fit into. There is enough material here to wrap you twice, perhaps thrice."

"More fabric provides more warmth when the nights turn cool, Your Grace."

He shifted, tugging a handful of dress and Jessica companionably against him. "Yes, more fabric does provide more protection against the weather. And combining our body heat is an advantage as well. Our mingled warmth is a comfort already."

Strangely, their proximity served Jessica as comfort, stimulation, and disturbance, all at one time. Watching her breath plume, she nestled closely into the man's body. Devlin touched his heels to the horse's flanks and Sweetness moved smoothly into a slow, rocking gait. The man fidgeted, twisting and turning.

"May I help?" Jessica asked. As she turned, his cloak unfurled on either side of him.

"Thank you, but our wrap is free now." He shook the cloak and, using one hand at a time, he pulled the sides around, enclosing himself and Jessica in its silk and woolen cocoon.

She forgot about the fictitious escort they were supposed to meet and slumped forward to take his weight. "Please lean on me, Your Grace. I am very strong."

"Yes, you are." His words sounded muffled and seemed to come with considerable effort. "Very strong for one so tall. And slender as a reed." He sat straight for a while, but eventually began to slump against her.

The strain in his voice indicated the duke was making heroic efforts to hold himself upright, but his strength was ebbing. "Please, Your Grace, rest against me. It is you who must sleep. I will watch for a while."

"It matters not whether my eyes are open or closed, all I see is darkness."

"The night is cold and you have suffered rough treatment. Your loss of sight may be your body's defense, just as we use the cloak to defend against the brisk night air."

His voice was husky. "Perhaps you are right. I've little doubt the problem is temporary." His words rang with conviction, but she wondered if his bravado was for her sake or his own. She had provided an explanation he seemed willing to adopt. He leaned more heavily and she suspected that his strength was failing along with his voice.

Jessica felt bolstered by one thought. She would not be around should her suggestion that his blindness was temporary prove wrong. This night had provided events that were rude assaults upon what she supposed was his soft, well-ordered existence.

As they advanced, Jessica fought the sleep that claimed her each time she let down her guard. When her head bobbed and she jerked herself awake for the dozenth time, Devlin jumped, startled, before he grabbed new handfuls of the cloak he held secure about them.

"Where are you from, child?" he asked.

"From Welter, Your Grace. I work at Maxwell Manor."

"Ah. That is one of my properties. Rather a peninsula forming the westernmost reach of my holdings. Thomas Maxwell is a supervising tenant left from my father's time." There came a lull and she thought he had fallen asleep. "I visited there last…let's see when…I would think it was about…" He hesitated.

"Four years ago, Your Grace."

"Has it been that long?"

"Yes."

"Did we meet, Jessica?"

She laughed. "I had just begun working there, mucking chamber pots. With the number of visitors, I was busy from dawn until night with little opportunity for socializing."

He croaked acknowledgment. "Sleep, Nightingale." His voice was a rasp. "Rest now, free from your servant's duties. Vindicator knows the way."

Exhaustion won. Against her will, bundled in the duke's arms, warmed by his body and the cloak they shared and the marvelous scent of both cloak and duke, Jessica knew little of the trip beyond that point until the horse's rocking motion stopped.

The sky had lightened with breaking dawn as Jessica squinted, only partially awake, bent beneath the weight against her back. A man shouted and she roused, alarmed to find people running to them like ants to a sweet.

She tried to shake off the cobwebs of sleep, but could not grasp immediately what was happening.

Figures clustered around talking and moving in a dreamlike state.

An enormous beast of a man stood immediately beside them. The giant's great paws yanked Devlin's cloak from their shoulders, exposing her warm body to the early morning chill.

Before she could react, those huge hands pulled the duke from the horse, almost capsizing Jessica as well. The giant caught her companion up in burly arms as if the nobleman were a babe. Then the monster carried his cloak-clad charge up broad steps and into the most superb house Jessica had ever imagined.

Two bustling women reached to draw Jessica from the horse. A groom held the animal's head, addressing Sweetness in tender tones.

The scene continued as part of a dream. Jessica felt as if she belonged there, returning to a palatial home, greeted by soft hands and strong arms and the unspoken promises of a bath and a clean warm bed where one could sleep for a fortnight.

Her dream ended rudely, however, as she was pulled from the saddle.

Chapter Three

The two ladies, maids judging by their costume, who had broken her fall and grabbed her as she toppled from the horse, obviously had plans for her. They chattered to one another as if Jessica were not there.

"Has his lordship ever brought a doxy into his mother's home before?" the scowling, middle-aged one said.

The older one returned the frown. "Nay, Nan, this is the first."

When the women had Jessica generally steady on her feet, they waved the groom to lead Sweetness away. Maintaining their holds on her, they scrutinized their charge. Both reacted with deepening frowns.

Jessica jerked her arms from the women's grasps. "I am no easy woman from the streets." Having clarified that, she could not think how to continue. She wanted to establish immediately who and what she was not. The woman called Nan made a face. "My, she's filthy."

"Needs a bath," the older one confirmed.

"What manner of clothing is this?" Nan lifted excess fabric floating about Jessica's frame.

"Stolen, I imagine," said the older one. "It doesn't look to be her own."

Jessica stared at the older woman, obviously the one to whom she should explain. It was difficult to frame an explanation as indignation exploded within, along with soreness in her backside as she stepped.

"Were I a thief, I would have pinched better clothing, at least something that fit."

The older woman nodded, and then looked at Nan, who bobbed her head in agreement.

"You need a bath," Nan repeated, this time addressing Jessica.

"No need," Jessica said, mellowed by their kinder looks and the fact they were addressing her. "I must be getting home. Which is the road to Welter?"

Each of the three serving women raised an arm, index fingers pointing south.

"Thank you." Jessica straightened and, summoning what dignity she could manage, working around the peculiar soreness in her bottom, pivoted and set her nose south, intending to follow that appendage until she either arrived in Welter or dropped alongside the road.

"Stop!" Devlin's hoarse but imperious voice roared from above and behind her.

Jessica turned clumsily to look back as the giant stepped up beside the duke on a second-floor balcony and reiterated his sovereign's intentions by shouting, "Stop that woman."

She'd been called girl, child, chit and, on rare occasion, miss, but she had never been called a woman. The term surprised her so that she turned fully around and peered at Devlin and his giant, the top of the master's head only reaching the other man's earlobe.

Devlin muttered something and the giant shouted, "Bring her into the house."

All three serving women grabbed Jessica's arms and hands as if they expected her to bolt.

"Gently," the giant amended, apparently prodded by the duke. The *house* appeared to be a palace, certainly like no dwelling she had ever seen before.

The walls looked to be of pink marble. The sunlight also created blinding glints from the floor-to-ceiling windows on three levels. Jessica jerked free of the women, as she looked to the balcony. "Please, Your Grace, I must be on my way. I have given all the time I can spare you this day."

Although he still wore around his head the crude wrap made of strips of her petticoat, his face looked scrubbed, his expression calm and he, remarkably handsome. "Jessica Blair, I insist you accept the hospitality of my home as a token of my gratitude."

The changing attitude of the servants around her was palpable as they withdrew and stared at her with new regard. He continued. "It would be common courtesy on your part to allow a person whose life you have redeemed to express appreciation."

The bandage impaired the one eye, but he kept the other closed. She assumed the giant and others realized his blindness. "Come inside, Jessica. I want to introduce you to the dowager duchess, my mother. She is eager to thank you personally."

Jessica was struck dumb. It had not occurred to her that this was a family home. Of course. He had a mother. One who resided here. With him. She should have guessed. She had a mother, one who, in fact, might be frantic at Jessica's absence, unless someone had stopped by to tend her. There was no one else to feed and bathe her, unless Brandon did. Jessica's older brother seldom visited the cottage, however, except when he was summoned, and then he rarely arrived promptly. Jessica could not leave her mother's care to chance.

Devlin called again. "Come inside, Jessica. Bathe, eat, rest a little. Then I will provide a proper escort to speed you on your way."

She drew a deep breath. Turning to look at the road yawning before her, she saw wisdom in his invitation.

"I cannot tarry long, Your Grace."

"No, my angel, I did not expect you would."

"Why are you on your feet?"

"Perhaps you could come inside and we could continue this conversation without inconveniencing the entire household."

A glance indicated many people, from stable boys to cooks to maids and butlers, were hanging on every word of their rather private exchange. Humbled by the rebuke, she said, "Yes, Your Grace."

The older serving woman led the way, flapping a hand, shooing the younger girl ahead with instructions.

Jessica tried to maintain some dignity and not favor the soreness in her lower portions as she followed. The tactless maid they called Nan trailed her up the broad sweep of stairs, through the immense doors held by liveried men at attention, men so well disciplined that they did not stare. Jessica had expected to be taken directly to the duke's salon for an interview with his family. Instead, she was escorted up one of the twin flights of stairs rising from the entry hall and down a broad corridor lined with the portraits of ancestors. A maid stepped ahead to open a door to a bedchamber.

The walls of the room were the color of ripening peaches, the trim painted a glistening white. Throw pillows on the ivory-covered bed and the upholstery of a small chair were embroidered with flowers in peacock blue. She might have designed and decorated this room in her dreams.

Too stunned to remark on the elegant chamber, or even to draw more than shallow breaths, she tried to commit the room to memory. As she did, the older maid busied about, fluffing pillows which were already plump, dusting imaginary wrinkles from graceful draperies siding leaded windows which were so clean they glittered.

Nan dashed about, too, opening and closing cabinets, and directing men who carried pails in and out of an alcove beyond the chamber where Jessica stood.

"I am Sophie," the young maid said quietly as she scurried by Jessica. "That is Odessa." She indicated the older woman. Moving officiously, Nan scurried from the room. Jessica caught disapproval in Sophie's voice as she said, "That is Nan."

Jessica offered to shake hands, but yanked the filthy appendage back before Sophie could accept. Not only was her hand stained with grit and grime, and even the duke's blood, her dress, too, was soiled so badly that most of the threadbare fabric was no longer blue but a dung-colored brown.

Jessica rubbed her hands down the dress and glanced at her feet. The battered, oversized boots were caked with mud. She lifted onto her tiptoes in an effort not to track from the polished wood floors to the thick rugs. She flinched as the younger maid nudged her elbow.

"Don't touch me," Jessica warned, startling the girl. "I am too filthy. I have no desire to befoul this lovely, lovely room or anyone in it." Wobbling, Jessica tiptoed backward.

Odessa set her robust frame between Jessica and the only avenue of escape.

"His Grace ordered that you were to have a steaming bath, which is just beyond that door." Odessa indicated a portal at the far side of the room.

Defensively, Jessica gathered fists full of her oversized dress, but the older woman seemed to read her thoughts.

"No need for concern, pet. Sophie and I have seen female forms more generously endowed than yours." She shot a smile at the younger maid. "Fact is, Sophie and I ourselves have more to display than you."

Both maids chuckled good-naturedly, drawing a smile from Jessica, who recognized truth in the boast. With these two for allies, her privacy was assured. She bent to remove the boots and release dirty, bare feet before she advanced several mincing steps toward the indicated room. She had heard of such facilities, but had never seen such a thing. This was the only opportunity she might ever have.

At the open doorway, Jessica stopped, closed her eyes, and inhaled. She longed to move closer to the freestanding tub of steaming water, the source of marvelous fragrances wafting about and warming the air.

The biggest, fluffiest towel she had ever seen draped the back of a small wooden chair to one side of the tub.

Drawn by the heavenly scent of roses when none were yet in bloom, Jessica eased forward; following her nose to thrust her face, stiff from dirt and the night's cold, over the water, thinking to absorb the steam without sullying the pristine surroundings. She filled her lungs, making no effort to hide her pleasure.

Following behind, Odessa said, "The bath is for you, my lady." Jessica's eyes popped wide. She saw a round of fragrant soap nesting on a washcloth on the broad rim of the tub. Odessa startled her in the midst of that dream by shouting, "Sophie! Now!"

On signal, both women swooped and tugged at the folds of Jessica's dress. She flapped at their hands, her efforts halfhearted. She wanted them to win, strip her, and toss her into that steaming tub.

"All right," Jessica said finally, unable and even unwilling to stay the serving women's hands. "But what use is it to scrub my body when I have no clean clothes to put on after?"

A knowing smile twitched the ends of the older woman's broad mouth as she looked to Sophie. "Martha is about her size, wouldn't you say?"

Sophie giggled and explained. "Martha is with child and not able to wear her frocks. The master insisted that you have fresh clothes." Sophie grinned. "He doubted we could do worse than what you are wearing."

Odessa eyed the layers of Jessica's discarded dress critically as she held it at arm's length. "Even blind, the man was right."

"You probably think he's right about most things," Jessica said, using her snippy tone, "since he is your lord and master."

Odessa narrowed her eyes, regarding the young woman who stood before her, arms folded protectively over her chest and wearing only what appeared to be boy's underdrawers. "He was mistaken about you. He told his mother you were a child of ten or eleven."

Jessica looked down at her nearly naked body, which had done unconscionable things in recent years. It was when those changes became apparent that Jessica's mother began begging Muffet's old clothing, even though other older girls closer to Jessica's size offered their castoffs.

Her mother insisted that while Jessica served in the manor house, working for Mr. Maxwell, she must wear the oversized clothing. It meant so much to her bedfast matriarch that Jessica saw little reason to object. Now, of course, Jessica had little choice. She would wear whatever was available, as long as it was decent. But why was Odessa staring at her with such open chagrin?

"No one else can know," Odessa muttered and waited for Sophie's nod before she grabbed the kettle and stirred a new supply of hot water and suds into the tub.

"Please, I must save these," she said, patting her underdrawers, making them jingle. "My purse." Both serving women nodded their understanding. Certain that the secret pocket sewn into her underdrawers was securely tucked; Jessica dropped that last item of clothing, and placed a foot in the steaming water. She closed her eyes and sighed at the pure pleasure of the warmth closing around her foot…her ankle…her calf.

Slowly, deliberately, she submerged the one appendage. The water rose to her knee. She hesitated only a moment before allowing the second leg to join the first. She stood basking in that pleasure for several heartbeats before she lowered her body, luxuriating in the warmth as it embraced her.

Jessica had never bathed in a tub, and considered herself lucky to dip in an occasional trough. In the summer, she swam as often as she could in the river. She loved feeling clean, loved having her long, thick hair free of debris and dust and accumulated filth.

She continued lowering herself into the tub, her chin, her nose, her forehead, the crown of her head. Completely submerged, she felt an epiphany, a baptism so thorough that she did not want ever to leave the watery confines. In moments that passed too quickly, she had to surface to breathe. One necessary gulp of air and she returned to the silence beneath the water.

A rap at the door to the bathing chamber startled all three occupants. Jessica's head popped out of the water as Odessa went to answer the knock.

"Is the child all right?" A woman's deep, melodic voice floated into the room.

"Yes, Your Grace."

"May I see her?"

Stiffening, Jessica heard Odessa hesitate before she stepped aside, swinging the door wide to admit an unusually tall, strikingly beautiful woman of advanced years.

Although matronly, the visitor did not seem to be nearly the age of Jessica's own mother, who was the ancient age of forty and four.

"Hello," the woman said, gazing at Jessica's face. "Welcome to our home, my dear."

As Jessica said, "Hello" and "Thank you," the woman's eyes drifted. She looked startled and dismayed as she surveyed Jessica's body, particularly studying the swells of her breasts that hinted of more hidden beneath the suds.

"But, my dear…I mean to say, my son said…Well, it's just that I thought you to be much younger. A child of nine or ten or eleven."

"Your son?"

"Devlin. The duke. Forgive me, darling. I am Lady Anne Miracle, the Dowager Duchess of Fornay. Devlin's mother."

Jessica realized she should stand and curtsy to a duchess, yet here she sat in a tub of water and bubbles, naked, displaying too much of herself, and no manners of any kind.

The dowager bit her lips and, for a moment, appeared to be overcoming good humor. Hastily she waved aside all thought of curtsies, obviously reading Jessica's mind.

"You are fine where you are, my dear. Perfectly fine. We don't seem to be observing any of the amenities. I would never have dreamed of barging in on a young woman guest while she was bathing. It's just that I thought you...Well, that a child might need reassurance." Her gentle words and pleasant smile dwindled, leaving only a frown. "How in the world did Devlin determine your age?"

"I don't know, Your Grace. He dismissed my repeated denials that I was a child. I told him rather persistently that I was a woman fully grown."

"It should have been obvious."

"He couldn't see and wouldn't listen."

"How old are you, Jessica Blair?"

"Eighteen, ma'am...er...that is, Your Grace...ma'am."

"Eighteen? Oh, but my dear."

Jessica was momentary perplexed before she had a thought. "Oh, please, Your Grace, don't be alarmed. I didn't come expecting reward or seeking work."

"Ah...well, no...of course I wasn't concerned about that, particularly." The duchess looked to Odessa, apparently seeking guidance.

"I believe our guest is unusually—charmingly so, of course—naive." Odessa shot a warning glance at Sophie, as if signaling. Jessica couldn't help wondering at the exchange.

What did that mean, unusually naive? She might lack formal schooling, but Jessica's parents were learned people. They had diligently taught her and her brother and sister to read the classics and to do their sums. Further, Jessica could tat, knit, cook, clean a house, and dress a variety of fish and fowl. And she had memorized most of what she considered the important verses of the Bible.

Things like that were not readily discernible when one was sitting naked as a babe. It was hard to make an impression crouched in a tub of water. "Madam, it seems premature and not at all fair for you to pass judgment on me or my abilities with no more information than you have." She didn't intend for her words to sound quite as curt as they did.

The dowager's vivid blue eyes twinkled as she lifted a handkerchief to cover her mouth.

At that moment, a rap on door between the bedchamber and the corridor announced another visitor and the duke called from the hallway. "May I enter?"

"No!" the dowager, Jessica, and both maids chorused.

"What is going on in there?"

The dowager hastened out the door from the bathing alcove, through the bedchamber and to the open doorway where Devlin stood. He sounded tired.

"Devlin, shall I see you to your bed?" his mother asked.

At the duke's side, the immense man called Bear loomed, having retreated only a couple of paces.

While her husband and all three sons held Bear in the highest regard, the dowager only tolerated him, thus, the huge man was seldom inside the house. Her attention turned back to Devlin as he responded.

"Madam, you have neither said my prayers nor tucked me in for the past twenty years, thank God." She took his arm and turned him, but he balked. "I want to see Jessica."

"She is bathing."

"It's perfectly proper. She is a child and I am a blind man."

"Well, then, you cannot see her anyway, so be off to bed and I will escort her when she is presentable."

"I didn't mean see her in the literal sense. I want to hear her voice so I may determine her well-being."

"Do you think you know her so well, my son, after a night's ride together, that you can discern her condition merely by the timbre of her voice?"

His shoulders squared, although the change in posture seemed to take great effort. "Regardless of your assurances, I wish to speak with her. Will you stand aside, or shall I summon Bear's assistance?"

She studied him a moment and wondered where her jovial, ever-obedient son had gone, giving his body over to this obviously spent but determined man.

Of the dowager's three sons, Devlin had always been the most compliant. Yet today, something about their unpretentious female visitor had aroused his protective instincts. Surely a country maid could not have acquired such influence after so short an acquaintance. Devlin had fended off courtesans far more practiced than this thin sprite.

As the duke drew a breath, pain etched his face. Seeing his effort, the dowager relented. "I will allow you to speak to her from the bedchamber, but you are not to venture closer."

"This is my home, madam."

"And I am your mother, Devlin. I will not have you address me in those lofty tones or I shall order the girl returned to her people immediately."

Devlin's shoulders bent as if under a sudden weight. Bear stepped close and said, "Please, Your Grace."

Neither Devlin nor his mother seemed certain to which of them Bear addressed his appeal.

"All right," Devlin said, first to yield. "I only want to hear her voice to assure myself she is not feeling threatened among so many strangers."

The dowager regarded him skeptically. "You think you will be able to determine that merely by hearing her voice?"

"Yes."

The older woman studied him another moment, acutely aware of his fatigue.

The duchess took Devlin's arm, led him through the bedchamber and positioned him at the door to the bathing room. She did not, however, allow him to stand where he would be able to see Jessica should his eyesight suddenly, miraculously return.

"Jessica," she said, needlessly summoning the girl's attention, "Devlin is here and concerned for your well-being. Please reassure him that you are all right so that we may return him to his bed."

There was a splash, followed by coaxing voices. Then he heard Jessica's musical giggle, joined by two other women whose laughs he did not recognize.

"Jessica? Are you being well served?"

Her giggling continued. "Yes, Your Grace, I am."

"What was that splashing? Did you fall?"

"I was alarmed to hear you speak when I am...when I was..."

"My voice frightened you?"

"I am not accustomed to the ways of a great house, Your Grace. In Welter, women do not converse with men from the bath or, well, when they are inadequately clothed."

His throaty chuckle prefaced a comeback. "Oh, I suspect such conversations do occur. I am pleased to learn, however, that you have not yet participated in those communications."

Her laughter pealed with his. "Perhaps they do occur, but as you rightly suppose, I have not experienced them, at least not until now. Would you please be away to your sickbed?"

"Only if you will come visit me, when you are adequately clothed, of course."

She peeked at Odessa, who had withdrawn into the corner but who nodded, granting a servant's permission for the visitor to interview the lord of the manor in his bedchamber when she was properly attired.

"I will be there before you sleep, Your Grace," Jessica said.

He muttered, "I am certain of that."

Hearing the aside, his mother peered at him and wondered at this son's peculiar behavior, marveling again that he had always been the most sensible of her three.

The eldest of her three boys, Rothchild, had been haunted throughout his short span by the prospect of someday assuming the duties of a duke. Studies came hard to Roth. He dedicated himself to pleasing his father, and her, too, she supposed.

Their youngest son, Lattimore, on the other hand, was frivolous, more interested in playing and hatching mischief among the servants or the livestock or the neighbors.

Devlin, the middle son, the moderate one, seemed more like her family, particularly her father. Devlin was the levelheaded one, the son who exercised the soundest judgment.

She guided Devlin back through the bedchamber, ignoring Bear, who waited silently a step beyond the outside door. She handed Devlin off to his valet Henry after extracting assurances the duke would be put directly to bed. Then she returned to the bathing room, eager to reevaluate this mysterious person who had entered their lives so unexpectedly and already exercised such influence on Devlin.

Jessica caught the dowager's perplexed look.

"Now," Lady Anne said, "you may continue with your bath."

Jessica brooded, sensing that her initial interview with the dowager had not gone well, even before Devlin's interruption. She didn't know exactly why not.

The noble woman returned to stand near the side of the tub and regarded Jessica oddly, as if she wished to resume their discussion. How had she offended the lady?

"I am to address you and your son both as Your Grace," Jessica said, attempting to discover where she might have misstepped. "That is correct, isn't it?"

The dowager bestowed a judicious smile and a nod, maintaining a probing look as if trying to fathom the girl's mind.

Jessica rescrubbed her face with the cloth, hoping to cleanse any residual smudges that might be the reason for the dowager's determined scrutiny.

"How do you think he is, Your Grace, beyond the temporary blindness, of course? I thought perhaps he was acting strangely, if you will forgive my saying so. Of course, I have no idea of how he normally behaves." She floundered for more to say. "And you do."

Jessica pulled the cloth down to watch as the studiously solemn face of the Duchess of Fornay broke with the most beautiful, infectious smile Jessica had ever seen. She returned the smile, blossoming in the glow of what appeared to be approval.

"Did I say something right?" Jessica knew her confusion showed in her face, which she suspected was transparent as always.

"You did, my dear." There was a lilt in the woman's words. "Devlin was absolutely right. You are quite disarming."

Gloom reformed in the duchess's face. "He has a nasty gash across the back of his head." The woman hesitated and Jessica nodded, indicating she was aware of the injury. "It appears to have bled profusely, which is probably a godsend. The doctor has seen him."

"My, your physician certainly came promptly."

The older woman again registered her approval. "Yes, Dr. Brussel is a friend and a neighbor, as well as our physician."

"Is the gash Dev...the duke's only injury?"

"They tell me he has bruises and scrapes, but nothing else of consequence."

In all the activity and conversation, Jessica had forgotten the pleasure of the tub. "What word did the doctor have concerning his eyesight?"

The duchess bit her lips. "He hopes the blindness is temporary. He said Devlin's eyesight can return in a blink, or it may return slowly, over time."

Jessica immediately adopted the woman's hope. "The condition probably will not be permanent. I've heard of that, temporary loss of sight after a severe blow to the head. Haven't you? Such injuries usually heal, with time and rest." She paused. Her words had come in a rush without allowing time for a response. Jessica wanted what she said to be true. She didn't want to entertain the other, bleak possibility. In truth, she had never heard of such a positive end, but nurtured hope that the duchess had. "Don't they?"

The duchess nodded, but looked distressed as she stared at the figured carpeting covering the floor at the side of the tub. She pivoted, crossed her arms and paced several steps without speaking, then said, "I have summoned his brother from London. Lattimore is a bright, cheerful influence, in spite of the fact he never lights anywhere long. Devlin may have need of Lattie's positive attitude."

Her eyes met Jessica's. "Oh, my dear, I did not mean to imply that you have been in any way remiss. It was wonderful of you to find and return Devlin to us. We appreciate your trouble and your dedication in seeing him safely home."

Jessica smiled. "I am not offended, Your Grace. As I am sure your son told you, I must leave immediately. My mother depends on me and I have other responsibilities as well." She saw no need to mention her hens, their care and feeding or the mucking out of their pens. A peer of the realm certainly had no need of information like that.

The duchess looked alarmed. "Oh my dear girl, you cannot possibly leave until you are properly rewarded."

The water was cooling around her. Although Jessica wanted to stay and continue enjoying the delicate fragrance of the soap, she felt obliged to forfeit the tub to provide what comfort she could to her hostess.

As she gathered herself and prepared to stand, however, the duchess called out. "Sophie, fetch the kettle to warm this water. And prepare the rinse kettles, as well."

Turning back to Jessica, the dowager said, "Stay just where you are, darling. You haven't yet had full benefit of the bath you so heroically earned." She hesitated, studying Jessica's dark, tangled hair. "Would you allow me to suds your hair for you?"

Stunned at the suggestion, Jessica didn't answer immediately, but ceased her effort to quit the tub.

"I'll do it," Odessa offered, suddenly reappearing from the far corner of the chamber where she had stood silently, allowing the two ladies uninterrupted conversation.

The duchess seemed to have attached her mind to the idea. "I had only three sons," she said, regarding Jessica's dark, abundant curls. "They, of course, had nurses and governesses, while I traveled with their father much of the time." Her thoughts seemed to wander, before her eyes focused again on Jessica. "I would consider it a privilege to wash your hair for you, Jess."

The dowager adopted the abbreviated form of her name others sometimes insisted on using, against her mother's wishes.

With that, Lady Anne Miracle, the Dowager Duchess of Fornay, dropped to her knees, pushed up the sleeves of her gold brocade morning dress and grabbed the round cake of scented soap.

Chapter Four

After looking in on a sleeping Devlin, Jessica spent the morning in a sort of stupor—her thinking dulled perhaps by her lack of sleep—waiting for the duke to rouse.

She paced to the broad windows of her chamber that looked out over grassy lots separated by fences. Sweetness grazed in one by the cart trail, the road the serving ladies indicated led to Welter. She should leave, but she wanted to see Devlin one more time, and then she would be away.

Turning from the window, Jessica eyed the full-length mirror, embarrassed to see herself entirely from top to toe. She moved closer to inspect her reflection in greater detail, gathered the length of her dress and pulled it up, little at a time, afraid of shocking herself with saucy revelations. She had never seen herself—not all of her, anyway. She felt vain admiring her reflection so brazenly, yet her appearance came as a pleasant surprise. She was more proportionate, more attractive, than she had imagined.

Twisting, she attempted to view the exposed backs of her legs and hips. After much repositioning and lengthy study, she smiled into the reflection of her own face.

She dropped her skirts and tugged the scooping neckline off of one shoulder for further inspection. Biting her lips at her own audacity and surprised by her lack of modesty, she squirmed to unfasten the dress and pull it down to expose the chemise. Nervously, she slid the undergarment down to examine her full, rounded breasts. She cupped and examined each one from several angles, blushing and smiling at her own effrontery.

Her curiosity sated, Jessica readjusted her clothing and promised herself that, if she ever undressed in a room alone, assured of complete privacy, in front of such a mirror, she would take full, unrestricted views of her person.

She needed to be getting home as soon as she saw the duke and said her good-byes.

Thoughts of that meeting and their conversation were interrupted by a commotion downstairs, like earlier ones that urged her out of her room to steal a look below.

More callers, like those who had besieged the house through the morning, bearing gifts and food and inquiring after the duke. Jessica watched the comings and goings undetected. The visitors made her realize the duke was well known and, obviously well enough, admired…maybe even loved.

Slipping downstairs, careful to avoid straggling visitors, staff, and family members, she marveled at the solarium, which might be a ballroom, if there were not already another vast chamber so designated. She stood in awe at the door to the great library that boasted four ladders extending to shelves high overhead.

When Patterson, the majordomo, caught her sometime later standing at the door of a small salon, she started and apologized.

"You are welcome to enjoy this room, as well as any others," he said. "This salon is for entertaining small groups of ladies making social calls. It is probably where you will entertain your guests."

She smiled at the idea of her friends calling upon her here. Penny Anderson would probably swoon dead away if she were escorted into such a chamber.

"And the duke's gentlemen friends? Where does he entertain them?"

Patterson indicated she should follow and led her to another salon near the library on the other side of the entry. "This is the duke's study and his office where he meets with businessmen from time to time."

"Where does he entertain his female callers?"

Patterson frowned. "He does not have female callers here, my lady."

She lowered her voice. "Will you tell me something of the older son, then, and how Devlin came to acquire the title? Was there bad blood among the three?"

"No, my lady." The man's face softened. "Master Rothchild, the eldest, was devoted to duty. He did things properly and well, groomed as he was from birth to be a duke."

Hoping this reminiscing might take a while, Jessica settled lightly on a window seat, prepared to listen.

"Master Rothchild was mortally injured in a duel over the reputation of Lady Jane Sequest, a woman who, it is said, maintains a list of men who died defending her honor. She added two names to her list that morning. Master Roth's opponent died, gasping for air around the ball lodged in his throat. The dying man's shot went through Roth's liver and pierced a kidney."

The old servant seemed to age, diminishing as his shoulders slumped with the memory. While Jessica did not like seeing his distress, she thought speaking of the death of a loved one sometimes aided the handling of one's grief. Also, she was curious about how the elder son's demise affected the family.

"The damage to either organ would have been fatal," Patterson continued, as if he were alone. "A London physician told us it scarcely mattered which failed first. The family returned to Gull's Way, the ancestral home."

Suddenly, he glanced into her face and regarded Jessica earnestly, as if concerned that she understand the import of his words. "Master Roth spent his final days in excruciating pain, not only his, but his family's.

"Until then, Devlin—that is, His Grace—had been the lighthearted middle son. He was a better scholar than Master Roth. Of course, he did not have the pressure that weighted Master Roth's efforts.

"As Master Roth lay dying, Devlin grew solemn as he anticipated a role he felt ill-prepared to take up. His father assured him, but the old duke's grief had himself tied in knots. He loved each of his sons equally, but he had not considered his second son might acquire the title."

Patterson paused and Jessica patted the cushion beside her. He eased onto the far end of the window seat. A glint of tears seeped from the corners of his eyes.

"Of course, Devlin had the intelligence and the courage to assume the responsibilities," she suggested, to waylay his sadness and keep him talking.

"You may be assured of that, Miss. He is, after all, a Miracle. Blood will tell."

"What of Lattimore? Did he share the family's grief?"

Patterson regarded her with what looked like annoyance. "Certainly, Miss, although Master Lattie was only thirteen at the time."

Quiet for a moment, Patterson smiled slightly at what seemed a bittersweet memory. "It was the youngest who said, 'At least a fatal injury, rather than instantaneous death, provided time for us to say farewell, and to adjust.'"

"Did his experience make his brothers more aware of the dangers in duels and other ridiculous gestures?"

Patterson gave her a wry smile. "No. Rather than making the young masters more cautious, Roth's passing made life the most intriguing gamble of all. His Grace, particularly, tossed life's dice fiercely, daring fate to take up his often-flung gauntlet.

"Eventually, Master Lattie, too, followed the pattern set by both of his elder brothers."

Patterson stood abruptly. "Please forgive me, Miss. I don't know what possessed me to confide this family's private concerns. I generally am not given to gossip."

Rising to her feet as well, Jessica smiled. "You are a discreet man, Mr. Patterson. You only disclosed as much as you thought proper and only to one you recognized as a friend who admires this family, though not nearly as much as you, nor for nearly so long. Thank you, Mr. Patterson, for trusting me. I will reward your trust with my own discretion."

He stiffened and regarded her down the length of his rather imperial nose. "You may address me simply as Patterson."

"That does not seem respectful, Mr. Patterson, what with the difference in our ages. Not unless, of course, you will consent to call me by my Christian name. I hereby give you permission—insist, even—that you call me Jessica."

His forehead wrinkled as his eyebrows arched.

"I am a scullery maid, sir, not a lady," she said quietly.

He snorted a half laugh. "I shall not mention your former position to a living soul, Miss, and I would advise you not to do so either."

"All right, it will be our secret. Now that we have shared such intimacies, will you call me by my name?"

Again, he appeared to think before his brow smoothed. "If I do, then you must call me by my Christian name as well. Tims."

She offered a well-scrubbed hand. Smiling broadly, he took it, sealing their bargain. Odessa, the housekeeper, chose that moment to exit the library, almost running into them both.

"Say, now, what's going on 'ere?" she asked.

Patterson's face resumed its closed expression. "Were you eavesdropping?"

Odessa looked as if she might burst before a glance at Jessica cut her anger. She regarded Patterson with a sympathetic smile. "This one," she indicated Jessica, "undermines a person's natural reticence."

Patterson drew a breath, and then exhaled as if surrendering. "That is an astute observation, Odessa. Now, kindly act as the lady's guide and show her the rest of the house?" He put emphasis on the word 'lady.' Jessica flashed him a conspiratorial smile as he abruptly turned and abandoned them.

Odessa giggled. "You do have a way with you, child."

"I am no child, Odessa."

"So you keep reminding us." Odessa nudged Jessica's arm and led her toward another set of double doors. The older woman babbled, spewing information as she guided Jessica through dining rooms—one large, one small—and into the kitchen, a vast space Jessica decided needed to be as large as it was if only to accommodate the number of staff in and out.

The kitchen contained cabinets and countertops, cook stoves, basins beneath pumps that brought water directly into the house, and a long trestle table flanked by equally long benches. Chairs graced either end.

Jessica left the kitchen as activity began with preparations for the noon meal.

• • •

She was his amulet, his charm, the spindly child with the long legs, tiny waist, and bony shoulders. He could almost feel again the warmth of her small, round bottom situated comfortably between his thighs. He was amazed by his mother's interest in and approval of the child. Of course, the dowager was partial to the female off-spring of her friends and even staff. Maybe she felt inadequate at having produced only sons, a feat which pleased his father.

His father, the eleventh Duke of Fornay, had been dead more than three years now. Some said he died of a broken heart after the loss of his eldest son.

Devlin didn't believe that.

Propped in his bed, bathed, comfortably drifting in and out of sleep, the nobleman smiled recalling his brothers and their youthful exuberance, how they pleased their father, each in his own way. They were none of the three alike, not in looks or dispositions or talents.

After Roth's death and before the old duke's passing, Devlin dedicated himself to enjoying life. He bought and raced horses, invested in and worked aboard cargo ships, dallied with well-bred ladies, all riskier than putting money on a gaming table. No chance was too great, no stakes too high.

He had been lucky, his every enterprise charmed...until now. He turned his head to press the side of his face against the pillow to hide an unexpected tear that seeped from the corner of his unbandaged eye.

Had fate at last been tempted beyond enduring? Was his blindness a summons, calling in payment for his recklessness?

Devlin swiped at the tear and rocked his head from one side to the other, trying to get comfortable, annoyed that Dr. Brussel, who had poked and prodded, hadn't been able to restore his eyesight or even to say with any conviction whether the loss was temporary or permanent.

Hot, he shoved his bed linens to one side. He wanted someone to come bathe his face and throat with the cool cloth. No, not someone. He wanted his Nightingale.

Devlin's restless movement stopped when he heard laughter in the hallway and voices. It was Jessica and one of the upstairs maids giggling about something young females giggle about.

Instead of annoying him, their laughter lifted his spirit. His Nightingale was sensitive. Obviously she was not concerned about his condition. She would not be laughing if his situation were dire.

Her laughter gave him a sense of well-being that came from having her in the house.

He clung to her spirit, a buoy in a rough sea; his good-luck piece, a tiny sprite who weighed less than seven stone, yet who had been clever enough to find and recover him, and strong and ingenious enough to transport him safely home.

• • •

Acceding to the dowager's request that she remain nearby until Devlin awoke, Jessica wandered outside, absorbing the early spring sunlight.

The gardens at Gull's Way were magnificent, and she wondered how they looked when the bountiful buds bloomed. Of course, she would be in Welter then, spending golden summer mornings in the dank scullery. If she remembered, she might imagine standing here, enjoying the feeling and fragrances of clean body, clean hair, clean clothing, and flowers about.

A horse's nickering called her from her reverie, and she turned to find Sweetness stretching his neck over a wooden fence near a wooded area.

"Hello," she called, happy to see a familiar face, even if it belonged to a horse.

As she approached his paddock, he wheeled and ran to the far side, kicking, propelling clumps of dirt her way.

"I am happy to see you, too," she said, laughing at his antics. "You appear to have suffered no ill effects from your night's burden." She lowered her voice. "Are you well rested, my hero? My Sweetness?"

The horse ambled closer in what appeared an attempt to hear her better.

"Silly. I know you cannot understand my words."

As if answering, he whickered softly, trotted to the fence and stretched his neck across, putting his head within her reach.

Rather than simply petting him, she climbed up two rails on the fence, wrapped her arms about his head, and pressed her nose to his warm, smooth neck.

Her mother recommended Jessica adopt a kitten to learn affection. Truly she loved Behavior, the cat, and the hens. After last night, however, Jessica knew the enchantment of true love, for she was bedazzled by her dark, compassionate hero; a horse of unconquerable spirit.

Behavior, the kitten, had grown into a cuddling cat. Jessica smiled. Her new pet probably would snuggle just as cozily in her lap, if his size would allow it.

Giggling softly at that image, she kissed the horse's long face as she scratched behind his ears, beneath his chin, and rubbed his velvety nose. Sweetness was the first true love of her life. Their meeting had aroused raw, disturbing feelings she had never known before, a longing awakened soon after she met the stallion.

Of one thing she was sure. The new excitement had not emanated from the man. The duke was too aloof. She shook her head to dismiss such an unwelcome suspicion.

A large bay mare trotting up and down the fence in the paddock one over issued a shrill whinny. The stallion's ears twitched against his head and he turned, baring his teeth, and answering with a shriek of his own.

"Uh-oh," Jessica said, smiling at the mare in spite of herself. "I think you have some explaining to do. Your lady doesn't approve of your spending time with other females, even one with only two feet."

The stallion tamped a forefoot, and turned his head back to Jessica, bumping her shoulder playfully with his nose.

Figg, the head groomsman, stepped to the stable door and whistled.

Sweetness whirled and threw clods of dirt, which Jessica dodged, as the huge horse crossed the lot, racing for the stable.

"Sorry, Miss," Figg sounded genuinely apologetic. "I didn't realize the lad had company. This here," he gestured toward the huge bay, "is the master's favorite mare. It's her time."

Looking uncertain, he caught Vindicator's harness and tugged him through a walkway between one paddock and the other. Tossing his head, Vindicator broke free and raised his nose, calling to the mare who turned her back to him. Figg propped a foot on the fence and watched the ritual as the pair snorted and sniffed and nipped at one another.

Turning her head so as not to observe the play too closely, Jessica walked closer to Mr. Figg. He continued watching the horses.

"Problem is; Meg here can't throw a filly. His Grace 'ould like to have a big old brood mare out of old Vindicator there. Meg's had three foals in three years, all of 'em boys."

He pointed to another paddock. "That one there's the last, the roan. Frederick's his name. Big like his folks. See. Feisty. A wonderful spirited boy. Devlin was here for the birthin' of all three. Not one of 'em black like their pa. Maybe this time we'll get us a big black filly."

Jessica drifted to Frederick's paddock, wondering that the stableman, Figg, referred to the duke by his Christian name. The colt romped to the fence and stuck his nose over.

"Hello, Freddie." She scratched his nose. Figg obviously had been around a while. He might be a good source of information, if she were there long enough to ask.

• • •

After checking to see Devlin continued asleep, Jessica returned to her room, stripped off Martha's fine clothes, down to the borrowed shift, stretched out on the massive bed, and fell into a deep sleep. She dreamed of green fields swarming with rollicking, spindle-legged foals with soft black noses, kicking their heels against stable doors, making an awful din.

She bolted upright with Sophie shaking her awake.

"Miss, Miss!" The young maid sounded frantic. "I been knocking. Wake up. It's the master, Miss. I think he's dyin'. Mr.

Patterson sent me to fetch you. Said I was to bring you quick. You must come now. At once."

Blinking against the afternoon light that invaded when Sophie threw open the draperies, Jessica felt disoriented. Her mind focused as she slipped her arms into the light dressing gown Sophie produced and held for her. The serving girl caught the sash ends and secured the robe's sides while she tugged Jessica, barefooted, through the door and into the hallway.

"Oh, please hurry, Miss," Sophie urged, pushing with a hand at Jessica's back.

Servants rushed in the same direction, sweeping toward the wing where the family slept. Caught up in a tide of humanity, Jessica coursed straight to the duke's bedchamber.

Sophie tapped lightly at the door which was flung open to Henry's grim countenance.

"He is restless with the fever again, Miss," Henry said, pulling Jessica's arm to propel her into the room, then closing the door abruptly in the faces of Sophie and other servants gathering.

"It broke a while ago, but now he is chilling, shaking with the palsy. He's calling for you. Let 'im know yer here. The doctor says the duke is strong but he has to keep calm. It's not good for him to thresh about like he's doin'."

Henry seemed to choke and cleared his throat with little coughs. Jessica gave him a hard look. The duke's personal valet didn't meet her gaze. When he did, the whites of his eyes were streaked with red, the lids puffy. He made several attempts before he spoke. Even then, his voice was husky. "He might be dyin', Miss."

Jessica grabbed the man's elbows, catching him totally unawares. "He is not dying!" She gritted her teeth and shook the spare, rather dignified little gentleman's gentleman. "Do not say that again, or I swear I shall flog you myself." She had never seen anyone flogged, but it had a good, brutal sound to it. "Do you hear me?"

Henry's eyes rounded and the man squared his shoulders, staring at her. "Most assuredly," he gasped. To her astonishment, a twitch which might have been a smile tweaked his thin lips before he regained control. "Don't waste vigor on me, Miss." He gestured toward the bed. "He's the one needs threatenin'."

She turned toward the duke.

Dying, indeed. Her stomach contracted. Did Henry think they were dealing with some lack wit from Welter? His Grace the Duke dying? This large, virile, haughty specimen? An outrageous, unconscionable notion.

Setting her jaw, fisting her hands, and scowling Jessica took long strides to Devlin Miracle's bedside.

Seeing him there beneath a mound of coverings, pale and shivering, Jessica pursed her lips and swelled to her full height before she said, rather too loudly, "You sent for me, Your Grace?"

One eye was hidden beneath fresh bandages. His free eyelid fluttered and opened, but no recognition registered on his face. A moment later, his hand snaked from beneath the covers. "Nightingale?" His voice was a rasp.

She kept her tone carefully modulated, adding just a hint of hauteur. "Yes, Your Grace. Is there something you require?"

"Am I...?" He frowned and turned his face from her.

"No, Your Grace, you are not dying, although I am sure you probably would prefer it, at the moment. Your fever has broken and you are chilling. In a while, that will pass and the fever will probably reoccur and peak again. It may go on that way for several hours, but you are strong. You will survive."

"I want you here."

"I am here."

"In here." Feebly he tried to lay the covers back.

"I am not a pet, Your Grace, to curl up in your bed to warm your feet."

His teeth chattered. "Please. Come to me as you did before. Put your warm little bottom against my belly and banish this infernal chill."

Jessica watched his muscular arm tremble and fail at the sustained effort to hold the cover open. A glimpse indicated he might be naked beneath the sheets, a shadow his only apparel.

Movement at one side of the room drew her attention to an older man packing vials and instruments into a dark case that sat on a table nearby. Until that moment, she had not been aware of anyone else in the room, yet, as she looked about, she also saw Lady Anne sitting stiffly in a rocking chair in a darkened corner wringing a handkerchief between her hands. The older woman did not look at Jessica and the girl speculated that the dowager duchess was probably praying.

"If you can, you need to do as he asks," the man whispered.

"Who are you to direct me?"

"I am Dr. Brussel, the duke's physician."

"Was it you who started that ridiculous rumor?"

"I asked Henry to send for you. Devin had asked for you. Henry's anxiety was contagious. I assumed he would enlist a maid to carry my message."

"So Sophia assumed...?"

Dr. Brussel stepped closer. "Devlin is ill, my dear, but as you so aptly said; he is a strong man who will, no doubt, overcome this scourge."

Jessica relaxed slightly. "Truthfully, sir, must I do as he asks?"

Brussel looked toward the bed. "If you can see your way to it, yes."

She gave the dowager another furtive glance, which apparently prompted the doctor to add, "His mother will remain here in the room. No one will suggest anything untoward about your being within the chamber, and they need not know of the other."

"Am I to assume a position here as family pet?"

"Have you been better treated anywhere, even in your father's house?"

Jessica considered his question for a blink before she answered with equal honesty. "I have not."

She gave the man a haughty sniff, rewarding his attempt at levity. She thought of Devlin's regard for Sweetness, another animal in his care, and then looked again to the bed. If he had looked weak or helpless, she might have agreed. Devlin's uncovered eye was closed, but he wore a somewhat supercilious smile that she found suspicious, although his occasional tremors appeared genuine enough.

"I will sit at the foot of the bed to warm his feet," she conceded finally, distrusting Devlin's expression.

Dr. Brussel finished loading vials of pills and powders and tapped the latch closed on his case. "That is most generous of you, Miss." He offered something in his hand to Jessica. "I'm leaving this." He placed a vial on the bedside table. Devlin is to drink two spoons of this every four hours. Will you make sure he takes the dosage and at the proper times?"

"Yes."

"His fever may come and go through the night, but I expect significant improvement by morning."

Jessica felt relief claw its way up from the pit of her stomach. The duke was going to be all right, and that was not just her uneducated, defiant declaration. It was a medical opinion from the doctor himself.

She indulged the urge to hug the somber physician and kiss his cheek.

The older man smiled and his eyes twinkled. "You assured me first, Jessica Blair. Now give the man whatever comfort you can and let me know if he's not better by morning. I don't expect to hear from you." Grinning as if he had a private joke, the doctor left, catching elbows and turning servants away from the door. "The duke is going to be fine. Just fine. He needs a good night's rest." Brussel pulled the bedchamber door closed behind him.

Jessica eased onto the foot of the bed where she remained stiffly upright for a time. Eventually, she lay on her side, cushioned her head on an elbow and curled around the duke's feet.

A sound startled her and she roused to see Lady Anne teeter forward in her chair, then jerk awake and right herself to keep from toppling to the floor. Jessica rose and tiptoed to the older woman.

"You need real sleep, Your Grace. It will not do to have two nobles ill in the same house. Go on to your bed now. I will see to the duke. I will summon you if we need assistance."

Lady Anne looked relieved for a moment, and then cast a worried glance toward the man sleeping soundly in the bed.

Jessica guided the dowager from the chair to the door and into the corridor to find Sophie slouched on a bench directly across the way. The girl leaped to her feet and hurried to give assistance.

Compliant, the dowager shuffled, transferring from Jessica's arms into Sophie's, and allowing herself to be escorted to her quarters, several doors down the hall.

Chapter Five

"No, no, no, fool." Nan, the officious upstairs maid, rushed to draw the window covering closed, jerking the cords from Jessica's hand. The long velvet draperies snapped shut over the sunlight, casting Devlin's bedchamber back into the pall of night, as well as cutting off the spring breeze that had whispered lightly about the room.

None too well rested, Jessica flushed at the maid's high-handed reprimand. Although little respected among the household staff, Nan had the audacity to call Jessica "fool" and attempt to instruct her on matters pertaining to her patient.

The impudence probably sprang from the household's confusion about Jessica's position. Much discussion had not settled the matter of how they should treat the young woman in ragbag clothing who had brought a peer of the realm home.

Jessica identified with the servants' dilemma, having no idea how she had obtained such a lofty standing, which is why she did not erupt at Nan's impertinence.

Patterson had a different standing, of course. The old retainer had helped rear all three of the Miracle's sons and treated the two survivors with thinly veiled regard when he agreed with their actions and disdain when they earned his disapproval. Patterson was regarded by the family as a venerable older relative, making him of more consequence than a servant.

Neither Patterson nor the dowager were present when Nan arrived and began noisily gathering soiled dishes on a tray, and snapping out fresh towels and linens. Jessica held silent until Nan turned her attention to the bed where Devlin had at last fallen asleep. Anticipating, Jessica intercepted the housemaid.

"That will be all, Nan."

The maid squinted as if to challenge the command.

Jessica raised her brows. "I wouldn't." While not threatening in themselves, the words convinced Nan to wait for another time to test this visitor's authority.

As soon as Nan clattered out the door, Jessica marched to the window and threw back the velvet draperies. She started as Devlin's deep baritone boomed in the silent room. "Good for you."

Jessica spun. "What?"

"Don't let them bluff you, Nightingale. Stand your ground. I will back you, even when you are wrong."

She tried to make her voice sound indignant. "Who is going to determine if or when I am wrong?"

As she intended, the arrogance in her question ignited his deep, throaty chuckle. Her giggling laugh mixed with his, lilting toward the rafters.

"I am glad you are feeling better, Your Grace. We—that is, your family and I…indeed, the entire household, of course—have all been concerned."

"You have been concerned for me, little bird?"

Jessica stealthily stepped to her right. His open, unbandaged eye did not follow. He could not see. Not yet, anyway.

"Certainly, Your Grace. I understand from all of this," she made a sweeping gesture, "that you are an important figure, not only to your family, but to the nation."

"Oh, am I?"

"Well, that's what everyone here seems to think."

"And you, my chirping little bird?"

"I know too little of politics or politicians to have an opinion, Your Grace."

Devlin struggled to prop himself higher on his pillows. Jessica rushed to offer her arm for his use in pulling himself upright while she reached behind to readjust the cushions.

He wrapped both hands about her arm and adopted a more serious tone. "You are strong, Nightingale, to be as thin as you are."

"Yes I am, Your Grace."

Steadying himself, leaning on her while bracing one hand on the bed, he used the other to finger the bandage wrapped about his head.

"Thank goodness," he said. "I thought I'd lost the ability to open and close my eye. It's only this infernal wrap. Perhaps the covered eye has regained its sight."

Jessica bit her lips together to keep from blurting the truth, certain that he was equally blind in both eyes, at least for the moment.

Jessica saw nothing to worry about yet. A sightless rich man could look forward to a far better life that a blind beggar. Jessica viewed the duke's situation as an inconvenience.

She glanced down on the top of Devlin's thick blond hair and realized he had grown perfectly still, his face pressed against her upper arm while she continued to hold him upright.

"Have you fallen asleep, Your Grace?" she whispered.

He stirred only a little. "You smell of the woods, of fresh air and pine, Nightingale. I was taking advantage of a quiet moment to breathe you. Surely you don't begrudge me the pleasure of your scent."

She shivered. There was something suggestive in the statement and in his manner. "No, Your Grace, of course not." The tenor of his voice puzzled her. Was he grieving, suspicious that the damage to his eyes might be permanent? Or frightened, perhaps?

No, not this marvelous man with his great house, vast expanses of land, family and staff to provide his needs and wants whether he could see or not.

He exhaled as he leaned back against the pillows, but maintained his grip on her arm. When she attempted to withdraw, his fingers tightened. "Stay."

"I am not a pet to answer to one-word commands, Your Grace."

He puckered and frown lines deepened at both sides of his mouth as his jaws flexed giving him a defiant look. "You will do as I say for as long as you are in this house."

She jerked the captive arm free. "Then I shall not remain in this house, Your Grace."

Heaving forward, he flailed at air and almost threw himself out of bed in his effort to retrieve her. She started for the door, and then looked back. She did not like seeing that big, beautiful man floundering.

Soundlessly, she eased back to position herself within easy reach.

His flailing hand found her shoulder and clamped it.

"I thought you had left me." The arrogance was gone from his voice as he lowered it to a whisper. "Nightingale, you must promise not to leave me. Not in this awful darkness."

"Is that a command, Your Grace?"

The stiffness leached from his back and shoulders as he wilted against the pillows. "A request. Please. Stay within my reach. Allow me the use of your eyes until mine are restored." His face etched with pain, he spoke softly, making her heart ache. "Promise me, Nightingale, that just as you did not abandon me on the road, you will remain with me until this nightmare has passed."

"Your Grace, I would stay gladly had I only myself to consider. However, others depend on me. I have responsibilities."

His open eye, the color as blue as the deepest sea on a cloudy day, fixed on her, as if he could see. "I will hire someone to take on your other duties."

She gave a mirthless chuckle.

Obviously hearing the derision, he said, "Where are your charges, my child? What are your responsibilities?"

"I am the sole provider for my widowed mother."

"Are you an only child then?"

"No. I have an older brother and sister, but they are otherwise obligated. I see to our mother: provide her meals and bathe her, change her clothing and her bed, take care of her personal needs, duties no one else cares to perform."

He snorted his disdain. "For the right sum of money, I can hire a dozen to tend your mother's needs while you remain here."

Jessica had never considered hiring anyone else to care for her mother when her own sister and brother refused to share the responsibility.

"Perhaps, Your Grace, we could hire that same dozen to see after you. The accommodations here are far more compelling than those in my mother's home."

He smiled. "I want you here with me and, because it is my wants I desire to satisfy, I am willing to pay to keep you here. Do we have an agreement?"

She wanted very much to remain in this grand place with the handsome, doting duke and his mother, yet her conscience gave her little choice. "No, Your Grace, I'm afraid not. Others also depend on me as well."

"What others?"

She was reluctant to say, thinking he might take offense or ridicule her, but he prodded her with his silence.

"Ten months ago, a fox got into the hen house at Maxwell Manor, where I work in the scullery. Cook ordered the injured hens killed and buried, afraid to serve them at table for fear the fox might have been diseased and infected the birds."

"I interceded on their behalf. My work day was over and I volunteered to take the damaged hens and bury the dead ones on my way home."

Devlin nodded that he understood the story to this point. Apparently feeling surer of himself, his grip on her arm relaxed. Moving a step closer to the bed, she straightened to her full height, although he maintained a hold on her near forearm.

The chamber door flew open and Nan rushed in. "Out, out, out," she hissed. "Get away from the master this moment. Who do you think…?"

Devlin's roar startled both girls.

"WHO IN THE HELL IS THAT?" His question reverberated off all four walls, the echo bouncing eerily.

Taken aback, Nan looked at Jessica as if trying to think of a way to blame her for the duke's outburst. Before either of them spoke, he roared again.

"I SAY, WHO CAME INTO THIS ROOM AND BEGAN ORDERING PEOPLE ABOUT?" His voice dropped to a shout as he continued. "Jessica, I demand that you tell me who the person is."

Jessica answered rather than risk exciting him further.

"It is Nan, a chambermaid, my lord. I am sure she was merely concerned that I might be pestering you."

"Does this Nan person appear to you to possess good sense, or is she addled?"

Jessica regarded Nan briefly before she answered. "It is difficult to tell, Your Grace, with only appearances on which to judge."

"Nan!" He barked the name, making the girl jump again.

"Your G-Grace?"

"You are never again to speak out loud in this house within my hearing, is that clear?"

"Yes, Your Grace." She began backing toward the door.

"If there is a fire, send someone else to alert me. Moreover," he said, increasing his volume and stopping her retreat, "Jessica Blair is my dear friend, the person closest to my heart. You are NEVER to address anyone else in this house in that surly manner, most particularly not Miss Blair. From this moment on, your employment is tentative. Your standing is that of a kitchen cat, tolerated but expendable. Is that clear?"

"Yes, Your Grace." Nan didn't raise her eyes, as she shuffled backward, again retreating toward the door.

"You remain in this house under a cloud, Nan." Again his words riveted her in place. "If I hear one complaint of your behavior or speech—even one—you will be discharged with no notice and without references. Do you understand?"

"Yes, Your Grace." With that, she turned, stumbled over the threshold, and pulled the door closed behind her. Before the latch snapped into place, however, another figure slipped through and into the room. The dowager tapped her index finger to her lips, indicating she wanted Jessica to keep her presence secret.

A pall hung upon the chamber, each of the inhabitants seemingly waiting for one of the others to speak.

Jessica finally stirred the quiet. "You were harsh with the girl, Your Grace."

"I did that for you, Nightingale. I want my family and every member of the staff to understand your position here." His facial expression changed to one she could not read.

"Exactly what *is* my position here, Your Grace?"

He disregarded the question. "I thought a damsel in distress would admire a gentleman who rallied to her defense."

This time her laugh was genuine. "I am a scullery maid—in truth, a scullery maid's assistant—in the manor house of one of your overseers, a man whose position is minute compared to yours. It is wrong for me to be an honored guest in your marvelous home, wrong for me to be here in your bedchamber conversing as if we were equals. Under ordinary circumstances, you would never have occasion to utter a word to me."

His rolling laugh interrupted her, at the same time he removed his hand from her forearm.

Jessica shook her head puzzling. "What was it I said, Your Grace, to cause such good humor?"

He sputtered attempting to speak, and Jessica couldn't help smiling as his hilarity infected her as well.

In a moment, as he became weakened by his attempts to articulate over a sudden fit of coughing, her gentle giggling merged with his. The dowager turned her back, her shoulders quaking with a similar shattering mirth.

The chamber door flew open and Patterson burst into the room, his face flushed, his mouth set in a decidedly disapproving frown. His gaze swept the room. He looked startled to see the dowager, who, in the throes of silent laughter, again tapped her finger against her lips silencing any acknowledgment of her presence.

"What has happened?" Patterson asked the room at large. "Is his sight restored? Can he see, in spite of the dire…?" The words trailed off along with the duke's boisterous guffaws.

"Who suggested I might be permanently afflicted?" Booming accusation was back in Devlin's voice. He again grabbed Jessica's forearm and his grip tightened. He sneered.

"Enlighten me, Nightingale. Did the physician tell you or my mother that my sight is permanently gone?"

She turned to face him squarely. "He did not, Your Grace." She wanted her response to be vigorous enough to be convincing.

Devlin's grip on her arm eased, but only a little. He lifted his face toward hers and his voice hardened, as if daring her to be bold enough to speak the truth. "Exactly what did the physician say, Jessica, and speak the words precisely as you recall them."

She looked to the dowager, hoping his mother might intercede. The older woman did not acknowledge Jessica's glance. The girl had no choice but to do as he asked.

"He said the loss of your eyesight was a result of the blow on the back of your head where there is a sizable gash."

She hesitated wanting to choose her next words carefully, but Devlin became impatient. "What else?"

"You would be better served to speak directly with him, Your Grace, or with your mother. I believe he discussed details of your condition with her."

"You are here. They are not." He squeezed her arm again.

Guessing how she might feel in his circumstances, she thought it only fair to enlighten him.

"He said your eyesight might return in a flash, or it might return slowly, as the damage to the inside of your head heals."

"Or?"

She dropped her voice. "Conceivably, it might not return at all. But, Your Grace," she hastened to add. "Of the three possibilities, two of them are favorable."

He rewarded her remark with a pained smile. "Well said, Nightingale. You have heard that I am something of a gambler, haven't you?"

"I have heard that. Yes."

"Did you consider that favored pastime when you couched your explanation in terms a gambler might like, the odds two-to-one in his favor?"

"I did consider it. Yes, Your Grace."

There was a long pause, during which the duke appeared to affix his most pleasant, most inscrutable expression. His face reflected changes as his thoughts tumbled about.

"And what of you, Nightingale? Are you a gambler?"

She grinned. "I believe life itself is a gamble, Your Grace."

"I want you to wager with me, Nightingale. Will you do it?"

She tried to decipher his meaning by his expression. Unable to, she responded with a reluctant, "Maybe."

"I want your word that you will remain with me until my sight returns."

She started to object but he obviously heard her inhalation and raised his open hand, touching her mouth with his fingertips and staying her words.

"This bet provides a large payoff. There will be a reward of five hundred pounds to you. I will see that you receive the full sum promptly on the day my sight returns. During the intervening time, however, from now until then, your eyes will serve as mine. You will be my companion, give me the benefit, not only of your sight, but your optimism, your exuberance, and your graceless honesty. I need to draw upon them, Nightingale."

She glanced across the room at the silent dowager who seemed fascinated, yet content to remain unacknowledged.

"I am a wealthy man, Jessica Blair, and a generous one. Although I do not know how I appear right now, in these circumstances, I generally am considered an attractive man. Right now, I need someone truthful to evaluate people for me: their movements and expressions, their furtive glances and inner thoughts revealed by a grimace, the glint of an eye, an unexpected smile."

"But what about...?"

He didn't allow her to finish. "Your mother is welcome to live here during the time you serve as my eyes." He hesitated, but not long enough to allow her rebuttal. "Your hens as well. I will have the gamekeeper build stout pens close to the house, so that you may feed and fret over them at your leisure. Or I will send a servant to look after your charges where they are.

"Think of it. When my sight is restored, your mother will not have suffered, you will be five hundred pounds richer—in addition to the clothes and shoes and any other benefits I may choose to provide during your stay. Your livestock doubtlessly will thrive under my protection. Now, what do you say?"

He freed her arm, indicating it was her turn to speak.

His offer was generous.

"Would I be a servant during this time?"

He looked startled at the suggestion. "You would not. You will be my...my ward." He smiled. "Unofficially, I will be your guardian. You will be treated as an honored guest or a distant member of my family."

"Your doxy is more likely what people will say."

He bellowed a laugh. "You hold rather exalted ideas of yourself, child. I may not be able to see, but my other senses are heightened by loss of the one. I am thoroughly familiar with the length of your arms and legs. I have rested for hours against your thin, muscular shoulders. Your hips snug against my crotch more closely resembled those of a young lad than a female."

She started to speak, but he continued.

"Don't bother to deny it. I have seen much of you with my hands, Nightingale." He paused as if to consider the possible insult in his words. "Of course, you are young. With age, I am certain you will develop womanly curves. Given your current attributes, or lack thereof, I think our friendship will be above reproach for a time."

She frowned down at her well-developed breasts, all the more prominently set off by her slender frame, then she glanced at the dowager who covered her mouth with both hands, her shoulders shaking as she again attempted to stifle her laughter.

Jessica didn't answer immediately, providing Devlin the opportunity to add, "You are usually captivatingly honest, Nightingale. Try to be as candid now, for both our sakes. Please."

Obviously he thought her younger than her eighteen years. Certainly she was slender, sinewy. True, her hips were not yet fully rounded, and her arms and legs long. The man had experienced no contact with her bust, which burgeoned out of proportion to the rest of her.

He had cast her as a child. For some unknown reason, he was enchanted with her, while, at the same time, dependent on her.

Again she glanced at his mother who regarded her with a peculiar twinkle in her eyes.

The duke had designated Jessica his good-luck charm and apparently wanted her to guide him through this current darkness, to remain for as long as he needed something or someone to advise and buoy him.

Perhaps she could arrange for someone else to perform her duties at the manor. If she made the offer sweet enough, her brother Brandon, two years older than she and unmarried, might agree to tend their mother until Devlin's eyesight returned.

Her most compelling argument for the duke's proposition had nothing to do with the properly fitted clothing, the gentlefolk running this household, or the ease Jessica enjoyed living in this place. The most persuasive consideration was Devlin Miracle himself.

Jessica was growing fond of this man, not of his title or his wealth, but of his humor, his kindness, his gentle spirit, his innate sense of fairness. She wanted to nurture him, even if it meant encouraging his arrogance and his irascible temper along with his boisterous laughter and his pride…him.

She would have to make arrangements first which meant she would have to leave him for a time.

Would he allow her to go away and trust her to return? Was their friendship yet that strong?

Chapter Six

The sun had cracked through gray skies by the time Jessica finished her breakfast in the kitchen, where a dozen servants gathered only to be brusquely sent back to their duties by Odessa.

"Jessica!" Patterson's voice, uncharacteristically raised to a bellow, reverberated down the stairwell.

Odessa's eyes popped wide. "Patterson never raises his voice."

A butler appeared, breathless, and stopped still when he spied Jessica. "The master must be passing over. Patterson is searching for you."

Patterson swooped into the kitchen and spied Jessica as she stood. "Quickly, Miss. He didn't like waking up to find you gone."

Jessica grabbed a clean cloth. Holding it by one corner, she dipped it in a kettle of boiling water, then touched it gingerly as she wrung out what she could of the surplus before following Patterson up the stairs.

"Where the hell have you been?" Devlin shouted as Patterson announced Jessica's arrival.

"Below stairs in the kitchen, Your Grace." She stopped inside his room. He sat straight, not slumped against the pillows as before. "You are looking well, Your Grace. Your bellow sounds fit enough."

His color had improved and his posture appeared ramrod straight. From the set of his stubbled jaw, it was obvious the man was stronger and not in a mood to be trifled with.

His shout became a roar. "YOU ARE IN THIS HOUSE TO SERVE ME, JESSICA BLAIR, NOT TO DALLY IN THE KITCHENS."

"What?"

His voice dropped back to a shout. "Is there something wrong with your hearing?"

Jessica's pleasant disposition dissolved.

"You forget yourself, Your Grace. I am in this house as your guest. You yourself said so. I believe you mentioned something about my being dearer to you than a blood relative."

Devlin cleared his throat and the change in his demeanor was visible. "Yes, well...I expect..."

"Do you demand abject devotion from your poor relations, Your Grace? Insist they grovel? It is not my idea to stay and if you no longer require my attendance, we are agreed."

She took three long strides closer, which put her still a dozen steps from his bedside. She glanced at the soaking cloth she carried.

"In my concern, I delayed coming long enough to dip a rag into a kettle. Though it scalded my fingers, I brought it thinking to wipe your brow." Her last words sounded harsh. Setting her jaw, Jessica packed the rag into a tight ball, drew back and hurled the wad at his head. The missile came loose to make a sloshing sound as it flew.

Devlin leaned to his right. The sodden rag slammed into his pillow directly behind where his head had been seconds before, spraying the area, including the duke's shoulder and arm.

As had become her habit since the child's arrival, Lady Anne clamped a hand over her mouth to stifle her startled laughter. The girl's temper was a match for her son's, even when his was at its best...or worst.

The dowager had once told her husband they needed at least one daughter to whip the male-dominated household into proper shape. Jessica proved the dowager's point, even though her arrival had been delayed.

Neither Jessica nor the duchess spoke as they watched Devlin feel for and find the sopping rag. He fumbled, trying to identify it without benefit of sight. Finally, he lifted it to the side, wrung it out, folded and placed it over his uncovered eye as he lay back against his pillows.

"Thank you, Nightingale. You are a thoughtful girl. I have a frightful headache. Will you be so kind as to fetch my Bible and read to me a little? I think perhaps something from Malachi. I may have need of a passage regarding penitence. Do you agree?"

Jessica was unable to contain the laugh that spewed between her lips, in spite of their being firmly clamped shut. Her voice sounded marvelously calm as she spoke.

"Perhaps we both might benefit from such, Your Grace."

• • •

"What color is your hair, Nightingale?" Devlin asked when the reading had them calmed.

"Brown, Your Grace."

"Brown like a thrush?"

"More like mud."

"Ah. And your eyes?"

"I believe they are green."

"You don't know the color of your eyes?"

"Some say they are gray or brown. Others insist they are green. For my part, I have never been able to see the true color. I do not own a looking glass."

"Surely you have a mirror in your bedchamber here, a large one which reflects your entire body."

"Yes, but I…I covered it, Your Grace."

"The mirror?"

"Yes."

"Why?"

"I found it embarrassing, seeing so much of my person in such a forthright manner."

His mother's voice broke the silence. "Her eyes are hazel and the color changes, depending on the sky, the hue of her clothes and her mood."

He turned his head abruptly. "How long have you been here, madam?"

"I have been in the room since shortly after you sent for Jessica."

He looked annoyed. "Surely you did not fear for her safety."

The dowager allowed a quiet little laugh. "No. I knew she was in no danger from you, my treasure. I was just curious to see how she might soothe you this time. Her methods astound me."

"Yes…well…I suppose."

His laugh emerged as more of a rumble deep in his throat and was swiftly joined by the giggling of both the dowager and his Nightingale as they recalled her hurling the sodden towel.

• • •

That afternoon, His Grace summoned four seamstresses and Mrs. Freebinder, the modiste, from the village. He ordered that they bring bolts of cloth with weaves soft enough for a child's sensitive skin and in every color. He particularly requested colors of the rainbow, the sea, skies, and meadows. Jessica objected to the fuss as the ladies measured her from tip to toe, the circumference of her wrists and throat and head, and insisted she select her favorites from two dozen bolts of fabric. She had never seen such an array.

"Will you make kerchiefs for my hair to match the dresses?" she asked. Her question obviously stunned the ladies, who were accustomed to outfitting nobility in his household—the dowager and her occasional guests. All females, even toddlers in a duke's family, wore bonnets trimmed in feathers and ribbons and jewels, not kerchiefs, which easily identified peasants.

Mrs. Freebinder, afraid of setting off the duke's famous temper, sought the dowager's advice: kerchiefs or bonnets? The duke's mother understood the dilemma.

"Kerchiefs will appease the wearer," the dowager said, "as long as Devlin is not able to see her. However, we had better have bonnets as well, to pacify him when his sight returns. Yes, we shall have both."

In her own statement, the dowager realized Jessica's optimism was infectious. She no longer doubted his eyes would recover.

Lady Anne retired to her private salon where she remained cloistered until she heard the dressmaker and her staff leaving. When she emerged, Devlin stood at the top of the stairs, tall and freshly shaven, his mustache and goatee trimmed to perfection. He took her arm.

"How did you know it was I?" she asked.

"Your fragrance, madam. Your scent is distinctive."

"I changed perfumes only this morning."

"I don't need your perfume to identify you. You are my mother."

Below, Jessica sat on a bench-like settee in the foyer pensively staring toward a window as mother and son reached the bottom of the stairs. Devlin turned immediately toward the brooding girl, surprising his mother with his uncanny ability to sense Jessica's presence without being able to see her. He said, "Come, child."

The girl afforded him only an icy glance before directing her frown back toward the window. "Your Grace. I am not a pet to heel at your call or whistle or the snap of your fingers."

He obviously struggled to subdue a smile. "I apologize, Miss Blair, for offending your sensibilities. My mother and I would consider it an honor if you would walk with us."

She stood and stepped to his side. "Your graceful apology is graciously accepted, Your Grace." She smiled at her permutations of his title. Her tone deepened. "What do you think you are doing on your feet?"

He placed a firm hand on her shoulder. "Walking upright, as a man should. Now turn around, you mouthy wench, and lead us out into the sunshine."

The dowager released his arm. "I have things to check in the kitchen." Without waiting for leave, she turned and departed quickly.

Jessica wanted to pursue his casual observation. "How do you know the sun is shining, Your Grace?"

"I can hear it in your voice, in the lightness of your step. You love the out-of-doors. I can feel you straining at your bit, like a filly, eager to be turned out to romp. Are you not that impatient foal?"

"Yes I am, Your Grace." She led him toward the front door a footman opened as they approached.

"Then why were you sitting there in the corner, glumly studying the day instead of venturing out?"

"Concerns, Your Grace. I have concerns."

His hand on her shoulder drifted up to her nape, which was bare above the scooping neckline of her muslin day dress, one of Martha's. Like his mother, Jessica had a scent of her own. At the moment, her fragrance suggested she had been in the kitchen near the stove when morning tea was steeping, the stables where she'd absorbed the aroma of hay and horses, and in the garden where she had garnered the scent of roses, pine, and honeysuckle.

"What concerns, Jessica?" His fingers brushed her soft flesh, following the curve of her swanlike neck. Her hair, tied back, brushed his hand. He wrapped the abundance around a fist and gave it a teasing yank before losing his fingers in the baby-fine coils. He pulled tendrils to his nostrils and inhaled.

Aware of his playful hand studying her, Jessica rolled a shoulder to interrupt its wandering.

"I need to go home, Your Grace."

He froze and held a moment.

"Just for a day or two to see that things are set right," she added. She heard the catch in his voice as his expression darkened.

"I thought we had an agreement."

"Yes. We have. Of course, but this is my third day away. I must see to my mother, make sure she has food to eat, someone to check on her every day."

He inhaled. "I am lost every moment you are out of my..." He stopped short of saying 'out of my sight.' "I cannot allow you to go." He hesitated. "What I mean is, I do not want you to go."

"I will be gone a day and a half. Two at the outside. You may discover, during that time, you've made a fool's agreement." She was baiting him. "If you change your mind, however, you must forfeit the reward anyway, as agreed."

He chuckled and the frown wrinkles smoothed from his forehead. "I have no doubt, Jessica Blair, that you are a vexation to every grocer and tradesman in Welter, harrying and dealing with the finesse of a seasoned monger. Is that an apt assumption?"

She bit her lips together and snickered away the question without answering.

• • •

Neighbors, tenants, two families from London who were staying at their country homes nearby, called that day, distracting the duke from his infirmity. Although Devlin felt as if they were there to gawk and satisfy their curiosity and gather gossip, he greeted them hospitably. Knowing the keep's layout as he did, it was fairly easy to move about, often making visitors forget his affliction.

When the ten-year-old daughter of a prominent noble family slid a chair away from its place in front of the hearth, however, Devlin bumped it rather decisively and fell back a step before he regained his balance.

Noticing the child's look of satisfaction, Jessica grew more watchful. She skillfully maneuvered Devlin around subsequent obstacles, annoyed that the little girl's parents seemed oblivious to the child's continuing, intentional mischief.

• • •

Devlin insisted Jessica travel to Welter in his private coach, in spite of her objections that his shiny black carriage with the ducal coat of arms would draw too much attention.

To her surprise, the giant called Bear was assigned to drive her. Devlin spoke to the man intently, as well as to Figg, assigned as footman, then summoned six outriders to issue them their instructions.

From what Jessica could overhear, the duke charged each one individually and jointly with Jessica's safety, ordering that each defend her with his life, if need be. He promised handsome rewards for their returning her safely and at top speed to Gull's Way.

The escort took his words to heart, allaying his concern that she make the trip to her home and back in safety. And with speed. He directed them to begin well before daylight the next morning and to have her back within his walls before midnight.

• • •

No longer wearing the bandage around his head, Devlin was present in the early morning darkness, using a cane to feel his way into the kitchen to prod the cooks to hurry with packing food for the travelers' journey.

"There is no reason I cannot go along," he said more than once, concluding by telling Jessica, "Wait while I dress. I'm going."

Jessica held silent while he worried aloud, but spoke up with his new pronouncement. "You are healing nicely, Your Grace. The jostling carriage might set your recovery back. Such a hurried trip would sap your strength, even if it did no other damage."

Standing in the roadway, he lifted vivid blue eyes to address her as she came down the stairs. She had never seen both of his eyes open and would have sworn at that moment that he could see her. However, those eyes did not follow as she silently descended several more steps. His gaze continued where her voice had been.

"This coach bears the ducal crest and I am the duke. If I say I am going, no yardarm of a girl is going to deny me."

She recognized his annoyance and his frustration. She lowered her voice to conciliatory. "Then I will not go…this way."

As her voice became quieter, his volume increased. "What do you mean by that?"

"I mean, I can make this day-long trip in the comfort of your carriage with food you have provided, and your trusted men watching after me, or I can strike out for home alone and on foot.

"I am not a servant in this house, nor subject myself to your fits of temper. If my responsibilities are going to add to your injuries, I must go and not cause you additional hardship."

Devlin opened his mouth, but stopped before any sound emerged. He paused, then said, "I don't like your threatening me, chit."

"Chit, am I?" She noted the quick glance that passed between Bear and Figg, but would not be distracted. You call me chit, implying I am as insignificant as a stray cat, or a minstrel to entertain you with foolish antics."

Her words came faster as their volume rose. "I am an intelligent woman with valid thoughts and opinions. Even a scullery maid can be concerned about her significance in the universe."

As she spoke, she tossed the hood back off her head, slipped the tie on her new, custom-made, ermine-lined pelisse, raked that garment from her shoulders and dropped it in a heap on the steps.

"I don't want your fine clothes or your generosity, with conditions. I will go where I will, when I will, with or without your leave." She practically spat the last word as she rolled the soft kid gloves he'd given her from her hands.

Attempting to move toward her, Devlin stumbled on the first step but kept his feet as he climbed swiftly, groping, guiding by the sound of her voice.

His tone became a purr as he approached. "No, no. Nightingale. Dear, precious creature. This show of ferocity is not necessary. You are not normally given to tantrums. Does my concern for your well-being offend you so deeply as all that?"

His flailing resulted in his grabbing one of her hands. His face stiffened. "Where are your gloves? It's too cold for you to be out in the early morning chill without your gloves." He groped up her arm to find she had no wrap. "Go back into the house at once. It is a brisk morning and you have need of both your pelisse and your gloves. What were you thinking coming out without proper attire? I personally ordered your cloak cut down from a favorite of my own. The cloak is woven wool and silk, the collar ermine. I had it made to keep you warm on this journey."

Her anger mitigated by his words and his concern, Jessica grew quiet. Her own mother had never shown such regard.

She looked to the dowager framed in the doorway. The older woman's gaze shifted from Jessica to soften with approval as it settled on her son.

The dowager then exchanged a pleasant, knowing glance with Bear. Jessica had thought the dowager did not like the giant. She needed to ask someone about the puzzling looks between those two.

"Will you let me go alone, as we planned?" Jessica asked as Devlin rubbed her chilled hands briskly between his huge, warm ones.

"Of course. Nightingale." He released her hand. "I was merely concerned. You are precious beyond price to me."

She thought herself an ungrateful wretch. "Thank you, Your Grace." She lifted her free hand to stroke his face. He caught the hand and pressed his lips to her palm.

"Now, where is your wrap, my darling little hen wit?"

She giggled. "Spreading the stairs beneath our feet."

His eyes were the color of sapphires, so brilliantly blue that it was hard to imagine they were sightless.

"While you were throwing your tantrum, you were tossing your clothing, casting my gifts at your feet like a spoiled young royal?"

Jessica hummed an affirmative, "Un-huh."

Devlin obviously tried to acquire an annoyed, fatherly expression, but he suddenly erupted instead, chuckling first, then shouting laughter into the early morning chill. "Temper, was it? It is as if we truly are related, Nightingale."

Henry, watching from the doorway, scurried down the steps to retrieve Jessica's cape, gave it a shake, and held it while she slid her arms into the sleeves. He then swept up the gloves and held each while she fitted her hands into them, her giggles burbling along with the duke's rumbling laughter.

"Are you laughing at me, Your Grace?" There was a cool warning in her tone that only fueled his mirth. He threw his head back to laugh toward the heavens. Henry steadied the duke who rocked precariously on the steps.

Devlin caught the back of Jessica's hooded head. "No, little cuckoo, I am laughing at myself. I find my own behavior absurd. I am the lord of this fine estate and of lands stretching beyond the horizon in every direction. I am temporarily incapacitated by an injury inflicted by ruffians, but the more serious blow has come from you. I have been felled by a slender girl whose primary resource is her own mettle."

She sputtered, but he waved a hand to prevent her interruption.

"To complicate matters, I adore you, quite hopelessly, even as you vex my soul." He sobered. "Truly, if you were older, I would defy my birthright, the Queen, the empire itself, and marry you simply for the joy you bring to my staid, orderly existence."

Nonsense, she reminded herself.

"This will be an endless day for me, here, without you, Nightingale."

"I prefer that name to the others which you call me, my lord: cuckoo, gosling, hen wit, chit."

"And I prefer that you call me Devlin, yet you refuse to do so. Perhaps one preference will prompt the other...chit. Now, take very good care of my eyes, since we are sharing yours for the present."

"Yes, Your Grace. I mean, Devlin."

"I will be in this same spot, waiting on these steps when you return, Nightingale."

"There's no need of that."

"You are my eyes, darling. What else can I look forward to, if not to seeing you?"

Chapter Seven

Jessica had never been complimented, catered to, never been so lavishly fed, quartered or attired. Pampered. It was the kind of treatment any woman would adjust to too easily, and Jessica knew a woman reared as she had been was even more vulnerable.

Away from this place, five hundred pounds was a vast sum, but it would not buy, even in her world, the homage she received here, in house and out, nor the joy of the dowager's constant approval.

Jessica had known the responsibility for care and feeding of her own mother since she was twelve. Her mother accepted her service as due, but it was never enough. Jessica supposed it was natural to bask in the dowager's approval. She had never known such appreciation before.

The problem, of course, was this wonderful life depended on Devlin's remaining blind, and she didn't want that. When his sight returned, he would no longer require her eyes, or her presence. Truly he did not require either of those now, surrounded as he was by a household of family and servants willing to do what little she did for him.

• • •

The coach clattered along the road, its six outriders ranging, two ahead and four behind, as its occupant pondered. She was lulled almost to a stupor when a commotion outside brought the coach to an abrupt halt.

An all-too-familiar voice shouted, "Jessica, my darling wife, step out here into the morning and explain yourself."

"John," she whispered. As if things were not complicated enough, John Lout had arrived to further confound her. An odd recurring thought again darted through her mind. Never was a man so aptly named as John Lout.

Although he sometimes appeared at inconvenient times, like today, John once had arrived at a most fortuitous time. At that event, Jessica had been desperately glad to see him.

Thinking, she threw off her gloves and the pelisse and opened the carriage door to find her betrothed and three other equally shabby riders, one astride a burro. "Yes, John, I am here, and it's glad I am to see you."

She poked her head out first, and then moved onto the step, clinging to the carriage door. "How do you happen to be out here so early?"

"Aye, lass, what are you doing in there at the same time, I might ask? Word is, you were abducted by another devil. I came to rescue you again." He gave Bear a suspicious glance, but the giant remained seated on the box and neither moved nor spoke as their eyes met.

Jessica looked into John's misshapen face on which excess flesh hung from his jowls. She schooled her own expression, to look both respectful and pleased to see him. "Thank you, John, but this time, as you may tell, I hardly have need of rescue."

His expectant look dissolved to disappointment. "I was told you needed assistance."

She smiled. "You are always my hero, John, even when I am not in danger. But you know that already."

Confusion replaced tentative anger in his stare as he remained astride the mangy horse that swayed beneath his brawn.

"Word came that you was being held against your will in a stronghold known as Gull's Way. We were in search of the place when one of my men saw ye. He recognized the paint on this here coach as that belonging to the cad holding you."

The ducal coat of arms. She knew that was going to cause trouble. Trying to maintain a look of calculated approval, Jessica broadened her smile. This situation bore cautious handling.

"The old duke was struck down by ruffians, John. He was robbed and left broken and bleeding on the road." She wrung her hands and changed her expression to regret.

"Hmmm." John appeared to follow the story.

"I found him lying back in the underbrush off the side of the road," she continued. "I delivered him to his home." She conjured a pitiful look, which must have been convincing as concern spread John's face. "He was blind, John, made so by an evil blow to the back of his head. I was the only one about to help him."

Satisfied with John's gloomy countenance, she continued. "While I may lack your depth of tenderness, John, I know how it feels to be caught and helpless, as you have reason to know."

He gave a nod and they exchanged a tender look.

While she was pacifying John, however, his band of three was getting restless, their mounts shuffling nervously at the approach of the trailing outriders.

"Are we to kill the buggers coming, John?" one asked.

"Maybe." Lout obviously didn't intend to be rushed to a decision.

Jessica ventured a quick glance at Bear and Figg. Both cast their attention at the team. They were leaving the handling of the situation to her, for now. She apparently was succeeding, so far.

She focused her attention again on her betrothed.

"John, the poor old duke was helpless. Abandoned. Blind. In just the little time it took for me to return him home, the man became quite attached."

John's scowl returned with a vengeance, but she threw up a hand to stop his next words.

"He's going to pay me, John, to serve until his sight returns."

Lout's eyes narrowed. "What services does his lordship intend buying with his blunt, and how much is he planning to pay?"

"A hundred pounds." She quibbled with herself, quieting her conscience. The duke's offer of five hundred included a hundred pounds, so she hadn't really lied…exactly.

John's eyes rounded. "For all that, I suppose he expects you to warm his bed." He looked as if he were considering his objections.

Jessica lowered her gaze. "No, John. He is a kind, older man. An honorable man. A peer of the realm, who has lost his eyesight, not his mind. The duke knows many beautiful, well-dressed, sweet-smelling ladies who, I am sure, would do the honors of his bed. He has no need of a peasant in tattered clothing."

John eyed her up and down. "'Pears to me yer clothing is not so tattered as it used ter be."

"There is a maid swollen with child. I have temporary use of her wardrobe." That, too, was true, although the gown she wore was made of fine new cloth and created specifically for Jessica by Mrs. Freebinder, the finest modiste in Shiller's Green.

John thought another long moment. The sounds of the approaching outriders grew louder.

"Has his majesty bid them come to his bed, these beautiful, sweet-smelling ladies?"

"Well, no."

"Was he the one put his babe on the maid?"

She cast him a hard look. "He did no such thing.

"I told you, John, he is old and frightened and crippled. A woman is the farthest thing from his mind."

Bear twisted to frown down at her. His look did not last long enough to let her eyes meet his.

She continued speaking, as much to provide information for the coachmen's ears as to explain to John.

"You know I have saved myself for marriage, John. You have proved your chivalry many times by helping me preserve that gift."

He straightened in his saddle and allowed a slight smile of, what…pride? Probably. Saving her virtue had given him certain standing, at least in his own mind. She didn't know why she was being smug. John had prevented her deflowering, even if he did so to protect property he considered his own.

Smiling with genuine regard, Jessica said, "You and I will soon have need of the money, John. The old duke has a reputation for being kind and generous."

When she glanced at Bear, he puckered his lips and nodded solemnly to confirm her words. Lout, too, took in the driver's response, and Jessica plunged ahead.

"Please, John, allow me to finish my sworn oath to the duke and earn the reward."

Without considering his companions, John nodded, provoking one of his men to say, "But, John, our plan was to…"

John's shout made Jessica jump. "Shut yerself up or I'll slit yer throat and stop yer blathering." The man quailed beneath John's glare. "This is between me and my lady. Has nothing to do with you."

"We was to get the money chest off the coach here and divvy up what's in it."

Bear looked alert, but spoke with uncharacteristic humility. "There's no money chest riding here, only the meager sum we carry in our purses."

"What's in the baskets there at yer feet?"

"Food to see us to the lady's home and back."

"Throw 'em down."

"The food baskets?"

"Right."

Bear did as he was told.

John turned in his saddle and squinted at his three cohorts, then looked back at the coachman. "Empty yer pockets then." He tossed a careless look at Jessica. "The three a' ya."

She reached back onto the seat for her purse. It contained ten ducats—her egg money.

"What's this?" John jingled the coins that were swallowed as he dribbled them into his hand. "The man's a duke, you say, yet he don't give ye any more than this for traveling?"

"That's not his money," she said, swelling with indignation. "I wouldn't take charity from any man, John. You know that. That's my money, from selling the eggs from my own hens."

His face twisted as he shook the ducats from his hand into his trouser pocket. "I'll hold 'em for ye, lass, return 'em when our time comes." He gave her a significant look and a wink.

Caught by surprise, she couldn't control the involuntary shiver and was glad he didn't notice.

John and his men yanked their mounts around, bounded into the woods, and were out of sight when the outriders came into view.

"Why are ye stopped?" one of the men shouted. "What's amiss?"

Jessica stared at Bear and Figg, wordlessly begging them to keep her secret, promising with the plea in her eyes to repay the money they had forfeited.

Shifting his eyes from her to the outriders, Bear said something about a loose harness.

• • •

Jessica's brother, Brandon, looked up from a kettle of wash steaming over a fire in the yard and stared at Jessica waving to him from the coach.

"Where've you been, girl?" He eyed the rig and the outriders suspiciously. "What's all this?"

He stopped stirring and wiped his hands on the apron covering his trousers.

Jessica absently allowed Figg to hand her out of the carriage.

"I'm here to ask a favor of you, Brandon," she said, ignoring her brother's questions. As his expression darkened, she rushed to continue. "The job will pay us a lot of money, if I can arrange things so I can do what is required."

Using the favorable responses she'd gotten from John Lout as a guide, Jessica repeated her description of the duke, again painting him as old and decrepit, temporarily incapacitated and willing to pay for her time until he healed.

"You're asking me to take care of this carping old woman by myself?" Brandon scowled as if not able to believe what he was hearing, and glanced toward the cottage.

"Yes."

Jessica didn't mention the duke had offered to let their mother live at the keep. After considering, she decided declining was the wisest course. She had trouble enough caring for her mother without having the woman pampered by a houseful of servants. Returned to their cottage afterward, her mother would, no doubt, expect Jessica to provide the care delivered by an entire staff, including frequent baths and fancy meals.

"He will pay me," said Jessica. "More than I could make off my hens and Mr. Maxwell in a year."

As she expected, mention of payment eased her brother's concern.

"She doesn't require much, Bran." Jessica used the childhood nickname and gazed up at him to remind him that he was taller and older and had done little lately to contribute to their mother's care or upkeep.

"You could live here for the few days required. The cottage is warm on a chill night. You can hunt. If you circulate word, mothers of eligible girls will bring all the food you can eat."

"And wag their pig-faced daughters to simper and flutter their lashes at me." He eyed Jessica skeptically. "How much?"

"Maybe as much as a hundred pounds."

Brandon's eyes rounded.

"They say the old duke is generous that way." She increased her volume. "Ask the coachmen." She turned appealing eyes toward the coach in the road a short distance away. Bear, again seeing the plea in her face, whether he had heard, or not, nodded assurance that whatever she alleged, was true.

"I'll do it for half," Brandon said, trying to appear sure of himself, but continuing to look ridiculous in his washer woman apron.

"Half?" She made her tone indignant. She did not want to promise any portion of her earnings before they were in her hands. Also, of course, Brandon would be suspicious if she agreed too easily. "That isn't fair. I do all the work and you get half the pay?"

"All the work?" He looked at the kettle of laundry still bubbling twenty feet from them. "You're expecting me to provide your mother's food, fix her meals, and clean up after her."

"She is your mother, too. Those are the things I do for her every day, with no help from you, Brandon Blair, much less pay."

"You're a woman. You're supposed to do those things."

"I'm supposed to do those things for a husband and family of my own, like Dulcie does for Clarence. You and she have left me responsible for Mum while Dulcie runs a home of her own and you run wild, cuckolding wealthy men, dipping into their wives and into their pockets while never passing a bit along to Ma or me."

"Wedding John Lout seems little improvement over what you do here for Ma."

"Marry John Lout? Whatever made you think I was going to do that?"

"You've been betrothed since you were tots, Jess. Everybody knows it."

"Being betrothed is no guarantee a man and a woman will wed."

It suited her purpose to encourage his thinking it. Only today she again had exploited the assumption. She had played similar scenes for similar reasons since he declared them betrothed, when she was six and he, ten. Brandon must be mad to think she would marry John Lout. She would die first, or disappear, which was nearer her actual plan.

To create a spirit of camaraderie, Jessica walked to the wash kettle and, with disregard for her fine, new apparel, she picked up the stirring paddle and began to work the boiling clothes.

As she manipulated the laundry, she also manipulated her brother, haggling until he agreed to one-third of the one hundred pounds she expected from the duke.

Calculating, she had bartered fifty ducats to John Lout and thirty-three and one-third to Brandon. How much would that leave? The actual promised five hundred pounds less eighty-three and one-third pounds. She smiled. The balance would allow her to leave Welter for good, once she consigned her other obligations.

Before hanging the clothes to dry, Jessica asked Brandon to loan her any money he had. Grudgingly, he produced three guineas. She walked to the carriage and handed Bear the money.

"Take your men to the tavern in Welter for food and drink," she said and fanned a hand to forestall his argument. "We no longer have food or drink."

Bear squared his substantial jaw. "The duke ordered us to guard you with our lives, Miss."

She put her hands on her hips. "My brother will watch after me, Bear. Besides that, we have only one squirrel to cook. One will scarcely feed our mother and Brandon and me, much less the eight of you."

With an annoyed look at Brandon, Bear nodded. "We'll be back after we've eaten. Be ready to leave when we return, by mid-afternoon. No later." His words sounded more like a threat than a promise.

As the carriage with the ducal crest rumbled off down the road, Jessica walked into the hut to greet her mother.

She removed the woman's soiled clothes and bathed her with warm water from a basin, listening all the while to complaints. Jessica changed the bed before preparing the meal.

When the hut was filled with the aroma of cooking meat and Jessica had made a pan of biscuits to serve with the squirrel Brandon had killed that morning, she mentioned her hens.

"Brandon, my girls need feeding while I'm away." She watched as her brother sopped gravy with a biscuit. "They are important to our income, Mum's and mine.

"You need to go to the pens mornings and evenings to throw them some grain."

Without looking at her, he said, "It'll cost you another ten."

"The hens provide food for your mother, Brandon."

"All right, seven, but no less."

"Five. You sometimes eat here, too."

"All right, five, and the thirty-three."

"Done," she said, offering a hand.

He took her hand in his greasy one and smiled. She smiled back. He had already forgotten the one-third pound. He might overlook the extra five when time came to pay him. Far be it from her to remind him. After all, she was the one earning the duke's award.

At that thought, a vivid picture of Devlin stole into her mind, momentarily blocking out the crude cottage and its inhabitants.

Earlier, she had visualized the old, feeble duke she described, first to John Lout, then to her brother. This sudden image caught her unaware, so vivid it nearly paralyzed her. No matter how she had described him, Devlin Miracle, the twelfth duke of Fornay, was in truth, the smartest, most devastatingly handsome, witty, virile, thoughtful, generous man she had ever met. The mental picture of him, so lifelike, distracted her, and she scurried to clear her plate.

"Jess-i-ca?" Her mother's wail summoned the daughter back from her illusion. "Have mercy, child, and bring an old woman a bit of tea to settle her stomach."

The image of Lady Anne was superimposed over Devlin's, and Jessica remembered that the dowager and Jessica's mother were nearly the same age. Of course, the dowager had enjoyed tangible benefits as well as the attention of a devoted husband. It wasn't fair to compare the two.

"Yes, Mama." She wiped her hands on her apron and hurried to her mother's bedside for her cup.

Leaning back, his feet crossed and propped in front of the fire, Brandon looked from their mother in her bed to Jessica.

"She could get up and fetch that herself."

Their mother flashed him an angry look. "I no longer have dependable use of my legs, Brandon. Jessica knows that."

"It's your own sloth, Ma, that keeps you bedfast. That and Jessica's energy. You have her fooled, but not me, and I'm the one's going to be seeing after you for the next…" He looked startled. "For how long, Jess?"

"Maybe as long as ten days." Seeing his scowl, she revised. "Maybe less, depending."

"Will he pay you more for a longer stay?"

"It is likely."

Brandon pursed his lips. "If it's a week, the old girl may be back on her feet and waiting on herself by then."

Their mother narrowed her eyes at him. Jessica recognized, for the first time, that these two, mother and son, were both accustomed to having their own way. The only thought worse than returning home to support her mother and argue with Brandon was the prospect of marrying John Lout.

Dear God, she hoped that did not happen. She needed money to escape—and find a way to provide for her mother without being physically present herself.

• • •

The coach had begun its return trip when Jessica signaled a stop. Figg leaped down, strode to the carriage door, and poked his head inside.

"What is it ye'r needing, Miss?"

"A moment's conversation with Bear," she said.

Bear clamored off the box. At Jessica's nod, he opened the door and offered a hand to steady her step down. She walked a little way before she motioned for him to accompany her.

They walked in silence before she turned to confront him.

"There are things I do not know," she began. "I might be of more assistance to the duke if I were enlightened."

He gave a series of nods, indicating he understood.

She looked into his eyes trying to decide if she should trust him. "What is your true name, Bear?"

"Ben Bruin."

"Ah, so that's why they call you Bear."

"That and my size, Miss."

"Will you tell me how you became friends with His Grace?"

It was like pulling teeth, but gradually Bear warmed to her questions.

He had been a wanderer and nearly thirty years of age when he tramped into Gull's Way some twenty years before.

"The old duke's sons were hellions back then," Bear said, smiling a bit as he drifted back in memory. "They were into every nook and cranny, every cave and hole—harmless places mostly, along with some that wasn't so harmless. The old duke and her ladyship needed help with 'em."

Jessica did not want to look at the man or distract him once she had him talking.

"The old duke asked me right off if I had a temper and I told him I had, but I kept it under control, for the most part.

"He asked if I was a decent hunter, a fisherman, and swordsman. He said I looked like a bonny fighter. I assured him I was all of those and more. That seemed to please him well enough. He shouted for Patterson to find Devlin and send him to us."

Bear grinned at the memory. "He told Patterson not to bother to have the boy wash. Told me the middle son—nine years old, he were then—wouldn't stay clean long enough to make washing worth our wait.

"As you might suppose, I took to Devlin right off, and he to me. The duke set most of his attention on training the older boy, Rothchild. He took little time or trouble with the younger ones.

"Lattimore—Lattie—he was only five years old when I come here. He mainly stayed with the nanny and the governess.

"But Devlin," his grin broadened, "was as fearless and adventurous as any boy born." Bear sent her a pride-filled glance while his grumbling words seemed to contradict his expression. "That's a bad combination in a youngster running unhobbled like he was." He stopped talking as if he were lost in his memories.

"You've been with them ever since?"

"Yes."

"Were you able to conquer Devlin's wildness?"

Bear laughed and shook his head. "Not so much conquered as reined it in a bit. I gave guidance here and there as I could. I never had no intention of breaking his spirit.

"The boy had a natural inclination with animals, particularly horses. He had no fear—not even enough to show a proper regard for wild things, in particular those a man is hunting. I sometimes helped best by letting him get into trouble. I only let him suffer enough to teach him to curb his riskiness some."

Bear touched the thin strip of his scalp where hair no longer grew. He smoothed his hair over with his hand so that the spot was covered. *Was the scar a memento of his own youthful excesses, or of Devlin's?*

"I tried to advise the boy before he stumbled into real danger. I helped him when he caught some of the hard lessons. If I didn't keep them from happening, I was there to pick up the pieces after."

"Like what?"

He appeared to approve the question. "Devlin broke his arm riding a waterfall that dropped fifty feet to feed the Longrine River."

"How old was he then?"

"I believe he was twelve, or nearly so."

"Did he cry?"

"Nah. He was trying to be a man by then. It took more than a broken arm to make him cry."

"How was it repaired?"

"I didn't bother the duke with it right off. I took the boy straight away to Dr. Brussel. He set the bone mending before nightfall. The excitement was past before we told the duke and duchess."

"Did you like all three boys?"

"God's truth, I loved each one for being just who he was, but it was Devlin who was turned more to my ways."

"Were you devastated when Rothchild died?"

He looked surprised. "Of course. We all was ruined for a time. Soon after, the old duke talked to me about how it was even more important that I watch closer after Devlin."

"And...?" she began but stopped as Bear glanced at the sun and interrupted.

"Here now, we need to get going."

They had a long way to go, yet she wanted to learn more of Devlin as a boy. As they walked back to the coach, she prodded Bear again. "Was Devlin more careful after his brother died?"

"No. If anything, he was more daring."

"How do you mean?"

"Not long after Roth died, Devlin intentionally offended the Black Tartan at the gaming tables. Tartan would have killed him for sure."

"You prevented that?"

"I drugged his drink."

"The Tartan's?"

"Devlin's."

"Oh."

Acknowledging her surprise, Bear's laugh rumbled. "The new heir to the title made quite a spectacle of hisself, sliding out of his chair and into a heap under the table. Dropped near a whole room full of drunken gamblers to their knees, rolling with laughter and bawdy talk about a boy with a mouth big enough to bait the Tartan being yet too green to hold his liquor." Bear hesitated. "I don't recall that I ever confessed that particular deed. I can't say I ever planned to. I'd just as soon you didn't mention it."

Jessica smiled, pleased that she and Bear shared a confidence. "Was he ever sickly?"

"Devlin? Nah. When he was, I nursed 'im through it, and through those heartbreaks a young man is bound to tumble into from time to time."

She felt as if a rock had hit the bottom of her stomach. "When he was in love?"

"Not that he ever was what you might consider in love, but he was a fair one to fall into infatuations easy enough."

"Have there been many women in his life?"

"He's had his share. He's a handsome fella'. Also, a' course, being rich as he is and with a title and property and all. Well, them's the sorts of things that draws the ladies like bears to honey."

"You don't think he has been in love?"

"No." He eyed her oddly. "Not before now, anyhow. Most of the ladies in polite society disappoint him when they turn out to be less than the ideal woman an impressionable young man dreams up in his own mind."

They reached the coach door.

"Did he ever make a fool of himself over a woman?"

"Once, maybe. It came down to a duel. It had been a duel that killed Roth, a' course. I was not gonna let that happen to the old duke's family again. I sent word to the prefect of police who was at the site waiting for the participants when we arrived.

"That policeman give the opponents a lecture. Told 'em about horrible diseases in his jail. He made promises, said he had no forbearance with young men with nothing better to do than challenge one another to duels. He said if they wanted to fight, they should buy theirselves a commission and go into the military. So that's what Devlin did."

"He did?"

Bear opened the coach door, caught the back of Jessica's elbow and rather firmly directed her inside.

"I went along, a' course. Our soldiering was cut short when the duchess sent word the old duke was dying. We went home in a hurry." He slammed the coach door. "Just as this party is gonna do right now."

• • •

The Twelfth Duke of Fornay paced the library. Instead of calming him, his mother's reading quietly in the chair near the window irritated him. Out of habit, he looked toward her and was soothed by the silhouette of her profile against the sunlight streaming behind her.

He stopped mid-stride.

It was the miracle he had sought. He could see. Not details, but shapes. Outlines of furnishings and his mother's form. The joyous shout nearly erupted before he thought. What changes might this miracle cause? He needed to put this into perspective before he shared it.

He should be jubilant. And he was, but if his sight had returned, he would no longer need Jessica's. He was not prepared to lose her—not yet. He wanted her near. Not just for her eyes.

As he pondered, a cloud blotted the sun. He lost the visual images and was once again blind.

The glimpse raised possibilities and, along with them, angst he did not expect. Return of his sight certainly presented new possibilities. He needed to harvest the benefits Nightingale provided—her exuberance, her optimism, her bright good cheer. The dowager was attached to the child as well. The entire household reflected her influence.

There were positive aspects for Jessica as well. He and the dowager could provide advantages for such a bright girl, establish her a place in society. Make a decent match for her.

Using his cane, Devlin fumbled his way back to his chair and sat heavily.

His returning eyesight presented a whole new realm of possibilities, not all of them pleasant.

Chapter Eight

True to his word, Devlin was pacing the steps of his great house as the coach bearing the ducal crest returned. It was nearing midnight and Jessica was exhausted but unable to sleep, excited by her return to Gull's Way. It seemed as if she had been gone for days instead of hours.

She doubted he would be waiting as he had said, yet she recognized the figure on the steps. He stood like a statue, bent slightly, both hands clasped on the cane in front of him.

Jessica threw open the coach door before the conveyance stopped and leaped. Her feet flying, disregarding pride and petticoats, she bolted over the graveled drive and bounded up the stairs.

Grinning, the duke tossed his cane to the side, opened his arms and braced himself. She leaped and he caught her up entirely, wrapping his arms all the way around her.

Then was the moment she had waited for, perhaps all her life. She was home for, surely, in all the world, this was where she belonged. It was a ridiculous thought, yet she embraced him, pressing her suddenly tear-dampened face to his jaw. She breathed in the familiar scent of him, and felt the tickle of his well-trimmed beard. Home at last.

As he touched his lips to her cool cheek, the rumbling in his chest brought her to her senses. She wriggled, but he did not immediately release her. Instead, he twisted so that her breasts scrubbed his chest. In her excitement, she had revealed what she had been determined to keep secret.

The man thought her a child. That first night, riding Sweetness, he had run his hands over her shoulders, trailed them down her arms, had even fitted her hips snugly between his legs as she sat the saddle before him. In spite of that intimacy, he considered her an infant. He disregarded her initial claims that she was a grown woman, capable of experiencing the sensuous responses any woman might to such a man.

Holding her closely in this unguarded moment, he would be aware of her prominent breasts, which she had been able to keep from his sightless scrutiny. In spite of her earlier declarations, Jessica thought it better he not realize her maturity just yet.

Heated by a blush, embarrassed by the joy of luxuriating for those brief moments in his arms, Jessica wriggled until she broke free. Devlin seemed reluctant to yield his hold.

"Oh, Your Grace, I am so sorry. It's a wonder I did not knock you down."

He cleared his throat. "Yes, well, your greeting may have provided a test of my recovery. I proved equal to the challenge, in spite of my surprise." His face took on that mischievous look as he added, "You might say, I was doubly rewarded."

She took his meaning. He had been made aware of her breasts. Perhaps they would no longer argue whether she was child or woman. The mystery of that misunderstanding was why other members of the household—his own mother included—who realized the duke's mistake, did not enlighten him, explaining that Jessica was not the moppet he thought.

Tangled in her web of thoughts, Jessica retreated two steps and caught one of Devlin's outstretched hands in both of hers to indicate her whereabouts, then she dropped a full awkward curtsy. She spoke breathlessly.

"Your Grace."

He sobered and adopted her formality. "Was your journey successful, Jessica Blair?"

"Yes. I accomplished everything I set out to do."

"Did you bring your mother home with you then?"

Tears threatened at his referring to his magnificent residence as *home*, speaking as if it were her permanent abode as well as his. He turned his face toward the carriage as if looking for her companion.

"No, Your Grace, my brother Brandon agreed to be responsible for our mother until you are recovered."

Devlin's expression became playful, but his unseeing eyes narrowed. "How much will Brandon's attendance cost you, Nightingale?"

Her laughter burbled at his usual perceptiveness. "I told him you were paying me one hundred pounds. He and I haggled over what his share should be."

"And?"

"He gets one-third of my purse, but believes that to be thirty-three pounds."

"Of a hundred pounds rather than five hundred pounds?"

"That is correct."

"Not thirty-three and one-third?"

She burbled another giggle. "Brandon is not particularly apt at sums."

"So, you are willing to take advantage of him, are you?"

She stiffened, wondering if his taunt were part insult, until she again noted the mischief in his expression.

"He is older than I, Your Grace, and able to see to his own affairs. He has taken the advantage of me often in the past."

Tugging her hand to pull her close again, Devlin turned her so that her back was to him and set his fingers on her shoulder indicating she should lead him into the house. Henry, the valet, retrieved the cane that had been tossed aside.

"Will he take proper care of your mother and your hens?" Devlin asked.

She assumed her usual guide's position, one step in front and one to the side.

"I don't know, Your Grace, but I realized today, Mum will be a fair match for him, even if the birds are not."

"Should I send someone to fetch your poultry, Miss Blair?"

She frowned, not so much at the question as the designation. "Why are you calling me by my formal name again, Your Grace?"

"There seems to be renewed confusion about our identities. My Nightingale calls me Devlin, rather than sir or Your Grace."

Before she responded, they were through the doors and into the great hall. The dowager duchess stood poised at the top of the staircase.

"Your Grace," Jessica said, bobbing a quick curtsy. "Why are you still about at this time of night? Are you ill?"

Apparently unaware of his mother's presence and thinking Jessica was addressing him, Devlin said, "I promised to be on the steps awaiting your return, darling, to demonstrate that I will always keep my word to you. Others trust me for that. You have not yet learned to do so." He squeezed her shoulder affectionately. "But you will."

The dowager looked from Devlin to Jessica, then back before she cleared her throat, giving notice of her presence.

"Hello, Mother." Devlin raised his face to the stairs, as if able to see her there. "What are you doing up and about at this hour?"

"Like you, I was concerned about the safe return of our gosling."

Gosling? Jessica realized the older woman's references often reinforced Devlin's mistaken image of her as a child. Why did the dowager help mislead her son into thinking Jessica was an infant?

Another curiosity to ponder later. Jessica seemed to be amassing a list of those.

• • •

When the ladies had retired, Devlin summoned Bear to his sitting room for an account of their journey.

Bear capsulized his report until he got to the part John Lout played in the day.

"Who is this John Lout?" the duke asked.

"A local ruffian from Welter."

"What interest does he have in our Jessica?"

Bear looked at the floor and shuffled his feet. Devlin could tell the man was uncomfortable with what he was going to say next.

"It seems, Yer Grace, that our young mistress is betrothed to the blackguard. He goes so far as to refer to her as his wife."

Devlin tried to hide his annoyance. "Describe this John Lout person."

"He's young enough, all right. Above average height, but soft around the belly. 'Pears to like his ale. The brigands riding with him defer to him. He bullies 'em. When me and the men went to the inn for a meal, I made inquiries. The man makes his living thieving and poaching. The keep said Lout's not to be trusted. He's a man little troubled with keeping his word or behaving in an honorable way. Knows nothing of the habits of gentle men and women."

Devlin locked his hands behind his back and paced. "Betrothed, is she? To a ne'er-do-well. I suppose I shall have to do something about that."

"Is that all you need from me, Yer Grace?"

Devlin turned his full attention on Bear. "When did you begin addressing me as 'Your Grace'?"

He could hear the grin as Bear brightened. "Since ye've begun behaving the part, Yer Grace."

"Does this change you detect in my behavior please you?"

"Aye. It does my heart good to see you maturing to the office you was born to."

Devlin stepped in front of his old friend and opened his arms. The two men hugged one another like two great bears, and then broke the embrace, laughing.

"Thank you for your years of patient instruction," Devlin said, clapping the larger man on the shoulders.

"It's been my own pleasure to have a hand in watching the boy of promise grow into the man he was designed by his Maker to be."

With a silent, unseen salute, Bear let himself out of the chamber as Devlin's face darkened and he returned to his pacing to contemplate this new information.

• • •

Jessica had been back for two days, days in which she cajoled and baited the duke out of his occasional doldrums into trying things others thought him incapable or unwilling to do without sight.

With Job-like patience, she taught him to tat and knit. His fingers were thick and cumbersome, yet he persisted, determined to please her. She enjoyed the shared intimacy of the lessons, during which their bodies frequently brushed one another, light touches of little consequence to anyone else.

Devlin had visitors, both social and business associates. After supper one evening as he entertained such guests, Jessica strolled out into the twilight, walking to the paddocks to visit Freddie. The colt came at a stiff-legged run when he saw her. As she stood rubbing his nose, she noticed two figures walking together along the lane. Not wishing to interrupt, Jessica stood still and continued murmuring to the young horse.

As the walkers drew close, she recognized Martha, her figure, swollen with child, distinctive in the failing light. Jessica did not, however, recognize Martha's companion, who wore gentleman's attire. He was a grown man, tall, his stride uneven. The couple stopped near the top of the lane and the man appeared about to take his leave. Before he did, however, he brushed a hand over Martha's protruding belly and laughed, rather raucously, before he put a light kiss on Martha's forehead, mounted his waiting horse, and rode off toward the highway.

Jessica had seen the man before. In Welter. She stiffened. Yes. A man like this one had ridden with John Lout. He was notable in Welter, for he dressed and carried himself like a gentleman. If it were the same man, what link could there possibly be between John Lout, a gentleman, and a chambermaid from Shiller's Green?

• • •

Early one morning, at the end of her second week at Gull's Way, Jessica looked out to rejoice in the unseasonable warmth and a bright sun. The air was crisp, but there were bees and tiny spring beauties dotting the lawns, hints of summer coming. She found it invigorating.

She raised her chin with a new idea. She would take the duke out into this bracing day. He was accustomed to riding wherever and whenever he chose. Perhaps being confined to the house placed an additional, unnecessary damper on his spirits.

Jessica entered the dining room dressed in a vivid blue riding habit to find Devlin standing at the sideboard, his empty plate poised as he inhaled the fragrances of the breakfast selections before him.

She called a light "Good morning," as she approached, but he was turning toward her before she spoke.

"Is it a good morning to you?" he asked. There was annoyance in his manner and his voice. "I'm glad you approve the day."

"I do approve, Your Grace, and so will you."

"Not I, Nightingale, for I cannot see it."

"Not see the gulls circling?"

He set his rock hard jaw in a belligerent line. "No."

"The gulls' antics are clearly stored in your mind's eye, are they not?"

He hesitated a moment before his jaws relaxed slightly. "Yes, well, I suppose so."

"The brilliance of the sunshine chasing early morning fog from these rolling, manicured lawns? Have you no recollection of that?"

"Of course, Nightingale. I've spent most of my life at Gull's Way. I am familiar with all the seasons here."

"Then those pictures remain clear in your head?"

"Am I to live the balance of my years on memories?"

"I would say not, Your Grace."

"Am I ever again to gallop Vindicator through the open fields, the sun and wind, rain or snow or sleet stinging my flesh?"

Jessica flashed the dowager a warning squint as the older woman entered the room to hear the wistful tone in Devlin's voice.

"I should think you would be happy to have an excuse for missing all that, Your Grace, as unpleasant as you make it sound. I suppose you will count it as loss that you will not have to endure any of those when you ride out today?"

"What?" He looked as if he hadn't heard her correctly. His mother held her silence.

"In spite of the glorious weather and your difficult attitude, sir, I think I shall take you riding this morning."

Devlin set his stubborn chin toward her, and snorted his disbelief. "I hardly think a child—particularly a girl with so little experience riding—is competent to look after a blind man on a horse out in the open."

"You have a short memory, Your Grace, if you do not recall that this child did exactly that one night quite recently, and subsequently delivered you safely into your mother's arms under conditions hardly as inviting as these."

All right, she was taking credit for having accomplished a feat for which the horse was responsible, but her comment had the desired result. She had learned that to motivate this haughty man, she need only prick his pride to draw him.

He fairly threw his half-filled plate onto the serving table, but she did not allow him to argue.

"Oh no, Your Grace, you need a proper breakfast. We'll not provide excuses for failing to keep up with a child, and a girl at that."

"If I am to ride today, Jessica, I shall do so in the able company of a groom rather than a snippy chit who refuses to demonstrate the proper regard for me or my station."

"No, sir, you will not ride out with any groom, unless you prefer to ride Molly, that dottering old mare you assigned to my use."

Devlin's voice became thunderous. "This is my home, you impertinent baggage. The staff here, the villagers, everyone within the influence of these estates yields to my bidding."

"Yes, well, they might be intimidated enough by your bellowing and bullying to do so, but I am not, and I, sir, am the one authorized by Dr. Brussel to serve as your eyes. Furthermore, he insisted that when you and I disagreed, as he expected we might, I should exercise my own sound judgment rather than defer to your demands."

She did not allow him an interruption. "Not only that, sir, but your esteemed Dr. Brussel passed that command to your mother and others in this household. You shall either submit to me, you overbearing oaf, or, by heaven and by doctor's orders, I will keep you prisoner within these walls for as long as it takes you to develop a proper regard for *my* authority."

Jessica had braced for lengthy, difficult negotiations. She was not prepared for laughter.

Sputtering, spewing, apparently unable to speak, Devlin, the Twelfth Duke of Fornay, picked up the plate he had discarded and, groping, spooned eggs and meat onto it.

Apparently she had won.

"Mr. Patterson," Jessica said, "please ask Cook to prepare a picnic luncheon. I shall be at the back door to collect it shortly."

Disregarding the gaping stares, Jessica lifted her chin and set out to convince Figg that the duke should be allowed to ride his fractious stallion. To put the man on any other mount would undermine the confidence Jessica was determined to foster, even if it were risky.

An hour later, galloping into the day, Jessica realized all her brassy decisions were correct.

To begin, Sweetness exhibited exemplary behavior. As before, the huge animal seemed to sense Devlin's limitations and waited until his rider was well seated before he began to prance, demonstrating his usual eagerness to be off. Devlin laughed aloud at his mount's vigor.

"I doubt you and Molly will be able to keep up today, Nightingale," Devlin said, not bothering to veil the challenge in his voice.

He did not know she was not on Molly, but Dancer, a long-legged, eight-year-old gelding, one of the few horses in the duke's stable with quality to match Vindicator. Dancer also was the stallion's familiar stable mate which Figg thought might encourage Vindicator's proper behavior.

"Lead off, Your Grace. We will attempt to keep you in sight."

Laughing again, for no apparent reason, Devlin yanked Vindicator around, sent him on a course heading east and gave the horse his head. The mount kicked his heels, as excited as his rider. Luckily, the duke was familiar enough with the course to adjust as Vindicator gathered himself and jumped the stone wall at the far end of the field. Devlin's laughter resonated as man and horse flew over the barrier.

Jessica smiled. She didn't know where they were going, nor did she care. More sure of herself in the sidesaddle after several riding sessions from Figg mornings and afternoons, Jessica easily held Dancer in check.

The duke and his mount waited for them at the edge of a small lake. Devlin's fair hair was tousled, his face flushed. His broad grin exposed large teeth that gleamed lustrously white. Jessica couldn't help smiling at how hale and hearty he looked.

"Is this the spot for our picnic, Your Grace?"

"Please, Nightingale, indulge me. Call me Devlin, at least while we are away from the house…and alone."

She wondered at the curious hesitation. Was he as conscious of their isolation as she? "Dismount then, Devlin, and secure the horses." She jumped down, rather gracefully, she thought, under the circumstances, and handed Dancer's reins into Devlin's hand.

"But I can't…" he began before he apparently remembered to whom he was speaking. "Oh, I see. This is your attempt to make me more self-reliant. Is that it?"

He seldom secured his own mount when he had his sight, so the work was unfamiliar. If he did not perform the task, however, it would fall to her.

He muttered and fumbled with the horse's reins while he dismounted. Jessica removed the pack containing their luncheon secured behind the cantle of Dancer's saddle.

Humming lightly, because she was happy, as well as to give Devlin an idea of her whereabouts, Jessica spread the cloth over a grassy patch near the water and arranged the assorted meats—chicken and slices of beef—and cheese. As she opened the loaf of bread, she wondered if the loaf was that fresh, or if it retained its heat by being so close to the horse's body.

"What horse are you riding, Nightingale?"

She smiled that he had guessed. "Dancer. He is more a match for Vindicator's range."

"Hmm. You have had instruction?"

"Yes, mornings while you hid yourself away in your study and afternoons when you met with business associates."

"I see."

After a brief silence, the duke introduced another subject. "What do you think of our young queen, Nightingale, or have you any interest in politics?"

"I have, and I admire her."

"Of course you do. She is not yet twenty herself. It is only natural that she would appear attractive to a female of your tender years."

Jessica set out grapes, opened a bottle of wine and wondered at his words, which reflected a man's haughty attitude.

"The queen is already a shining example of the dignity we have missed in our royals in recent years," she said.

"You did not approve of King William?" It looked as if Devlin were making a valiant effort not to wave his hands to feel for obstructions as he made his way toward her.

"Victoria is much more dignified."

"In rather a frumpish manner."

"Attractive enough to entice a prince."

"He is her cousin."

"Yet I think they are in love."

"What? Royals do not marry for love, dear child. As the dowager would say, it simply is not done."

"You are practically stepping on me, Your…Devlin. You are on the quilt and may sit directly on that spot, if you like."

He dropped to his knees on the blanket, used his hands to determine his location, rolled onto his hip and stretched out on his side. One leg crossed over the other, he propped himself on an elbow. He looked completely at ease.

"What would you have first, meat and bread, cheese, or fruit?"

He ignored the question and new resonance in his voice alerted her to something changed.

"Will you marry for love, Nightingale?"

"Possibly."

"Do you mean to say you love this John Lout person?"

She giggled. "John Lout? No." Suddenly, realizing what his question revealed, she sobered. "What do you know of John?" Before he could answer, she added, "Furthermore, what business is he of yours?"

"Bear mentioned your meeting with Lout and his men. Bear enlightened me regarding your betrothal. I was disappointed you had not mentioned your lover." He paused, but she offered no explanation, nor did she correct his assumption. "Of course, such commitments can change when they involve someone of your tender years. I was merely curious."

"And you, Your Grace? Will you marry for love or will your marriage suit your sovereign?"

"Victoria is my sovereign. If you are correct and she married for love, I doubt she would demand less of those in her court."

"Would you like some grapes?"

"No." His expression turned serious. "What I would like is to see your face, Nightingale."

She lifted her chin, posing, casting her eyes heavenward. "Look all you like."

"While I cannot see you at this moment in the usual way, perhaps you would allow me to view your countenance by touch."

She lowered her chin, drew one breath, then a second before exhaling. She studied his face, looking for unwelcome intentions. She saw none. He appeared to be sincere and to harbor no evil design. She swallowed hard, the effort clearly audible in the quiet afternoon.

"All right." Her voice had a whispery quality that surprised her as much as her nervousness appeared to please him.

Devlin rolled onto his knees, gained his balance and reached for her. He advanced both hands at shoulder level, wiggling his fingers, inviting her to come within his grasp, then he ceased his suggestive motion and waited.

Rising onto her knees, mirroring his position, she bumped forward, a difficult maneuver as her riding habit tightened about her legs. Adjusting it, she inched closer.

When he made no attempt to grab at her, she took his right hand in both of hers and guided his fingers to her face. He raised his left hand with his right as he began, benignly enough, surveying her hairline, measuring with his thumbs to her brows.

"Some say a high forehead is a sign of intelligence," he murmured as he brushed his fingertips down her temples.

"An old wives' tale, Your Grace." Her voice sounded unsteady.

"Devlin," he corrected.

"Devlin," she repeated, her volume less than his.

"In your case, the old wives are correct. You are quick-witted, Nightingale."

His fingers followed her brows and traced her nose, making her extremely self-conscious. She twitched.

"Your nose is not nearly as long or as angular as I imagined. It is rather pert. Are you a comely girl, Jessica Blair?"

She felt the heat sweep upward and warm her face.

Feeling the heat, he smiled. "Ah, I've made you blush."

"Perhaps we should eat."

"But, my dear, I have not concluded my survey. Ah, I see that you have wide, round eyes. Tell me again their color?"

She recalled quite distinctly his mother telling him her eyes were hazel. Apparently he had not considered it information worth remembering. Her shoulders rose and fell with disappointment.

"No, Your Grace." She watched his expression closely. "They are rather drab—sometimes green, sometimes brown, sometimes a soulful gray, I'm told."

He didn't seem disappointed. "They change with the light or the color of your clothing?"

"Yes."

He bent forward a little, his face closing on hers as he reached for her hair. She turned her head and shrank back to remove the country maid's kerchief securing her coiling tresses. When she again put herself within his reach, he wound both hands into the long, unbound abundance.

"Did the milliner not design one of those ridiculous little hats to match your riding habit, Nightingale?"

"She did. Yes. A delightful bit of fluff, and very costly."

He slanted a disapproving look. "You did not choose to wear it for me?"

"I do not do it justice, and you are not able to appreciate it yet anyway."

"Ah." He smiled and nodded. "I see. What color is this wild tumble of hair?"

Before she could answer, he took a fistful to his nose and inhaled. "You smell of the out-of-doors, Jessica, of the woods and the flowers and the earth. The scent of you inspires me."

"Inspires you to what, Your Grace?"

He flinched at the title, but did not correct her as his fingers resumed exploring. "The color?" he repeated.

"Disappointingly, it is not as fair as new-mown hay, like yours or the dowager's. It is brown."

"Your cheeks feel warm, Nightingale." His playful expression turned to concern. "Are you ill, darling? Do you have a fever?"

He started to rise, but she put a staying hand on his shoulder, encouraging him to hold their positions kneeling before one another. She was again aware of the difference in their sizes as he loomed above her. She might be feverish, but the heat had nothing to do with her health.

"No, Your Grace, I am quite well. It must be the sun warming my face. Or the wind. Or the exertion of the ride. I am fine. Are you finished?"

He appeared to doubt her explanation, then the confusion left his face.

"No, dear heart. I find this game fascinating. I want to continue familiarizing myself with your features. Besides, I do not yet have an appetite for food. Have you?"

"No, I suppose not."

"Is there some other activity you would prefer?"

She gazed toward the stream. "We could fish, if you like."

He grinned broadly, as if her flimsy attempt to distract him had been just that—flimsy.

"First I would like to finish my study." He held his fingers poised, waiting for her to place her face again within his reach. "I have established that you have large, inquisitive eyes, which are green, gray or brown, depending on your garb, the weather, and your mood, and that you have a profusion of dark, coiling hair. Are you sometimes mistaken for a gypsy, Jessica?"

The word 'gypsy' raised bad memories. Jessica barked a sharp denial. "I am not." The words emerged clipped in a tone higher than her usual speaking voice.

Devlin caught her face between his hands, steadying her. "You have had an unpleasant experience with gypsies?"

She twisted, an effort to free her face, but he held her fast. "Yes."

"Tell me about it."

"No, Your Grace, it was a long time ago."

Devlin gave a strand of her hair a playful tug. "Was your problem with a man?"

"Yes." Her brusque retort extinguished his teasing grin.

"Did he steal you?"

Her voice dropped to a whisper. "Yes."

The duke's smile vanished. "Did he...?"

"No, he did not violate me, although that was clearly his intention."

Devlin's jaws flexed and his expression became granite hard and unyielding. "How did you avoid the assault?"

"John Lout, the man to whom I am betrothed, rescued me. John followed when he heard of my capture. He is a hunter and the best tracker around Welter. He arrived in time to save me."

Devlin lowered his hands to his sides and silence hung thick between them. "I wish I had been there, little bird. I wish I had ridden to your rescue and earned the devotion you feel for John Lout. I have been curious about your reason for promising yourself to him."

They remained like that, kneeling face to face, neither touching the other, for several moments before Devlin placed his hands again on either side of her head and ran his thumbs over her lips.

Closing her eyes, giving herself over to his gentle study, Jessica drew a deep breath.

"You have a broad, generous mouth," he murmured, "though it's often given to an excess of words."

"Yes, Your Grace, so I've been told."

"A pointed chin, perhaps too short to make you bewitching. More cherubic, I imagine."

"Yes." She continued with her eyes closed, caught in the hypnotic cadence of his voice, the smooth appraisal of his fingers that followed the rims of her ears and down her lobes. Gently, he stroked the nape of her neck, before following the line of her shoulders out and back to her throat. As he drew his fingers to her collarbones and started to explore lower, she jerked away.

"What are you doing?"

"I am looking at you."

"You've seen enough."

"Not so, my little gosling. If I had my eyesight, I would have looked you over far more thoroughly than this."

"I would never have given permission for that, Your Grace."

He seemed oddly sober. "The eyes look where they will, with or without leave. Furthermore, I thought we agreed you would call me by my familiar name when we are alone."

"I think perhaps we should continue observing the amenities." She eased back to sit on her feet, "Particularly when we are alone. Perhaps, too, we should not ride out unchaperoned."

His voice was low and taunting. "Do you want me to kiss you, Nightingale?"

His confidence put her off. Her answer was brusque. "No, I do not want you to kiss me."

"You would tempt any man, darling. Your innocence, your candor. I have known you were a lovely young woman from the first night."

"You did not suppose anything of the kind. You thought me a child."

"I have some experience with women, Nightingale. I realized immediately that you were an attractive young woman."

"Then why have you pretended to think me a moppet?"

"Prudence at first. I felt vulnerable and thought you might be in league with the thieves who attacked me."

"Later, then? At Gull's Way, when you practically ordered me into your bed."

He flashed a roguish grin. "I wanted to see if you would accommodate a man of wealth. I wanted to know how far you had gone with other men."

"Once you realized my…lack of experience? Why did you not admit then that you knew I was a woman grown?"

"I didn't want to frighten you away."

Of course. He enjoyed toying with her, did not want to make her bolt while he had a use for her.

She yearned at that moment, to prove her womanhood; to throw her arms around his neck and press her lips to his, to rouse his manly instincts, which seemed to lurk close to the surface in most men. She could entice him, encourage him to roll up on top of her and do those things that occur in private between men and women, things she had heard of and read about.

Her behavior at this moment might dictate a direction for the rest of her life. She did not intend to be deflowered by any man, noble or not, and left by the wayside. Not like Martha....His hands shifted to her waist and he grinned as he tugged, pulling her forward and off balance. Rolling onto his back, he carried her with him.

Sprawled on top of him, Jessica braced her hands on his chest and pushed herself away, but he held fast. They struggled before he caught her face in his hands and brought her nose to his nose. Chuckling, he tilted her face down and planted his lips firmly against her forehead.

"You are my own angel, Nightingale, sent to me from God in Heaven. I would not defile you, had you the allure of Salome and Bathsheba combined. Although I am totally enamored, you are safe from my base appetites and shall remain so."

He rolled, pushing her off to the side, away from the food.

"You might have squashed our lunch," she admonished, clambering to her feet and straightening her clothes.

"I would never have done such a vile thing. Our food is on my left, well away from our tussling. I knew exactly where it was. I may not be able to see, my darling little twit, but there is nothing wrong with my sense of smell."

Under the circumstances at that moment, Jessica was not certain whether she preferred his considering her a temptress or a twit.

Chapter Nine

The dowager duchess regarded them curiously as Devlin and Jessica came through the front door of the house. Devlin swung the basket containing the remains of their lunch. He appeared windblown and disheveled, but moved with a light, jocular step.

With a quick greeting, Jessica dashed up the stairway.

Lady Anne couldn't be sure, but their friendship was developing precisely as she had hoped it might—her primary concern that it not progress more quickly than was seemly.

"Devlin, I want to go to London." Receiving no adverse reaction, she continued. "I want Jessica to accompany me."

A pall settled over the foyer and its two occupants. The dowager thought Devlin's frown an inappropriate response to her happy announcement.

"No." His curt tone surprised her. "Jessica's trip to Welter and our outing today were enough to curb her appetite for travel. She's had quite enough gadding about."

"At her age," the dowager said, nullifying his objection with a wave, "Jessica has energy to sustain her on a dozen jaunts like those."

He squared his shoulders. "She stays with me."

"Here? Without a chaperone? That would not do. Today is an example. It is not proper for the two of you to go traipsing off alone, even here at Gull's Way."

He puffed up. "I will have you know, madam, that I was there to chaperone, ready to protect our young lady from any threat, man or beast. I consider seeing after her my solemn duty."

She wondered if he were trying to misdirect her or if his statement indicated an effort to mislead himself.

"I see. Well, you've explained away my concern in that regard." She wanted to be diplomatic. "In that case, I suppose Jessica and I shall have to allow you to accompany us to town."

"Hmm." He frowned. "I don't recall your ever requiring my protection on your trips to town before, Madam. Why do you consider it important for Jessica to go to London?"

Her hauteur waned. "Oh, Devlin, first because she has never been to town. Oh, darling, it would be such fun. Also, of course, she needs proper clothes. Although she is delightful in the frocks made with the limited resources available locally, she is going to require fashionable attire, the latest styles from a London modiste. Something befitting her rank."

"Precisely what rank is that?" He sneered.

Disregarding his question and his disdain, Lady Anne pursued her own thoughts. "I want to introduce her to people in town, smooth the way for her entrance into society."

"Madam," Devlin said, raising his voice, "might I remind you that Jessica has no rank for her clothes to aspire to."

"She is too lovely, Devlin, too winsome, her mind too quick, to remain buried in Welter. Also, I might point out that, just as you yourself have said, she is not yours to control. She is neither your child nor your ward nor any relation to you whatsoever, so please do not dictate to me how she should be outfitted or introduced."

As Devlin shook his head and frowned, the dowager studied her son and contemplated not what he had said, but the significance of what he had not said. While he artlessly granted that Jessica was a nobody, he did not suggest she continue to live in anonymity. With that in mind, Lady Anne thought she needed to tread carefully on his feelings and proceed tactfully.

"Of course, darling," she cooed, smoothing the feathers she had ruffled, "to be accepted, she must be seen with you."

Having changed her clothes, Jessica came back down the stairs. Lady Anne beckoned her to join them, preceding them into Devlin's study as she continued talking.

"As an added benefit, Devlin, if you travel with us, we shall have an opportunity to consult with Dr. Connor, the ophthalmologist, about your eyes." She addressed herself to Jessica, as if signaling for her assistance. "Ophthalmology, my dear, is a brand new area of medicine specializing in diseases of and injuries to the eyes."

Jessica touched Devlin's arm. "That sounds like a wonderful idea, Devlin. Your mother wants to go to London and it would be an opportunity for you to see this specialist."

"You are my eyes, Nightingale. If I go, you must go also."

Jessica hesitated. She had not been out of her own river valley until she brought Devlin home. Likely, she would never have another chance to visit London, certainly, never an opportunity to travel there in luxury.

"I would be happy to accompany you and your mother to London."

Devlin pursed his lips and appeared to consider the plan that had the endorsement of the two most influential women in his life. Finally, he raised and lowered his shoulders and gave what appeared rather an indifferent nod.

"All right. We shall all go to London."

"When?" his mother pressed.

"Could we allow time to prepare, madam?"

"Of course. Let us plan to leave on Tuesday next."

• • •

After a good night's sleep, a result, he supposed, of the ride in the fresh air and flexing wills against an able, and thoroughly delightful, opponent, Devlin rose with a new sense of well-being. His could see the forms of furnishings and even Henry's narrow physique as the valet moved about the room.

At the breakfast table, light drew the duke's eyes to the chandelier. He could see the candles flickering. He shifted his gaze to Jessica as she entered the room. He was eager to see the waif, the female whose importance increased daily, not only to his household, but to him personally.

As he attempted to focus on her, however, his erratic sight failed and he was again plunged into darkness.

Still, brief glimpses of light several mornings in a row indicated Jessica's original optimism might be justified. His sight seemed to be returning, if only in annoying, fleeting snippets. He resolved again to keep the incidents secret until he could be more certain they signaled recovery. He did not want to arouse the false hope in others that was taking root in him. Also, he did not look forward to females fussing or any other repercussions.

Jessica and his mother and Dr. Brussel all might have been correct in prescribing rest as the best medicine, yet he felt compelled to travel with Jessica and his mother to London, strain or no. Like his mother, he was eager to see Jessica's reaction to the comforts and luxuries of his town house, as well as the sights of London. He rather fancied the idea of squiring her about, showing her off in society, even if he were not able actually to see the envious glances of other gentlemen.

Yes, the benefit of having his Nightingale in town among old friends and neighbors would definitely lift all of their spirits.

Devlin also enjoyed the prospect of continuing in the close company of these two most important people and to protect and guide and advise them.

He couldn't recall how long it had been since his mother had sought his advice or guidance. Devlin smiled at his own conceit. He had not realized humility had been absent from his life until Jessica came to raise his awareness of that.

• • •

"Another fine day for a picnic, wouldn't you say, Jessica?" the duke inquired as he finished breakfast.

"I thought we might attempt a different kind of outing today," Jessica said.

Devlin smiled, anticipating any suggestion she might make. "What do you have in mind?"

"I think it is time you became reacquainted with mother earth." Seeing his smile waver, she hurried on. "You often remark, in a complimentary way, that I smell of earth and fresh air and roses. Toiling among the flowers is gratifying."

"I imagine that is true, if one is a gardener," Devlin said.

"The joy of horticulture is not limited to the lowly gardener, Your Grace. I understand that you successfully cultivated the soil when you were a youth."

He chuckled. "True. My efforts produced an abundance of mud cakes. Properly dried, they were ammunition against unarmed brothers and unsuspecting grooms."

Jessica's light laugh joined with his. "Yes, well, fortunately, we have some cuttings from the most robust yellow roses in your gardens. I want to plant them beneath the windows and along the walkway from the door of the small salon that serves as your study."

He frowned as if he had difficulty recalling the site.

"It is an area clearly visible from your desk. Do you remember it?"

"Vaguely. How do you know it wants planting?"

"I often slip through your study and out that way when I cannot sleep. That garden is protected from the North by the great wall. The house and that wall often retain the days' warmth. It is a serene place where one may say her prayers."

He looked puzzled. "I see."

"I would like your help placing the slips in the ground."

"Jessica, I am a duke."

"Yes, and are allowed to participate in any activity you choose. Is that not correct?"

"Well, yes, I suppose." He appeared to be genuinely perplexed. "You believe I might benefit from planting roses?"

"Yes. Of course, there is one stipulation."

"What is that?"

"No mud cakes."

"What of your theory that I am the duke and entitled to do anything I like?"

"It is a matter of your image, sir."

"Mud cakes might tarnish my reputation?"

"I am certain of it."

"But what if...?"

"I have a supply of mud cakes myself, prepared only yesterday, to prevent this very speculation on your part."

"What speculation?"

"The plan you are hatching as we speak."

His mischievous smile warmed her through. Their laughter twined in unison through the dining room. Listening, the dowager smiled as she often did at their exchanges.

Devlin and Jessica spent the morning on their knees, digging in the soil. He drew surprising pleasure and finished with a feeling of accomplishment, basking in Jessica's praise of his work. His back felt strained, he had blisters on both thumbs, and the muscles in his legs twitched objections. In spite of all that, he breathed deeply as Henry helped him bathe. He ate a hearty luncheon.

• • •

Before the rooster's crow, Jessica awoke to the sound of alarmed, muffled voices downstairs. She grabbed a wrapper and hurried to quiet the commotion before Their Graces were disturbed.

The front door stood wide open and a buzz of conversation issued from the broad sweep of steps just outside.

A crowd clustered about an object on the stairs. Jessica shouldered her way in to find Martha lying there.

"Has she fainted?" Jessica asked. Without waiting for an answer, she said, "Quickly, someone bring a cup of water."

Kneeling beside the fallen figure, Odessa glanced up, her eyes round. "She's dead, Ma'am."

"But she looks…" Jessica didn't finish as she studied the peculiar way Martha's head was bent. "Did she fall? Why was she out here so early? Will the baby…?"

At that moment, Sophie pushed through the gathering and dropped to her knees beside her unmoving friend. "Oh, Martha, what have you done?" She clamped both hands over her mouth as Odessa stood and pulled the younger woman to her feet.

"There, there, Sophie. She's gone now and comfortable as any of us can be. You go along inside. Go on into the kitchen and brew a strong pot a' tea. We'll be needing it."

On her feet, Sophie started to speak, and then apparently changed her mind. With a quick glance back at Martha's form on the steps, she scuttled into the house.

Jessica watched Odessa. The older woman looked distraught, yet began issuing orders. "John, fetch Mr. Patterson. Dolan, get out there and build us a decent coffin."

When the dozen or so staff people remaining turned as one, Jessica followed to find the dowager and Devlin negotiating the steps arm-in-arm. While she wanted to intercept them, she hardly knew what to do about Martha's body without their input.

Everyone began speaking at once until Odessa raised a hand to silence them. In a clear, calm voice, she stated what she knew. One of the horses was foaling. It took two stable boys to help. Afterward, they saw a shadowy presence on the stairs. The boys found Martha dead. It looked as if she had fallen.

"Strange though," Odessa said, "Martha has stayed to the back of the house these last weeks, not wanting to make too much of her condition. I know of no reason she should be on the front steps, 'specially so early in the day."

"Perhaps she had a caller," Jessica suggested.

Everyone regarded her strangely, but no one spoke as the dowager described the scene to Devlin in low tones. He assumed command.

"Set a cot in the solarium. Two of you carry Martha there, bathe her and lay her out properly."

"Patterson, send word to her family. We can bury her here, or they can retrieve her for burial with her people. We need to know their preference right away."

Jessica watched Odessa bite her lips, either holding back comments or grief.

Later, Odessa motioned Jessica from the music room.

"Will you help me prepare Martha's body? Usually Sophie helps, but she and Martha grew up together. This is too sudden."

"Yes." Jessica had helped prepare dead bodies before, in Welter. It was part of the village ritual for a girl to learn such things as she matured. She was not prepared for Odessa's grief as they bathed and dressed Martha's body. Odessa sobbed openly.

"Were you very close to her?" Jessica asked.

"It's the babe I grieve for, never able to breathe. Martha's people, if they come, are going to be sad and embarrassed, too. She had not told 'em about the babe."

"Odessa, do you know who fathered Martha's baby?"

"No, and neither does Sophie, Martha's closest friend, only that he has noble blood."

Using a rag and warm rose water, Jessica washed the dead girl's face. As she brushed Martha's hair back, she noticed bruising around her throat.

"Odessa, look here."

The older woman peered at Martha's neck a moment before the discoloration registered. She stepped closer to examine the abrasion.

"Strangled, it looks like."

She straightened. Who could say Martha's killer was the father of her babe? Surely she had shown the father he had no need to silence her. She had not revealed his identity, even to her closest friend.

On the other hand, those closest to Martha—her family—had not been informed she was with child. Perhaps Martha was afraid to confide in them, less they make some claim against the nobleman.

Jessica retired to her rooms, sat in the small rocking chair and rocked fretfully.

There was a light rap on the door.

She cleared her throat. "I am indisposed," she called to whoever was knocking.

"Nightingale, it is I," Devlin said quietly.

She wrapped her arms more tightly and rocked harder. She adored this man. Her admiration extended far beyond his physical beauty, although that reason was enough. Devlin was her hero. His generosity, his integrity, his basic honesty. He did not need to display those qualities. They were born in the strength of his own character.

"Nightingale?" he called. "Open the door." He rattled the latch, verifying that the bolt was in place. "I want to speak with you."

What a coil. She remembered the stranger walking with Martha near the stables. He had seemed gentle as he planted a kiss on the maid's forehead. Martha had raised onto her tiptoes, obviously offering more.

Jessica paced to the door. Would Devlin knock again? No, he was the soul of patience. She slid the bolt and opened, then stepped back as the duke entered, studying her face as if to read her thoughts. "I saw Martha with a large gentleman near the stables three nights ago," she blurted, turning and presenting her shoulder.

Devlin settled his hand gently, and then slid it to her neck. "Are you cold?" he asked.

"No. I'm upset."

"About the maid? Martha?"

"Yes. Did you speak with Odessa?"

"Yes." He spoke softly, as if dealing with someone addled. "She told me of your speculations."

"The marks on Martha's throat are obvious."

"We do not need to discuss it now. I am more concerned about you at the moment. I feel responsible that you have had to suffer any part in this."

"Devlin, please listen to me. These suspicions must be confirmed or disproved. Please lend your…" she shuddered. "Your assistance."

He straightened as if resigned to do as she asked. "All right. May we sit while we talk?"

She glanced around, realizing they probably should not be in her bedchamber alone, but these were special circumstances, requiring privacy. She led him to the wingback chair near the hearth. After he was seated, she eased into the small rocking chair. He smiled as the chair creaked signaling her whereabouts.

She didn't stay seated. Instead, she popped up, pacing and wringing her hands.

"No one knows the identity of the father of Martha's baby. She said only that he is of noble blood."

Devlin shook his head as if denying an accusation.

"Some speculated so at first, Your Grace, but they quickly deferred to the denials of your household who know your character well."

He leaned back in his chair. "That is some comfort, at least."

"Do not be smug. Not all of that is to your credit. Some knew your mother would not allow any babe fathered by a man of her blood to be raised a bastard, assuring the babe did not spring from you or Lattimore."

"Yes, well…Who might the father be, and why should his identity matter now that the babe and its mother are dead?"

"Who would be more motivated to rid himself of unwelcome responsibility to either Martha or her child?"

"I see. You believe a cad enjoyed her body, then dispatched the woman to rid himself of the inconvenience."

"Exactly."

"Which you believe is what makes the tender scene you witnessed near the stables significant."

She brightened, relieved to have his attention on the matter. "He was a large, slow-moving man. When they said farewell, Martha tipped her face up to receive his kiss. The man put a gentle stamp to her forehead, instead."

"Perhaps it was her father or a brother passing through."

"No, he was not a peasant, not outfitted as he was. Also, she didn't mention having had a visitor. My point is, if the figure with Martha that night was the father of her baby and if he assaulted her, we must find out who he is and hold him accountable."

Devlin nodded. He, too, had heard rumors that the man was a nobleman, but he put little stock in that, after assuring himself Lattimore was not the culprit. His lack of concern piqued Jessica's ire all over again.

Devlin stood to leave. Although she found their interview unsatisfactory, she did not prevent him. Nor did she escort him to the door.

Two days later, Martha's kin arrived, loaded her coffin onto an open wagon and left the household to wrestle with the perplexing, unanswered questions.

• • •

Another day and a dozen domestic projects later, Devlin was in fine spirits, the matter of Martha's death dismissed, as he entered the small salon late Monday morning to find his mother alone.

The dowager studied her handsome son a moment. "Jessica has gone to the stable to admire a new litter of kittens, darling, if you care to join her."

Smiling and shaking his head, Devlin declined. He had already been forced to bathe after having spent much of the early morning in the kitchen with Jessica and Cook learning tastes and fragrances and experimenting with herbs and spices.

Lady Anne opened a new subject as she turned her attention back to her needlework.

"Devlin, what would you think if I petitioned Victoria to make me Jessica's guardian?"

He paced to the long window and gazed out, marveling again at the miracle of eyesight as he surveyed the gardens. His vision returned for longer periods each morning now, as he awoke, rested and untroubled.

Also, gradually, he was able to discern more detail. Still, he was reluctant to share the good news with his mother or with Jessica. If the girl knew he was healing, she might try to leave, even before the trip to London. He was troubled by his rather annoying, ever-increasing fondness for the girl—her perpetual good cheer and unflagging energy and, yes, her undisguised regard for him. In spite of his insistence that she remain at Gull's Way after he was well, she seemed determined to abandon them when that time came.

She had voiced no objection to making the trip to town with his mother, leaving him behind, an example of Jessica's willingness to be separated from him.

For his part, their relationship had become mysteriously significant. He was more and more attached—more dependent—on her, even as he healed.

She had him experiencing new things: cooking, dealing with tiny newborn animals, weeding and tumbling dirt with his hands. The most surprising upshot was, he enjoyed it.

Evenings, she made him play the spinet or knit, of all things, keeping him physically occupied as she read aloud, books he never knew existed, ones she drew from his own library.

Sometimes, he caught her strumming at the spinet when she thought no one else was about, picking out notes of melodies that haunted or cheered, then adding bass accompaniment to produce music that soothed his soul.

She had become as much a part of him as his…his eyes.

Of course, she still served as his eyes most of the time, but her presence was so much more than that. With her, he enjoyed an inner peace he had not known before, content with himself and his circumstances—even blind.

A natural restlessness he thought born in him, eased at her touch. The sound of her voice allayed anxiety. She was a tune he hummed as he toiled at the tasks she assigned.

He rode Vindicator every day now. Although he had been unsteady at first, he had grown comfortable again in the saddle, riding out with one of the grooms, enjoying the confidence she instilled.

Further, he had begun identifying his staff by their voices. He had never gone to the trouble of putting names to faces of new people when he had his sight. He had grown more attentive, sensitive to their opinions. He now heard undertones and asides to which he had been deaf in the past.

To Devlin's surprise, he found that, in spite of the majordomo's advanced years, Patterson was not the dottering old fellow the master sometimes supposed. The old retainer wielded firm control over the men of the household staff and those who toiled outside as well. Although patient, the man had little tolerance for sloth. Layabouts did not last long on Patterson's staff.

The man delegated similar authority to Odessa, who supervised the women working in the kitchen and the chambermaids.

Devlin's mother and father chose well when they set Patterson and Odessa managing Shiller's Green and the staff for the house in town. Devlin assumed households ran themselves. Patterson and Odessa had been overseeing things all his life, creating that impression.

Suddenly, his mother's words registered and he responded. "Make Jessica your ward?"

"Yes, darling. Haven't you heard anything I've said?"

"She has family. A mother and two older siblings. I don't think it would be possible without her mother's consent, and perhaps the permission of her brother and sister."

"That's what I just said, Devlin. I'm sure her mother would be reasonable, if you provided adequate incentive."

"Oh, I see. Unable to produce one of your own, you want me to buy you someone else's daughter. Is that your idea?"

Lady Anne pursed her lips, glaring at her son's back. "No such thing. Surely, my darling, even you have noticed how the atmosphere here has changed under Jessica's influence."

He clasped his hands behind his back, but continued staring out at the small garden beyond his study doors, an area he tended with his own two hands. As he considered it, he made a mental note: A brick border might set off the roses.

Of course he had noticed the changes. He had probably been more aware of them than his mother had.

Her voice became quieter and he assumed she had bent again to her handwork. "If her family will allow it, I want Jessica to be my ward."

"I doubt the Queen will consent. She is little older than Jessica herself."

"Then, you must petition to be her guardian. Victoria will do it for you, particularly if you mention it to Peel and soften him beforehand. Robert admired your father. As prime minister, he has Victoria's ear."

"On what am I to base this petition?"

"You owe this girl your life. You want to provide for her future out of appreciation for her help during your crisis."

"What will people think, Mother? That I could not have found my way home without the help of a slip of a girl?"

"If they do, they will be correct. You might have happened upon the same ruffians, or worse. With neither your sight nor a weapon, it would have been easy for them to finish the job and eliminate a witness who could send them to the gallows."

"Yes, well, I might not have been as easily dispatched as that."

"Do you believe they would have armed you and called out their positions to allow you to attack them?"

He snorted at her speculation. She made his argument sound ridiculous.

"Then what will you do with her, assuming the petition is approved?" he said, bringing her back to her request.

"We will employ a tutor to polish her musical skills, a duenna to teach her to entertain, to walk properly, to speak on subjects popular in Court, to eat and drink at table. Then we shall present her."

He gave another snort. His eyesight was beginning to blur and, disappointed, he wanted to summon Jessica, but he did not interrupt his mother. Besides, he was warming to the idea.

"Mrs. Freebinder loves fashioning clothes and hats for her," the dowager continued. "She finds Jessica a charming subject. My modiste in London will be overjoyed. Lattimore and his friends will appreciate having such a delectable young woman enter their realm."

Suddenly, Devlin had a new thought. "You will offer Jessica to the likes of Lattie and Marcus Hardwick and Peter Fry? Mother, have a thought. A girl like Jessica could not endure an evening with any of those buffoons; much less agree to marry one."

"Marcus and Peter both are in line to inherit titles. Hardwick will be a marquis and inherit nice estates."

"Jessica is not interested in presiding over grand estates."

"No? How do you know that?"

"Because I know her and what she considers of value."

"The fact you still consider her a child is indication enough that you know very little about her, indeed."

"What, exactly, is this depth of her I do not know?"

"Devlin, Jessica is a lovely, lovely young woman. She is eighteen years old, elderly for an unmarried girl from a village."

"She has had opportunities at wedlock."

"That would be exactly what marriage to a villager would be for Jessica, with her sensibilities. Wedlock would be cruel punishment. She is a winsome child. Like you, I do not want to see her broken by the drudgery of life in a place like Welter with a man like that Lout person."

His sight almost completely gone, Devlin wheeled and took two strides toward his mother, stopping beside her chair. "What do you know of John Lout?"

"I've overheard the servants. Just as we think them sometimes invisible, they are not always aware that I am present. Some of the girls live in fear of a John Lout in their futures. Others find him attractive with animalistic appeal. Jessica refuses to speak of him, as if she is resigned to the inevitability of marrying him."

The dowager's voice took on an edge. "Devlin, I simply cannot allow that beautiful child to fall into that brute's filthy hands."

Filthy hands? A brute with dirty hands? That probably described most men in the countryside, yet that was Devlin's impression of the man who had delivered the blows that knocked him out of his saddle that night. The harsher beating had come after Devlin was on the ground, from a gentleman's boots, and hands beneath fine leather gloves.

Wouldn't that be irony, for Jessica's intended to have caused the injuries that resulted in Devlin's fortuitous meeting with his Nightingale?

He gave a short, mirthless laugh. "How much would be required of me in providing the cocoon for this caterpillar whilst she transforms into a butterfly?"

Lady Anne clapped her hands and he heard a subdued wheeze of pleasure. "You will need to pay for everything, of course."

"Of course."

"When she is properly schooled and introduced, you will need to squire her to parties and balls and the theater and serve as her chaperone."

"A blind man? You jest. Perhaps you can have Lattimore play the lady's sponsor and guard dog."

"No, Devlin. I have other plans for Lattimore's role."

"What might those plans be, dear Mamma?"

"He is only a little older than Jessica."

"Twenty-five to her eighteen. Seven years."

"She is more mature and far more responsible than he. If we can arrange the match, she could influence him toward improvement."

"They are not a match, Mother. She is too…"

"What, Devlin? She is too what?"

"If you are set on marrying them, why the trouble and expense of introducing her?"

"Because Lattie would balk if I paired them directly. He must be encouraged into this. He must see other men admire her and offer for her before he realizes what a treasure she is, one living within his own family. Please, Devlin, say you will help me."

"What of John Lout? Will he allow you to disregard him?"

"Yes, well, that is another thing you might manage."

"Must I keep reminding you, Mother, I am blind. It hardly seems fair to make so many demands of your sightless son in order to arrange an agreeable match for your sighted one."

"I know, dear, it seems insensitive, but you may benefit from all of this too."

Somehow, he didn't see how he was going to benefit from paying for everything, coaxing his dunderheaded brother into a marriage Lattimore did not want, and losing his Nightingale in the bargain.

When had he begun thinking of the girl as *his* Nightingale?

Of course, neither he nor his mother had considered Jessica's opinion. She was a practical soul. He doubted she would object if the proposition were presented well.

Lady Anne rang for Patterson who immediately opened the door to the study.

"Yes, Your Grace."

The dowager hesitated, but Devlin had no intention of initiating her plan.

"Patterson, please ask Jessica to join us here."

The girl arrived breathless moments later, her face the color of a ripe peach. She stopped just inside the door and dropped a quick curtsy.

In spite of not being able to see her, Devlin swallowed a smile, as the scent of hay wafted into the room. He pictured her by her sounds—her noisy entry, the staccato steps which stopped abruptly, the rustle of her skirts as she curtsied, and the breathless, "Yes, Your Grace, you wanted to see me?"

"My dear, Devlin and I have been speaking of your future. We have come to agreement and would like your impression of our thoughts."

He heard Jessica turn to him. "Is this your idea, Dev...er, Your Grace?"

He tried to look severe, his arms folded over his chest as if he had final say over her destiny, which he knew he had not. He would never impose his will upon her, no matter how concerned he might be, and, he conceded, he was concerned.

"I cannot take credit, Nightingale. The dowager has concocted a scheme and I have agreed to help. It is of considerable importance to her. I ask only that you hear her out."

She rustled again, obviously turning attention back to the dowager, who began in low, dulcet tones. "Come sit beside me, child."

He heard the rustle of skirts settling before his mother began to speak.

As if addressing someone she loved, the dowager outlined her plan. Jessica listened without interruption until the conclusion.

"I have given my word to John Lout, Your Grace," Jessica said, and Devlin heard regret in her voice. From their earlier conversations, he understood that Jessica had no intention of marrying Lout, so why use him as an excuse?

"Yes, well Devlin mentioned that. I wondered if we invited Mr. Lout here to see the advantages available to you as my ward..."

"I doubt that, ma'am. You see John has a habit of knowing and doing what is best for himself. He has little concern for the needs or wants of others, including his own mum and dad."

Devlin felt compelled to interject a thought. "Mother, you may recall that, historically, surnames come from occupations, physical attributes, or behavior. The name Lout might have been assigned to the man's ancestors due to certain familial traits."

The dowager duchess was quiet for several ticks of the clock before she advanced another thought.

"Do you suppose a sum of money might make him release you from your promise?"

Jessica's thin laugh had a bittersweet timbre. "I suppose it would, Your Grace, but he is sly enough to recognize an advantage. He will overprice the goods and rob you, if he can."

Rob her? Devlin's thoughts raced. He wondered if the robbery Jessica anticipated might not be the first John Lout had perpetrated upon the Miracles.

"Devlin," his mother said, "will you negotiate this matter?"

"Aye, I will, but only if I am accompanied by armed and trusted eyes."

"Bear and how many others?"

He allowed an easy laugh, an attempt to quell the concern in her voice. "Bear and I, even in my current state, probably can manage the negotiations."

"I prefer that you take two or three others along. I have lost one son contesting over a woman. I don't intend to make that two. Speaking of which, perhaps I should send another messenger to town for Lattimore. I cannot imagine what is delaying him. We may be in town before he arrives."

"I am sure important matters of state are holding him."

The dowager's face twisted at his sarcasm. "Or a pretty face. I wish I had produced one daughter to populate our homes with giggling girls eager to gain her brothers' attention."

Devlin smiled at Jessica. "You see, Nightingale, my mother is determined you be the daughter she has coveted all these years."

"Am I also to be the sister you have always wanted?"

His smile faded. Receptive to the idea of a daughter for his mother, he had never wanted a sister. Women seemed more difficult to command.

Considering her question, he realized his feelings for Jessica were not fraternal. What were his feelings toward his Nightingale? Seeking an apt definition for their relationship, he became restless. He supposed his unease indicated he had need of a woman. It had been some time. Perhaps he should arrange to see the winsome Lady Elaine.

No.

While Elaine had once satisfied his desires, a man eventually required more.

Mercedes, then, with her beautiful face and voluptuous hips, widowed twice, rich in her own right, and certainly one of his ardent admirers. She seemed determined to be a duchess, having advanced by stages, first marrying a viscount, and then an earl in her prior nuptials. Her desire for a ducal title was flagrant.

No, thoughts of Mercedes no longer appealed. Maybe it was not a woman's company he needed.

As he pondered, he heard the rustle of skirts. The two women in the room were moving. He caught Jessica's scent. According to the blended fragrances, she had been at the stables and the rose garden. Oh how he would love to pull her into his lap and study in detail her myriad bouquets.

His body stiffened with desire.

He did need a woman, but why did his body not respond to thoughts of other women, and then rouse with the scents of this child? She was not a child, of course. She was eighteen and of an age to marry.

He and his mother agreed in thinking Jessica should not wed John Lout. Their views differed about Jessica being a bride for Lattimore. She would suit, but Lattie was a rake and a gambler and interested in his baser appetites. Besides that, he would probably take a commission in the Queen's navy, a profession particularly hard on a waiting wife, producing and rearing children by herself, confined to her home for months, even years at a time.

Devlin did not consider Lattie too old for her. She needed a mature man, to provide a stable home, a steadying hand for her whimsical kindnesses, a man who was patient and affectionate.

Chapter Ten

An excited hum developed as the staff scurried about preparing to transport the family to London. Anticipation accelerated in the predawn darkness as the travelers loaded onto the conveyances.

As they rode in the covered brougham, Lady Anne and Jessica sat comfortably side by side facing Devlin. The duchess filled the air with details and reviews of individual dressmakers and milliners.

She rattled off ideas regarding styles she expected to set trends in the coming season. Jessica assumed Lady Anne was speaking of clothes for herself, amazed that one woman needed so much—three or four riding habits, a dozen ball gowns, morning frocks, dresses for afternoon teas, either entertaining at home or going out.

Listening to his mother describe the various lords and ladies, their foibles and reputations, and Jessica's frequent questions, Devlin felt a dark premonition.

Earlier, satisfied that his sight was returning, he had felt buoyant, pleased at traveling to town with two such delightful companions. Beyond his private darkness, all seemed well, yet as they drew closer to London, the inexplicable foreboding grew heavier.

As morning stretched into early afternoon, the convoy—the ducal coach and a second carrying household staff, followed by a wagon filled with luggage and foodstuffs from their country larder—finally stopped for luncheon from a huge hamper.

Thoughts of sautéed quail and accompanying fruits and breads had tantalized the ladies for what seemed like hours before Devlin finally ordered the stop.

They had just escaped the confines of the coach and were strolling about, stretching, when Bear appeared at Devlin's side.

"Could I have a moment of yer time, Yer Grace?"

"Certainly, Bear. Will you have a drink or a bite of luncheon first?"

"Nay, my lord. I need to speak privately with you." He glanced at the women and dropped his voice to a growl. "I'm needing your advice on the rigging."

Bear led the puzzled duke toward the front of the coach and, as a ruse, guided his hands to the straps. "There's a man following us, Yer Grace."

"Has he been with us long?"

"Ever since we left Shiller's Green. I directed Figg's attention to him."

"What do you think he's about?"

"Donno' as I could speculate about that, Yer Grace, but no need for you to worry about you or your ma. That's what I'm doing here."

"And will you protect Jessica Blair as well?"

"Nay, my lord. I only got two eyes and they're already taken."

"I see what you mean." Devlin ran his fingers along the straps. "Well, then, I suppose it falls to me to watch after the fair Jessica. Is that how you see it, Bear?"

The man stared at the duke. "Not to put too fine a point on it, Yer Grace, but it looks a heavy task to keep what you might call a proper watch on the lady when your eyes don't see nothing at all."

"It does present a challenge, but what else can I do? You will keep the fellow off of me and I will pass the favor along by keeping him away from Jessica."

Bear cleared his throat. The girl would come under his protection now, whether she deserved it, or not.

Less than three hours after that conversation, Bear's new burden grew weighty.

Late in the afternoon, Devlin signaled the driver to pull to the side of the road to allow the passengers to stretch and refresh themselves. After the two outriders ranging ahead determined a likely spot to accommodate the ladies' needs, Jessica and Lady Anne retired into a thicket for privacy. When they had finished, the dowager returned to the carriage, but Jessica saw the iridescent flutter of a bluebird and wandered hoping to glimpse the elusive prize.

She heard a rustle in the underbrush, but before she could turn, a huge, calloused hand clamped over her mouth as a matching arm caught her about the waist and lifted her high so her kicking feet met only air.

"Hush up, my love," a familiar voice hissed. She grew still. There were better ways to deal with John Lout than a physical struggle.

"Oh, John, thank heaven it's you. I was frightened nearly to death."

The arm locked at her waist relaxed and he lowered her feet again to the ground. "Ah, Jess, I am relieved to hear yer glad it's me. Is the old duke treating you badly, then?"

She set a warm smile on her face. "No, John, the duke thinks of me as a pet."

"People are saying coarse things about you and this duke fella'. They say you warm his bed at night."

"As I told you, he has never suggested intimacy." This statement was not altogether true, if one counted Devlin's teasing.

John's voice lowered a third. "I would kill him if he did. I might go so mad as to kill you, too, before I got meself under control."

"What if he offered to pay for the privilege, John, more than the hundred he already promised for my care and company? What would you say then?"

Lout rubbed his chin and his eyes narrowed. "I'm a reasonable man, Jess. Has he offered money for the favor?"

"No. He hasn't."

"Will he, do you think?"

She shrugged; disheartened that even John could draw the correct conclusion. "No." She looked toward the coach. "I need to return before anyone realizes I am gone."

But their private tête-à-tête had been discovered. In spite of his size, Bear moved through the underbrush with the stealth of a cat.

When his mother returned without Jessica, Devlin sent Bear for their missing member.

Bear grudgingly did as he was bidden, tracking back the way the duchess had returned.

He heard rustling and the girl's startled yelp when Lout grabbed her. Bear listen, placated by the fact that she did not sound alarmed.

Staying to the cover of the trees, Bear crept close to hear their conversation.

"Does the old duke know we are betrothed?" Lout said, stalking her as she began walking back toward the road.

Bear studied her face and decided the man spoke the truth about their impending nuptials. At the same time, he was curious. Jessica's expression was not that of a bride gazing upon her beloved.

"If that's the case, I'd better take you meself now," Lout said. He lunged, but she sidestepped agilely, staying well beyond his grasp.

"It's likely you shall have me, John, but not before the appointed day, after the words have joined us as man and wife. You agreed."

"All that prevents us now is the speaking a' the words?"

"I intend to have say over my own body until the vicar's words join us."

Lout tramped close, a determined look in his eyes.

The girl might not realize her peril. Bear saw the man's intentions. He thought of his orders not to intervene unless she was threatened. Did the order anticipate protecting her from her own beloved?

Lout raised an arm.

No longer ambivalent about his sworn duty, Bear lunged, grabbing a fallen log.

Jessica stood boldly. Lout was nearly on top of her when she squatted and covered her head with both arms.

As the length of dead wood from Bear's hand broke over his head, John went limp. His massive body folded over itself with a whoosh.

Hearing the unexpected thud, Jessica peered from between her fingers to see the huge man crumple. She saw Bear and her terror spiked. She shrank again.

"Don't be scared, milady. I'm here to serve you." Bear held out his open hands. "It's me. Bear." He spoke softly, as if to mollify her and, at the same time, keep a watchful eye on Lout. The downed man groaned and began to stir.

"I recognize you, Bear."

"I thought ye might be too scared to know it was me, Miss. Come, then, let's be leaving."

"No. You must go, and quickly, before he rouses."

"How will you explain the lump on his head?"

"I will tell him a branch fell out of the tree. I will tend him sweetly, soothe his wound and gentle him with my caring ministrations, while you run for your life."

Bear swelled to his full, height, over six foot three, and flexed a massive arm. "I do not run from fights, Miss, for sure not from a scuffle with no two-footed creature."

"For my sake, then." She knelt and began stroking Lout's brow as he groaned. He raised thick, searching fingers to his head only to encounter Jessica's delicate hand.

He mumbled without opening his eyes. "Am I dead?"

Jessica bit both lips to stifle a laugh. "No, but you were no match for the tree."

"What happened?" His eyelashes fluttered. Jessica raised a pleading look to Bear.

"You have felled many trees in the woods, John. I suppose it was only a matter of time before one took revenge."

There was a slight rustling of underbrush as Bear slipped into the thicket, where the sounds of movement stopped. Jessica knew he had not gone far.

"What does an injury to me have to do with you, Jess?" John groaned.

Seeing the bully humbled, she felt a stir of tenderness. "I do not wish any man ill, especially you who will be my husband, make my living, provide for my table, warm me on cold winter nights in our bed."

His eyes rolled as he tried to focus, his face contorted with a silly look of tender disbelief.

"No, John, I do not wish to see you injured."

His tender look became alarm. "Did you hear something?" Squinting but obviously unable to see clearly, he pointed to the place where Bear had disappeared.

"The wind, John. Come now; let's see if you can stand."

"Nay, not yet."

She started to rise, but he caught her wrist in his great paw. She smiled. "I'll fetch water to wash your face and help you come fully awake."

A giddy smile bowed his lips.

Jessica glanced toward the woods as she scurried to fetch a jug from the carriage. Perhaps she could see Bear's form in the underbrush, but maybe not, camouflaged as he was by the trees. Then a hand appeared, floating, and waved.

She flapped a hand back, as if shooing an insect, in case John saw her and wondered.

• • •

Because of the distance and the size of their party, Devlin knew his entourage would not reach the city in one day. He had arranged for accommodations at the Greymont Inn, a relatively clean place, respectable, host to many of the gentry when they spent a night on the road.

As the ladies freshened themselves and prepared to sup in the tavern below stairs, Bear led the duke to the stable, beyond the hearing of others, to report Jessica's meeting with Lout.

"When they spoke of their agreement, did you take it to mean they were referring to their betrothal?" Devlin asked.

"I'm not certain, Your Grace."

"Was she terrified of him?"

"Not so much terrified, as not altogether pleased."

"Perhaps she was startled by his sudden appearance."

"That may be, mixed with annoyance. Her concern rose as they spoke, eying each other like two warriors about to do battle."

Devlin rubbed his chin briskly. "There was no tenderness or affection between them?"

"None." Bear added. "Well, none until I dropped him."

"You say she attended him when he was injured?"

"Yes."

"Of course she did." Devlin mumbled, as if speaking to himself. "That is what she does. Attends the lost and hurting."

Bear felt ashamed that he might have drawn Jessica and Lout closer, which might have been a good thing, under other circumstances. Obviously that consequence did not please Devlin, however, and what did not please His Grace, did not please Bear.

• • •

In his youth, Devlin had not shown good taste in his choice of women. Bear had, on more than one occasion, worried that some temptress would fool the lad with her wiles, but that had not happened.

This one—this Jessica—was different. She slipped into Devlin's heart as she had into almost every other heart in the household.

At first, Bear did not trust her for allowing the sightless Devlin to believe her a young girl rather than a lass of marriageable age. She did not behave like a girl in search of a husband.

Bear was better satisfied with her behavior when he saw her with the horses, the kittens in the barn, her exuberance with the hounds that showed none of their usual mistrust of strangers. He liked her exchanges with the household staff as well. She treated them as equals, in spite of her preferred status, yet she did not let the officious ones take advantage of her.

Mostly, however, he liked how she was with Devlin, respectful, watchful, not overly sympathetic, pushing him but not expecting more of him than he could manage.

He also liked that she didn't sidle close or rub against the duke, as many a lass had done, even when he had his sight, to draw his attention.

There was quality, character and conduct worthy of respect in this Jessica Blair. When Devlin asked Bear to keep an eye on her, he accepted the charge with more than a little curiosity of his own.

• • •

In the tavern below stairs for supper, the duke dismissed his concerns as he and his mother and Jessica finished their meal. He ordered extra glasses of a surprisingly good wine, which, the keep boasted, he made himself.

Noisy new arrivals shouted and shoved benches that scraped and toppled thunderously, disrupting the cozy atmosphere. Devlin did not want to show his annoyance, particularly when he felt Jessica, on his left, stiffen as the rowdies fairly took over the establishment.

Devlin placed a steadying hand on the back of her neck and put his mouth close to her ear. "Do not be alarmed, Nightingale. They are just off the road. There is no cause for concern."

"I am sure you are correct, Your Grace."

She remained stiffly alert and Devlin was prompted to ask, "What is causing you such discomfort, darling?"

"Nothing, Your Grace. I am just being silly."

"Are you overly fatigued?"

She insisted she was fine, shushed him, and fell silent as his mother continued her running account of who was who in London society, but where Jessica had asked questions and expressed genuine interest earlier, she grew tense and did not speak.

"Jessica, are you tired?" the duchess asked finally.

"What? Oh, yes, Your Grace. The excitement of the day and the long ride has finally caught up with me. I am embarrassed that you and the duke are able to outlast me."

Lady Anne laughed lightly. "We have had years of conditioning. In town, people often welcome the dawn before seeking their beds."

"How does one endure it?"

"We sleep away the morning, a practice foreign to you. Just as well. I doubt it is one that will be available to any of us tomorrow. In keeping with country hours, I suppose we should be up the stairs and to bed."

Instead of listening to his companions, Devlin had tuned his sensitive hearing to private conversations, particularly to the last noisy group, for their talk seemed to be about the nobleman and his ladies. He didn't like the men observing his party so closely.

Then the deepest, most graveled voice overcame the others as all conversation in the room fell to whispering.

Devlin knew his concerns probably were unwarranted. Still, he would feel better having his charges upstairs and bolted. He would put both ladies in one room and assign Bear to the door. Also, he decided to tell Ned, a sturdy, well-trusted footman, to mind the back of the tavern, the area between the inn and the stable, as another precaution.

"Jessica," Devlin said quietly as she guided him up the stairs, his hand, as usual, on her shoulder, "would you mind very much quartering with my mother tonight?"

Her exhale sounded like relief. "Certainly, Your Grace."

No questions? How extremely unlike her, but she had been behaving strangely since the band of men entered the tavern. Perhaps they had expressed unwelcome interest, had cast lurid looks her way, and she had been uncertain about how to spurn their attention. He didn't bother asking. She would no doubt deny her nervousness in an effort to allay his concerns.

As they reached the top of the stairs, Devlin sent Ned to tell the innkeeper to set either a second bed or a pallet in the dowager's room, then to summon Bear from the stable where the men had settled for the night.

When Bear arrived, the duke heard him riffle a hand of playing cards. "Bear, will you bring your blankets and sleep in front of my mother's door tonight?"

"Do you believe the dowager is in danger?"

"I don't know, but something is amiss. I don't want to take any chances. I might hear an intruder's approach, I might not be able to prevent any...unpleasantness."

"I will see to it, Your Grace." Bear had retreated several paces when he spoke over his shoulder. "I'll get my things and be right back."

"Thank you. I am grateful, particularly as you were otherwise pleasantly occupied."

Bear riffled his cards again with a thumbnail. "Not so pleasantly as ye might believe. I was bluffing. By now the buggers 'ave figured it out. They can manage fine without my blunt. I expect this little interruption may provide protection for my purse as well as your mum."

Devlin smiled and Bear chuckled. No one eavesdropping would have heard their earlier conversation or would have suspected they were having any but a light discussion.

• • •

Bear slept sitting up, his back propped against the door to the ladies' room, his pistol loaded, his thumb on the hammer. The way his hat dipped over his face, a person could not tell if he were awake or asleep.

The dowager and Jessica prepared for bed, laughing and talking like schoolgirls.

"Jessica, I want to give you something." The duchess rummaged in her satchel and produced a cameo often worn by unmarried girls from wealthy families. It hung from a delicate gold chain. "This was mine when I was a girl. I would like for you to have it."

"Oh, Your Grace, it is lovely, but I seldom wear jewelry. I could not accept such an exquisite necklace."

"Posh. I planned to give it to my daughter, but God saw fit to bless me with sons."

"Then you must save it for a future daughter-in-law or a granddaughter."

"Look closely, my dear. The face on it is yours. The resemblance is amazing. Since the likeness is you, the piece must be yours. I hope you will wear it always."

The duchess indicated Jessica should turn. She fastened the delicate chain around the girl's swanlike neck.

"It's a little long," the duchess said.

"Which means it will hang concealed where it will not be scratched or broken…or envied."

The duchess caught Jessica's shoulders and turned her around. Tears in the older woman's eyes silenced further objections or mention of Jessica's return to Maxwell Manor.

• • •

As Bear prepared the duke's coach for travel the next morning, Devlin again heard the graveled voice he recognized as the leader of the noisy bunch from the tavern the night before. Fatigue—or perhaps worry—prevented the duke's usual morning glimpses of light.

Jessica's shoulder beneath his hand trembled at the sound of men's voices as she led him down the stairs. Her reaction made hairs prickle on the back of the duke's neck. He would pay much for one look at her expression when she spied the man with the grating tone.

At the bottom of the stairs, Devlin realized the graveled voice was coming closer. Judging by the volume and the man's odor, he imagined the fellow to be a farmer in his late twenties; tall, burly, and a bully, by the way he ordered people about. It sounded as if people deferred to the fellow's noisy demands.

The innkeeper's voice appealed quietly, a tone below the bully's. "I have your bill here, Your Grace."

"Thank you." Devlin removed his hand from Jessica's shoulder. She inhaled sharply and her skirts swished as she moved quickly toward the door and out. "Where are you going, child?"

He heard a whispered exchange before she answered a little too loudly. "To the coach, Your Grace. I will send your valet back to provide escort." The door slammed.

Since Jessica had been in his household, she rarely referred to the servants by titles or occupations. She called them by name.

Why had she said she would send his valet back when that same valet, Henry, was one of her closest friends?

. . .

In step beside her, John Lout grabbed Jessica's arm and whisked her around a corner of the inn. She did not object as he shoved her against a wall where they were hidden from the duke's men preparing the coach.

Using a falsetto voice, Lout whined, "Yes, Yer Grace. No, Yer Grace. Kiss yer ass, Yer Grace?" Then the graveled hiss was back. "I won't have any woman a' mine squallering between another man's sheets, especially no rich man's bed, for no paltry hundred pounds."

Reminding herself of possible danger to the dowager or the duke, Jessica tried, but lost the battle against her rising anger. She yanked free of John's grasp.

"You forget yourself, John Lout. First, I am not 'any woman of yours'. Not yet. And let me tell you, if this is the kind of behavior I can expect if I take you as husband, then I am not going to be your woman. Not in this lifetime. I will die first."

He retreated a step, but she followed, rising onto her tiptoes, propping her fists on her hips, and spewing words directly into his face.

"I told you before, in words I thought even you understood, the duke would not have me in his bed. He has other, more important considerations. He is blind as a bat. Beyond that, he is too old and too experienced to be interested in easy ladies or urchins off the streets. As you can also see for yourself, he is easily thirty years of age, practically in his dotage.

"Another thing," she continued, not allowing him a word, "I am as much a paid companion to his mother as I am to him."

Scowling, Lout attempted to interrupt as he retreated, staying close to the wall but moving toward the rear of the building. Her temper unleashed, Jessica continued her stalking tongue-lashing.

"Do you have any prospects of making one hundred pounds, John Lout? Any that will not finish with you swinging from the end of a rope?"

He held silent and withdrew another step.

"No, you have not! I have! And I am willing to share my good fortune with you. If this brutish bullying is how you respond to my womanly regard, I will reconsider my plans for us."

John jutted his chin at her and stood his ground, as if he felt finally, safely beyond her reach.

"I don't want 'im putting 'is filthy hands on ya."

A glance at John's hands and her eyes popped. How could he even speak such words?

"His hands are never filthy, John, never so dirty as yours…or mine either. He puts one hand on my shoulder to steady himself and I lead him. In his dark, unseeing world, he thinks of me as a child. No one, not even his mother, has convinced him that I am a woman grown. That information has no bearing on his interest in me or on our business relationship. He does not consider me a person, male or female. I matter to him only as a guide to lead him through his current darkness. I will not tolerate your bullying like this and behaving like a complete oaf. I will not have my intended embarrass me."

Lout drew a quick breath as if signaling he wanted to be heard, before his frown deepened with the sting of her words.

Seeing his expression darken, Jessica checked her aggression. She made a conscious effort neither to quail or retreat as she saw the change. Perhaps she had carried her attack too far.

John's hands balled into ham-like fists and he spoke through clenched teeth, edging closer to Jessica as he whispered.

"I'm going to kill the bastards." He glanced around. "The big one first, that one they call Bear. Once he's gone, the rest'll fall easy—the fancy old dame and that strutting peacock of a duke, too."

Jessica did not want John to see her fear at the threat.

"Killing an old gentle woman and a blind man would take little skill, John Lout. Those would be the acts of a coward, not behavior of a man I could marry."

She lowered her eyes and adjusted her posture to make her appeal seem more feminine. Easing closer, she placed her fingers gently on one of the forearms he had crossed in front of him. They stood a moment before a smile twitched his lips. She had been waiting for a sign she had retaken control of things, including her temper. Only then did she allow her eyes to engage his.

"I could not endure if you killed either of them, John. If you committed such a heinous act, it would be better if you murdered me as well. The disappointment of knowing you had slain such gentle, harmless creatures would shatter the tender regard I have for you."

"If I swear not to kill 'em, will ye vow here and now to be my wife?"

She started to speak, but he eyed her suspiciously. "I have pledged it a hundred times, Jess, but you never did. Not once. What I'm saying is, if I let their dainty highnesses go, will ye give yer word we'll wed before Michaelmas?"

Jessica stared at his quivering jowls. His face was ruddy and puffy from heavy drinking the night before, the distortion emphasizing his bulbous nose and low forehead. Promise to wed him? And do it before September was ended? So soon as that?

An image of Devlin superimposed itself over John's face—the duke's well-defined jaw, his straight nose and high forehead over Lout's pudginess.

She visualized Devlin's full lips outlined by the manicured mustache and the narrow beard that emphasized the sensuality of the man's mouth. She could almost hear the coaxing tones he used addressing his mother or her. She got goose flesh recalling the warmth of his hands. She rejoiced in the memories of his impeccable manners and gentle ways, even when he dissolved into those—now infrequent—fits of temper.

When John was under stress, he became abusive, using any means available, weapons or fists, to annihilate obstacles, particularly a weaker foe.

Devlin utilized his wits to quell a challenge more often than he used his considerable physical skills. It was another of his most admirable qualities.

Could she lie in her marriage bed with John, free of the mental images of Devlin Miracle?

As she contemplated John's suggestion, he drew a knife from his belt and thumbed its well-honed edge. It was the same weapon he used to skin and butcher game. Slowly, he raised his gaze to hers. She saw his intentions. With a word, she could prevent the spilling of noble blood.

John was sly. He and his ruffians would give no warning. Devlin's beloved friend Bear would be their first victim. A wise choice, she supposed. Felling Bear first would make it easier to finish the rest of the duke's party. Devlin would be dead before the ruffians could harm his mother.

Michaelmas was weeks away. Devlin might recover his sight before that. If not, surely he would grow tired of their arrangement before then, pay her the five hundred pounds and send her away.

Unlike the nobility, Jessica had no qualms about going back on an extorted promise.

When she was free of her obligation to Devlin, she would take her share of the money, leave the agreed sums for Brandon and John, arrange for her mother, warn Bear of Lout's threat, and run.

She would never dishonor a pledge made voluntarily, but an oath given under threat was different.

She would turn her coops and livestock over to Penny, her friend, and the other Anderson children. They would care for and reap the benefits of her birds.

If Devlin had not recovered and sent her away before then, she would explain her dilemma and, with his permission, leave him to his mother and his servants and his life of ease.

Brandon and their mother and even the scullery at Maxwell Manor would have to manage without her. She could vanish with a clear conscience, change her name and become a governess. She could adopt the surname Nightingale. That had a familiar ring.

"What's it to be, lass?" John said, interrupting her thoughts. "Do I kill this mob and take you wi' me now, or do we postpone the spilling a' noble blood this day, wish 'em well, and let 'em live on to their happy dotage? It's yers to say."

She straightened to her full height and raised her chin. "Yes. All right. Michaelmas it is. September twenty-ninth will be our wedding day."

He eyed her suspiciously. "If ye try to squirm outta' it, no matter how sound yer reason, his honor the duke and his mum die. I'm just making sure we both understand the terms o' this here agreement."

When she didn't respond, he raised his voice.

"I'm trying to assure meself things between us are clear, Jess. Are they, then? Clear?"

She looked down at her silk shoes designed to fit her feet, far more delicate and comfortable than the cast-off boots John provided. "Yes."

Lout sheathed his blade, puckered his lips and bent from the waist, tilting his lumbering hulk closer. Jessica stepped quickly aside and rounded the corner of the tavern, putting herself again in full view of the duke's people readying the team, loading the coach, and preparing their departure.

John trailed her. As she passed the tavern door, Bear stepped out, placing his considerable bulk between Jessica and John. The two men stood eye to eye, taking one another's measure. Although they were of comparable heft, Bear, taller and more mature, exhibited hard, tested muscle while John, not quite so tall, looked heavier and notably softer.

Bear glowered at Jessica, then at her companion before setting inquisitive, perhaps sympathetic eyes again on the girl. "His Grace asks if yer ready to continue the journey." His gaze followed as hers shifted to John and back. Bear's stare narrowed and fixed on the other man as if visually daring him to speak.

Lout remained silent, but offered a smarmy victorious grin and did not flinch as he returned the stare.

With another glance at John, Jessica flicked her tongue over her bottom lip. "Yes, thank you, Bear. You may tell His Grace I am well ready to be away from this place."

When neither Bear nor Lout moved, nor yielded their visual lock, Jessica attempted to initiate dialogue between them. "Bear, this is John Lout, a friend of my brother's, from Welter. John, this is the Duke of Fornay's most trusted friend…"

"Friend, is it?" Lout glowered insolently at the older man. "Slave, more like. Nobility don't have friends. Don't need 'em. They hire what bodies they want around 'em. Don't have to put up with giving something a' themselves to get something in return like the rest of us."

Bear's eyes narrowed and John thrust his chin forward, mutely daring the older man to dispute his words.

Unexpectedly, Bear opened his great cavern of a mouth and roared; a sound so loud it rattled the inn's great oaken door.

Jessica started and John staggered, obviously taken aback. Bear studied Lout another long moment as blue twinkled in the deep-set cavities of his weathered old eyes.

"Come along, Miss. We'd best be going." Glancing back, he grinned again at Lout and, taking Jessica's elbow, turned her toward the carriage. "You can show His Grace yerself ye'r truly ready."

She heard John curse as he wheeled to join his men.

Chapter Eleven

"Your sight will return, or it won't," Dr. Emmanuel Connor said rather philosophically while Devlin rebuttoned his shirt. "There's nothing I can do to make it happen. No therapy. No medicine. No surgery. Your heart is strong. You're a hearty specimen. Rest. Stay fit and well fed and avoid aggravations for a time and we'll see if Mother Nature will help. Indulge in pleasant pastimes. Spend your days with people whose company you enjoy." He paused, and then lowered his voice. "I don't know that I would enjoy myself too much with the ladies for a time, if you get my meaning, what with the strain involved in that particular pursuit."

"I understand. Thank you for your reassurance."

"As to those glimpses of light and shadow you're experiencing, I find that very encouraging. Even if you weren't to regain your full ability to see, those wee peeks indicate the parts work. No doubt, some of your vision will be restored. If you will take proper rest, your attitude and stamina will do more for you than any physician can."

Dr. Conner turned to put away his stethoscope, and then looked back at Devlin. "Entertain healthy thoughts. Laugh. Laugh out loud as often as you can. A cheerful heart makes a healthier man."

Devlin again thanked the doctor as he finished dressing and joined the ladies in the physician's outer office.

"What did he say?" the dowager asked as Devlin took her arm with one hand and placed the other on Jessica's shoulder.

Seeing the concern in his face, Jessica was interested in his answer.

They strolled through the door and followed the narrow stairwell to ground level, and then outside to the duke's crested coach waiting at the curb. They were settled inside the vehicle, the ladies side by side, before he repeated the physician's prognosis and advice. He did not mention the glimpses of light, or the doctor's optimism about what those events might foretell.

Jessica sensed something hopeful, but the duke's spoken account didn't reveal it. Devlin's mood was noticeably lighter, however, as he gave the driver an address for their next stop.

"I know of a gifted milliner who might be able to transform our sparrow here into a cockatoo with a proper crest. But first to the modiste. Our little bird's feathers must outshine the rest."

Lady Anne Miracle smiled at Jessica. "Yes, we should do that. The three of us together. I am sure Mrs. Capstone will not object to a blind man accompanying us. You are sure you have no sight at all, Devlin?"

He gave her a roguish grin. "Now would be a good time for a miraculous cure, madam, but it has not occurred as yet. I will let you know the moment it does."

Jessica tried on dresses already pieced and needed only fitting to be hers. The girl slipped in and out of soft, silky garments and stiff ones as well, as Mrs. Capstone and her helper, an older lady, tall and angular, toiled, obviously uncomfortable in Devlin's presence. When they commented incidentally on the girl's figure, the assistant, a Miss Todds, became more fidgety and required repeated reassurances from Lady Anne that the duke was totally sightless.

Sitting stoic and sightless, his other senses fully alert, the duke felt put off by the unfairness of it. His pique was fueled by a series of foreign emotions. His most prominent and prevailing response was scarcely recognizable to himself. He had little experience with jealousy.

Brooding, he felt a consuming, irrational annoyance with everyone who enjoyed the benefit of seeing eyes. In addition, he did not appreciate being ignored as Jessica and his mother chatted amiably with these insipid women, fawning and cooing over every fabric and color, not including asking after his comfort or seeking his opinion. He was expected to sit patiently ignored until it was time for money to change hands. They would look to him for the necessary payment, of course. It would serve them all right if he refused.

He heard the approaching rustle of skirts and recognized the mingled fragrances peculiar only to one person. Jessica. He smiled without intending to. A bit of sheer fabric floated over his hand and up to skim his face.

"Am I being besieged by butterflies?"

"Devlin, in truth this cloth is like a butterfly's wings. It is the sheerest, loveliest fabric I have ever seen, yet Mrs. Capstone insists it be used only for undergarments."

"Perhaps a nightgown then. Would it be comfortable for sleeping?"

He heard Jessica's clothing swish as she whirled. "Oh, yes, Mrs. Capstone, could I have a nightgown made of this?"

The older woman cleared her throat and he realized her answer was directed at him. At last, someone was soliciting his opinion.

"It is very expensive, Miss. It would not be practical as it would require several yards to sew a proper nightgown. In addition, the fabric is too sheer to provide any warmth to the wearer. As you can tell, it is transparent, too bold to be worn by an unmarried lady. What would be the use in a single lady owning such an expensive, impractical garment?"

Devlin didn't realize he was smiling, until his mother put his own thoughts into words. "I think, Mrs. Capstone, we might benefit from a man's input here."

Quite surprisingly, the lone man in the room had the mute attention of all the ladies present. He tried to darken his look to emulate the wisdom of Solomon, but Jessica's giggling indicated the abrupt alteration of his expression of eager anticipation had come too late.

"He is, after all, the one paying for all of this," the dowager reminded them.

"Yes," the modiste said, "of course. If you commission it, Your Grace, knowing the cost, I will craft this wisp of cloth into a marvelous, flowing gown."

"Oh, all right. Do it," he said, forcing reluctance into his tone. Secretly, he rejoiced at being able to give his young charge something impractical she valued so highly. "Make her one in each color."

"Oh no, Your Grace," Jessica objected, genuine concern in her voice.

He waved a hand in her direction. "How many will you have then, my pet?"

"One is sufficient. You are most generous to provide that."

"If you think to send me to the work house with your extravagance, Nightingale, you will have to spend far more than you have done so far."

He puzzled that she did not answer and by the fact she remained painfully quiet to the end of the fitting.

As they left the establishment with their bags of finished clothing and instructions to return for final fittings two mornings hence, Jessica remained uncharacteristically silent. Devlin placed his hand on her shoulder and spoke softly. "What is wrong, darling?"

"It was never my intention to send you to the work house, Your Grace."

"You shan't, my little cuckoo. I want you to have your heart's desire, whether it be clothing, coops for your hens, or gems to rival the crown jewels. I want to spoil you. I suspect I am the first."

She shot an alarmed look at Devlin, and then at the dowager, who again appeared to be, not only pleased, but laughing behind her hand, as she did often when Jessica and Devlin had their exchanges.

To the duke's astonishment, at that precise moment, as he prepared to follow Jessica into the carriage, he experienced another momentary glimpse of light.

He nearly stumbled, so enthralled was he in studying Jessica's shapely backside. Idly, he considered again the cost of the transparent nightgown. The expense suddenly became of even less significance than it had been before. Devlin smiled as his fickle vision dimmed again.

• • •

Mornings in town, refreshed from nights of sound sleep and the pleasant company of his companions, Devlin's incidents of sight came more often and his fleeting glimpses more detailed. Yet those opportunities never occurred when he could get a full, unobstructed view of Jessica. One of the few things he did not enjoy about being in town was a young stable boy to whom Jessica took a liking.

With her apparent approval, the boy, with the unlikely name of Latch Key, brought his performances inside where he was heard day and night entertaining cooks and staff in the kitchen with his jokes, juggling, musical ditties, and antics.

Devlin had never liked humor that ridiculed. Although he occasionally overheard Key performing or got reports of his wit, he was not annoyed enough to act until one afternoon when he heard Jessica's laughter bubbling forth from the kitchen with others.

Puzzled by a flush of anger he could not define, Devlin could not decide what action would be least misunderstood. Normally, a stable boy's behavior, even if he enjoyed rousing popularity with the staff, was not enough to merit the duke's attention. Jessica's approval presented another element.

Devlin did not deal personally with the estates' staffs. He left the matter of discipline to Patterson's impeccable judgment. In this case, Patterson, who often took his lead from Jessica, also seemed to be prey to the boy's antics.

One morning, as the duke strode into the large solarium downstairs, Latch caught Jessica's eye, then noiselessly fell into step behind the nobleman, exaggerating his stride, gliding and swaying with the master's distinctive glide and sway.

Jessica giggled at the boy's mastery of the duke's characteristic walk. Devlin stopped abruptly, almost making Latch to run into him, and turned to confront Jessica.

She bowed her head and covered her mouth, but could not muffle the sound of her laughter entirely.

"What are you sniggering about, Nightingale?" Devlin asked, smiling. "What makes you so jubilant this morning?"

"Nothing, Your Grace" she sputtered as Latch threw her a terrified look, before he ran on tiptoe to hide behind the draperies. He slithered through an open window and disappeared.

Devlin peered down as if able to see his own clothing, and smoothed his trousers with both hands. "Have I something amiss? How have I provoked such hilarity?"

She bit her lips to stop the giggling. "You are perfectly turned out, as usual, Your Grace."

"Why are you addressing me by my title? Are we not alone?"

She froze.

His jaws tightened. "I expect a prompt, civil answer when I ask a question, Jessica. What about me has caused your uncontrollable laughter?"

"It's your walk, Your Grace."

"My walk?"

"Your method of walking."

He cocked his head slightly. "What is it you find amusing about the way I walk?"

"It is graceful for a man, Your Grace."

His frown became a glower. "What does that mean?" When she struggled and failed to respond quickly, he continued. "I've been told I have a bold, innately masculine walk."

"Who mentioned your manner of walking?"

His chin jutted. "People."

"Ladies?" She slanted a speculative glance.

"Yes, ladies…and gentlemen who said they envied my stride. Why?"

"It seems an odd subject for the most important people in the realm to spend their time and intellect discussing."

He stared with unseeing eyes as he moved closer. "Certainly it came only after they had dissected the budget, the Queen's conservative choice of clothing, and other significant issues."

Jessica giggled, knowing his examples signaled a diminishing of the tension that had flared between them.

He gave an answering smile and dropped his voice to a coaxing tone. "Now, what about my walk do you find amusing?"

Arching an eyebrow, Jessica reduced her girlish grin to the sultry smile, one a scullery maid might bestow upon a footman who sparked her interest. She had learned that, even though Devlin could not see her facial expressions, they influenced her tone of voice, which rang clear to him. As she studied his open expression, the duke's face relaxed like the stable boy's had earlier, and Jessica marveled at the ease with which men could be brought to heel.

"Your walk is more of a glide than a stride, Your Grace," she ventured, speaking perhaps suggestively.

"Show me what you mean." He stepped close, grasped her shoulders and turned her back to him, then positioned his hands just below her waist. She gasped at his familiarity and waited until her breathing slowed before she spoke.

"Like this." She directed her toes outward and moved studiously, swaying, an exaggeration of Devlin's stride, as if she were skating on an icy pond. At the same time, she rolled her shoulders, rotating from her waist, and was pleased to achieve a stride very like his, if somewhat overdone.

"I do not walk like this." His volume resounded off the stone walls of the solarium as he concentrated on her hips beneath his hands.

The chit pleased and vexed him, in turn, as no one, male or female, had done before. He felt an unexpected stirring in his groin as her small, rounded hips swayed beneath his hands.

She stepped twice to one side and pivoted, thinking the demonstration finished. He tightened his grip.

Quiet crept like a fog and stayed until Jessica addressed him over her shoulder. "Yes, Your Grace, you do walk that way, although my version is not as accomplished as yours."

He measured his words. "Do you have any idea how offensive your portrayal is, even when I cannot see what you are doing?"

"The demonstration was not intended either to offend or to flatter."

"You thought I might be flattered?"

"No, Your Grace. I thought you would be...informed."

Hearing her usual artless honesty, Devlin rocked his head back and shook the walls again. This time they reverberated, not with his shout, but with his laughter.

He secretly mourned as he allowed her to slip his grasp.

"I may want to pursue this later, Nightingale, but for now let's adjourn to the library where you may abandon your study of my stride and practice your marvelous reading skills instead."

She said, "It seems rather early in the day for you to be in need of a nap."

He grinned. "Ah, you've discovered my secret. The problem is, of course, that you read well, and seldom need me to decipher or pronounce. Does my little deception trouble you?"

Her voice lilted. "No, except I am often tempted to follow your example."

"Are you concerned that someone will find us napping together, alone, in the library?"

"Not at all, Your Grace. I often find your mother and her cat nodding off together in that same location. I imagine the household considers our relationship much like theirs."

A smile teased Devlin's broad mouth. For a moment he seemed to regard her skeptically, then, as if the spell were broken, he stepped up, apparently to precede her into the corridor. Suddenly, he stopped and waved a hand motioning for her to pass.

"I do not want to corrupt your walk, Nightingale. I will try to remember to follow rather than lead when we stroll together."

"Your stride is distinctive, so unusual that in combination with your height and your striking physique one is able to locate you, even in a crowd."

"Have you ever looked for me in a crowd, Nightingale?"

"I have, and have always been successful."

In truth, she could pick him out of a crowd not only by his movements, height, and stature, but also by the depth and resonance of his voice, which she seemed able to hear, regardless of the noise or commotion around them. She recalled the biblical passage about a sheep who knows his master's voice and smiled fondly to herself as she preceded the duke down the cool, dim hallway and into the library.

Maybe they would read a little scripture this morning. She would keep the inflection out of her voice, an effort that often induced him to doze. When he slept, his defenses fell away and his manly features relaxed giving him a look of vulnerability. It was a game she enjoyed, lulling him to sleep, for while he slept, she drank her fill of his handsome face; his large, warm, capable hands; his chest rising and falling as he breathed. In those private moments, Jessica indulged in private dreams of things that could not be.

Chapter Twelve

"I cannot allow you to marry John Lout." Devlin began their luncheon conversation by firing the opening salvo.

How could he know of her approaching nuptials? No one else knew. She had no idea who could have told him.

She looked to the dowager, but found no ally there. Lady Anne seemed fascinated with her soup.

"I beg your pardon, Your Grace."

"One of my people overheard you speak privately with the ruffian at the inn before we left. The fellow suggested you planned to wed on Michaelmas."

The duchess shot a quick glance at Jessica, and then returned to the hypnotic soup.

Jessica wasn't certain how to respond. When the duke's mother indicated by her silence that she did not plan to intervene, Devlin adopted a reassuring tone.

"As a peasant's wife, Nightingale, you will be worn out with drudgery and childbearing before you are thirty. I can feel the softness returning to your hands in only the weeks you have been with me...with us. Your calluses are giving over to cool, smooth flesh. You cannot tell me you prefer life as a country maid to that of a lady."

"Certainly I do not, Your Grace, but a girl born to a poor scholar has little opportunity to live in a great house where she is required only to coddle a sightless duke, and that a temporary position."

Devlin rested his knife on his plate. "We will address coddle later. For now, what do you mean temporary position?"

"I mean when your sight is restored, you will have no further use for mine or for me."

"Do you sincerely believe I would outfit you while intending that you should wear your new wardrobe in the kitchens at Maxwell Manor?"

"No, Your Grace. I supposed the clothes were…on loan."

"Are they not fitted exactly to your figure? Is it not your coloring they flatter? Are they not designed and sewn to your preferences?"

"Yes."

"Would your clothes fit any other female in my home?"

"Perhaps Sophie or Nan."

"A lady's silken finery for an upstairs maid?"

"A maid's clothes were good enough for me when I arrived. Mine should do for them."

Devlin drew a breath, and then hesitated. "Yes, well, I hadn't thought things out quite that far. What a practical, frugal girl you are. Have you foreseen this eventuality from the first?"

"Of course."

"When you were being fitted?"

"Yes."

He lowered his voice, signaling change to a more intimate subject. "Jessica, do you fancy yourself in love with John Lout?"

A spewed, scoffing laugh exploded. "My father said I had a gift of imagination, but the talent is not sufficient to instill love in me for John Lout."

"Then why do you entertain the idea of marrying him?"

"Truly, I do not expect to marry him."

"Then why in God's name are you betrothed to the man?"

"You have no way of knowing this, Your Grace, but John is a large man, nearly as tall as you, though heavier." He nodded. "He was a large boy. When he was ten and I was six, he announced publicly that I would be his wife. To save my brother from a beating that day, I agreed.

"By the time I was twelve, he had repeated the statement so often and so broadly that even adults assumed we would wed.

178

John bullied other children, particularly the boys, into echoing his declaration. He became an able hunter and fighter, although he never became in any way handsome. He is physically energetic, but intellectually lazy. He didn't bother with reading or sums."

"So he is illiterate?"

"Yes. He thought it a waste for both of us to develop the same skills when we would be husband and wife. He is an accomplished woodsman. They say he can track and kill or capture even the largest, wildest beasts. And, of course, he is a grand fighter, having grown up belligerent and having built his confidence by overpowering small animals and children.

"When he was sixteen and I was twelve, he beat Brandon severely for informing him, at my urging, that I had no intention of honoring the marriage promise he had announced when we were young.

"Soon after that, John bullied Brandon into publicly declaring that John and I truly were betrothed."

"And so you were browbeaten into accepting him."

"Well, that was the case until I was fifteen." She saw a subtle, expectant change in Devlin's expression. "Gypsies came to Welter peddling goods from wagons. You may recall my alluding to the incident. The son of the family took me, against my will, to a cave near the river.

"People who had seen me taken, screaming and clawing at the man, reported to John, before they even notified my family."

Jessica paced to the windows that overlooked the rose garden where the buds popped blood red before they opened to crimson.

"John tracked us through the woods and came directly to the place with little delay. Deterred by my struggling, we arrived only moments before John.

"In spite of the circumstances, when I saw John's face, I was terrified for my assailant who had not had time to subdue me.

"I had known John all my life. I had seen him furious, but I had never seen him as angry as he was in those moments.

"The trader's son was not a large fellow, but he was strong and quick and wily. I am sure some women considered him attractive, but that was before he met John that horrible afternoon.

"I had been frightened for my virtue before John's arrival, but that turned as John thrashed the gypsy. I did not intercede, at least not as soon as I should have. John beat the man long after he was defeated."

Recalling the gypsy's mangled face, she raised her eyes to the duke's flawless features.

"Then what happened?" Devlin asked.

"Although I could have walked, the cave's floor was rough and I stumbled as we began our return. John lifted me into his arms, as if I were an injured pet, and carried me all the way back to Welter."

Devlin looked as if he could see her. "What became of the brigand who carried you off?"

"They say his mother, who had countenanced his abhorrent behavior toward other village girls, did not recognize her son when he returned to their wagon during the night."

"Did that incident make you feel more kindly about marrying Lout?"

"I felt obligated to him, not merely by a promise coerced from a child and years of public declarations, but by honor. John saved my innocence that day. I am indebted to him in a sum I cannot repay."

"Surely gratitude is not enough to induce you to sacrifice the rest of your life to the man."

She rubbed her hands together. "It does sound rather extreme when you put it that way. In spite of his heroic effort, I have no real intention of marrying him. I do plan to give him a cash remuneration." She rolled her index fingers into her gown, fidgeting, movement Devlin apparently heard and interpreted.

"If you prefer, Nightingale, we may change the subject."

"All right. What shall we discuss?"

"Perhaps you should discuss my unique walk with my mother." He flashed a playful grin. "Wasn't that the subject the maids were discussing prior to my arrival in the bedchamber before luncheon?"

"This morning. Latch was in the solarium after breakfast, walking behind you, mimicking your stride. He didn't imagine you would know he was in the room. Later, he was telling the maids."

A scowl replaced the duke's smile. "I distinctively heard the term 'La-de-dah.' Can you explain that?"

Jessica hesitated.

"Come, Nightingale, the whole sordid story, if you please."

"Hardly a 'sordid story,' Your Grace. Latch has a rather inflated idea of himself. He needs bolstering."

"At my expense?"

"He needs to feel superior, Your Grace."

"And the snapping noise. What was that?"

"Nan was popping the spread above the sheets, making it flutter as it settled over your bed."

"Is that the same girl you confronted in my bedchamber the first morning you were at Gull's Way?"

"Yes."

"What were her exact words to this Latch person, if you please."

"It was silliness, Your Grace. No one considers the prattle of servants."

"I want to know what they said, Nightingale, and I expect you to tell me."

"All right, if I can remember such inane remarks. Nan said something like she could tell—by your walk—that you were a 'la-de-dah gentleman.'"

"And…"

"Sophie described how the ladies of the court fawn over you. She had never heard one rumor about your having an appetite for anything but ladies, and that something of a rapacious one."

"And Nan's retort?" he asked.

"Only that one can never tell about the appetites of a nobleman."

He looked more satisfied than annoyed. "I gather they did not know you were nearby."

"Nor you. I said they were behind schedule and suggested they would increase their productivity with less conversation."

"What was their reaction to that?"

"Nan said I was as much a servant here as she. She often addresses me as 'Your Highness.' I suggested you might give her references if she wanted to look elsewhere for employment."

"Let the wench go, by all means."

"Nan likes it here. She says the atmosphere is pleasant as there is no threat to a girl, no matter how beautiful she may be, in a house where the master is 'sissified.'"

His eyes narrowed with new understanding. "I thought you were using this Nan's words to discredit her, Nightingale, but that is not the case, is it? You are challenging me." He arched an eyebrow. "Are you trying to determine if I am the sissified man Nan believes me to be?"

"Certainly not. Why would I care whether you were as masculine as you appear? I relayed my conversation with her, at your insistence. If you did not want to hear it, you should not have been so relentless."

The dowager rose with a clatter of silverware. "I think I shall retire."

Devlin came to his feet. Likewise, Jessica stood. Seeing the look on his face, she retreated a step as Devlin walked his mother to the corridor. The sound of scurrying feet indicated some unseen person had been listening outside the door.

As the dowager moved into the hallway, the duke kept his hand on the door, then shoved it noiselessly closed and waited. The bolt snapped into place. With a feeling of foreboding, Jessica advanced toward that door, intending to exit the room before Devlin began chastising her.

Maybe she had baited him...a little. She hadn't intended to imply he had anything to prove. Not to her. Had she not retreated quickly from his teasing on their picnic? Yet, she couldn't help being a little curious, particularly hearing speculations from the women in the kitchen.

Devlin had never made any serious sexual advance on her, or on any of the females on the household staff, as far as she knew. Many of them, including Jessica, had wondered about that. It was common for the lord of a manor to foist himself upon the girls in service, particularly young, pretty ones. Did the duke lack the usual male predilection? Perhaps, as Nan suggested, his taste ran to young males, although no one had tales from the stable boys. Perplexing.

Jessica had not intended to interrogate him, exactly. Who was she to question the behavior of a duke? She had merely intended to slake her curiosity. At the moment, however, she did not like the look on his face. It was almost as if he felt challenged to prove something. Perhaps she had pushed too far.

Frowning at the floor, Devlin locked his hands behind his back and paced to the windows, looking for all the world as if he could see. Even safe in the knowledge that he could not, Jessica blushed and sputtered. "I need to be about my duties, Your Grace."

He strode slowly back to the door and pivoted to face her. His expression was not exactly threatening, but neither was it altogether benign. "Not just yet, Nightingale. I need your assistance with something first. I need you to advise me, provide me the benefit of your usual candor." He moved toward her, exaggerating his usual glide, keeping his body between her and the primary exit as he came. "Do you find my walk effeminate? Is it off-putting to you as a member of the gentler sex?"

"No, Your Grace, not at all. As I believe I mentioned before, I find your walk appealing. That is to say…"

His lips turned up, but it was not a genuine smile. "Prettily put." He continued advancing on her. "Will you be so kind as to allow my fingers to read your face as we talk, Jessica?"

Withdrawing another step, she tried to think of an excuse to keep him from touching her. If he touched her, he would detect the heat of her rising blush, be aware of how she trembled when he stood so dangerously close.

"As I said, Nightingale," he crooned, drawing to within arm's reach, "I cannot, in good conscience, allow you to marry John Lout."

She was not able to follow the erratic conversation. "You should encourage our union, Your Grace. Dedicated to honor as you are, you should insist on my keeping my word."

He reached for her. She sidestepped, dipping her shoulder to avoid his hand. He seemed uncannily attuned to the swish of her skirts, however, and followed her retreat, his stride never faltering as she scampered and slithered just beyond his grasp.

"I said I cannot allow it."

"Yes, Your Grace, I heard you clearly enough. Did you not hear me as well?"

He grabbed for her with both hands. She slipped deftly to one side, beyond his fingertips, and darted toward the other door in the room, the one to the adjoining library.

"Your Grace, you are only a lord of the realm. You are not God to dictate people's lives."

He matched her stride for stride. "Ah, but Nightingale, I do not wish to dictate the course of the lives of everyone under my authority." His voice dropped to a threatening hum. "Only yours." He continued his skating gait, again closing on her. "I want you to stay here when I am here, and at Gull's Way, when I am there. I want you within the sound of my call." He stared at her with eyes dark, vivid gray-blue, the color of a stormy day. "I want you be, at all times, within my reach," he flashed a taunting smile, "if not my grasp."

She glanced behind and realized he was driving her as a dog drives sheep, into a corner.

"Under what pretext would you keep me, sir? Will you adopt me? No, I am too old. Perhaps retain me as your nanny? Your education is too advanced to name me your governess."

She skimmed lightly around the long couch. Her patter continued, an effort to combat her nervousness. "Do you think some night you will stagger in drunk from an evening of gaming at your club and, in the heat of the moment, force yourself upon the resident country maid? Transform me from servant to mistress?"

Circling the wingback chairs paired at one side of the hearth, she shot another quick glance at the couch. Could she scramble over it before he caught her? What if he captured her mid scramble? He moved quickly for a blind man, his hearing honed to an astonishing level.

Somehow, her last suggestion stopped him. What had she said? She didn't recall. It was part of her nonsensical chatter. His handsome face twisted, looking as if he had been injured.

"You trample my sensibilities, you ungrateful chit. Do you imagine me capable of such vile, loathsome behavior toward someone—a child—living under my protection?"

Jessica felt her own volatile emotions bubble from simmer to boil. "I am not a child, Your Grace, as you well know." She felt a victim to her own overwrought emotions. "Although I am not your equal, I will not be bullied or forced to endure your tempers, no matter how you might justify them in your own highborn conscience."

Patterson stepped to the library doors that stood open between the library and the corridor and peered at the noisy combatants.

Neither the duke nor Jessica noticed him. A peculiar smile flitted over the old retainer's mouth before he stepped into the room and collected both doorknobs. Soundlessly, he pulled the double doors closed. He then stationed himself in the corridor outside and folded his arms over his narrow chest, his body language effectively barring observers. Personally, the majordomo considered this confrontation long overdue and the adversaries, despite their individual strengths and weaknesses, evenly matched.

Meanwhile, the tension in the room escalated as Devlin again began to stalk his unrepentant charge. Jessica dodged one way and another, avoiding his hands that periodically slapped at the air in front of her as he drove her relentlessly toward a far corner.

"Mistress?" He chortled, firing Jessica's indignation. "What would an unschooled infant like you know about being a mistress?"

He heard the intake of breath as she prepared to flay him with her knowledge of the duties of mistresses. At that prospect, he lowered his voice, changing his tact to defuse her verbal explosion. He was, after all, a peer of the realm, compelled by rank and upbringing to be gracious to underlings.

"Nightingale, I have no doubt that one day you will be a desirable, sought-after woman." He stopped moving toward her and she froze, standing stiffly, not wanting to end this discussion cowering in the corner of the room. "Until that time, I do not want you to squander your unripened charms on John Lout. Even as an adolescent, you are too fine a match for him."

He waited for her retort, to evaluate how his less threatening demeanor might change the tenor of their exchange.

As she delayed, he shifted, subtly realigning himself. Something distressed her. Initially, insisting she not marry John Lout, he intended to flatter, not frighten or offend her. She was still a child, a joy and a vexation, a puzzling bundle of contradictions.

He wanted to maintain her refreshing naiveté. His purest instincts were to shelter and protect her for as long it was in his power to do so.

He wanted to reduce his chaste intentions to words, but something restrained him. Perhaps his hesitation had to do with her pricking his pride with her vile suggestions.

He opened his arms. "Dear Jessica, come here. Let me hold and comfort you as a doting father would console a well-loved child."

"A father's well-loved child, am I? You are insufferable. How can you suggest assigning us those roles?" She stamped her foot and fisted her hands on her hips. "I am not a recalcitrant child who seeks your lap for solace, Your Grace. I am a woman grown, fully capable of coping with the rigors and responsibilities of husband and home."

His indulgent smile only heightened her temper. "There, there, little bird. I keep offending you when I intend to soothe." His kindly tone stymied her; therefore, his lunge caught her totally unaware.

She yanked her wrist out of his grasp, but not before his free arm wrapped and pinioned her waist. Pummeling his shoulders, she refused to yield, even knowing her struggle was futile against his superior strength and size.

Ensnared, she recalled strategy that had worked on zealous fellows in the past. She went limp, allowing him to win their pulling match and, hopefully, put him off his guard, as he had done to her seconds before.

Surprised, Devlin staggered but, unlike the others on which this ruse had worked so effectively, he did not yield his hold but pulled her with him as he staggered backward under the burden of her unexpected weight.

Retreating, his heel caught the edge of the rug, throwing him off balance. He staggered several steps before he toppled.

He dropped directly onto his backside on the floor, still holding firmly to Jessica's waist. Their joint momentum propelled her down on top of him. The back of his head made a resounding thud as it hit the wooden floor beyond the edge of the thick Persian carpet.

Then he went still, completely motionless. The deadly silence in the room was broken only by their respective gasps. Jessica disregarded Devlin's arms firmly locked around her waist as she lay sprawled atop his unmoving body.

"Your Grace?" She prodded, her voice breathless from exertion. "Devlin? Oh, please, say something."

She flattened her hands on the floor on either side of his recumbent body and attempted to push herself up to relieve him of her weight. His hands were locked and, oddly, he seemed unable or unwilling to release her.

His eyelids fluttered, but he did not respond as she called his name. "Devlin? Devlin? Can you hear me?" Shifting her weight onto one stiff arm, Jessica used her free hand to pat his face. "Oh, Devlin, tell me I have not murdered you."

Reluctant to summon help until she could reposition them, she spoke in an earnest whisper. "Devlin. Devlin. Please, say something." Urging, she patted his face with more energy before deciding she had no choice. She must summon help. As she opened her mouth to wail, Devlin's eyelids fluttered.

"Devlin," she pleaded. "Oh, please wake up. What should I do? How can I help you?"

His voice was a rasp. "Kiss me."

She stared at his face, then at his mouth outlined by the narrow, neatly trimmed mustache and beard. Her gaze swept the hard planes of his face, appealing in his supine position, to his long, dark eyelashes feathered against his cheek, his unseeing eyes closed.

This is not John Lout, she reminded herself curtly. This is a gentle bred man. A blind man. Perhaps not altogether harmless, but honor bound by birth. She was the one with no identity, a servant in this household—a position that required unquestioning compliance with this man's wishes. Was it not her duty to meet his requests, without regard to her own preferences or misgivings?

Wasn't it?

Gazing at his face, not wanting to examine her motives too closely, Jessica wriggled upward and carefully pressed her lips to his jaw, the part of him most accessible.

His eyelids fluttered, responding positively to her effort. She repeated the gesture. He turned his head slightly away from her, as if avoiding her lips.

Encouraged that he seemed unaware of what she was doing, she ran staccato kisses along one jaw earning hums of approval, a sound like a large cat purring.

So caught up did she become in prompting the purr that she was not immediately aware of Devlin's hands tugging, relocating her upon his fallen body until she was squarely fitted to him, except for her legs, which straddled boldly as she tried to shift some of her weight onto her toes. Her efforts forged a peculiar intimacy between them.

She squirmed again, thinking to lever herself up and off of him, but with her movement, Devlin's arms tightened. When she ceased to struggle, his hands caressed her back from her shoulders to her waist, and he murmured again, "Kiss me."

If that was a command and he was toying with her, she would not obey.

He whispered, his voice like a summer breeze through saplings. "Please." Then more quietly still, "Please, darling."

The words seemed not a command, but a request. Now that was altogether different.

Her position, while untenable, was not exactly perilous, particularly since there were no witnesses.

What if someone passed in the corridor?

She raised her head to peer at the entry's double doors to find them securely closed.

When had that happened? No decent unmarried female would allow herself to remain in a closed room with the master of the house, unchaperoned. She was not exactly a servant to obey commands, was more like a friend of the family. In that role, she should heed the dowager's teaching regarding the proper deportment of young ladies. While she continued puzzling, Devlin spoke again. His whisper sounded suspicious as he repeated, "Please."

She needed to get up, to pursue more productive activities, but she found this scandalous situation…well…stimulating. She tapped a quick little kiss on his cheek, then curiosity overcame judgment and she pressed her lips to the lobe of his ear, whereupon, he thrust his chin high giving her access to his throat. He looked vulnerable and terribly accessible, so she kissed him there as well, inhaling the marvelous scent of the man.

Suddenly she recalled the resounding thud when his head met the floor. "Are you injured?"

He didn't open his eyes, but allowed a slight smile. "No, my little hen wit. Women have kissed me far more violently than this, and I have not suffered damage from it."

"I doubt the genteel ladies in society ever hurled you to the floor and leaped upon you before kissing you."

"No." His eyelids fluttered again. "It could become quite the rage, once the landing is perfected."

Giggling, Jessica again tried to push herself up and off of him, but he groaned with her effort and she felt his manhood stiffen between her legs. She seemed to be inciting him. Hardly the response one might expect a man to have toward a nanny or a governess…or a child. She wondered if he realized what was occurring in his nether regions.

One of his hands swept down her back again, then ventured lower to cup her bottom.

He definitely was aware of his body's interest and was even encouraging it. She reached back to slap the offending hand, but her movement cost her the prop and brought her chest down hard on top of his.

"Umph," he groaned, then smiled again, looking smug.

"You great oaf, let me go," she said, annoyed with her increasingly untenable situation.

"Do you wish to alter our positions?" he asked with feigned concern. "Darling, you had only to ask." With his usual catlike quickness, he rolled.

Before she could recover, she was pinned beneath him, the prod pressing even more firmly between her legs that remained sprawled on either side of his. Was he playing, or was he seducing her?

"Ah. You were right, Nightingale. This is better. That floor is rather hard." He flashed a mischievous smile. "And that's not all that's hard, is it?"

She had heard her brother and his friends crow about their manly erections, something in which men seemed to take inordinate pride. No woman with half a brain lavished compliments on a man who all but insisted upon them. At least, she did not.

"Get off of me."

For his part, Devlin seemed to be enjoying their game. While the stumbling entry had not been a noble way to accomplish it, he did, finally and at long last, have her securely in his arms. The blow to his head as he fell had precipitated pinpricks of light that spread. With the sun-lighted windows at his back, he was able to see something of her, though she was concealed by his own shadow.

Tussling on the floor with an innocent young female might catch on as an enjoyable afternoon pastime. It certainly beat wagering at the horse track—even when he won.

Although he held himself braced over her, each time she wriggled, her breasts caressed his chest. His hips moved of their own volition, pressing more firmly to her. He no longer required eyesight to view this charming companion. Royals were famous for affairs with their servants, but he was not cut of that cloth. Also, Jessica was no servant.

As she continued struggling, he shifted his weight to his knees. Unburdened, she flailed about to gain her feet, before turning the full force of her fury on him.

He rolled to a sitting position, bent a knee to prop his forearm and regarded her. If he squinted, he could almost see her features, her dark hair limned by the sunlight, a short chin beneath a generous mouth. Huge eyes dwarfing her pert nose.

"You are a bully," she charged, her hands on her hips. "A brigand disguised as a gentleman." He marveled at how provocative she looked. "Furthermore..." Her harangue stopped. "Are you all right?" Her tone was tinged with suspicion and concern.

"I am. As I recall, we were engaged in what was part minuet and part hand-to-hand combat when I fell. You leaped upon me and..."

"Leaped upon you? You scoundrel! You who knocked me down with all the grace of an overzealous wolfhound."

"I was a wolfhound, was I? You were the one licking her victim's face."

"My victim?" She gasped. "Those, sir, were kisses. They were not bestowed voluntarily, but at your command."

He regarded her thoughtfully, secretly rejoicing that he could see blurred expressions—confusion, relief, pique—playing upon her face.

"Do country folk learn kissing from the lapping of animals then?"

She stamped her foot, wheeled and started for the doors. "You make me very angry, Your Grace." She spat the title as an insult.

His response only heightened her rage, for he rocked his head back, watching her from the corner of his eye, and barked a laugh at the ceiling.

Muttering, she stomped to the doors, grabbed the handles of both and threw them open.

Patterson, just on the other side, jumped, startled by her abrupt, untidy appearance.

Equally astonished to find the majordomo immediately on the other side of the doors, Jessica staggered back into the solarium.

Witnessing—able to observe—the stunned, mirrored responses of Jessica and Patterson, Devlin shouted renewed laughter at the ceiling and flopped back, bracing himself on his elbows, sobering only a little beneath the girl's venomous glare.

Instead of the invectives he expected, she seethed, "I pray you get your eyesight back before the sun sets this day. It will serve you right!"

The words hurled as the worst kind of threat, only added to Devlin's hilarity, as he dropped flat on the floor, and howled.

Chapter Thirteen

Devlin had not mentioned his brief glimpses to anyone but the ophthalmologist, so he maintained his silence regarding his sight during his tussle with Jessica.

Although his vision returned for longer periods each day, it was not fully restored; he rationalized in not sharing the news.

After Jessica left the library, Patterson helped the smiling duke to his feet and tidied his clothes. Devlin sobered as he thought of other aspects of his returning sight. He wanted to see again. He should be grateful that Jessica and others prayed for the restoration of his eyesight.

He smiled recalling her pique, and then grew thoughtful. His recovery would cost him dearly if it cost him her. As she said, without his handicap, he would no longer need her. She would return to Welter—to her ailing mother, her shiftless brother, her hens, and John Lout.

She should realize that as long as she remained with him, she had many alternatives.

What a ridiculous coil. He had lost his eyesight, but she was the one blind to what the future might hold for a bright, beautiful woman with intelligence and an enchanting face and form.

He raised his eyebrows remembering her curvaceous form. That was unexpected. Perhaps eating and sleeping at Gull's Way and here in town had put meat on developing bones. He had been misled by her long arms and legs and narrow waist. Originally, he had mistakenly concluded that she was young and sparingly made. Her figure—and her clothing, too—made her a scarecrow to a blind man that night.

Why hadn't anyone corrected his error?

She tried to tell him, of course, but none of the others in his household had verified that. Why had they not?

"Patterson?"

"Yes, Your Grace."

"Why did you not tell me Jessica was a fully developed young woman?"

Patterson, intently straightening the hem of the duke's trousers, hesitated for a brief moment, long enough to raise Devlin's suspicions.

"Quite naturally, Your Grace, I assumed you knew."

"How would I have known when I could not see?"

"When you arrived, you were wrapped together rather…shall I say…rather intimately. I assumed you had taken the liberty… that is, the opportunity…to, ah…That is…I supposed you were aware of her dimensions." Patterson finished with the trousers and stepped back, studying the duke's countenance. He saw bewilderment as Devlin nodded.

"Had my prior reputation with ladies anything to do with your conclusion?"

"Yes, Your Grace, it had."

"I see."

• • •

Devlin's eyesight returned the next morning and lasted until noon. He did not mention it to either his mother or Nightingale. Nor did he speak of it the next day, when his sight continued into the afternoon.

He felt guilty about the ruse, but each time he started to confess, he stalled, thinking one more day might be enough for Jessica to realize she had changed. Like a caterpillar metamorphoses into a butterfly, Jessica had transformed, from peasant girl to noblewomen, a fit companion for a peer of the realm.

In the next several days, the three of them—Jessica, Devlin, and the dowager—took open carriage rides in the park. Jessica drove the matched pair of grays, so the trio dispensed with a driver.

Shyly at first, Jessica responded to the waves or called helloes of other members of the ton as "the Miracles" became a familiar sight on the riding circuit. Occasionally Devlin or his mother introduced Jessica as a distant cousin from the west, near Shiller's Green.

One afternoon, Lady Anne pleaded a headache and declined to go, though Jessica argued the fresh air might ease her pain. Vindicator and Dancer had been brought to town. When his mother begged to stay behind, he suggested he and Jessica ride mounts rather than drive the buggy. Their riding unchaperoned did not raise an eyebrow.

The girl had a place in his family. He liked his household the way it had evolved. In spite of his occasional rants to the contrary, Devlin liked the way she made fun of him when he became what she termed, "overly majestic."

One evening when he had been particularly obnoxious, as Jessica prepared to go up to bed, she said, "Sleep well, Your Pomposity."

"What did you call me," he asked, looking toward her.

"Your Pomposity. It seems an apt title when you behave as you have this evening."

"The title I carry was bestowed on my ancestor over two hundred years ago by a grateful king. Historically such a title commands respect." Devlin was trying to maintain control of his temper and impress Jessica with the importance of his background.

"You were born into a titled family."

Swelling to sit more erectly, he gave her a regal nod.

"Just as I was born to a scholar."

His lordly posture relaxed. "Well, yes, I suppose."

"Do I brag that I can read and write when those abilities are rare among villagers?"

He held hard to his anger. "It is not the same."

"How is it different? We were each born from a mother's womb. Does any babe receive credit for a feat that everybody who breathes achieves? No," she answered without allowing him to speak. "We who survive share a common achievement that is neither to our credit nor our blame. We arrive without so much as swaddling, blessed only with our individual gifts. Will you argue with that?"

He rose and began walking toward her voice. If only his eyesight might return at that moment, his anger might propel him to do more—to take the waif across his knee and school her in the proper regard for the difference in their stations.

She wasn't, however, through antagonizing him. "You were born a second son who could anticipate living on the generosity of an elder brother or the hope your father might purchase you a commission in the military. Isn't that correct?"

Damn her eyes and that quick little mind. Why didn't the snip stand still? He continued to slide his feet in what he hoped were unnoticeable steps. If he got his hands on her, she would learn a valuable lesson regarding his sensitivity and his position, aspects she determinedly ignored.

He heard her gown rustle as she attempted retreat. Was she frightened or merely moving on instinct? He did not imagine her afraid.

He moved toward the rustling. "But my older brother died and I fell heir to the title and its inherent responsibilities."

"A title earned by a long-ago ancestor who did murder or thievery or some other scandalous act to earn his liege's pleasure," she taunted. "What have you done to deserve the homage you demand?"

"Demand? My staff here and at my estates, the villagers and the overseers in the manors to Welter and beyond, have sworn their fealty to me."

"To you? Do people even know you? Would they recognize you if you walked into a pub in Welter without your ducal crest announcing your identity?" She hesitated a moment. "Or, perhaps, you are recognized. Perhaps they did know who you were that night on the highway, riding a grand horse, clothed in finery. Perhaps they resented that you had so much and they so little and they attempted to beat you, or perhaps take your life."

He bristled. "The brigands who attacked me were after my purse, not my life. Had they known it was I, they might have offered assistance."

"Not bloody likely."

His tone exploded in a shout. "You will not use that common language in my presence."

"Have I offended your sensibilities again, Your Grace? I have overheard you swear using words that fairly scorched my tender ears.

"Furthermore," she continued, not allowing him time or space to respond as she continued dodging his grasp, "your title is only what you make of it. No one honors a word, which is all 'duke' is. People subject themselves as they choose. If your subjects choose to hold you in high esteem, they are exercising their God-given free will, not the dictates of some puffed-up prig who, by accident of birth, is heir to a title."

She spun away from him as he grabbed close, and continued her verbal attack.

"A parent, a man, even a duke, must earn the regard of his children or friends, not demand it. Neither your name nor your title are enough to make one uneducated villager pay homage."

Suddenly her bombardment ceased. There was no sound in the room at all, except that of their heavy breathing. He stood still, stung by her words. Was what she said true? Had his father and grandfather, all the men in his background, received the title, and then set about earning obeisance?

He did not know about prior generations, but his father had prided himself on dealing fairly with the people who worked his lands. Lady Anne still drew shouts of praise—villagers threw flower petals occasionally—when she passed. Her answering smiles and waves reflected her regard for them. The duchess had risked her health in the past to take poultices and elixirs to treat the ill or injured. She sent beef and vegetables from estate stores to help in times of famine or poor harvests.

The people responded in kind. They grieved as if they shared the family's loss when Roth and then Devlin's father, the old duke, died. Their sympathy was heartfelt as they showered the new widow and her remaining sons with bouquets, food and gifts.

Perhaps Jessica had a point. Perhaps there was more to a title than accepting admiration. The title did not bring allegiance. The holder of the title needed to demonstrate an answering regard.

He had not forgotten Jessica as he digested this new aspect of his authority. Feeling chastised, he grumbled. "Furthermore, I do not swagger, and I resent your saying I do."

Her lilting giggle washed the anger from his soul as a glass of wine might clear his thoughts. His self-effacing laugh joined her heady one. Humor often soothed harsh words between them.

Unschooled as she was in the ways of court, Jessica knew how to plow into his soul, wring his heart, and tickle his fancy with a gesture, a musical laugh, or an aptly worded argument.

Over time, she had interceded between him and staff members in both residences, softened his edicts by volunteering an occasional explanation, or clarified a servant's reasons for why something was done differently than he prescribed.

He found her too sympathetic with the staff, an attitude he considered inappropriate. She made the effort to be as understanding with them as she was with him and his mother. Yet, although she had neither title nor authority, people within and without the walls at Gull's Way and here in town adored her.

She had captivated Patterson and Odessa from the beginning. Sophie, and even Bear, no longer complained about her. She had a surprising rapport with everyone, from the stablemen to the villagers, to the peddlers outside the gates. And with his own mother.

What of Devlin himself? Wasn't he, too, one of her devotees?

What other explanation for the stirring he felt as he awoke each morning, pleased at the prospect of seeing her? She had stimulated him when she sat before him on Vindicator's back that first night—her willowy body warm, her hands cool and comforting when he burned with fever the following day in his own chambers.

He was surprised that she bore no grudge toward Nan, the upstairs maid who had been officious with her in his rooms that first day. He harbored more resentment toward the haughty chambermaid than Jessica did.

Such thoughts mellowed him. "Come here, Nightingale. Let me see you."

He heard the familiar rustle and sensed her before him. He lifted his arm and she curled under it, putting her back to him in anticipation of leading. He swept his hand across her back from one thin shoulder to the other before he clamped that hand upon her neck. She allowed herself to be pulled snugly to him.

Her face against his shoulder, her warm, sweet breath on his neck, he wrapped her tightly in both arms and smiled when her sigh preceded his own. Smoothing over an argument with her was like the early morning calm after a night of storms. He rocked, aligning her body with his. This was perfect contentment. Ease spread through him, bringing to mind the look on his father's face when the old duke held his duchess close and watched their young sons romp. Devlin experienced such tranquility.

As he and Jessica stood silently locked together, light filtered through Devlin's unseeing eyes. He blinked. It was nearly twilight. Since the accident, he had not seen a single sunset. Here it was. He looked around, unwilling to disturb the woman snuggled against him.

The gilt mirrors reflected chandelier candles so bright he had to squint. The pattern in the wall covering was distinct. He had never properly appreciated the beauty of glorious, everyday things taken for granted.

He bent his head to Jessica's hair, able to see that dark mass, candles reflected in its highlights. She tilted her face. Her eyes met his and she started, almost pulling out of his arms. He tightened his hold. "Stay, Nightingale."

"You're looking at me." Her words rang with amazement, accusation and reverence. "You can see!"

"Yes. Your face is the first thing I have seen clearly in long weeks of darkness."

She wriggled out of his arms to stare into his face and he into hers.

"Is this a miracle?" Her smile was tentative. "I have prayed for this moment, Your Grace."

He stared, unable to draw his gaze from her enchanting face, her perfect features, the intelligence—and something more— shining in her gray, fathomless eyes. In her innocence, she awaited his answer, expecting the truth.

"I have had glimpses in recent mornings." He caught her hand as she pivoted. "But, no, I have not been able to see detail until this moment."

Tears glistened in her eyes as she bowed her head, hiding her face from him. "Have you told your mother of these glimpses?"

"No."

She blinked, keeping her face turned, but trying to peer at him from the corners of her eyes. "You've told no one? Why not?"

"I did not want to raise false hope." True as far as it went.

She caught one of his hands in both of hers. "I am so glad…for you." Her voice broke. "I honestly am, Your Grace. I have prayed diligently…for your sight to return." Her shoulders shuddered. She gave a muffled sob, dropped his hand, whirled and darted away, stammering. "I shall pack my things and…and prepare to leave at once." Without looking back, she launched herself through the doorway and disappeared.

His world dimmed, this darkness bleaker than before. His sight likely would return, but what joy if it cost him his Nightingale? She must not leave, yet he could not hold her against her will. What inducement could he use? What promise could he make?

· · ·

That night Devlin lay wrestling with his conscience into the wee hours. He was groggy when a commotion arose at sunrise, and several of the staff scurried into the small dining room. They escorted Jessica in the tide. Each one seemed eager to be first to notify the duke that his brother Lattimore had arrived and was in the front hallway, he and two traveling companions being welcomed by Patterson.

As he heard the excited reports, Devlin's smile was forced, and Jessica's senses, already on edge, sharpened. Watching his face, she realized, first, that his erratic eyesight was gone again, and secondly, that for some reason he was not overjoyed at the news of visitors. The duke's younger brother might require watching, maybe as closely as the mischievous child who had played nasty little tricks on a blind man when they received visitors at Gull's Way.

Bracing, renewing her resolve to protect Devlin, Jessica was hardly prepared as Lattimore Miracle and two other strapping young gallants, dressed in evening attire, strode through the dining room door.

She knew immediately which of the three was Devlin's brother. In spite of a marked difference in coloring, their square jaws, straight noses, and animated brows were remarkable.

The baby of his family, Lattimore, at twenty-five, was still seven years Jessica's senior. She thought him handsome, his hair dark, rather than straw colored like the duke's or the dowager's.

Like Devlin, Lattimore wore a stylishly thin beard and mustache that circled and emphasized a generous mouth as he smiled, revealing large, even teeth, strikingly like his brother's. He had dark, playful eyes with a familiar twinkle when he turned them on her as Devlin made introductions.

Lattimore stepped close and collected both of Jessica's hands in his. "So you are the wench wreaking havoc in my family and its households."

He was shorter and more sturdily made than his brother. The crown of Lattimore's regal head came only to Devlin's chin as the two men stood side by side.

Lattimore's voice had a teasing, singsong quality to match his movements, his tone higher than Devlin's. "I have come, my dove, to bring gaiety into your dismal little life."

Disregarding his companions, who were appraising her, awaiting their own introductions, Lattimore turned to Devlin. "If I had had any idea, brother, that the reports were true, I would have sped to your sickbed. The servants in every house buzz with stories of our cousin." His eyes stayed on Jessica. "I will also claim kinship with this winsome creature to assume my place as escort and chaperone."

Devlin's expression dissolved from pleasant to displeased at Lattimore's teasing. "Jessica is no concern of yours, little brother."

"Surely, you will not keep her tethered here? She is too young, too beautiful, too alive, to be buried in this mausoleum with you and Mama when there are parties and plays and historical sites to enjoy."

Jessica stiffened. "I am in this house, your lordship, to assist, not to be entertained."

Lattimore turned a stare on her. "You are one of those cheeky, educated girls, full of sass, are you?" He laughed as if his words rang with exceptional wit. "How utterly delightful."

Jessica glanced at Devlin to see his face darken with an expression she had not seen. If the duke were concerned with her throwing in with his younger brother, he assumed wrongly. She had some experience with too-handsome brothers who thought of their own wishes first, last and always, and who had little regard for the needs of others, including ailing relatives.

In brief seconds, she considered battle lines drawn. She would remain at Devlin's side, whatever the cost, and would not admire Lattimore except as was necessary.

She was hardening her resolve when the dowager swept into the room.

The rakish expression on Lattimore's face lifted in boyish glee as he hurried forward, threw both arms around the dowager duchess and lifted, twirling her round causing her skirts to billow in an undignified way. Rather than upsetting the Lady Anne, his antics set her giggling like a maiden.

Jessica couldn't help smiling at the dowager's happy response. Perhaps she had been premature in her harsh appraisal of Lattimore Miracle. His genuine fondness for his mother counted much to his credit.

She glanced at Devlin to find his expression, too, changed to pleasure. A family together. A wonderfully handsome threesome. At its head a man who obviously had the good sense and intelligence to bear the mantle of authority. Could the old duke possibly have been any more stately? Or the elder brother, Rothchild? She could not imagine men better qualified in looks or disposition to assume the title's responsibilities.

After Lattimore set his mother back on her feet, Lady Anne's voice carried over the company. "Let's go into the solarium. Patterson, please bring us some refreshment."

Arm in arm, Lattimore and his mother led the company into the room bright with morning light filtering through leaded windows.

When Patterson returned, however, he looked grim. He stepped close to Devlin and whispered. The duke sobered. He whispered a question or two, and responded. Patterson retreated crisply to the hallway.

"What is it, brother?" Lattimore asked, having released their mother to allow her to welcome with kisses on their jaws the two young men in his company, ones she apparently knew well.

Devlin turned, giving no indication that his vision was impaired. "Are there more in your party than the three of you?"

"At this hour?" Lattimore laughed. "It's early, brother. Only impudent family or brazen friends come calling this time of day. Why?"

"A boy reported three men followed you here. They seem interested in our garden walls, as if looking for a breach. Odd, wouldn't you say?"

Lattimore's two friends sobered as quickly as Devlin had, but his younger brother chuckled. "Devlin, we are not at Gull's Way. Thieves and villains do not frequent this neighborhood. You are under siege only by these three present, a civilized mob that includes your own, sometimes ill-mannered brother." His smile faded. "What measures would you take if we were about to be set upon?"

"Bear has been notified." Devlin's expression lightened.

Laugh lines appeared again at Lattimore's mouth and eyes, mirroring his brother's. "Then we are indeed fortified. I have not seen Bear in years. Does he still have his teeth?"

Devlin's grin broadened. "Yes, in spite of his advancing age. Years toughen the man's hide, sharpen his eyes and wits, and improve his skills."

Obviously the brothers shared regard for the giant they both affectionately called "Bear." He was another of the enigmas in Devlin's life that Jessica did not understand. For people like Bear and Lattimore, she supposed she would trust Devlin's instincts.

"Nightingale," Devlin said, summoning her with a hand, "come here and greet my brother. He often does not think before he speaks, or consider how his words might be perceived. Don't stand back, child. Step up here and curtsy."

Jessica glared suspiciously as Lattimore cut his eyes, arched his brows, and gave her a look a hungry man might give a meat pie.

She dropped a curtsy, tried to smile, and inclined her head, exhibiting all the hospitality she could muster. She gave similar acknowledgments to the other gentlemen when they were introduced, Peter Fry and Marcus Hardwick. There was something familiar about Fry, an overly tall, clumsy man who offered a silly grin. He reminded her of a friendly, overgrown dog. Jessica couldn't think where she had seen him before, but his buffoon's behavior did not fit that memory. Certainly he had not worn this ridiculously decorated military uniform. He and Hardwick both, for that matter, appeared to be in costume.

After introductions, Jessica excused herself, saying she needed to return to her duties. In truth, she had no tasks, except packing, of course, but she wanted to allow the family and friends to converse in private. Also, she did not care for Lattimore or his friends whose eyes made sly lascivious sweeps as if visualizing her form beneath her clothing.

When she made her excuse, neither the dowager nor Devlin urged her to stay.

• • •

"How much longer will the wench be with you?" Lattimore spoke with more than his usual indifference.

Devlin did not pretend to disregard the insult implied in the question. He was already put off by Lattie's undisguised interest. Other conversations in the room stilled as everyone attended the duke's answer.

"A while. Why do you ask?"

"How long do you expect to need her…ah…services?"

Devlin moved to the tea tray and biscuits Patterson had brought. He poured himself a cup, as if he could see. "Is our reunion limited to an interrogation about my guest, or are we to have personal exchanges? How are you getting on these days?" Devlin took a sip of his tea.

Lattimore laughed congenially, but pressed on. "I understand you know little about her."

"Enough to trust her with my life." Devlin dropped his voice. "I was required to do exactly that, you know. She proved reliable when I was my most vulnerable." After a length of silence, Devlin's smile dimmed. "Lattimore, Jessica is dear to me…and to our mother. I intend her to live permanently beneath my protection, although I have not yet mentioned that to her. I would like to provide everything she needs or wants, from now on. She has earned all it is in my power to bestow."

Lattimore glanced at his friends who appeared to be intent on the exchange. "Devlin, I do not believe we have ever before had brigands sizing up the walls."

Devlin returned his cup to the tea tray. He locked his hands behind his back and assumed a thoughtful frown. "Correct. We have not experienced such a thing, at least not before you and your party arrived. I doubt anyone beyond these walls is overly interested in one insignificant girl. Have you enemies, brother?"

"My poor, deluded duke, if you think your guest an insignificant girl, you have lost your sight, and your sense of touch as well."

"Be careful, Lattie. Jessica is an innocent and will be treated so by this household and all who enter here."

Lattimore shot a quick glance at their mother who had settled on a settee near the hearth away from the group. Fry and Hardwick hovered over a decanter, eavesdropping without even pretending to pour the libation.

"How can you know she's so innocent if you've neither seen nor touched her?"

Devlin eased into a chair, leaned back, and propped an ankle on the opposite knee, demonstrating a lack of concern. "I knew more of that child without seeing her, than I have known of ladies I have entertained in my…residences." Both brothers, one seeing and the other not, cast harried glances their mother's direction. "I know that she is tall and has rather…ah, well…attractive proportions."

Lattimore gave a snort. The duke continued, but shifted, suddenly uncomfortable in his chair. "She is an honorable, intelligent child, Lattie, even for one so young. She has a marvelous sense of humor and amazing skills with people. She communicates with stable boys and scullery maids as easily as she does with Patterson or the dowager or me."

"As I asked, how long do you expect to keep her here?"

"For as long as she will stay. How does our arrangement bear on you?"

Lattimore shouted an artificial laugh. "The most outstanding beauties in the court have blossomed beneath your attentions, brother. They grieve at your absence. It has been rumored that even in her raw form, this one may prove the most dazzling of the lot. I suppose it takes more than a blind man to see the potential for trouble in this situation."

"You are saying you find her comely, then?"

"Surely you already knew that."

"How could I, sir? As I mentioned, my appraisal is based on regard and camaraderie. Without sight, I adore the cheerful, mischievous imp that she is. Nightingale's unfailing optimism lifts me to the light even while I endure this abysmal darkness."

After a moment of silence, Lattimore cleared his throat. "First, Devlin, let me clarify: your Nightingale is not a child. She is a woman, brilliantly made. Her face is a pleasure to look upon and her form willowy and graceful. She walks as if music accompanies her steps."

Devlin remembered grappling as they struggled through the thicket back to the horse, the intimacy of her rocking between his thighs on the ride to Gull's Way, and, of course, he savored the memories of the picnic, and of their recent tussle on the library floor.

During the time she had been his guide, his hand on her shoulder, he had been aware of her regal carriage, the swan's long, graceful neck, her straight, strong shoulders and back providing a live crutch on which he had come to depend. "A woman brilliantly made" sounded right.

Chapter Fourteen

Jessica trudged up the stairs. She hated leaving Devlin with those men, none of whom were his friends.

She paused, suddenly remembering where she had seen Peter Fry, at least a silhouette of him. He was the man she saw walking with Martha, the maid who died at Gull's Way.

Jessica realized that she might have seen him even before that; in Welter, with John Lout and his ruffians. A strange coincidence that the man had been in Welter, then at Gull's Way with Martha, and reappear here as a friend of the duke's brother. Could he be the nobleman whose baby Martha carried? Might he have murdered Martha to keep his identity a secret? Jessica stopped in the upstairs hallway. Was this Fry a man who could dispatch a lover and his own unborn child with a murderous blow?

Jessica felt new concern for Devlin. Closed in her own room, she paced. She was the duke's truest friend, and he liked her. She admired the duke as she had never admired any man. She wished him able to see again. To see her, perhaps to enjoy looking at her as she enjoyed looking at him. When his sight was permanently restored, however, she must leave. Wasn't she even now supposed to be packing the borrowed trunk?

She threw herself across the bed to ponder an old thought. Was this longing she felt, the excitement when he appeared, or when she heard his voice unexpectedly, the heated breaths, the accelerated heartbeat...could the cause of these disruptions be love? The idea was outrageous, of course, but she suspected its truth the moment it first occurred, at Gull's Way that first day when he lay fighting the fever.

She doubted she was the first scullery maid to fall in love with a nobleman. Her rich imagination ran beyond that, for in her dreams, he returned her love. Devlin's affection for her more probably resembled what he might feel for a kitten in the barn.

Jessica had considered what it might be like to love a man, yet she was too practical for such frivolous speculation. She might have stayed out of love with the duke, if she had not first fallen for his friend and companion, Sweetness…er…Vindicator. Perhaps she should seek his counsel.

Jessica got up, left her room, marched through the upstairs corridor directly to the kitchen stairs and down, hurrying, on her way to a rendezvous.

Out the back door, she strolled to the paddock, suddenly eager to see her four-legged confidant. When the stallion saw her, he galloped into the lot and charged the fence, then came to a shuddering stop and stood, his eyes rounded, his ears straight up.

"Oh, Sweetness." Jessica launched herself onto the fence.

• • •

From the solarium, Devlin heard Jessica's footsteps in the upstairs corridor to her room. He also heard her emerge a short while later. His curiosity piqued when her pace quickened as she neared the back stairs.

As his companions filled his mother with gossip, Devlin stepped to the doorway to listen as Jessica trotted down the kitchen stairs and out.

Where was she going?

Without calling attention to his departure, Devlin stepped into the corridor, and then followed. Through the kitchen he heard the outside door slam. He followed, visualizing the way—three steps down, then the path.

He heard her running. A sniffle, punctuated by an occasional sob drew him further than he intended to go. If she looked behind, might she see him?

He heard a horse's hooves, then Jessica croon in low, loving tones. He suspected at first she might be meeting a stable boy, until he heard the familiar nickering and snorts.

Her assignation—his rival for her heart—was with Vindicator… or…Sweetness.

Devlin's flailing hand made contact with a tree, a place to observe without seeing or being seen.

A duke might best a stable boy for a woman's affection, but could he compete with a horse for a young girl's love? Devlin bit his lips.

A nobleman should not vie for a scullery maid. If he did, he should have the confidence, the experience, and the God-given gifts to woo and win her.

He recalled a conversation once about how girls adored their fathers first. Some had trouble transferring love for a father to a younger man. The brother of a specific young beauty said his parents facilitated his sister's transfer of affection by giving her a horse. Her love for the horse served as a bridge enabling her eventually to develop regard for a young man.

Was Nightingale such a woman? She obviously loved Vindicator, but could a man use that to make her a loving, dutiful wife?

Why should he care how she bestowed affection? What did that have to do with him?

He exhaled and his shoulders rounded. Perhaps he esteemed her more than he should. Of course, his interest was probably stimulated by his mother's regard for Jessica.

As he stood behind the tree, less than an hour after his last glimpses of light, his sight returned, enhanced by the brightness of the noonday. He peered around the broad oak that was his refuge, to see Jessica use a dainty lace kerchief to mop her nose. The fragile swatch was not intended for such practical application. Devlin subdued a laugh.

Smashing the handkerchief to her nose with one hand, Jessica patted Vindicator's muzzle with the other, her murmurings muffled.

"Oh, Sweetness, whatever shall I do? I was resigned to my fate." She sniffed and tilted her head, murmuring words Devlin could not hear. Then: "I was glad to have work, even in Maxwell's scullery." She tugged her sleeve down to dab her eyes. Devlin smiled again.

He lost her next words, muttered into the sleeve, then picked them up again. "...different now. In Welter, I do as I am told... well, most of the time I do. Here Lady Anne and Devlin encourage me to think my own thoughts and exercise my own judgment; to proceed boldly."

The horse whickered as she continued stroking him. "I love who I am here. Oh, Sweetness, the me I was before is gone." She sniffled again into the flimsy piece of lace. "I must leave, but I cannot abandon Devlin. How could they protect him—his fragile mother and his staff, ignorant of the wiles of people who pretend friendship—maybe his own brother."

Devlin strained to remain silent as her weeping turned into wrenching sobs. "Sweetness," her voice quivered, "you are the only one who can share my feelings." Her voice squeaked. "You have my heart, but he owns my soul. Oh, Sweetness, what am I to do?"

Who was this he to whom she referred? A stable hand? A servant? Devlin ventured another look.

The stallion stretched his neck and lifted his nose high as Jessica sobbed. She threw her arms around the horse's offered neck and smashed her nose against his silken warmth.

Devlin stepped from behind the tree trunk, wanting to comfort this tender shoot. He might have run forward and scooped her into his arms, but for his capricious eyesight, which chose that moment to desert him once again.

Cursing quietly, he groped back to his place behind the tree and agonized listening to her choking sobs.

The man to whom she had given her heart must be an imbecile. While Devlin did not want her to leave his home or his protection, he wanted to make things right for her, even if it meant losing her.

If John Lout were the man, she would have him. Devlin Miracle, the Twelfth Duke of Fornay would see to it.

After her comments, it seemed unlikely that Lout inspired this longing.

Lattie? He grimaced. His younger brother was attractive enough, in a sturdy way, but Devlin doubted his brother had captured Jessica in those brief moments of their meeting. Who then?

Peter Fry or Marcus Hardwick? She would hardly be impressed by those ridiculous uniforms designed by the wearers and adorned with those farcical ribbons and medals affixed as decorations. Hardwick might be all right, but Devlin never particularly liked Fry. There was something sinister about the big, lumbering fellow.

There was a breathless quality to her voice when they were introduced. The younger men probably looked dashing, and she was an impressionable country maid. Devlin felt a duty to protect her where they were concerned. Someday she would thank him for not allowing her to throw herself away on either of those fellows. No, neither of them was worthy. Not of Jessica.

Later, when she was feeling less emotional, Devlin would invite her to discuss her situation. He would console her; encourage her to consider more reliable chaps. An older man might be best for her, one willing to school her patiently in her wifely duties.

Reared in the country, she naturally understood basic reproduction, but the girl appeared naive about the raptures of making love. He would be honored to tutor her on the fine points of physical expression between a man and a woman.

He leaned against the tree. Now where had that come from?

He bore no guilt when the girl wandered into his dreams at night arousing carnal desires, but this waking consideration was unconscionable. In his dreams, when he removed her clothing, one item at a time, he was not accountable. Those dreams likely resulted from his being so closely involved in the purchase of that clothing.

Facing her mornings after such dreams, however, his fingers sometimes twitched with latent urges.

Still pressed against the tree, Devlin realized he had a new problem. He seemed to be as emotionally overwrought as she, without the tears. Unseemly thoughts would vanish when his eyesight returned for good and he could observe her everyday features and expressions.

He smiled, thinking how happy he would be to watch her lips when she spoke, particularly when she was vexed. He would like seeing her laugh, or study her rapt attention to her knitting, or watch intimate conversations like the one she was having with Vindicator.

His desire to see an attractive woman's face was not the primary reason he wanted his sight restored. He hadn't thought of seeing the flawless face of Mercedes Benoit, a woman some thought a beauty.

This was the first time he had thought of Mercedes since the note from her a fortnight back. For a time, Mercedes was important in his life. Pressed by his mother to take a wife, he had thought of making Mercedes the mother of the future heir to his title and estates.

Now that thought seemed ludicrous. He had not mentioned it to the dowager. He understood that considering one's mistress as a wife often displeased one's mother.

Mercedes might surprise him, but when she spoke of marriage, she sounded more interested in his fortune and title than in heirs.

There was a remarkable difference between his feelings for the willowy Jessica and the voluptuous Mercedes.

He peeled a piece of bark from the tree. Jessica had begun singing to Vindicator. As the sun warmed the day and birds warbled, Devlin was content, trapped against the tree.

His attitude toward Jessica vacillated. Some days she vexed his soul with her feminine ways. When she wept as she had today, thinking she was alone, a primitive feeling rose in his chest, one that made him want to take her to some remote place where he could please her, perhaps for long days and nights. Alone. His motive was to nurture and encourage her, release her from every inhibition and influence except, of course, his own.

He wanted her to remain as independent as she was and, at the same time, be totally submitted to him.

She had begun speaking again in a low conversational tone.

He could not hear her words, but her placating croon was clear. He continued to absorb the air. He loved the spiky breeze with its hint of winter coming. He needed to return the household to Gull's Way. One of the things he loved most about winter in the country was the isolation, the feeling of being shut away from the world and its demands.

The coming winter would be more enjoyable with Jessica there to play chess and with her determined attempts at the pianoforte. He loved her inflections as she read passages of poetry or Shakespeare's plays. He imagined himself dozing by the fire listening to the click of knitting needles beneath quiet conversations between Jessica and his mother.

When it came time for bed, he and Jessica would climb the stairs together, arm in arm.

Where was the dowager in that image? Absent. He scowled at such inappropriate thoughts, yet, once his mind went there, he pursued the image, thinking of Jessica in the sheer nightgowns

Mrs. Capstone had made and which had cost him so dearly. He had a right to see them on her, hadn't he?

No. No man not her husband deserved to see an innocent like Jessica in frothy confections, even the man who paid for their creation.

Thoughts of marriage had seldom entered Devlin's mind beyond his mother's prodding, before he met the little hoyden from Welter. After that night, the idea of joining himself to one woman for a lifetime visited often. His mother loved Jessica as she would a daughter of her own; indeed, she wanted to petition the Queen to make her Jessica's guardian.

The child herself admittedly enjoyed living in his household. She was content at Gull's Way. When the duke needed to be in London on business, he could continue his life and activities here unhindered, perhaps even see Mercedes, if he wanted.

He scowled. Mercedes had not visited him, nor had she expressed condolences on the loss of his eyesight. In her only missive, she urged him to return to town in time for the season. She needed an escort.

She could not visit the keep when his mother was in residence. Mistresses, even those whose existence and identity were known, were not welcome in the home of a man's legitimate family.

Thinking of Mercedes and his mother and Jessica together gave him an unpleasant jolt.

Lady Anne was of untarnished character, a quality that seemed to encompass Jessica by association.

Jessica and Mercedes. The one a breath of spring, the other sultry summer nights. One was gangly with arms that wrapped the neck of a horse and scooped up abandoned hens…and dukes. When Jessica asked a question, she listened to the answer, evaluating.

Mercedes, on the other hand, lured him with fragrances and touching, teased until his physical need defeated thought. She knew the natures of men. When she asked questions, she rarely heeded the answer if the subject concerned anyone other than herself.

Jessica genuinely thanked him for providing the clothes on her back. Mercedes considered it her due when he bought the jewelry she selected.

While Mercedes expressed no interest in him during this difficult time, Jessica had set aside the duties of her own life to serve him.

Of course, he would pay for Jessica's devotion, yet he had not offered to do so initially. The robbers had left him nothing, yet she had helped him anyway.

Knowing the dispositions of the two women, with which should a man share his title? His wealth? His bed?

He heard the swish of her skirts and the accompanying thud of horse's hooves moving restlessly in the paddock as Jessica came back down the path returning to the house. Scarcely breathing, Devlin maneuvered around the tree, keeping the trunk between him and the sound of Jessica's footsteps, hoping Vindicator would not give him away with a whickered greeting.

The stallion's usual restless tamping stopped. Devlin supposed the stallion had seen him. Jessica continued her ongoing patter as she moved beyond his tree and toward the house.

"I'm not going tonight, but when his eyesight is restored permanently, I will go." She was silent for several steps, then murmured again. "I shall miss you, and Lady Anne, of course, and Sophie and Odessa and Patterson and...well, I suppose I shall miss him, too," her voice fell, "perhaps most of all."

The horse whinnied and pawed the ground.

"I doubt I could bear never to see you again. Perhaps I will sneak back to see you some dark night."

Her voice dropped a third. "Oh, Sweetness, how shall I live without any of you? She is the mother every woman wants to become. And he..." Devlin held his breath, hoping her words were about him. "I've already prattled on too much about him. I don't see how I can ever marry another, when my heart and my soul will always belong only to him."

Marriage? She was entertaining thoughts of a less-than-joyous marriage, not to Lout, but to whom? Not to Devlin, of course. A noble did not marry a commoner. It simply was not done. What of bloodlines?

On the other hand, it was within the prerogative of a duke to marry anyone he pleased. Conceivably he could argue that her father's liaison with the German baron's daughter created a link with nobility. It was rather sketchy, but might silence some.

No. What was he thinking? Pledging himself to a scullery maid for the rest of their lives? To ride out with her surveying his lands, to take her to church, to waken beside her, to give her babes to inherit her dark coiling hair and laughing eyes. He smiled, having contemplated other eventualities with less pleasure.

It might be a thought for when he lay restless in his bed at night. Or, perhaps not. Nocturnal thoughts of Jessica stimulated rather than lulled him.

Her footsteps quickened as she neared the house, unaware of his overhearing her private revelations shared with Sweetness... that is, Vindicator.

His mother wanted to dress Jessica in the grandest clothes, teach her the courtesies of society, show her off. Perhaps exposure to society would rid the girl of the idea of the inappropriate match with Lout or any man of his ilk. Perhaps the dowager might find a young, eligible man from a prominent family, someone worthy of a Nightingale.

That was it. His mother could find a proper husband for the girl, a perfect solution. The dowager's choices would require his own thorough scrutiny. The idea definitely had potential.

His conscience would not allow him to claim it as his. After all, hadn't his mother offered the same solution on prior occasions? What difference did it make whose idea it was? It obviously had merit. Yes, he would find her a suitable husband. Now, how to implement the plan.

Chapter Fifteen

Devlin realized he had not been missed by his family or their guests. The duke poured himself a sherry and was aware of a change in the room as Jessica descended the stairs, identifiable by the fragrance he recognized as hers.

Devlin suddenly had a clear view of the solarium, the hall, the stairways, and every occupant. He started as he caught his first full view of Jessica.

On the stairway, she was limned in light from windows on the landing, tall, stately, aglow in the pink frock he had glimpsed earlier. The cut of the gown accentuated her long, graceful throat beneath a short defiant chin, splendid collarbones, and promising swells at the neckline. Dark, unruly ringlets emphasized wide, trusting gray eyes locked upon his face. Devlin feared she would realize he could see her and mention it.

Lattimore was right. She was magnificent, fully developed. That revelation only muddied Devlin's already confused thoughts concerning Jessica.

She glanced at Lattimore and bit her lips together, an obvious effort to veil her thoughts, but the energy was wasted and her disapproval showed. Devlin could scarcely conceal his pleasure at the girl's lack of admiration for his brother. While his sight lasted, he turned toward his mother, who sat poised to one side of the hearth enjoying a bright give-and-take with Lattimore's friends. Fry and Hardwick, cousins to each other, both the younger sons of their respective families, stood as Jessica entered the room. They had impeccable manners, yet wore—as he had guessed— ridiculously bedecked military costumes. They would probably have military careers, as Lattimore likely would do.

As darkness threatened to reclaim his sight, Devlin shifted his eyes again to Jessica. If he were never to see again, he wanted his last image to be of her.

She looked at the young men who continued conversing with the dowager, even as they stood, and her transparent disapproval continued.

Did she know either of the men? Perhaps. Yet, as far as he knew, neither Peter nor Marcus had been to Welter. The village was too primitive and remote for their tastes.

The darkness closed and he was imprisoned again with his questions. He might be able to find answers, if he could study the faces of the visitors and of his Nightingale. Alas, he would have to manage on verbal inflections, at least for the present.

• • •

Lattimore suggested they go calling in the afternoon. Devlin declined without making any excuse. Smiling at his mother, Lattimore did not insist.

Lady Anne went up for her afternoon rest, leaving Devlin and Jessica alone.

As they strolled through the ballroom, Jessica wondered whether to share her suspicions about Fry. Perhaps after Devlin's sight returned permanently, she would. Besides, her suspicions were based largely on speculation and instinct.

To distract herself, she walked over to examine the sporting foils displayed over the mantle above the massive fireplace.

"Men, with their superior strength, often have the advantage of women," Jessica said, stretching onto tiptoe to finger the swords.

Devlin perked up, curious.

"With the lighter foils, an agile woman could compete with a man, if the combatants are equally armed."

"You are mistaken, my pet," Devlin said, rising to the bait. "Even a weak man has more strength than a strong woman, no matter how dauntless the lady might believe herself to be."

She worked one of the rapiers free and, taking it in hand, slashed the air. "He may have superior strength, but that could be counterbalanced by her greater quickness."

"A man properly trained would be more likely to issue a fatal blow when a woman, reluctant by instinct, might hesitate."

"Then she should train like a man; condition herself to overcome such instincts."

"Idle conjecture."

"We have weapons here, Your Grace. Perhaps we should endeavor to prove our points." She whipped the air with her foil and laughed. He grimaced at the pun before a slow grin took his face, making him look a handsome rogue.

"All right. Retrieve the foils, milady, and let us proceed with your enlightenment."

She emitted a half snort, half laugh. "You may be a lord of the realm, Devlin, but you are blind…for the moment. Are you not?" She regarded him skeptically.

"Yes."

"Have you accepted the limitations of your disability?"

"I do not require sight, Nightingale, to best a child with a capped blade. Even blindfolded, I am an excellent swordsman."

"I am surprised you have had success as a swordsman, Your Grace, if you underestimate your opponent in such cavalier fashion."

Again rising to the bait, Devlin recovered his voice and a smattering of his pride. "One could say the same of you, my pet. A lord of the realm could hardly boast about throttling a babe. Touché."

He raised his voice. "Patterson, bring us padding to protect our vitals and check the blunting on these foils." He lowered his voice, but continued as if the message were for Patterson rather than aimed entirely at her. "I am going to provide our guest a much-needed lesson in humility."

Patterson appeared immediately carrying the requested pads as if he had been prepared and only awaiting the command. "He is an excellent swordsman, Jessica."

Devlin's expression darkened. "Who gave you leave to call the lady by her Christian name?"

"Why, she did so herself, Your Grace," Patterson said, taken aback.

The duke's glower deepened as he turned toward his charge. "You must not give servants permission to call you by your given name, Jessica."

"Devlin, I am all but a servant here myself, yet you insist I use your familiar name."

He bowed his head, struggling to beat a smile ignited by her usual impeccable logic and candor. The lines between family members and servants had grown less distinct since her arrival. When his sight returned, he would rectify the lapse. For the time being, he would muddle along with lines between servants and nobility wavering like his sporadic vision.

Even as he entertained those thoughts, his sight came again, allowing him to see Patterson's shadowy form as he helped Jessica.

Devlin stepped to one side, blinking, again eager to see as much of her as he could.

Her profile grew distinct. He saw the shine of her dark hair pulled back and bound at the crown, before it cascaded down her swanlike neck, and over her ramrod straight back. He was impressed again by her posture and stance. Her carriage was regal.

She was lifting something dark in both hands. It was the breastplate to shield her fragile body, not only from the duke's blade, but from his perusal as well. Patterson stepped behind her, fitted the plate and tied the laces at her back.

As Patterson fitted the same protection to the duke, Devlin marveled that his eyesight lingered longer than before. He squinted, straining to bring her features into focus, but they swam before him. Because the wavering made him nauseous, he closed his eyes.

A moment later, he whipped the air with his blunted sword, and opened his eyes again, still able to see. Jessica stepped directly in front of him. Damn, her angelic face was hidden behind a mask.

As they saluted one another, he said, "You must talk or hum, Nightingale, so I will know your whereabouts."

"What opponent is going to give you that advantage, Your Grace?"

He was more annoyed with the return of the familiar darkness than by her ongoing ridicule.

"This one," he quipped.

Patterson spoke as he returned to the chamber. Devlin was not aware the man had left. The servant carried a tiny bell which he had attached to a length of yarn.

"I suppose we agree then," Jessica said, continuing their banter, "for Patterson has brought a bell, at my request, and is tying it around my neck to facilitate your search."

"That will be helpful. My thanks, Nightingale."

As they circled, each moving to his right, the bell tinkled joyously. "How like a man to claim every advantage," Jessica taunted.

Devlin pivoted to keep her positioned squarely in front of him. "You have a light step," he said. "Most male opponents tread heavily, breathe loudly, or grunt or boast as they wield their swords."

"In this instance, Your Grace, silence and stealth could be among my few allies."

"Then let's have the best effort you and your allies can muster, or is it your plan to wear me down with dancing and idle chatter before our swords ever cross?"

She lunged and he parried more gracefully than she thought such a sizable man capable of doing.

"Ah, Your Grace, you perceive my strategy."

Again they circled, before he jabbed a point at her mid section. She sidestepped, too nimble for the blade.

Admiring their skills, Patterson considered that their swordplay resembled a dance choreographed for the theater, with two well-rehearsed performers.

Henry, the duke's valet, scurried by in the hallway, but the scene within brought him back and he slipped into the room to stand beside Patterson.

"They make a fair match," Patterson whispered without taking his eyes from the performance, inhaling sharply when Jessica jabbed but caught only air as the duke did a neat pirouette, dodging the move.

"Well done, Your Grace." Jessica wanted to be chivalrous, thinking to veil her chagrin at this blind man's ability to avoid her blade. She intended him no harm, of course, but she grew angrier with each miss, and the pique induced her to greater risks.

Overly eager, she misstepped with a determined thrust and teetered too close as she slashed at his vexingly elusive middle.

Grinning and aware of her disadvantage, Devlin raised the hilt of his blade and brought it down, thinking to thump the top of her head in retaliation for her vigor.

The blow, intended to be only a tap, miscalculated her height, however, and connected with a resounding thud.

Patterson and Henry, joined by a gaggle of maids and one wandering stable boy, all of whom had slipped into the doorway behind them, gasped, yelped, and groaned as Jessica gracefully wilted to the floor. The tinkling bell went silent.

"What happened?" Devlin called. "Jessica? This is no time for playing. Where are you?"

Flailing, his free left hand swiped back and forth to meet only thin air as Devlin slid his feet, nearly stepping on the form crumpled on the ballroom floor.

"Patterson! Someone, come quickly," he shouted, adding to the muffled confusion as servants prodded one another, fearful that the master would discover they had been idly watching the sham combat, yet frantic to aid the fallen contender.

"What has happened? Any of you! Someone speak up."

The stable boy swallowed a lump in his throat, ducked low and scurried into the room. He skidded on his knees to a stop near the fallen Jessica.

"You dropped 'er like a rock, Yer Grace," the boy said, admiration evident in his tone. "She's down."

"And out," a female voice volunteered.

Hearing soft groans, Devlin stopped flailing and shouted to the room at large. "Where is she?"

"Down here, Yer Grace. At yer feet. Watch now, if ye don't intend trampling 'er to finish 'er off."

Jessica groaned. Devlin tossed his foil, which skidded over the floor as he dropped to his hands and knees. His concern for appearances forgotten, he crawled, closing on those pitiful sounds. In a moment, his groping hands caught one of hers. He clasped the captive wrist and felt for a pulse. It seemed slow and even compared to the pounding of his own. Her groans and her breathing sounded muffled.

The mask. He pulled closer to her and fumbled with the ties securing the mask against her face. After some blundering and fending off the assistance of other hands, he freed the safeguard and tossed it aside.

He ran his fingers over her thick, coiling hair, searching frantically for the sticky ooze of blood.

"Patterson, tell me, have I killed her? Is she bleeding? Speak up, man. I command you to tell me: how serious are her injuries?"

The majordomo hurried back into the ballroom, a wet towel dripping in his hands. "You thumped her nob with rather more energy than was altogether necessary, I should say, Your Grace."

"What?"

"Your playful tap knocked her unconscious, but there is no open abrasion."

Devlin pulled on her captive arm and lifted her body to wrap his arms around her, enveloping protective breastplates—his and hers—as well. He lifted, braced her against his leg and began fumbling with the ties at her back.

"Quickly, someone, help me get this thing off her so she can breathe."

With Patterson's help, Devlin grappled with the laces, but each man seemed only to cancel the progress of the other. Yielding, Patterson unfastened the duke's protective shield.

Jessica mumbled. Unable to understand her words, Devlin stopped struggling with the laces to listen.

"What? What is it, Nightingale?" Straining to hear, he bent close. Again unexpectedly, vision returned to allow another startling glimpse of things directly in front him. She was there, vivid, directly in his line of sight.

He saw her pulse beating in the hollow of her throat, the milky white flesh, dark curls coiling around her flushed face.

"Lord God," he whispered reverently as sight continued, allowing him to study his protégé, to assess each delicate feature. In her unconscious state, she was beautiful beyond anything he had imagined. A perfectly formed young woman. Her features flawless.

"Don't be alarmed, Your Grace," Patterson whispered, patting the man's shoulder. "I don't believe she is badly hurt, only fainted away a little."

Without opening her eyes, Jessica raised an unsteady hand to the knot on the top of her head, touched it and whimpered.

Devlin's mercurial vision faded, then heightened, allowing him to view her porcelain-like arm, the long, delicate hand and fingers that swept up to hide her face. He caught a fleeting glimpse of the slender column of her throat. Surely she was, in truth, too young, too innocent to be aware of the stirrings she aroused in him in those brief, tender moments.

As he nudged her hand away from her exquisite face, sight again abandoned him. He groaned. He wanted to feast his eyes upon that face, but fate gave him no choice as the familiar darkness enshrouded him. He would have to be patient again, and remain in her vicinity until the next opportunity. He resumed groping for the chest protector which Patterson had partially removed.

Devlin shifted to lay her over his arm and turn her, giving him access to the last tie, freeing her. As he lifted the shield, her breasts, confined in a chemise and a man's shirt buttoned to her throat, exploded into his hands.

Her moan and his groan came simultaneously. He recognized immediately the supple heft of a womanly breast, covered, but easily identified by a man with some experience with women. Such an abundant breast felt out of place on someone with her delicate anatomy.

He let his hand span the middle of her, a thumb on one set of ribs, fingers at the other. Cautiously, he slid the hand toward her throat, verifying.

"Here, gov'ner, let me help you with that." The stable boy's voice warbled with excitement.

"Away!" Devlin shouted. "Go for help. Have them summon the physician, and the dowager duchess. Move, imbecile, or I'll have you quartered for the spit."

The boy jumped and ran, leaving Patterson, who had shooed the rest of the observers back into the hallway, to deal with the duke. At Devlin's ear, Patterson spoke quietly. "She is breathing normally, Your Grace."

Devlin wondered if the old servant had witnessed his fondling and hoped if he had, he believed the breach inadvertent.

"Yes, I can tell she is." He was unable to keep from again brushing a wandering hand over those full, perfect breasts to confirm his discovery.

• • •

Rousing, Jessica blinked. All she could see was a fair haze. Reaching, she laced her fingers into the tangled mass of Devlin's hair. He cursed and she yelped before she realized his head was that close, blocking her view of anything else.

"Jessica?"

She groaned and, at the same time, redirected her wandering fingers to probe gently at the knot on her crown. "Ouch."

"Is she bleeding?" he asked the room at large, as he threaded his fingers into her hair tangling with combs and pins.

"Stop that, barbarian. You are hurting me."

He froze.

Jessica wriggled free of his arms and rolled onto her hands and knees. She railed against his offered assistance and protested as he stood and lifted her, with surprising ease, to set her on her feet.

She sputtered apologies, which sounded as if she were embarrassed. He hoped her discomfort was caused by the event and not her realization that he had touched her inappropriately.

"Darling pet," he crooned, smoothing her hair from her face and caressing her shoulders. In spite of his renewed honorable intentions, he could not forget the feel of those firm round breasts that so perfectly fit his hand. He wanted to touch her again, but knew witnesses in the room, the hallway and, yes, throughout the household, already had grist for gossip regarding the incidental encounters between his hands and her form. Part of what he felt might be guilt, rather than lust, he supposed. He had injured her.

That was a bitter dose for any man protecting a delicate flower like Jessica.

Odessa's voice commanded the room as the housekeeper swooped upon them like an avenging angel.

"Away. Get away from her. All of you." In her distress, the woman gave no quarter to anyone, titled or otherwise.

Devlin shuffled back, out of the way of the overwrought housekeeper.

. . .

When Jessica appeared in Devlin's study late in the afternoon, she found him gazing out the window. Although her skirts swished, she cleared her throat to announce her presence.

"Nightingale, how are you feeling?" he said, turning his chair to face her.

"I am fine, Your Grace. I apologize for my behavior and manners earlier—and for Odessa's as well. Can you see right now?"

"No, but I've had sight several times today. Thank you for asking." He heard her clothing rasp and assumed she had raised a hand to her poor injured head. "You showed admirable restraint in not pummeling me when you roused after my unconscionable behavior." He struggled to control his mingled relief, guilt, and good humor at having her up and seeking him out. "As to your apology, it is I who should beg forgiveness for thumping you. It was not a malicious blow. I misjudged your height."

"Are you saying I was partially at fault for being taller than I ought to be?"

He smiled dutifully at the self-effacing humor in her voice.

"My height is a fact you have mentioned on more than one occasion, Your Grace. You might have allowed for it."

His good humor increased as he pushed back from the desk, but remained seated. "Would you care to sit in my lap, my offended pet, and allow me to console you?"

"Console me?" She lowered her voice, "or fondle me, Your Grace?"

He held a roguish smile in check. When she did not pursue the subject, he couldn't tell if her reticence was modesty or uncertainty. As dizzy and disoriented as she had been, perhaps she had not realized how his touching her had come about.

Her nervous laugh prompted a new grin. Obviously she was sufficiently recovered not to need pampering. He expected offering his lap to prick her pride and set her on the attack. Still, he would have enjoyed holding her, if she needed or wanted his attention.

"Is the hunting party returned?" she asked, referring to the young gentlemen who had gone visiting, scheduling themselves at the homes of what Devlin described as vapid, wealthy, young women—potential heiresses.

"Lattimore and Hardwick are entertaining Mother in the music room. Mr. Fry is, I believe, in the library. Would you like to join them? Mother probably would enjoy some whist. She is a wicked player. They need a fourth."

Fry was in the library alone. This might be her opportunity to confront him and perhaps judge his unguarded reactions.

"I might take a moment to see what Mr. Fry has found to read and ask if he cares to join the others at cards. If not, then I will be glad to."

•••

"I remembered you," Jessica said, opening her conversation with Fry rather brusquely.

Lounging on a sofa, Fry did not stand, demonstrating his lack of regard. "I wondered if you did. From Welter, was it?"

She advanced into the room. She intentionally left the door to the hallway ajar as an escape path. "Gull's Way, as well."

"Oh?" He did not appear concerned. Did he mean to imply she had not seen him at Gull's Way or did he think her notice of little importance? Was his lack of interest pretense, or did he not realize he had been seen with Martha? Or was she mistaken and he had not been Martha's shadowy visitor? She needed to press, even if it risked arousing his annoyance.

"Tell me—" she was pleased that her voice did not tremble with her distress, "—were you one of the brigands who waylaid the duke on the highway?" She retreated a step as he straightened to stare at her. "Are you thinking to finish the evil deed here because the duke is blind and you consider him as vulnerable as a lone man set upon by a mob of thieves?" She glanced around to judge the distance to the open door. "If so, you are wrong again. The duke is not defenseless here. If you attempt another attack on him, I shall tell about you and your associates in Welter."

Moving more agilely than she anticipated he could, Fry threw his book and stood. His long legs consumed the distance between them. Jessica's quick response stopped him when he realized she could reach the door before he could reach her.

"What do you know of my associates?" he hissed.

Jessica saw fury in his distorted expression, but she met and defied his gaze. "You recruit ne'er-do-wells to waylay travelers and lighten their purses to line your own."

His jaws clenched.

Surely an innocent man would react with indignation and sharp denials. She waited.

"Do you have proof of these accusations?" he asked, casually shifting his gaze to the book he had tossed.

"If I had, you would be lounging in gaol rather than enjoying the hospitality of a nobleman's home."

At his next look, every nerve in Jessica's body sang an alarm. He studied her a long moment, gathering himself before he hurdled the divan, his ham-like fists swinging but catching only air. His landing shook the room. Close up, the man was enormous. Was he thinking to kill or maim her right here in the Miracles' home, in their library, mere yards from the family?

Alerted by his fury, Jessica was ready and skittered back, staying well beyond his reach before she turned and bolted through the open library door.

Fry grappled for her as he fell. His size threw him off balance. She shot into the hallway several seconds before he could block her escape.

She fairly flew to the music room seeking the safety of company. As she ran, Jessica entertained ghastly thoughts. If Fry were a friend of Lattimore's and of noble blood, his word would be considered more reliable than hers. She needed evidence to accuse him. Further, as flustered as she was, the others might think her hysterical, yet, it seemed certain that the big, bumbling man was responsible for recent attacks on lone travelers near Welter, including the attack on Devlin, and for the murder of Martha the chambermaid, and her unborn child.

Jessica slipped into the music room without drawing notice. Fry followed immediately behind her, casting ominous looks she took as threats.

Was Fry the instigator of the attacks or did he take orders from someone else? Someone who did not care to participate in the assaults? Did Fry rob and murder to prevent witnesses? Certainly, the man's size would be easy for victims to describe and identify should they see him again.

Did his gang rob any wayfarer, or were they specifically sent to attack Devlin? Murder him? Thinking, she did not return the looks of any in the room, certainly not Fry's dark leer.

If Devlin had died that night by the side of the road, Lattimore would have inherited the title and the ducal holdings. Taking speculation another step further: had Fry allied himself with brigands like John Lout, or was he an agent, one who would benefit from Devlin's demise? Could Lattimore Miracle be the mastermind behind the assault? Might Hardwick also be involved in the evil activities?

Jessica glanced at Devlin's too-handsome brother. She did not want to think Lattimore wished the duke ill, yet once the thought occurred, it seated itself firmly.

It was only wild conjecture, yet Jessica felt an urgent need to confide in someone. But who? With nothing but unsubstantiated accusations, how could a scullery maid lodge charges against members of titled families?

On the other hand, what if she didn't speak out and Fry were here, welcomed into the bosom of the family, to finish the deed? How could she protect Devlin by herself?

She couldn't. She needed an ally. A strong one. Her closest friends and confidantes were Lady Anne and Devlin. If she could not speak of her suspicions to them, then who?

• • •

Both Jessica and Devlin were pensive through the evening meal. Fry's glower continually directed at Jessica got no response.

As they finished eating, Hardwick was telling a long, involved account of an adventure in Scotland, when Devlin interrupted to excuse himself, saying he had business to consider.

Jessica watched him climb the stairs. Almost immediately, Henry scurried from the duke's chamber, having obviously been dismissed.

Staring at the stairway after Devlin disappeared, the dowager quietly—speaking beneath Hardwick's narrative—suggested she and Jessica retire to "sit by the fire" in Lady Anne's chamber and "leave the men to their stories and their brandies."

As she had conscientiously ignored Fry's ruthless squints and thinly veiled verbal threats, which had become less and less subtle through the meal, Jessica was happy to leave. While she was not concerned about Fry for herself, she felt restless about Devlin's safety.

Disregarding Fry, Jessica nodded at the dowager's suggestion, stood, and left the room without excuses or wishing good evening to the others.

Although Jessica and the dowager each took needlework, neither seemed inclined to it.

"I don't like Devlin's sudden dark mood," Lady Anne said. "I'm surprised. I expected Lattimore and the others to lift his spirits, not send him plunging back to the depths." She held quiet for a moment or two. "Jessica, do you think the change in his mood signals a relapse?" She slanted a glance at the younger woman. "I thought we were beyond that. If it hadn't been for you, my dear, he would not have managed as well as he has until now. You perform a vital service in this household, dearest." When her companion did not respond, Lady Anne tried again. "Do you think we came to town too soon?"

Jessica laid her handwork aside. "May I be excused, Your Grace?"

"Certainly my dear. Do you have a headache?"

"No, Your Grace." Without further explanation, Jessica rose and walked listlessly to her quarters directly across the hallway.

Lady Anne was curious about the behavior of both of her usually vibrant companions. Questions begged answers. She did not like to interfere in the relationships of others. This was neither her business nor her responsibility.

If not hers, then whose? Thinking her way to a conclusion, she set aside her knitting and, whipping her mind to resolute, walked to Devlin's rooms.

He did not respond to her light knock until she identified herself. After another moment's delay, he called for her to enter.

He stood in the center of the room, his hands fisted behind his back as if he had been pacing. The dowager duchess studied her son's expression and wondered at the tension in his stance as she entered and closed the door quietly behind her.

"Jessica has gone to her rooms. I suppose we all need rest." She advanced the innocuous salvo as a peace offering.

"I see." He scowled at the rug as if entertaining troubling thoughts. "Lattie's arrival changes things."

The dowager's concern deepened. "Oh, darling, they are just here for a couple of nights, to check on us and as a respite from living at their club."

"And to inspect Jessica."

"It is quite natural for Lattie to be curious about a person we have taken into our home and our hearts. Perhaps he was concerned she might be a different sort, cunning or someone with evil intentions."

"Do you think he believes neither you nor I would recognize evil intent? We would need the baby to rescue us?" Devlin grimaced. "Don't be ridiculous, madam."

She didn't care for his tone, but thought it best to disregard it for the moment. "Regardless, Devlin, they are leaving soon, going to the Hardwicks' country home in Bristol."

"To Bristol?" He pivoted to face her. "The way is near Shiller's Green and Welter. They said none of them had been that direction."

"Perhaps they did not realize the proximity. They are going to deliver a new brougham and team purchased by Marcus's father, and to visit his family, of course."

"Does Lattie go to Bristol often?"

"I don't know, Devlin. If he did, I think he would stop in on us when we are at Gull's Way." She glanced away. "Although Lattie says the keep holds too many sad memories. He is terribly sentimental about your father and Roth. Losing them was a terrible blow to him, coming during his formative years." She looked again to her elder son. "What does it matter who goes to Bristol or when?"

"I was on the road from Bristol when I was attacked."

"Darling, I doubt one thing has to do with the other."

"Still, it seems a curious coincidence."

"People from London travel west all the time. Are you worried about Lattie's safety? I hardly think thieves would attack three of them. If they did, the brigands probably would get the worst of it."

Devlin gave a thoughtful frown. "Yes, I suppose." He appeared to shake off his dark thoughts. "All right, madam, what activities have you scheduled for you and your charge tomorrow?"

"I thought we might take a day or two away from the gadding about and let Jessica rest?"

"Rest? Why? Has she complained of fatigue?"

"No, darling. I thought she might need to recuperate after your brutish behavior." The dowager was casting a line to test his response.

He recognized the ploy. Did his mother know? Had someone mentioned his inappropriate behavior? He needed to cover his confusion. "If that is your concern, madam, perhaps you should have this conversation with her. She may prefer not to be in my presence after what transpired."

"Darling, Jessica knows it was an accident." She drew close and patted his shoulder.

"The thump on her nob?" Obviously the dowager did not know more than that. "Yes, I am sure she does."

"She has a forgiving nature. Your friendship will endure."

"I suppose." Still, he was troubled.

"You did apologize, didn't you?"

"Of course."

"Was she aware of your apology?"

He shot her an incredulous look. "What do you mean?"

"Was she addled?"

"When do you mean?"

"When you apologized."

"Oh, that. Yes. Well, I mean, I think she was conscious and completely aware of…of what I said." He lowered his voice. "Not, perhaps, of my bizarre behavior."

Sensing something amiss, the duchess adopted a conspiratorial tone. "What is troubling you, Devlin?" She started to suggest possibilities, but deemed it better to wait.

He dropped into a chair. Deferring to his obvious distress, she forgave his rudeness in not inviting her to be seated first.

"For a few moments today, Mother, I had sight."

Lady Anne was sweeping her dress to one side preparing to sit, but his words jolted and she remained on her feet. She blinked hard to stanch the instantaneous tears of joy. Noting his troubled look, she swallowed percolating joy, and responded instead with a soothing, "Darling, that is wonderful. How grand to have your sight back."

"It isn't back. It merely comes and goes, rather whimsically."

"Oh." She had no idea why such happy news had made him so miserable. She decided to delve further. "When did it happen?"

"Today's occurrence was not an isolated incident. I have had glimpses of light beginning even before we left Gull's Way."

"Did you mention this to Dr. Conner?"

"Yes." He bit his lips. "For the most part, I have had teasing glimpses of light and form. Recently, they are more distinct and last longer." He shook his head. "This one came when Jessica was injured on the floor, barely conscious."

"Seeing her in that condition, is what has upset you so?"

"No, Mother. I couldn't see her at first. She was concealed behind protective gear."

"Her face too?"

"Yes."

"Yes, well, I knew you could not be annoyed seeing her face. The child has quite a pleasing countenance." She waited for him to agree or comment. When he did neither, she continued. "What was it about the incident you found disturbing?" She watched his expression darken. "Darling, she is all right, you know."

He flapped a hand at her, as if her conjecture were a swarm of gnats. "No. You miss the point."

"Perhaps you could enlighten me." She was annoyed by this sparring. "Jessica would be miserable if she thought her behavior had added to your burden." The dowager crossed the room, moved a straight chair to position it directly in front of his and sat.

As soon as she was settled, he leaped to his feet and resumed pacing. "The glimpse I had enabled me to reach her. I fumbled to remove the protective mask to facilitate her breathing."

"I see."

"Yes, well, then I unlaced and removed the breastplate."

"Was she properly clothed beneath the protective pad?"

"Of course. She is not a wanton, for heaven's sake."

Baffled by this even-tempered son's mounting agitation, Lady Anne held her tongue. Obviously he needed to get this out and seemed to be mincing his way toward it.

"Then what happened?" she prodded.

"My sight failed. I intended to listen to her heartbeat. That was the reason I…" He stopped pacing and stared at nothing with his sightless eyes, before turning to face his mother.

"Is Jessica…well is she…ah…unusually well-developed for a female her age?"

She was so relieved, she suddenly felt like laughing. Instead, the dowager pressed her handkerchief to her mouth to muffle any telltale sound. So that was what was troubling him. Finally, he had discovered the truth: that Jessica was not the hatchling he had assumed, but was instead, as the girl herself so often declared, "a

Sharon Ervin

woman grown." The revelation was one Devlin was not prepared to face. The dowager had wondered when and how this discovery might occur, yet now that it had, she hardly knew what to say.

Candor was probably best. "How old do you believe Jessica to be?"

"I thought her a child of ten or eleven at first, as I told you. Later I thought perhaps as old as thirteen."

"Devlin, Jessica told you she was a grown woman."

"Yes, but I thought she was putting on airs. Her interests—her devotion to her hens, for heaven's sake—marked her as a person of tender years."

"Her naiveté provided your conclusion?"

"It was convincing enough, but add to that her behavior. She mounted and rode a strange stallion—astride, mind you. She crawled through brambles, slithered on her belly, to find me. She devised ways to cope with me and persist, in spite of my own obstinacy." A smile played at his mouth as he detailed Jessica's efforts. "No mature woman of my acquaintance would have attempted any of that."

He began pacing again, head bowed, hands locked behind his back. "Once I was on Vindicator, she bid me farewell as if she were glad to be rid of me. I could not allow her simply to go trudging off afoot, unrewarded, but I had a devil of a time convincing her. She resisted, but I had the impression she was frightened, perhaps of being abandoned alone in the dark. Besides my own reluctance to leave, Vindicator refused to budge without her.

"When I finally had enough of bickering, I ordered her to ride. My assumption that she was a child was confirmed when I grasped her wrist to haul her into the saddle. It was like lifting a bag of thistle down."

As if he thought his description demeaned Jessica, his voice grew earnest. "She was strong, but sinewy. I even commented about her being built more like a young lad than a girl."

241

Again he paused before he continued. "How old is she, Mother?"

Lady Anne lowered her tone to match his. "She looks to be the eighteen years she claims, Devlin, just as she told you."

Devlin raked both hands into his thick hair and gave an agonized groan. "I thought she was pretending, just as she played at being competent to order me about. I made her vow to stay with me until my sight returned. Sometime during my delirium, I entertained your very thought, that I should make her my ward and provide for her until some unfortunate knave took her off my hands."

"If it's a knave you want to marry her to, Devlin, why not the one to whom she is already betrothed?"

"Don't be ridiculous."

The dowager was drawing insights. Devlin Miracle, the Twelfth Duke of Fornay, with little knowledge of innocent, unsophisticated females, wanted to take custody of this one. He wanted to make her part of his family, establish her in society, provide a respectable dowry, and find her a proper husband.

At Jessica's age, she was no waif. She was a woman whose reputation might be sullied by association with an unmarried gentleman. Lady Anne did not speak her thoughts.

"Her reputation is not ruined for rescuing you."

"How about spending the night in my arms, unchaperoned?"

"On a horse? For the time required to return an injured man to his home? For attending your wounds? If anything, the reputation of a scullery maid would be enhanced by reports of her courageous efforts on your behalf that night."

He stopped pacing and considered his mother's words. Since she had him reevaluating, Lady Anne continued.

"Devlin, I want her to stay. I want to spoil her just as badly as you do."

"I made an agreement, Madam. Gave her my word. As soon as my sight returns—returned—I am, was, to pay her five hundred pounds and provide safe passage home."

"Darling, we cannot allow that dear creature to go back to Swelter."

"Welter, Mother. The village where she comes from is Welter, not Swelter."

Lady Anne dismissed his correction with a wave. "Since Jessica has been with us, I have served as incontrovertible chaperone. Because I have always been aware of her age and of your regard for her, I have made a plan. We will announce that she is a cousin whose family is on hard times. We shall host a ball, a closed affair with carefully selected guests, to introduce her. We shall do it soon, while so many are out of town. We might make a fine match for her in some lesser family."

"Wed her to some dolt? Absolutely not. Jessica shall have no less than a baron." He frowned. "He must be a man schooled as a gentleman." His shoulders slumped. "That was perhaps a better possibility before today."

"What transpired today to change things?"

"The servants saw me fondle her."

"Surely you did not touch her intentionally. Besides that, neither Patterson nor any of the household staff would…"

"A stable boy was there. The one called Latch."

"What was a stable boy doing in the house?"

"I don't know. I only know he came running, offering to help when he saw me groping."

"Do you suppose your handling of her appeared practiced, as if you were familiar with…with a woman's anatomy?"

He smiled for the first time. "Here I was worrying about her reputation, never suspecting mine might be in jeopardy. You do know, Madam, that I have a reputation as a connoisseur of ladies. Mine will be the one sullied if word spreads that I handle ladies as ineptly as I did this cousin today. I was so astounded as to flush. The shock must have shown in my expression and heightened color." He spewed an involuntary chuckle, laughing at himself.

The dowager gave him a stern look before her laughter joined his, echoing about the room.

Their laughter subsided as mother and son settled into chairs side by side. Lady Anne was first to break the reverie. "I would like to host a ball to introduce her to a few friends."

Devlin's good humor dimmed. "To what purpose?"

"To make a match. She would be a lovely consort to any eligible man at court."

"You think to foist a peasant girl off on a gentleman?"

"Her father attached himself to a German baron's daughter. We could hint that Jessica has a connection to the aristocracy through that."

"Strange, I had a similar thought myself."

The dowager's smile freshened. "Is the son as scheming as his mother?"

He laughed. "I abandoned the idea. It was too outrageous, linking Jessica to nobility through her father's mistress. I would say Jessica was a victim of that union rather than a beneficiary."

"Then, it seems fair that she should get some benefit from his defection in payment for the suffering it caused her."

Devlin snorted, indicating disregard for such a duplicitous scheme, then he sank low into his chair.

His mother was not usually devious. Except for the shaky claim to nobility, the idea had merit. In London, he, Devlin, would entertain offers for Jessica's hand. Although he might not be an expert, he was wise enough not to join a flower like Jessica to a brute like John Lout, or some addled, aging gentleman.

"All right," he said. His mother drew a long breath. "But I will consider only offers from gentlemen."

"What of his appearance?"

He waved a hand. "Of course, he must be handsome, after a fashion, but his looks or taste in clothing will be of lesser importance than his wit or intellect."

"Have you told Jessica that your eyesight is returning?"

"Yes." He raised a hand, palm out. "Do not get out of sorts. I did not tell her first. She caught me staring into her face and guessed. I would appreciate your not discussing it, not even with her."

"Darling, she will be so pleased about your progress. She has been so certain you were going to get well."

"When I am, she probably will leave. What then of your plans to see her well married?"

"I cannot bear the thought of her leaving. Oh, Devlin, she has brought sunlight into my life." She cast a look at him and realized he shared similar thoughts. "That is part of your concern, isn't it? Does the idea of Jessica leaving trouble you?"

He did not speak, nor did he indicate he had heard her questions.

"It is obvious, darling, that you want her to stay, perhaps as badly as I do. That is correct, is it not?"

Again he didn't respond, but spoke as if he had not heard. "Perhaps you had better see to your hatchling, Mother. I am a grown man no longer given to sharing his innermost thoughts with his mama."

Lady Anne started to chastise him, then decided that his grief at the prospect of losing Jessica was punishment enough. She might have a word with Jessica before retiring.

Devlin recovered his manners and stood to escort his mother to the door. Lady Anne turned and he bent allowing her to press a kiss to his forehead.

"Sweet dreams, darling," she said, then held him as she gazed into his face—a face she had loved since giving birth to him nearly twenty-nine years before. He rewarded her lengthy silence with a smile.

The duchess went directly to Jessica's rooms. When the door opened to her light rap, Lady Anne marveled that the girl's troubled expression nearly mirrored Devlin's.

"How are you feeling, darling?" Lady Anne began as they sat in chairs at either side of the small hearth in Jessica's rooms.

The younger woman had changed into a dressing gown, but she appeared more stimulated than fatigued.

"Do you have a headache?" the dowager asked.

Jessica touched her injured crown tenderly. "Only a little one."

"I am certain Devlin will offer recompense for his wretched behavior."

"He has already apologized."

The dowager studied her. "He seemed uncertain about whether you were alert enough to be aware of his apology."

Jessica stared at the small blaze brightening the room and wondered again at the strange sensations she experienced as she had revived that morning in Devlin's arms. Had he touched her as intimately as she thought, or had that been a beautiful dream?

She had never allowed any man to caress her as she imagined he had, and she had been shocked by her own responses, whether it was real or a dream. Instead of being offended, as would have been proper, she had felt exhilarated. When he withdrew his hand from her breast, she groaned with disappointment. She had wanted him to continue touching her.

A sharp rap at the door startled both women. Jessica hurried to answer, opening to Devlin. He stood there, still in his clothes, his hair mussed as if he had run his hands through it, repeatedly. She hoped neither he nor the dowager would notice how she flushed. If so, maybe they would attribute it to sitting near the fire.

"Is my mother here?" he asked brusquely.

"Yes. Come join us." Jessica felt a leap of pleasure when he reached for her shoulder before she realized he only required guidance. As was their habit, she turned her back, presenting the shoulder for his hand so she could lead him to a place by the fire.

"I'll stand," he said, aware of the hearth and sliding his hand from her shoulder to the mantle. She chastised herself for her silly sense of abandonment.

Away from him, Jessica tried to regard him critically. Tall and solidly built, he was too handsome by half; too haughty, likely spoiled by his station in life and by women, too. Adoring females included his mother who expressed unmitigated pride in this son. Jessica continued evaluating as his mother filled the silence.

"I was just asking Jessica how she felt. I assured her you would make recompense for the mishap this morning."

Seeing the look of chagrin on his marvelous face, Jessica burst from her reverie to laugh lightly. "How is he to atone for my abasement, Your Grace?" She threw a lazy glance his way only to see his expression darken at her choice of words. Surely he did not think he had done her any real injury. She needed to heighten the jest to show him she bore him no malice. She giggled, a sound she hoped he would interpret as lightheartedness. "Shall we fit him with a collar and a leash and allow me to lead him about for a time?" Jessica punctuated her taunt with another laugh. "A little subservience might benefit the man."

The dowager's low chuckle, mingled with Jessica's tinkling laughter, prodded him. He leaned closer to the girl and spoke in a low voice. "If it's a collar for me, then perhaps we can manage a muzzle for you, little fox."

Her breath caught, indicating his words startled her, as he intended. Giggling, she placed a hand on his forearm. Her laughter coupled with the gesture, appeased him. He could not control the smile that spread from his heart to his face.

"Perhaps I exaggerated my injury," she said, laughter trilling in her voice. She turned to his mother to prevent her speaking of it again. "Please, Your Grace, what matter did you come to discuss?"

The dowager looked from Jessica's imploring face to Devlin's half smile, and yielded.

"If you feel well enough." She cast a quick, meaningful glance at Devlin. "We have an idea to discuss with you. Is that agreeable, Devlin?"

He shrugged, giving tacit approval without speaking.

Chapter Sixteen

Jessica tried to lie still, listening to Sophie snoring softly on her cot at the far side of the room. She wished she might join her maid in that world of dreams, a place where a scullery maid-turned-lady could go for solace. As she lay listening, Jessica's angst increased.

She needed to tell someone about possible danger to Devlin, then she needed to leave, return to Welter and her mother. To John Lout. To her duties in the scullery at Maxwell Manor. There she could no longer hurl accusations against Fry or Hardwick or Lattimore Miracle.

How, her conscience begged, could she walk away from the safest haven she had ever known? How could she surrender the hot baths, clean sheets on soft beds, marvelous food and wardrobe? There was the money, too, as if she could allow Devlin to pay for luxuries a girl such as herself should never have known.

She pushed off the covers. If she were honest, it was not sweetness of life holding her. It was sightless blue eyes that reflected the skies when he smiled or laughed and, occasionally, the storms gathering over the sea when he was annoyed, or when he touched her.

She sat, stood, and shuffled to the door, grabbing a wrapper to cover the sheer night rail, one of those Sophie laid out for her to wear each night. Her hair hanging loose was an annoyance. She stepped to the vanity and fastened the unruly tresses back with combs.

Soundlessly, she lifted the latch and slipped into the corridor, easing the door closed behind her, then drew a breath.

This was not the beginning of her flight. No, this was just an outing. She would need to plan and prepare for the longer journey. No female would set off in clothing as scant as that she wore.

She slipped her arms into the wrapper's sleeves, lapped the sides and secured the tie at her waist.

The chatter of birds anticipating the dawn encouraged her as she traversed the long walkway, ran down the stairs, and turned to cut through Devlin's study to access the yellow rose garden, her favorite. There sweet smells and gentle breezes mingled behind a north wall. Recently someone had placed a bench where a wanderer might enjoy the sunlight or even sit protected from a light rain. She was grateful for the foresight of that person.

Inhaling the crisp night air, she squinted down at unopened buds of a bush she had planted with her own two hands. She had been watching the addition for signs it was satisfied in its new home. She knelt and, with cautious fingers, touched the new growth.

"Yes," she whispered. "I knew you would like it here."

A familiar voice spoke quietly, as if trying not to startle her, as it did precisely that.

"What are you approving with sweet murmurs out here this time of day, Jessica?"

She stumbled to her feet and whirled, fumbling with her sash to make sure her covering was secure. "Oh, Your Grace, I apologize most sincerely. I did not imagine anyone might be here so early." She began backing toward the door.

His smile was scarcely visible in the predawn darkness, but she could see the gleam of his teeth as he emerged from the shadows.

"This garden may be small, but I believe it can accommodate two visitors at one time." His voice sounded of suppressed laughter.

"Yes, I suppose it can." She peered at him, entertaining a new thought. "Unless one is at his prayers or seeking privacy."

"Were you?"

"What, Your Grace?"

"At your prayers, kneeling and whispering."

She rewarded his guess with a little laugh. "No. I was speaking encouragement to the buds, Your Grace. I suppose praising a flower is a prayer of sorts. A compliment to its Creator."

"The one who planted it?"

She laughed again. "No. The originator."

His quiet laughter joined with hers. She squinted into the darkness trying to make out his face. "Have you sight this morning, Your Grace?"

"Devlin. Call me by my Christian name, Jessica."

"I do not think familiarity shows proper regard for your station, particularly in front of our—that is, your—staff."

"Are any members of the household present now?"

"No, no one else seems to be up."

"Then, if you please."

"Devlin."

"Yes. Thank you for your interest, Nightingale, I do have sight this morning."

A smile spread her face just as the playful breeze teased one unruly ringlet from its hastily affixed anchor to drop over her forehead, giving her a mischievous look.

"A miracle is a grand way to begin a new day," she said, and noticed that he looked both pleased and amused, like a youth not yet burdened with a man's responsibilities. A broad smile broke his wondrous features, turning his into the most beautiful face she had ever seen.

"Nightingale, on some subjects you have the wisdom of Solomon. On others, you remain hopelessly naïve."

She couldn't help returning his smile, in spite of the little vexation she felt at his words. "To what are you referring?"

"Your lack of knowledge about men."

"I have a brother and had a father, Your…Devlin. I've had opportunity to study the male of the species and his behavior. Of course, I have been around villagers, men in Welter, all my life. In what way does my training appear lacking?"

Devlin's smile waned. "What experiences have you had with the men of Welter?"

"I have grown up with some, talked and laughed and done business with others. I've been friends with several and have made genuine effort to endure others."

"What kind of behavior is required to endure men in Welter?"

She tried to fathom what she had said to have darkened his mood so.

"Well, when I am making effort, I try to be respectful and not talk more than necessary so as not to annoy them. I make it a point to be meticulously honest in my business dealings, in selling my hens and eggs." She arched her brows. "Of course, I feel compelled to call the grocer to task when he puts a thumb on the scale weighing out flour or sugar. I insist a merchant be as meticulously honest with me as I am with him. Sometimes I am required to prompt his honesty with rather a terse reminder." She hesitated. "That doesn't happen as often now as it once did."

The smile again bowed the duke's broad mouth. "The merchants being…?"

"The grocer and the fish monger, occasionally the smithy."

"Are these married men?"

Her frown deepened. "The grocer's wife died last June. I believe he is out of mourning. The monger smells too bad to woo a proper wife, and the smithy is too hairy. I have suggested he wear more clothing to conceal some of that hair if he hopes to win a bride."

"Did the smithy take your advice?"

"Yes, for a while, until he began attracting ladies whose interest he did not want."

"Were you one?"

"Great heavens, no!" She laughed incredulously.

"Did the smithy solicit your interest?"

"Not that I noticed. He has always been kind."

"As you grew, did you notice men being kinder and more meticulously honest with you?"

She puckered her lips. "I had not realized it myself until you asked."

"Perhaps, while you are in my care, Nightingale, I should teach you about the thinking of men."

She glanced back at her blooms. "Perhaps I might repay the kindness by teaching you something of flowers."

"But not about women?"

She heard the teasing tone in his voice. "I know you to be well instructed on that subject. Judging the way women behave around you, I doubt you have been denied many secrets by ladies of your acquaintance, Your Grace."

She stooped to pull bits of grass and weeds sprouting among her flowers, becoming more visible with the dawn. She did not feel threatened when the duke moved closer.

"You see, Nightingale, it is not wise for a young woman to make herself available to a man alone, in the predawn hours of morning."

She giggled and blurted, as if speaking to the bud she was examining. "Of course, if we had observed a silly rule like that when we met, you might have perished."

"Yes, well, there are exceptions, of course, but, perhaps it is not wise for a young woman, particularly one as attractive as you…"

She pivoted, but remained hunkered, and looked up. "You have never said you thought me attractive. Is this a new opinion?"

He cleared his throat. "No. I have always thought you attractive. When you are not vexing my soul, you can even be quite a charming, beautiful…child."

She turned back to the plants. "I am a woman, Your Grace."

"As you have told me several times. I can see that for myself now, even in this muted light." He glanced toward the bench. "Come and sit a moment so I may have your full attention."

She took his extended hand, stood, and followed him to the bench. She loved his touch, regardless of the reason. Maintaining his hold on her fingers, he waited for her to sit, before he settled closely beside her.

"Jessica, you entice men, both with your beauty and your naiveté. It is a powerful aphrodisiac."

She frowned, unclear as to his meaning. "I see."

"It is a wonder you have come this far without losing your… innocence."

"You mean my virginity." He looked stunned so she provided a definition. "You mean because I have not shared my body with a man?"

He cleared his throat and said a slightly strangled, "Yes."

"How did you surmise that?" she asked. "Are you able to envision a person's past?"

He gave her a fatherly smile. "Your innocence about men, my darling, is obvious."

"To your well-trained eye?"

"Well, yes, I suppose."

"Are you offering to remedy that? If so, let me assure you, a dozen have offered before you." She looked around. The darkness was lifting. "Of course, those invitations came near a haystack, in a stable or an isolated field, rather than in a rose garden."

"How did you answer those offers?"

"Sometimes I mentioned John Lout would be furious. Men and boys around Welter knew John."

"Were any of those willing to risk his wrath?"

"Some, but, of course, John has been telling everyone for years that he deflowered me when we were children, so they considered drinking of the same well of little consequence."

Devlin's hands clenched into fists in his lap. "Is the claim true? If so, I will see him brought up on charges."

She touched his fists lightly with her fingers. "No. I boxed his ears more than once for trying. I would not give the privilege of my body without a priest first speaking words over us."

Imagining the slender child defeating the brutish John Lout, the duke bit his lips but couldn't suppress the laughter that escaped expressing his genuine joy with unexpected volume.

Jessica came to her feet. "Shhhh. You will wake the house, Your Grace."

He brought the laughter under control. "You're right. This is a private conversation. We wouldn't want others listening."

She gave him a puzzled smile and nodded.

Sobering, he stared for a moment at her wrap, and then fingered the sleeve. "What is this you are wearing?"

She retreated. "It is the covering for my night rail."

"So you are wearing more adequate clothing beneath this?"

"I don't imagine anyone would consider it more adequate exactly."

"What do you mean?"

"Do you remember the gossamer Mrs. Capstone showed you?"

"Of course, but I was not able to see it then."

"You instructed her to make me nightgowns of that in every color and she did. I am wearing one. Do you remember the texture?"

"It was vaporous, as sheer as butterfly wings."

"Yes."

"I would like to see it now, while my sight is upon me."

She glanced over her shoulder at the doorway. "I will bring one for your inspection."

He caught her hand before she could leave and tugged her back to stand in front of him. Mutely, he peered into her face. "You understood my meaning well enough, didn't you?"

"Perhaps."

"You knew I didn't intend you to bring me another example of the weave?"

"I suppose not." She refused to meet his gaze.

He put his hands at her waist and tugged, separating his knees to draw her within their perimeters. As he untied her sash, she drew a quick breath, but did not object. The sides of her wrap opened, framing her body.

"I want to see you, Nightingale. I have grown feverish in my bed imagining this moment. Though I examined your face with my fingers, I had no idea your features might be arranged in such fascinating order. While I have some idea of your appearance, I did not imagine a voluptuous form." He pushed her wrap to either side to expose her torso, scarcely concealed by the gauze of her gown. "Alone here, now, I want to look at the form that houses your bright, astonishing spirit."

Jessica shivered, but did not speak, wondering why she was allowing this man to stare at her as she stood before him, practically nude.

Through the filmy fabric that floated with her every breath, he regarded the swells and hollows, the most intimate parts of her supple young form. He stared at the dark circles where her breasts peaked. His breath stopped when his gaze drifted to the shadowy vee marking her femininity. His eyes followed her hips and down long, shapely legs.

Delicately, he placed an index finger at the beginning of the swell between her breasts.

"Lesson One: You must never allow any man who is not your husband to see or touch you below this point. No other may experience you with his eyes or with his hands and, most forbidden of all, his lips."

He saw the shimmer of awakening desire in her eyes. She moistened her lips and her mouth remained open. Her breathing became ragged and she nodded her understanding.

He groaned, ashamed of himself but not able to control his own burgeoning pleasure as his finger descended. She inhaled and her breasts swelled, encouraging his touch. She trembled.

"Are you afraid, Nightingale?"

"No, Your Grace. I know your intent is honorable, that you wish to school me."

He chuffed, a half cough, half laugh, as his unrestrained finger circled one of her breasts, tracing it round and round like a corkscrew, winding to a stop when it reached the tip. There he trapped that sensitive nub between his thumb and forefinger and squeezed ever so slightly.

She gasped, staring into his face, but made no effort to prevent him.

"Do not allow any man to do this, Jessica. Tender touching mesmerizes. Do you understand?"

"Yes, Your Grace." Breathless, she shivered again, then shifted, inviting him to repeat the lesson with her other breast.

A smile twitched the corners of his mouth as he attended the second, marveling in how sensuous she was. His breathing, too, became uneven before he leaned forward to press his nose to her midriff. He felt her warmth, a stunning heat with only the gossamer between his flesh and hers.

Reaching low, he caught both her ankles firmly and heard her breath catch.

"Even if you should feel willing, and allow a man to fondle your breasts, you must never, ever allow him control of your legs. It will suggest you lack the character to stop his prying them apart, like this."

"Y-Your…" Her voice broke as he slid his hands up the backs of her calves. The gossamer caught on his forearms as they ascended. His hands stroked behind her knees and slithered up the backs of her thighs, easing her feet wider.

"Your Grace." The two words were a plea.

"You must never allow a man to touch you this way. These long, lovely legs protect the core of your womanhood, the center of your being, and of his, if he is the man worthy of being your husband. You may allow this privilege to only one man in a lifetime."

Jessica stared at him as if under a spell, asleep with her eyes wide open. "But, Devlin, you are a man," she whispered.

"Yes." He continued staring at her midriff.

"How are you taking those liberties that I am not to allow any man not my husband?"

He nodded solemnly. "There's no help for it now. I suppose I shall be that man."

A bird chirped. Abruptly the spell over Jessica was broken. Devlin tilted his face, bringing his wondering gaze to lock with hers, as if he had been startled by the thought spoken aloud in the silence of the awakening day.

Jessica's glance darted to the tree where the bird had lighted before she began flapping both hands, escaping the duke's grasp as she stumbled out of his reach.

With an audible groan, Devlin dropped his hands. At the same time, Jessica became shockingly aware of the transparency of the fabric covering her, stunned by the realization that she stood before this man draped in the sheer nothingness.

Accusation darkened her eyes. "Am I the most thoroughly ignorant female you have ever met?" She did not allow an answer. "I underestimated your cunning, never expected reprehensible behavior from you. Was that the point, to tutor an ignorant country girl and, at the same time, exploit her?"

He tried to clear the cobwebs from his mind, as she sneered. "The mantle of honor placed upon a nobleman's noble shoulders. Did you swear an oath to protect those who are dependent upon you—the children of peasants, and foolish women in your own household?"

Devlin jutted his chin becoming defensive. "You scald me to the heart, you...you ungrateful..." He stopped, staring at her. She returned the look, seething. When he finally spoke, his words were deliberate.

"Dear one, do not ever trust any man's pledge or his will where your delectable body is concerned. You must assume sole responsibility for keeping yourself chaste, to protect what you alone may bestow. Do not be lured to private places." He looked directly into her eyes. "Under some circumstances, proper or improper, all men are bounders and cads. We are none of us to be trusted with the allure of a beautiful woman."

She took advantage of the ensuing silence to ask, "Are all men able to...to arouse...shall we say...sensations in women?"

He smiled the teasing smile she had grown to love. "To what sensations do you refer?"

She blushed from her wrapper to her hairline and spread all ten fingers in front of her torso. "Those that raise goose flesh," she ran her hands up her arms, "all over. Those sensations."

Looking defeated, Devlin stood, bowed slightly from the waist, and strode to the door to his study. Before abandoning the garden completely, however, he turned to face her. He did not allow his gaze to meet hers. Instead, he frowned at the ground.

"My apologies, darling. A man...particularly after a rather a restless night...No, my angel, that is incorrect." He interrupted himself, then delayed a long moment. "I have no excuse. I behaved improperly." He drew a breath. "Perhaps my sight will continue through the sun's course. If it does, when evening comes, I will pay you the five hundred pounds and you may return to Welter with no further imposition from me."

He wheeled and disappeared into the house.

Jessica shivered silent ascent, even though he was no longer present. Fumbling, she caught the sides of her wrap and lapped them before securing them with the tie. She looked down verifying her efforts, but she was unable to see anything through the sudden, blistering tears.

The distractions during their time together sent all thought of Peter Fry flying straight out of her head. She had intended, on their next meeting, to tell Devlin all she had observed and suspected and solicit the duke's thinking. Now, there might not be another opportunity, particularly as he had cautioned her against solitary meetings with single men, including him. She did not want to discuss the matter in anyone else's hearing.

• • •

Devlin spent the morning in a black mood. His mother worked quietly, surprised when he remained in the same room with her. His gloom was, no doubt, precipitated by something Jessica had done or said or thought. He was attuned to the young woman's humors, and she to his.

The dowager could guess the cause of their mercurial ups and downs. If and when Devlin's eyes were healed, he would have no further excuse for insisting Jessica remain. Losing the girl was a dismal prospect for the entire household. Both the dowager and the duke benefitted most from Jessica's effervescence, her optimism. Why, her very presence could lift the spirits of a room, salon or scullery.

Lady Anne set aside her knitting and watched her son stare at the same page of a book as he had been doing for half an hour without turning a page. Perhaps he could not see the words, his reading pretense.

"Will you miss her as desperately as that?"

He didn't bother to look up. "Yes." His voice sounded brittle. "I am afraid I shall."

It was a wonder, the dowager supposed, that he had mentioned his returning sight to anyone at all. Had he realized the depth of his feelings for the girl and entertained thoughts of maintaining the deception of his blindness?

No, he was not a man to rely on artifice. Certainly, he had enough experience of women to know his feelings for Jessica were different than those he had felt for any other. As she thought about it, no women had held his interest for long, particularly no woman with whom he spent time.

Jessica was different. She was important to him.

Did he mean as much to her?

Lady Anne smiled, thinking of how they cast secret glances, how they bickered and challenged one another. Also, she conjured mental pictures of the beautiful children they would produce, intriguing mixes of his blond good looks and flashing blue eyes and Jessica's dramatic dark features.

Their regard was mutual, but did they realize it? She would like to be the one to point it out, but perhaps it would be wiser to allow them to discover that on their own.

The duke's recovery signaled separation, unless they negotiated a new agreement.

Lady Anne stood, placed the fingers of both hands at her waist and massaged the stiffness in her back. She hoped there was not too much pain involved in the metamorphosis they must all endure. Still, the anticipated joy might justify some little discomfort.

• • •

Jessica avoided the yellow rose garden. She chose, instead, the small herb patch beyond the kitchen for her sojourn into the brisk twilight. Her midnight blue slippers pinched her little toes, so she kicked them off, and removed her stockings.

Her feet had become sensitive to the tiniest pebbles, no longer toughened to the abuse of briars and stones. Rather than tromping around the meager space, she propped herself against the wall of the cistern, set her shoes and stockings on the ledge, and crossed her arms over her middle curling into herself.

An ant on his way back to his hill, took a shortcut over her foot. Drowsily, she saw him stop. She yelped when he stung her, dusted him off, then laughed at the insect's unmitigated gall. Had he thought to kill her with one sting, making him hero of the colony?

"He showed poor judgment," she muttered to the closing darkness. "One should devise a plan and summon an army before such an ambitious undertaking." She wondered if, in the ant's position, humans would be as bold. Would an ambitious man recruit allies to guarantee success? Had Devlin's enemies united to overcome him?

She must discuss it with someone, but who?

The urgency diminished a day later with the abrupt departure of Lattie and his two friends.

Chapter Seventeen

As the ladies made afternoon calls, the dowager was subtle, introducing her protégé and mentioning the dowry the duke had placed behind "this dear, lovely, creature." She spoke of the dowry only to her close friends, careful to do so within the hearing of select members of their staffs—particularly those known to have a penchant for gossip.

Also, she let mention of dowry slip at the dressmaker's, disregarding ladies eavesdropping from the next fitting room.

Jessica's wardrobe was not completed before she began receiving invitations from single men—young and old—for carriage rides in the park, and other off-season events, properly chaperoned, of course.

More curious than flattered by the flurry of attention, Jessica sought Devlin's advice when they met incidentally in the library one morning as Patterson supervised the arrangement of new books on shelves there.

"Is your mother weary of me that she tries to auction me to every household with an eligible male?"

His eyesight present for most of each day now, Devlin saw the perplexity in her lovely face and was scarcely able to keep himself from telling her not to pucker that captivating mouth. His restraint did not extend to denying himself entirely and he opened his arms.

Neither of them seemed to retain any memory of the tutoring session in the yellow rose garden. She looked to assure Patterson remained in the room before she sidled to the duke like an obedient pup and, like that soulful whelp, wriggled close.

Devlin thought his affliction was almost worth the closeness he and this young woman had achieved in past weeks, particularly since his blindness wasn't permanent. He wanted to tell her his sight was almost fully restored. Now, perhaps, might be a good time.

"You look lovely," he began.

She snuggled closer. "I saw you watching me at supper last night."

"I have been able to see with very little lapse for the last two days."

She tilted her head back to look into his face. "You do mean see. You don't mean with your fingers?"

He returned her gaze, diving into the shimmering pools as her trusting eyes stared into his with genuine concern.

"No, darling, I mean my sight apparently has returned."

She had prayed for this day, and dreaded it, too.

She pushed out of his embrace, and withdrew several paces. He saw her turmoil.

"That is wonderful," she whispered. "Truly it is." Her forced fervor turned to anguish. She swallowed, an obvious effort to get control of volatile emotions. "Although it is wonderful, the return of your sight is devastating; for me, I mean. Nor may it bode well for you entirely."

She shot a quick glance at Patterson, who did not seem to be paying any attention to them. Her expressions changed comically. Devlin couldn't help smiling at her distress as she stammered. "I mean of course, it is the answer to all our prayers." Her voice dropped. "Truly it is." She kept blinking as if she could not see clearly.

"Nightingale, it does not have to change our arrangement. You may continue living with the dowager and me, here and at Gull's Way." He reached for her shoulders, thinking physical contact would help convey the sincerity of his message.

She shrugged out of his grasp and lowered her voice. "Devlin, hear me." Her voice rose as she spoke, frantically reeling out a confused tale of a shadowy figure she thought was Peter Fry walking with Martha at Gull's Way the night before the maid's violent death. Jessica was more definite in naming Fry as the man she saw in Welter riding with John Lout and his minions.

"I think Fry hired John Lout to attack you on the road that night, perhaps even to murder you."

Devlin cast her a disbelieving look. "What reason would Fry have to do such a thing?"

It was just as she thought. He didn't give her theory credence. "Perhaps to provide Lattimore your title."

He began shaking his head, his expression concerned, as if she had taken leave of her senses. Desperate to convince him, she stammered, which made her sound addled, even to her. "I thought possibly Lattimore was involved, that he might have asked Fry to hire John to perform the awful deed."

Devlin regarded her strangely as she spun what he obviously considered a fanciful tale. Frantic to lend credibility to her account, she continued.

"It was Bear who discovered how much influence Fry wields over Lattimore. Devlin, the man holds gaming vouchers from your brother in the amount of eight hundred pounds. With that amount of leverage, he could have coerced Lattie into attempts against you to give him the wherewithal to pay that outrageous debt."

Devlin's look of incredulity deepened again as she hurried on.

"Fry may plan to manipulate your brother, if he can give Lattimore the title."

Telling him all this was breaking her heart, suggesting his own brother might be responsible for an attack that might have left him permanently injured, if not dead. She swiped at her eyes with the back of her hand, struggling to maintain her composure. "Don't you see, if I'm right, you are in mortal danger."

He saw her fear, but considered it as he would the bleating of a kitten trapped in a tree. The indulgent smile that broke over his face only fueled her despair.

"Darling, darling child." He clasped her shoulders and stared down into her face. "First, contrary to your opinion, eight hundred pounds is not a significant sum of money."

"Not to you, maybe, but certainly to John Lout and even to Peter Fry. Perhaps to your own brother, it may be…"

"Shhh, shhh." He tried to pull her close, but she put her hands on his chest and stiffened her arms. He let her prevail, holding his position. "You have let bits and pieces of would-be evidence spur your imagination into fanciful theories."

She blinked, but try as she might, she could not stop the tears. They ran down her cheeks. Her voice quivered and broke. "Your life is in…danger. I must…I simply must…make you see your peril." She grabbed the front his coat. "You must believe me."

Patterson turned a curious look, then returned to his cataloguing of books as if Jessica's angst and Devlin's cool responses were matters of indifference.

"Darling, you are overwrought," Devlin crooned. "Is the return of my sight what has brought all this on? My being able to see again can be a good thing, my lamb, for all of us. You do not have to conjure up imaginary danger to stay. You may continue living with the dowager and me, searching for an appropriate match or a respectable position."

She wilted, as if a pin had been inserted, releasing her courage, her determination and her energy all in one whoosh.

"Devlin, please," she whispered.

He swallowed his smile. Maybe he should take more serious note of her concerns. It was probably insensitive of him to dismiss them without at least pretending they could have merit.

He tugged her shoulders, but she staunchly refused to let him hold her. She appeared to have lost control of her emotions as she stood there, nose and eyes dripping like well-primed pumps.

Studying her, he felt flattered. Her distress seemed centered on regard for his safety. That was the illuminating aspect of this discussion. Perhaps he could comfort her best by reminding her that he was no longer vulnerable to unseen attacks. With sight, he could defend himself ably, as he had all his life. The next step, of course, was to convince her that Lattimore had never aspired to the title.

He might have better success if he answered each of her accusations calmly, one at a time.

"Let's sit down over here," he offered, indicating the pair of high-backed chairs across the room and, perhaps, out of Patterson's hearing.

Having dissolved into sniffling and blowing her nose into dainty handkerchiefs, Jessica moved reluctantly as Devlin nudged her toward the chairs.

"First, dear one, I suspect John Lout and his ragamuffin cohorts are the ones who attacked me on the road that night."

"What?"

He nudged her into the chair and put a footstool under her feet.

She sat stiffly. "Robbery on the highway is a capital offense, is it not?"

"Yes, but Lout's involvement is conjecture on my part. I have no proof."

She bowed her head over clasped hands, relieved and troubled. "You would not bring charges anyway, would you, against the man to whom I am betrothed?"

"Your alleged betrothal to John Lout is altogether another matter and will demand its own thrashing out at another time." He waited for her to agree before he continued.

"My second point on the subject is my younger brother has little ambition and absolutely no desire for any responsibilities other than seeing to his own amusements. Lattie's greatest aim in life is to enjoy himself and provide entertainment for his mates. Your intuition told you as much on your first meeting. You said he reminded you of your father and brother as you cast aspersions on all too-handsome men. I remember the sting of those words, implying you did not consider me attractive enough to qualify."

She sputtered to come up with an explanation, but he held up a hand to prevent her. "The point is, I do not believe Lattie considers either you or me a threat to his goals."

Disregarding his hand, she said, "Certainly I am no threat to him. He assumes my greatest ambition is to be a maid in a fine house."

"I doubt he envisions you as anything so lowly as that." He liked the fact he was coaxing her away from her dark imaginings. "You would be a gifted governess, Jessica, not only meting out information, but infecting children with your verve for life; with your optimism and energy.

"As an alternative, you may choose to marry one of the swains inundating our home with invitations and flowers and poetic declarations of undying devotion."

She looked stricken and struggled to stand, stepping around the small stool at her feet and keeping beyond Devlin's reach.

"I must return to Welter, Your Grace, to my mother, my birds…my life." Her voice caught. "And leave you to yours."

He, too, stood, but did not step toward her. "Dearest, you have a new life now. It is here, for the time being at least, with the Lady Anne and me."

"I cannot stay here and watch you…"

"I am going to continue as I always have, Jessica, seeing to my own needs and those of people I love." Suddenly the prospect of life without his Nightingale seemed real and bleak. "No one has evil intentions toward me. You will neither endanger yourself, nor be a threat to me, by staying." His voice took on volume and authority. "You belong here, Jessica." He sounded more desperate than he wanted. To dispel the urgency, he lowered his voice. "You are part of our lives now, and we of yours."

"Devlin, did you think to recreate me? To empty my mind of my family, my experiences and memories, and refill it with frocks and sweet-smelling baths and vapid people? Did you think to expunge my true responsibilities?"

Her lack of gratitude—her entire attitude—had begun to grate. Devlin kept his arms at his sides by sheer force of will. "Now, see here, Jessica, I like to think I rescued you from the mire of a destitute existence, dusted you off, outfitted you with lovely clothing and presented you into the bright sunlight of my world, reborn."

"Think again, Your Grace. It was not you who rescued me. I was the savior whose efforts linked our lives, if you will recall."

She could see his temper rising in the flush of his face, yet she felt no regret for speaking the truth.

"I see," he said, the words clipped as the muscles in his jaws flexed. "So all the time you have been here, you have pined for that other existence. No wonder you fought the bit like a foppish colt. You were eager to get on with the business of mucking up after a bunch of misbegotten hens, catering to a mother who relies on fictitious ailments for attention, pining for John Lout, and continuing in service to a scoundrel like Maxwell. All of that should be clear to me, now that I have my sight."

Jessica's eyes rounded and he could almost imagine steam coming off the top of her head, venting the anger about to detonate within. He retreated a step, uncertain about the explosive potential of his companion's wrath. At the same time, he was acutely aware of his eyesight growing more distinct. Colors became more vivid with the heightening tenor of their exchange.

Her voice seethed with contempt. "I don't know why I concern myself for you, Devlin Miracle. You are a vain, useless bit of fluff, very like a bright feather atop a lady's hat. Your entire existence has no more significance than a bit of frippery."

He lunged for her, but she sidestepped, staying beyond his grasp as she continued, her words spewing venomously. "What good do you perform anyway? You have so much," she swept a hand indicating the expensive accoutrements in the library, "yet what effort do you make toward the good of common men and women? You have a wealth of talents. God has blessed you richly. Yet, what benefit is any of it to Him or to His creation? What contribution do you make?"

She glanced about startled that she had worked herself into a corner. As Devlin closed on her, he raised a hand. She ducked, as if expecting him to strike her. He propped that raised hand on the mantle and froze in place, glaring at her, his face flushed, his free hand fisted at his side.

"How can you shrink from me? Have I ever, ever given you cause to cower from me?" With the flinch, she had offended him more deeply than either of them thought possible.

"How can you speak to me in that tone or accuse me of doing no good, when you have reaped every benefit I have been able to bestow upon you? How, when you have been closer to me than anyone has ever been? You have been cherished. You've seen the work I do, the effort I make to benefit commerce every day?"

Her temper answered his. "Your efforts add more wealth to your coffers, but you do not care about people or their lives. You deny the members of your household the one greatest compliment you could bestow, as limited, as crippled as you are by your own conceit."

"What compliment?"

She dropped her voice as if the point were too important to be shouted. "How long has Patterson been in your employ?"

"Don't be ridiculous."

"How long?"

"He worked for my father and my uncle before him. Patterson has been here longer than I have. The man has been like another father to me."

Her voice was barely a whisper. She shot a glance at Patterson, who was midway up a library ladder and appeared to be completely absorbed in his work and oblivious to their conversation. "This man whom you consider as close to you as blood kin, can you tell me his first name?"

A deadly silence settled over the room.

A stray voice from above startled them both. "Tims, Your Grace. My Christian name is Tims."

The man, supervisor of all the workings of Gull's Way, the townhouse in London and every other estate held by the Duke of Fornay, gave Jessica a withering frown as he descended the ladder. "There has been no occasion for the master to know my familiar name, Miss. The noblemen in this family and I have long honored our respective stations. I, for one, prefer it that way."

Duly chastised, Jessica ducked her head, slipped past the duke, darted by Patterson into the hall and flew up the stairs. Both men watched her departure in somber silence.

Jessica scarcely hesitated as she reached a decision. It propelled her along the second floor hallway, down the back stairs, through the kitchen, and out.

. . .

Arriving at the stablemen's quarters, Jessica knocked on the door. Moments later, she asked Latch, who opened the door, to summon Bear. She needed to speak with him.

When Bear appeared, she motioned him to follow.

"Devlin's sight has returned," she began and her dreary visage defeated the older man's joy. "He may go to his club to celebrate. I am afraid for him. I fear the thieves who beat him before may not be thieves at all, but friends, maybe even family. I fear they want him dead and his authority in other hands."

She stopped short of suggesting a course of action. Peering at her down his bulbous nose, Bear nodded. "I'll see to it, Miss. I'll keep 'im safe. Don't fret yerself."

"Bear, suspect everybody, particularly Peter Fry. I'm almost certain I saw the man in Welter, riding with John Lout and his friends. He may have been the father of Martha's baby. Perhaps he could be the person who murdered her. I suspect Fry initiated the attack on Devlin. There may be others involved, more influential men who commissioned him. Maybe Marcus Hardwick as well. Fry could even have been acting on orders from…from…someone closer to the duke. A man who has far more to gain from Devlin's demise than Fry."

Bear regarded her a long moment, and then spoke as if reading her thoughts. "I doubt Lattie has thrown in with them, Miss."

"But you will protect him from Lattie as well, if it comes to that?"

"Aye, Miss. I will."

• • •

Having seen the duke settled at Dracks, Bear went directly to the stable where Marcus Hardwick boarded his horses. It did not take him long to coax the story from Hardwick's groom.

"It was Mr. Fry's plan," the man stammered as he wiped a trickle of blood from the corner of his mouth, a result of Bear's coaxing. Leaning against an upright, the man kept a jaundiced eye on his interrogator. "The two a' 'em, Fry and Hardwick, met here on their way to Welter that night. They knew the duke was headed for his country place and he was alone. He likely would be stopping from time to time to quench his thirst, don't ya know."

"They said all this in front of you?"

"Well, not to my face, if that's yer meaning. I was nearby and they was talking, keeping ther voices low, but not so low as I couldn't hear 'em. I wasn't precisely included in their conversing."

"And what else did you hear of this plan?"

"Fry was the one wanting to waylay the duke and lift 'is purse as a way a' paying off debts young Lattie owed 'im, don't ya see? Said it was also in the way a' doing a favor for a friend."

Bear nodded, encouraging the man to continue.

"Hardwick didn't want no part of it and said so. Mr. Fry knocked him off 'is feet, left 'im laying right there about where yer standing."

"Did Fry go alone then?"

"I doubt he did. He said he'd git some local fellas to help 'im with the business once he was down in the country."

Bear handed the groom a cloth to mop a trickle of blood from his nose. "Did Fry say who else might have been involved?"

The groom looked confused for a moment, dabbing the cloth against his nose and regarding it closely in the dim light. "No, can't say that he did, except maybe the friend he mentioned. I remember wondering why he didn't just go beat the blunt outta the duke's brother, which was the one owing 'im in the first place, but I figured then maybe he give the markers because he didn't have the money, so Fry was going to collect from the duke who did, don't ya see?"

Bear knew Fry had not gone to Welter to demand payment. He had attacked Devlin when the duke was riding alone at night on a remote highway. From Devlin's injuries, it appeared to Bear that the assailant had meant to do more than injure him, and might have succeeded, if things had gone differently.

Bear scowled at the groom, who suddenly broke for the door. Lost in thought, Bear didn't follow. He liked Hardwick, but he had bad feelings toward Fry. If Fry had hired riffraff at Welter to help him attack Devlin, John Lout would likely know something about it.

Setting his jaw, Bear squinted hard at the stable door the groom had slammed shut as he left. Bear would keep a watch on Devlin until the duke was tucked in for the night; then he and Figg would travel to Welter to have a talk with Lout. If Lout was involved in the attack on Devlin, Bear hoped he would resist. He owed Lout for frightening Lady Jessica. If this were another debt—Bear opened and closed his fists and his face took on a sinister frown— he would enjoy setting things right.

. . .

Late in the afternoon, Devlin slapped his cards face down on the table, rocked his chair back, balancing it on its back legs and cast his eyes toward the ceiling.

"What has come over you, Devlin?" Lord Gadspar asked, gathering the playing cards to shuffle and redistribute them. "The lovely Elsabar is newly widowed, and you are newly recovered, yet you've not joined the pursuit?"

Devlin continued regarding the ceiling. "Elsa had some allure beyond her virginal years, but she has been too well ridden of late and her dalliances reported too broadly."

"Which probably only means she has learned methods to please a new beneficiary."

"I suppose." Devlin had no interest.

"What of the newest lady coming to court and to the attention of every man in the ton? Is she of no interest to you either?"

"Who might that be?"

"The Lady Jessica, of course. Surely you have heard of her." Gadspar threw his head back and shouted a laugh at the ceiling as if his words were riotously funny.

Surprised that there was a new lady about with his Nightingale's familiar name, Devlin smiled. "I know nothing of a Lady Jessica." His voice reflected idle interest, but he remained rocked back and impassive.

"Come now, man. The last two seasons have produced some well-dowered ladies, but few beauties, a situation that has caused complaints among the young gentlemen. Now a most fetching female living under your own roof promises to be the belle of the coming season and you disavow knowledge? What are you playing at?"

The two upraised legs of Devlin's chair hit the floor with a thud as he pushed upright.

"My Lady Jessica? You are speaking of Jessica Blair? Are you saying that she is a member of the aristocracy?"

Gadspar gave his companion a suspicious glance as his eyes narrowed. "That is the lady. Your cousin, if rumors are true. She is the rage among the young swains, and even a few of the old ones. I hear the Earl of Steen is smitten and prepared to offer for her."

Devlin glared at Gadspar, forcing the man to yield another bit of gossip.

"I know, Steen has a reputation as a rogue, Miracle, and he is old, but the man is as rich as Croesus."

"And a slayer of wives, if servants can be believed."

"That may be true, but he first swaddles them in silks and jewels and spoils them lavishly as he toys and plays with them, sometimes for years, before he tires of her."

"Then he murders them."

"He is of the old school, Miracle. He considers a wife as chattel. I understand he never intends harm, only grows a little exuberant at play. You and I both know that as a man ages, it takes more stimulation to bring him to performance level."

"Great God in heaven, what have we come to, that we consider murder an acceptable prelude to intercourse?" Devlin stood and shoved his chair, which fell sideways with a resounding thud. "If you are speaking of my ward being wed to a blackguard like Steen, then you…" Seeing amusement on his friend's face, Devlin stopped abruptly. "Never mind."

Gadspar grinned broadly. "You are in exceptional voice today, Your Grace. I don't believe I have heard you expound so fiercely on any subject in all the years we've been friends. Is it the girl? Is she arousing you like this? I say, old man, no wonder the dandies rhapsodize. Has a simple country maid worked her wiles even on you?"

"Don't be ridiculous."

Effecting a dismissive shrug, Gadspar said, "I suppose it would be of no interest to you, then, that Steen plans to steal her away as soon as Saturday, from Benoits. He has hired a pair of scoundrels to ambush his carriage after he spirits her from the house. They are to take the couple to an unnamed location and hold them captive a full twenty-four hours."

Devlin bent to pick up his toppled chair. "A full day?"

"Long enough to ruin her reputation and…"

Grabbing the much-abused chair by one leg, Devlin hurled it against the wall with enough force to startle men playing cards at the other end of the lounge. The sturdy chair shattered, a leg flying one way, a broken slat another.

Undeterred by noisy objections and grumbling from bystanders, Devlin raged. "Does the man intend to leave me no choice? Shall I be forced to kill him?"

Gadspar shook his head. "Action which would further damage the lady's reputation. No, I suspect he intends to make it impossible for you to refuse his offer, to force you to allow him her hand."

"Never."

"What other option will you have if you are to preserve her reputation, and your own?"

Studying Devlin's face, Gadspar retreated; placing himself safely out of reach of the duke's clenching fists. He marveled then as Devlin's expression softened.

"Ah, friend Gadspar, thanks to you and your timely warning, I shall not allow Steen's theatrical farce to take place. I will simply negate his plan with one of my own."

Gadspar took a step closer to ease an arm around Devlin's shoulders. "Glad to have been of help, old friend. Actually, I thought you might be relieved to have the girl off your hands."

"Who or what made you think her a burden to me?"

"Let's see now. You are a man seasoned in the strategies of females. I, and others of course, naturally assumed this novice to be of no interest to you. I supposed she was pretty enough. The watchers say she was a bit ungainly immediately following her arrival, but has taken control of her length and looks quite well in her clothing. Still, I would hardly have thought her a match for a man of your exotic tastes."

Devlin shrugged the other man's arm from his shoulders. "Then you and I, Gadspar, are not all that close these days, are we, that you should be familiar with my taste in women?" With that, Devlin turned on his heel and strode toward the exit.

"I thought you were one of his most intimate friends?" a man at the near gaming table observed, glancing up from his cards.

"Yes." Gadspar chuckled good-naturedly. "It has been my experience, however, that love can make a beast of a reasonable man, a stranger to even his closest friends and family."

The five men at the table regarded him soberly, their interest obviously piqued as he continued. "I confess I have never before seen this man in love. What a peculiar being it has made of him. In spite of his experience, he seems surprisingly unaware of his condition. This situation bears watching. I think I shall attend Benoits' ball Saturday night and follow this drama. See where it leads."

• • •

Devlin stood on the stoop at Dracks, squinting toward the setting sun and reviewing his conversation with his old school chum. He might need to go back inside and apologize. Just as he decided to do so and pivoted, he heard a familiar pop as a missile ripped the air just below his ear. Fingers pressed to the spot came away sticky. Blood. He had been shot, or at least grazed.

That was the trouble with civilians carrying firearms. There was a constant danger of inadvertent discharges, which was the reason he preferred not to carry a weapon when he was in town.

Dabbing at the scratch with his neck cloth, Devlin hurried to his carriage, parked at the curb, and ordered an overwrought Latch, who had seen and recognized the sound of a gunshot, to take them home.

Meanwhile inside Dracks, members, unaware of the incident on their doorstep, talked noisily of wagers.

"Mark my words, the Miracle matter will end in a duel between the duke and Steen," one man said.

"Nah, Steen's too old and too wily to allow things to progress that far," said another.

"Devlin may offer for the girl himself," Gadspar speculated quietly, staring at the door that had closed behind Devlin.

"I'll wager a hundred pounds against that," one shouted, his bet prompting joyous shouts of agreement and challenge as men gathered in the lounge.

The noisy debate escalated but Gadspar, looking skeptical, walked out the door wondering where he might find Lattimore Miracle. He wanted to discuss this rather surprising turn with someone who knew the duke and the girl. What was her name? Ah, yes, Jessica Blair. A perfectly respectable English name. His mother knew some Blairs. Maybe they had people near Welter who could throw some light on this mysterious little coil. He would inquire.

• • •

It was twilight as Devlin blasted into the foyer and blew by Patterson without a greeting, instead snapping a question. "Where is Jessica?"

"She is with your mother, Your Grace, in the South rose garden. Shall I summon her?"

"That will not be necessary." Devlin's tone and body language warned it might be best to let this gathering storm blow through unhindered.

The duke thundered into the rose garden.

His mother carried a basket while Jessica stooped to cut long stems of blood red roses to lay across it. Their murmured conversation ended with Devlin's shout.

"Jessica, I forbid you to attend Benoits' ball on Saturday. Is that understood?"

Devlin seldom addressed her these days in any but the most gentle tones. His sudden, unreasoning belligerence seemed undeserved.

"What?" both women said, almost in unison.

The dowager was first to challenge the statement. "We sent our acceptance a fortnight ago, darling. Jessica and I will be attending together. She will be well chaperoned."

"She needs to be more circumspect about her attendance at these things," he said.

"But, darling, why should she deprive the Benoits? She is the most popular young lady of the coming season. Men flock to her like bees to clover. She is well-spoken and makes a lovely impression, not only on the young men, but on their mothers and fathers as well. She is exquisite on the dance floor, executes the newest steps with a grace I have not seen, even in Vienna."

Devlin's expression darkened, a rare occurrence when he addressed his mother. "She is my responsibility and under my protection, Madam. I do not intend to explain myself to you, to her, or to anyone else on earth, except perhaps the Queen. Jessica is not to attend Benoits and that is final." He held up a hand signaling he would entertain no further discussion. With that, he turned on his heel and left the two women standing speechless.

"Well," the dowager said finally, straightening to her full height and looking both indignant and confounded.

Jessica's eyes fairly sparked. "I am under the man's protection. I am not his bondservant, nor am I an upstairs maid to be ordered about with no civil explanation." Her piercing eyes, pewter gray and glittering with righteous indignation, met the dowager's.

"You and I have accepted the Benoits' kind invitation and I fully intend to honor that commitment. You do not have to accompany me. If you prefer not to, I shall invite…" She considered a moment, then continued. "I shall require Mrs. Conifer to attend with me. A duenna is perfectly acceptable as a chaperone, isn't that correct?"

The dowager studied her charge. "No, darling, our accepting the invitation is as much my commitment as yours. We are absolutely in the right in the matter. We cannot go about playing willy-nilly with our obligations."

Jessica frowned her confusion at the basket of long-stemmed roses. Even the sight and aroma of those did not ease her annoyance. She did not know what in the world had come over Devlin, but ever since he regained his eyesight, his moods had been capricious and increasingly difficult to fathom.

Chapter Eighteen

Devlin did not join them for their evening meal, nor did he appear in their box at the theater; although, to their mutual astonishment, Lattimore slipped in shortly before the curtain rose.

"Good evening, ladies," he said, sliding into a chair behind them.

They both greeted him amiably, neither able to imagine what could have induced Lattimore to attend "Romeo and Juliet." He might be expected to endure one of Shakespeare's darker dramas, but habitually complained about plays about what he termed "the buffoonery" of romantic love.

Each time Jessica glanced back, Lattie was scanning the other boxes, as if he were searching for something—or someone. Yet when she looked toward him, he favored her with one of his devastating smiles.

Escorting them through the crowds after the play, Lattimore chatted companionably. His banter dwindled shortly before he asked, quite nonchalantly, "Will you be attending Benoits Saturday?"

Jessica looked to the duchess for their response, refocusing Lattie's attention by indicating his mother should be the one to answer.

"Perhaps," Lady Anne said. "Will you be there?"

He dimpled. "If you and Jessica will be, I wouldn't deny myself the excitement."

"Whatever do you mean by that?" Jessica asked, annoyed by his answer.

He looked all innocence. "Nothing, my sweet. Nothing at all."

"Lattie," his mother said quietly, "what is all the to-do about Benoits? You seldom show any interest in such galas."

"That's not so, Madam."

"Exactly how many balls have you attended this preseason?" his mother pressed, her curiosity piqued.

He nodded, yielding the point. "None, but I have been remiss, and this one promises more entertaining than the usual."

Lady Anne Miracle drew breath as if to pursue her questioning, as two young men crowded close, clearing their throats, almost as one, and addressed the threesome.

"Good evening," one began, bowing to the dowager.

"We would consider it an honor if you two lovely ladies would accompany us to Decatur's for supper," the second one said, offering his arm.

As Lady Anne turned a gracious smile on the pair, sons of one of her dearest friends, she accepted their invitation and the arm. Jessica caught a glimpse of Lattie's coattails as he melded into the throng of theatergoers.

• • •

A scurrilous wind brought the duke's carriage to the curb to collect him from his club just as the rain began that night. The driver, wrapped tightly in his cloak, bent low against the onslaught. Hurrying to dodge the elements, Devlin leaped into the vehicle and slammed the door, presuming the welcoming torches had been snuffed by the nasty weather.

He felt unsettled, vexed by an ominous disquiet. He didn't like having to disappoint his mother and Jessica about their plans for Saturday night, but he was responsible for their safety and was conscious of that. That was probably the cause of his unease.

If the chit had not challenged him, he might even have provided a reason for his order, but damn it, she needed to trust him to have her best interests at heart and not question his every decision.

Perhaps the ladies would be about when he arrived home. Why in hell was Latch driving so erratically? And where had Figg got off to on such a night?

Devlin pulled the leather rain curtain back to peer out.

This was not the way home. They were racing pell-mell toward the docks. Not a place for either his ducal carriage nor its occupant on this sinister night.

"Latch," he shouted, "where in blazes are you going?" The man did not answer. Perhaps the wind had deflected his inquiry. Devlin sat forward on the seat and thrust his head out the window. In doing so, his hand brushed the side of the carriage. Where was the raised ducal crest? He ran his fingers over the side where the crest should be. It was not there.

This was not his coach, though it was similar. And this driver, pushing his team much too fast over this badly cobbled street, just as obviously was neither Figg nor the lackadaisical Latch.

Devlin did not delay. When the carriage slowed for an uneven turn, he jumped, shoving the door closed as he flew, the noise of his departure apparently lost in the howls and rumblings of the storm. He stumbled into a shadowy doorway where he paused to brush off his clothing. He watched the carriage career, continuing its wayward flight.

The circumstance loomed too peculiar to be chance. Could someone have arranged for him to be spirited away? Who? Who would benefit from his absence, be it temporary or permanent?

John Lout came to mind, but even if this effort were not beyond Lout's mental capabilities, which he considered it to be, it likely was beyond his purse.

Were the thieves who had accosted him on the highway all those weeks ago making another attempt? Perhaps there had been another attempt on him. He dabbed at the place where a shot had grazed his neck. The theory seemed a reach. What could possibly be at stake? He thought of Jessica's imagined fears and wondered if she had guessed better than he knew.

These efforts had required prior planning and payments, if he were, in truth, a target.

The coach clamored to an abrupt stop in the lamplight of a warehouse in the second block down. Two men darted out as the driver leaped from his perch and ran to fling open the coach door.

Although Devlin could not make out their words, the men all shouted at one another before an overly tall, familiar person emerged from the warehouse. His muffled command silenced the men who followed as he led them back inside the darkened building.

Devlin pulled his hat down and rolled the collar of his greatcoat up around his face, then hunched his shoulders against the driving wind and rain. So Peter Fry was somehow involved in this little drama. Devlin could think of no reason Fry might wish him ill. Perhaps the man was a hireling. If the evil attempts were not done at Fry's initiative, the intriguing question was: whose?

The duke flagged down a commercial carriage when he had had his fill of walking and contemplating. On stepping into the house, he asked Patterson to summon Bear, if the man were in his quarters above the stables.

"Are my mother and Jessica at home?" he asked the majordomo.

Patterson smiled. "No, Your Grace. It is common knowledge among the servants in the various households that the Miracle ladies are the most popular in the ton. I expect they will not return until shortly before dawn. And Bear is…away for the evening, Your Grace."

"When he arrives, have him come to my study."

Bear did not appear until the wee hours of the morning, whereupon, Devlin closed them in the study for a private conversation.

• • •

The clock sounded half past three before Devlin dismissed a yawning Bear to seek his bed. The duke doused the lamps and sat alone with a brandy, staring into the fire. He did not reveal his presence below stairs when his mother and Jessica arrived sometime after the clock in the hallway chimed four.

At sunrise, having decided on a plan of action, the duke freshened himself and his clothing, and left the house long before businesses opened in town.

• • •

Lattimore arrived at the house before noon and gave his mother a genuine smile when she invited him to stay for luncheon. Her invitation fit his plans.

"Jessica," he said when the younger woman appeared, "I understand you are a horticulturist." He took her arm as the three of them wandered into the salon, and turned her toward the garden door. "Mother tells me you have particular success with yellow roses. I would like to see them, if you would be so kind."

She glanced at Lady Anne who nodded, both ladies inferring the dowager was not included in the invitation. Jessica mimicked the nod and smiled at Lattimore. She thought him pleasant, even handsome, for a man who appeared to lack the character apparent in his brother. "Certainly."

Lattimore expressed no interest in the roses or any of Jessica's other horticultural successes. He seemed instead to be terribly tense. "Darling?"

Jessica's startled gaze sought his face when she registered the endearment.

He regarded her soberly. "Will you marry me?"

"Certainly not." She stood, her response as abrupt as his question.

"I am serious."

"So am I."

"Why would you refuse without giving the question thought?"

"Because you obviously have not given the question enough thought yourself."

"I want to marry you."

"Whyever for?"

He intertwined his fingers, the gesture of a recalcitrant child. "Rumors say the dowager and Devlin are determined to make a match for you." As Jessica considered how to respond, Lattimore signaled silence. "Allow me to continue, if you please."

Jessica bit her lips. Patience was her most pronounced shortcoming and she warred with it in an effort to think before speaking.

"It would simplify matters," he said.

"It would complicate things for me."

He continued as if he had not heard. "I have property, although my holdings are not as vast as those belonging to the duke. I am not destitute, and Devlin is generous." He looked pained at making that admission. "He would never suffer me...us...to live in poverty."

He hurried on, not allowing her opportunity to argue. "I have funds put by to purchase a commission in the army. I am twenty-five years old; mature enough to take a wife. The dowager adores you. I am certain she would insist you live with her while I am away on military campaigns. Your life would go along much as it is now. Assuredly you would continue to enjoy the comforts of the ducal estates."

She held up a hand indicating she desired a word. "Why would you want to marry me?"

"Would you believe me if I said I love you?" He raised his eyes to her face, as if curious to see how those words might be received.

"No."

He flashed an admiring glance. "What makes you think I don't?"

"What makes you think you do?"

"This is a ridiculous conversation."

"At last, a reasonable statement. Your first."

Lattie ignored the gibe. "Devlin shows no interest in taking a wife. If he does not produce a legitimate heir, our children—yours and mine—would inherit the title, the estates, and all that goes with it. There is always the possibility of some tragedy befalling Devlin, taking him prematurely, in which case, the title would come to me. Perhaps you find being a duchess compelling."

She stared at him. Had Lattimore hired the men who waylaid Devlin on the road? Could a man reared by Lady Anne Miracle sanction such a deed? No. Yet, Lattimore sounded as if he could be jealous of his brother and of the title. She tried to conceal her suspicion.

"So you plan to force Devlin to support me and any children I might produce while you perform your military duty until either you or our hypothetical offspring inherit his title and property? A convoluted scheme. Surely there are more direct ways to rob your brother of his birthright." She had not intended to use the word robbed. It just slipped out.

Lattie's eyes narrowed. "If you were a man, I would demand satisfaction."

"If I were a man, we wouldn't be having this conversation."

His jaws clenched. "See you no virtue in me at all, Jessica Blair?"

She did not answer, afraid of what she might reveal either by her words or her usually transparent facial expression. Certainly he had virtues, though she had scarcely looked closely enough to determine what those might be.

Finally, Lattimore filled the awkward silence with what seemed private musings spoken aloud. "Truth be told, the title was not Devlin's birthright. It belonged to our brother, Rothchild, the eldest."

Was that how a younger son justified hiring men to attack, even murder an older one?

Lattie looked to the sky, crossing his arms. "What if I told you marrying me would save Devlin's reputation? Maybe even his life?"

She inhaled. "What do you mean? What have you done?"

His fury at her nefarious question made his hands fist and caused sweat to break out at his upper lip. "You have heard the rumors?" he asked quietly.

"Not rumors, more bits of information pieced together."

"There are those who believe I would be more malleable than he; that if they were to provide me the title, I would be grateful enough to squander all that goes with it."

"How would our marrying change that?"

"Those desperate souls, who would rather I bore the title, have heard you hold sway over Devlin, thus, if I controlled you as your husband…"

"Who are these desperate souls?"

"I am not at liberty to divulge that information to you, even if I knew, which I do not. I have only rumors relayed through friends trying to prevent further tragedy in this family."

Jessica's eyes narrowed. "I would have to hold evidence behind such rumors in my own two hands before I would believe them."

"What's that supposed to mean?"

"It means I am not interested in participating in any schemes to dupe the duke." She swelled to her full height and turned toward the door to the salon. "Unless you produce such evidence or name names, I want no part of any plotting."

"Yes, well, I can see my proposal and my best arguments for the proposition have taken you by surprise. I was afraid of that. I even told…"

She turned an unbelieving look on him and he flashed a charming, boyish grin. "Let's say mutual friends verify that you are refreshingly outspoken, which is a reason for my suit. I don't believe I have ever met a truly honest woman—the dowager, perhaps, being the exception."

"Then, it may be time you reevaluated your choice of friends." She paused to think. "I would appreciate it if you would demonstrate your regard for my honesty with like honesty."

"How?"

"First, recant. You do not love me."

His grin became sheepish. "No. Nor do you love me, which is the way people at our level of society form such liaisons. Among members of the ton, a marriage takes more the form of a political alliance, like a treaty between nations. Sovereigns with like interests band together for mutual benefit, which is precisely what I am proposing you and I do. I see that you admire Devlin. You've made that clear. It seems right that he should be a beneficiary of our joining."

Jessica shook her head. "Thank you, Lord Miracle, for the truth, although I do not see what benefit I might bring to such a union."

"I would at least like to report that you have agreed to think on the idea."

"Report to whom?"

"It is better you not know."

She wondered about his character, his ambitions, his opinion of his remaining brother and, mostly, about his friends. Had he chosen them or they him? And to what end?

Lattimore appeared to take her silence as an affirmative response and looked pleased, until she spoke.

"No. My answer is and will remain no. I will not make an alliance with you, most certainly not with any of the questionable sorts you represent."

His expression soured. "Do not entertain illusions about Devlin, Jessica. Do not mistake his kindness or his generosity. You are attractive. He may dally with you, but a duke does not marry an untitled, undowered girl, no matter how fetching her face or form."

She felt the sting of his words, but the implication was a new thought to her. "No, I don't suppose he does. Nor would this untitled, undowered woman consider marrying him, a possibility you failed to factor into your hypothesis."

Again, she turned to leave. Lattie quietly intoned one word. "Wait." She hesitated. "What about the danger to Devlin? As I said, a sacrifice on your part might protect him from attacks on him and, quite literally, save his life?"

"I think you are gulling me, or your friends are, through you, preying on what you hope are my tender feelings for your brother."

Tired of the exchanges, she brushed by Lattimore, hurried through the salon, down the corridor, and up the stairs. She asked that a luncheon tray be brought to her room rather than enduring any more of Lattie's company.

• • •

The younger Miracle decided to stay at the town house. Lattimore was his usual charming self when he joined the dowager and Jessica for tea late in the afternoon, as if their earlier conversation had not occurred. He focused his charm, however, on his mother. Jessica accepted the rebuff with relief and growing concern for Devlin's safety.

As she recalled Lattie's proposal, she couldn't imagine why he had more need of an untitled, impoverished peasant wife than his brother. How would Lattimore benefit from such a joining? What about his scheme might save Devlin's life? Was he being overly dramatic, or had he heard some evil rumor?

• • •

It was not unusual for Jessica to visit the stables, but she felt unusually restless that afternoon. When, eventually, she saw Bear, she invited him to walk.

"Lattimore suggests there are people who want him to be the duke rather than Devlin."

"Yes, mum."

"Have you heard the same?" He had her full attention.

"Yes, mum."

"Has Lattie spoken with you, too?"

"No, mum."

She poked his upper arm with her fingers as if nudging him might release information. "You must tell me what you know, Bear, or I shall go out of my mind with worry."

"Yes, mum, and I will, just as soon as ye leave off talking."

She waited what seemed like a dozen heartbeats before Bear met her searching gaze. "I talked wi' young master Hardwick's groom." He took a long breath. She remained silent. "It was Mr. Fry hired the men who attacked Devlin on the highway."

"And Lattimore?"

"Knew nothing of it."

"Is Hardwick's groom reliable?"

"Yes, mum."

"What did Fry have to gain?"

Bear waved a hand indicating she should listen, not speak. "It was Fry who hired John Lout fer the job."

"Oh."

"It was Lout that stopped that nobleman from finishing 'im."

"That sounds like one of John's boasts. Did he tell you that?"

"No, mum, it came from Hardwick's groom who was on the road hisself."

"Was Hardwick in on it, too?"

"Nay. The groom was returning from carrying a message to Hardwick's country place. Happened into 'em at the tavern. Tarried for a drink, then rode alongside 'em thinking it was better to be in company than by hisself on that stretch at night. There'd been stories of riders alone being robbed. As it happened, he was riding with the very ones he'd been warned against."

Jessica sighed. "I still don't know why Fry would want Devlin gone and Lattimore to inherit?"

"I s'pose fer the markers."

"The eight hundred pounds?"

"That's right. I'm fair certain Fry thinks like you, that eight hundred pounds is a pile of money. I've seen the old duke's sons lose that and more in one night a' gaming. The lad has no sense of money. Fry probably thinks to hold the markers over Lattie's head supposing to make 'im follow orders."

"Is that not possible?"

Bear snorted his disbelief. "No."

"Eight hundred pounds?"

"Nor eight thousand. If Lattie knew Fry's scheme, he would stop it."

Jessica spun and started back toward the stable, intending to go straight to Lattimore, but Bear caught her.

"This is men's business, Jessica Blair. Not for you."

"But something needs to be done. We must get this whole connivance out in the open."

"Maybe not, miss. Maybe we'll let Mr. Fry play his cards and catch 'im in the deed."

"Another attempt on Devlin's life?" She shivered at the prospect.

"Or yers."

She looked into his face. "Mine?"

"Ye'r said to influence everyone in the family. It's a wide-held opinion."

"So someone might try to murder me on the chance anyone listens to me? That's crazy. I'm not worth it."

"I'm studying on it, keeping my eyes and my ears open. You begged me to tell ya and I did. Thought I could trust ye to hold steady."

She enjoyed the warmth of Bear's good opinion reflected in his words. He had made the sons of this family into men by allowing them some difficulties. Perhaps Devlin's strong character was a result of Bear's not making his road too easy. Should she trust his judgment now? She did not want to risk losing his regard just as she had discovered it.

"All right." Her voice sounded thin.

He grunted approval and remained at the stable as she whirled and walked stiffly back to the house. It would take her best efforts not to reveal what she had learned.

• • •

"Lattimore said you refused his suit."

Early that evening, the others absent, Jessica and Devlin sat together in his study. As he spoke, he did not look up from the ledger where he wrote numbers. His comment broke her concentration and she lost count of the row of knit and purl.

Handwork annoyed Jessica. Even the simplest pattern required her undivided attention. "Yes," she said without looking up, trying to determine the duke's mood by his tone and, at the same time, recount stitches. How much had Lattie told him of their conversation?

"He said you are too ambitious to settle for the second son, that you want a titled husband."

"Of course he did." She glowered at the handwork thinking her displeasure might make the yarn more cooperative and free her gnarled thoughts as well, but something in Devlin's sudden sharp attention pulled her glance his way. The blue of his eyes darkened when he was angry. At that moment, they became sapphire as he stared at her, as if he expected her expression to verify or disprove his statement.

"Drat and damn." She dropped the needles to her lap. "I can fashion coops from barrel staves and scraps of rope, but I lack the ability to knit the simplest shawl."

"What did you mean 'Of course he did?'" Devlin asked, the vee between his disapproving brows growing more pronounced.

"I meant that of course Lattimore would absolve himself of blame for a woman's lack of interest."

"What do you mean by that?"

"Simply put, Lattimore and I do not share his generous regard for himself. Neither do we value people's strengths or weaknesses the same."

Devlin closed his ledger on a finger to mark his place and set his attention on Jessica. The intensity of his gaze unnerved her a little, yet she remembered his regard for honesty and waited for him to speak.

When he did, the duke sounded defensive. "Lattie comes from a good family and has wealth of his own. He doesn't need a title to insure his place in society."

"No, he doesn't. Nor could a title repair the flaw in his character that stifles my interest in him as a husband." She shot him a quick look. "That is, if I were looking for a husband, which I am not. I happen to have one potential husband too many already, if you recall."

"Are you telling me Lattie falls short of criteria set by the exalted John Lout?"

"Do not pretend to be dull witted. You know my situation perfectly well."

Devlin's visage was hard to read, but as she watched, his anger appeared to dissipate. "To what character flaw are you referring?" His gaze held steady on her face.

She wanted to be cautious, at the same time, forthright. She would not lie, even to maintain their camaraderie.

"Lattimore cavorts through life like a willful child. He is not inclined to duty nor to serious endeavors, nor does he consider the consequences of his behavior on the lives of others." When Devlin did not speak, she continued. "He disclaims responsibility for his own actions or words or the mischief they may inspire."

"And you consider yourself an authority on men who avoid responsibility?"

She straightened in her chair, clamped her fists about the knitting needles and fought the familiar rise of temper. "I do have knowledge of that particular shortcoming. My own father was similarly disposed. He married above himself and happily fathered the three of us, yet my mother carried the full responsibility for supporting our household.

"My mother's father was an earl who earned his rank and acquired his wealth on battlefields. Mother had brothers to inherit from him. After my grandfather died and his estates were divided, nothing came to his only daughter except the occasional charity handed down by her brothers, neither of whom was inclined to be generous.

"My father was a handsome man, and charming—like Lattimore, I'm afraid—not inclined to physical labor. Indulging his intelligence, Father read. He was a virtual storehouse of information. Unlike most peddlers, a learned man can demand only small wages for providing knowledge carried about in his head."

She paused to find Devlin gazing as her as if absorbed in her rhetoric. When he didn't attempt to talk, she continued.

"His learning, attractive appearance, and charm drew the interest of other men's wives who, though they enjoyed the benefits of wealth, were often bored by their rich but unlearned and sometimes negligent husbands. Father became an acceptable solution.

"While he basked in the reflected light of his knowledge and the attentions of wealthy wives and daughters, Mother tutored and gave piano and voice lessons to children of the gentry."

Realizing her hands were perspiring on the wool, Jessica set her knitting aside, stood, and rubbed her hands together as she walked to the window. A fine mist had taken over the evening.

"Eventually, Mother did mending for the families of her students. That evolved to doing their washing and ironing." She turned a hard look on Devlin. "This was a woman who spoke three languages and could conjugate any Latin verb in a blink."

Devlin's mouth puckered. "How did your father react to his learned wife becoming a laundress?"

"He read more devoutly and pretended not to notice or take responsibility for the deterioration."

"Of course, he taught you and your brother and sister to read and write and do your sums."

She softened. "Yes, and he provided us a genuine love of literature." The frown returned. "Right up until the day he left."

"Left? I thought he was deceased."

"He is now, but that came after he abandoned us. I was devastated. Brandon and Elizabeth scarcely seemed to notice his defection."

"What about your mother?"

"At first she pretended indifference. There was, after all, one less mouth to feed from her meager earnings. Her lack of concern lasted until we learned he would not be returning.

"Word reached us that he had run away with one of Mother's piano students, a rather plain, dull-witted girl of nineteen, the only daughter of a wealthy merchant, someone who could afford Father's continuing pursuit of wisdom.

"Mother did not speak of him from that day on, neither ill nor good. She worked harder, taking on more students and laundry and drudged along one day after another. Three years after he left, we received word that Father had died, alone, in a pauper's flat in Paris.

"Mother took to her bed. By then, my sister was married to a curate in the church." Jessica looked at Devlin, but could not read his expression. "My brother tries to emulate our father. He pretends to be intelligent, but his conversation reflects his own, often baseless, opinions rather than those of wiser men. Brandon is handsome and spends every shilling he earns on clothing. He entertains women who are willing to support a man who makes a good appearance. I learned an important lesson. A woman must not marry a man she loves. She must marry a man who loves her, preferably to distraction."

Devlin's frown deepened. "You think Lattimore is like your father and brother?"

She turned from the window feeling the weight of unresolved anger and frustration. "I don't know, but I have no desire to research the subject. Lattimore is handsome enough, but he lacks depth. I will not shackle myself to a man who may have those all-too-familiar flaws."

"Would it help if I guaranteed to support you during your life together?" Devlin asked the question gently.

"No." The word carried more venom than she intended. "I can support myself, thank you."

"And John Lout?"

She gave him a bittersweet smile. "John is…manageable."

"What does that mean?"

"While John may have little ambition, he has energy and character. He knows I'll not bear any man's children only to have them abandoned. He vows that if I produce, he will support our offspring."

Devlin cleared his throat with a cough. "By highway robbery?"

"I did not specify how he provide, only that he do so."

"So you are not interested in a titled man, either?"

Her eyes narrowed. "I did not say that."

Their gazes met and locked. "Then you would entertain an offer from a titled gentleman?"

"Only if he were a man of unquestionable character…and loved me beyond anything."

"In that case, what of your agreement with John Lout?"

"I would explain the situation in terms he would understand."

"You would offer him money."

Her smile approved his statement. "Yes. Bribery is something John understands."

"I see. How much will it take to make Lout cry off?"

"He and I have spoken openly of that very thing."

"What is his price?"

"If there is no intervention from people who do not normally deal with the likes of John Lout," she cast him a warning look, "he would be willing to terminate our relationship for one hundred pounds."

"One hundred pounds? He will sell his betrothal to you for one hundred pounds?"

She laughed lightly. "I thought it a good price for an overly tall, unemployed scullery maid's assistant." Her giggling sounded self-deprecating.

Devlin's eyes twinkled. He regarded her a moment before his rumbling laugh enhanced hers. He rose and went to stand beside her at the window.

As their laughter diminished, they pivoted to smile into each other's faces. Devlin opened his arms and Jessica moved into the familiar embrace. He gathered her close and, propping his chin on the top of her head, swayed.

Peeking from the corridor, Patterson allowed a slight, mysterious smile and a sniff, waggling his head as if the scenario were of his own making.

Chapter Nineteen

"Yer honor," John Lout said, welcoming Devlin into Solomon's Tavern, located between Gull's Way and Welter. The place smelled of smoke and sweat and strong drink, as it had when Devlin visited there last, less than an hour before he was set upon, beaten and robbed. "It's pleased we are to have you among us again, gov'ner."

Lout eyed Devlin jovially at first, but the man's expression sobered when Bear entered the tavern, along with two other large men who looked as if they, too, were in the duke's party.

"What can I get ye?" another voice intervened.

"Have you a private room?" Devlin asked, addressing himself to the barkeep. "Mr. Lout and I have business."

"Yes, Yer Grace. Right this way." The man's feet thudded against the pegged wooden floor, which would have made it easy for Devlin to follow if he had still been blind. He had determined before this trip that it might be to his advantage to pretend he remained sightless.

He closed his eyes as he trailed the tavern owner through a doorway, then heard a chair slide and correctly assumed it was for him. He fumbled a little as he sat.

"Begging yer pardon, Yer Grace," Lout said, sliding a chair out for himself and settling on Devlin's right, "but we heard ye'd been wounded in a fight and was healed, but the bout had left ye blind as a bat. It's grand to see ye'r recovered from that little set-to with the ruffians, 'cepting fer the damage to yer eyes, o' course."

Other than a slight smile, Devlin disregarded the comment. "Mr. Lout, I am here to present you with a business arrangement I think you will find to your benefit."

"Well, then, milord, feel free to get on with yer presenting."

"First, I think my men and I will have some ale. Barkeep!"

The innkeeper scurried through the door. "Yer Grace?"

"Ale for my men and me and freshen Mr. Lout's drink as well."

Lout looked around as if surprised to realize he'd left his glass at the bar. "I'll have a new one, my man," he said, ignoring the keep's scowl. "Now, what's this business you have with me, yer worship?"

Lout's addressing him by the mixed bag of wrong titles galled Devlin, but he schooled his expression not to reflect his annoyance. "Mr. Lout, I understand that you are betrothed to Jessica Blair of Welter."

"Yer information is good, yer honor. Of course, the bans is a formality. Miss Blair and me consummated our joining years ago, as I am sure ye've cause to know." He winked at Bear and seemed taken aback when the duke's man returned a harsh stare with no change of expression.

Momentarily deflated by Lout's airy besmirching of a lady's good name, Devlin took a deep breath, another effort to guarantee no negative reaction showed on his face. "I see." He thought of Jessica, of her spontaneous blush, her nervousness when he had initially placed his hand on her shoulder for guidance or any time he ventured too close to her. She obviously was not accustomed to any man's proximity, much less the intimacy of a man's body. Lout was lying and doing so in cavalier fashion, in a public tavern. That behavior might be one of the many things about the man Jessica considered unacceptable.

The tavern owner chose that moment to return with their ale.

Bear grabbed a glass, drained it noisily and set it back on the sideboard before the keep left the room. Noticing, the barman gave him a curious look. Devlin's old mentor nodded, answering the mute question, indicating he would take another.

The duke began again. "Lout, as you may know, Miss Blair has been in my household for some time now."

"Yes, yer lordship, we heard about that. A sweet, active little tart to have romping 'tween yer sheets, ain't she?"

Devlin stared at the man, hoping his eyes continued to look sightless. "I would thank you to watch your tongue where the lady is concerned," His voice lowered to a threatening growl, "or you risk leaving here without it."

Confirming the threat was serious, Bear squinted at Lout, whose demeanor and facial expression became apologetic. "I didn't mean no offense, Yer Grace. My mistake entirely. I just figured having a plum like Jessica about…What I mean to say is, a man couldn't be blamed fer squeezing 'er like."

"I assure you, sir, Miss Blair has been treated as a lady in my home, with the utmost respect."

"So, maybe I ain't understanding ye clear, yer honor. Perhaps we should get on wi' the business we're to conduct."

Devlin took his indignation in hand, but made a mental note that this was another insult for which he owed Mr. Lout repayment.

"My mother, the dowager duchess, has grown fond of Miss Blair over the last weeks," Devlin said, pleased that his voice did not betray the raging upheaval of his temper. "The duchess wants to make Miss Blair her protégé."

Lout looked genuinely puzzled. "What's that, gov'ner? The word's not familiar."

"Her student. My mother wants to train Miss Blair for a profession."

"A profession, is it?" The sarcasm was back in Lout's tone. "Just what kind of profession is yer ma thinking might fit a gel from the village betrothed and taken when she was no more than six year old?"

Devlin struggled to let the lie—a vile, odious attack against his angel—pass. He tallied one more mark against Lout. Once this business was over, he promised himself he would beat the man more senseless than he was.

"I assumed, Lout, that you wanted what would provide the best income for Miss Blair's future."

Lout's eyes narrowed as the suggestion took root. "Are we talking money here, yer worship?"

Again Devlin struggled to hold his temper. In spite of his pretense, Lout knew the correct way to address a duke, but refused to do so with any consistency.

"Schooled as a governess or a teacher, Miss Blair would have opportunities not now available to her." Devlin again felt pleased that his annoyance did not taint his words or his tone.

"I suppose that'd mean she'd have free run of rich men's houses."

Devlin didn't like the implication, but again steeled his facial expression. "Naturally." He could almost see the wheels of larceny turning in Lout's brain, obviously believing Jessica's access to rich men's houses might be his entree as well.

"Couldn't she do this protégé thing married to me as well as not?"

He wouldn't let the man sally off that direction. "Hardly. She would need to be unencumbered. Probably she would live with a wealthy family and be paid handsomely to educate their children."

"Now, see here, yer honor, that plan would deprive me of my one true love. Can't you see what you and yer ma is asking me to give up?" Lout looked startled and began stammering. "I didn't mean no offense by referring to yer seeing, Yer Grace."

"No offense taken. I assumed you would be pleased at Jessica's opportunity to improve her situation. I thought the advantages would make you eager to allow her this opportunity by making some small, perhaps temporary, sacrifice as a contribution to her future."

"How much would yer ma be willing to pay me fer this sacrifice, Yer Grace, for making this, whatcha call this here small, temporary contribution?"

"Do you intend to sell your betrothal to Miss Blair for cash?"

"Think of it as ye'r providing me compensation fer her bit o' well being, yer honor."

"How much compensation?"

"How does a hundred pounds strike ya?"

Devlin was prepared to go as high as five hundred, but apparently Jessica knew this adversary and his values well. Perhaps he should follow her advice. Not wanting his relief to be obvious, he gave the request a proper scowl and a moment's thought before he cleared his throat and said a grudging, "Yes, well now, you see, Lout, one hundred pounds is a considerable sum of money."

"Not to a rich man like yerself, yer lordship."

The duke risked a direct look into Lout's eyes and saw the man had more spark to him than Devlin expected. "Of course, we are asking you to sacrifice your marriage to an attractive young woman."

"Yes, well, there's that to consider too, yer honor."

Now that they were down to it, Devlin realized he wanted Lout to relinquish all claims to Jessica. The offered money had mellowed Lout, had him sounding agreeable. It might be wise to raise the ante.

"A sum like one hundred pounds should guarantee more than temporary restraint."

Lout eyed him suspiciously. "Begging yer pardon, gov'ner, I miss yer meaning."

"What I mean is, for one hundred pounds, I would expect you to renounce your betrothal, along with any other claims you might have upon the lady."

Lout's frown indicated thoughtful consideration before he grunted what sounded like acceptance. Devlin wanted to be sure.

"Do you agree?

"I do, yer worship."

The many wrong titles Lout used gnawed at Devlin. He wanted to correct the man, however, he didn't want to upset negotiations when they were progressing so well, so he held back.

"Exactly what is it ye'd expect of me for yer blunt, your lordship?"

"You will release Miss Blair from her betrothal and…" He added as an afterthought, "you must give your word never again to speak of your past association with the lady."

"One hundred for me letting 'er out of it permanent, free as a bird, so to speak?"

"I thought the offer of a prosperous future for a woman you profess to love plus one hundred pounds extremely generous."

Lout gazed at his hands fisted together on the wooden table and shook his head. "If it were only up to me, I might be willing to walk, ye see, but there's my ma and pa to consider, too."

"Is Miss Blair obligated some way to your parents?"

"Not so's anyone else would know, but she loves my folks like they was 'er own kin. They've been counting on 'er to be the one to bring a herd of young Louts into ther lives to brighten ther last dreary days on this earth."

Devlin recognized the story for what it was: a credible, spontaneous, fabrication. Lout was more facile mentally than the duke had anticipated.

"I didn't realize there were family obligations involved. Obviously I have overstepped." Devlin slid his chair back, annoyed with himself for underestimating his adversary. It was not the thing a seasoned campaigner would do, exposing his position like that.

Lout was on his feet quickly, his tone apologetic. Devlin took heart as he saw Lout wring his cap in his meaty hands. "I can settle it with 'em for ye, Yer Grace, if ye could see to parting with a wee bit more—say another twenty pounds?"

The man did know the proper means of address and had been vexing Devlin intentionally with the other designations. Concerned the duke might walk away from the deal, Lout leaped to bargain for more. Devlin felt victorious, but kept his face a blank.

"I want this to work, Lout," Devlin said, "but it is of more interest to others than to me. I was willing to give it a modicum of my time, and a reasonable amount of cash, but not an inordinate portion of either." He paused. "All right, an additional twenty, but not a shilling more. Do you and your family relinquish all claims upon Jessica Blair for the total sum of one hundred twenty pounds?"

Lout nodded, but studied the duke suspiciously making Devlin wonder if he had revealed too much. He had decided to renege on the additional twenty pounds when Lout said, "I'm thinking ye do well at the tables, Yer Grace."

"I'm not much of a gambler. I usually avoid gaming."

Lout continued nodding and eying him. "Ye may have missed yer calling, Yer Grace."

Chapter Twenty

Carriages came and went Saturday morning. Patterson noticed that Devlin was out of his study on an unusual number of errands, which kept him circulating, greeting the parade of suitors coming and going.

Patterson surprised the duke once listening at the closed salon doors. "Your mother is with them, Your Grace, if you are concerned about the young lady's reputation."

Devlin grimaced, but did not abandon his post. Patterson, too, stopped to listen a moment to the simpering voices of several admirers in that chamber, driveling on about Jessica: her luminescent skin, the silky shine of her hair, her charm, her wit, her manners. The old retainer arched his eyebrows and smiled to himself. If anyone knew the minds of those young gallants, it would be the duke. Patterson rather enjoyed seeing Devlin's agitation. The duke knew how to thwart inappropriate posturing. He had seen—maybe even practiced—similar ploys for years.

Devlin gritted his teeth, exercising already tense jaw muscles, clenched and unclenched his fists in and out of his trouser pockets, and paced. As the number of Jessica's suitors increased daily, the duke's patience diminished at a like rate, and the list of those he considered suitable husband material dwindled with equal dispatch.

The dowager, on the other hand, grew more cheerful with each name Devlin or Jessica crossed off the list, much to Devlin's surprise. Lady Anne appeared to have decided on a husband already, and was biding her time until Devlin and his ward came to her foregone conclusion. Everyone abandoned thoughts of preparing Jessica as a governess.

Through the morning, Devlin recognized several voices: Pearce Rockwell and Clement Browne, both too old; Peter Fry, too devious; Marion Criswell, a notorious gambler and card cheat; William Touchstone, a rake who had maintained the same mistress for a dozen years and doubtless would continue the liaison after he was wed. Voices he did not recognize made the duke edgier than those he did.

One thing he knew: thus far, not one showed worthy of the prize.

He stepped back into the alcove, in the shadows beneath the stairs, to allow a group to pass, then launched himself into the face of Touchstone the Rake.

"Do not come here again." The duke's flashing eyes conveyed clear warning indicating argument might lead to bloodshed.

"See here, Miracle, the girl likes me."

"She doesn't know you, Touchstone. Before supper tonight, she will. Do not return, and do not let me hear you have spoken her name in any company. Is that clear?"

The visitor glanced at Patterson stationed by the front doors. The butler kept his eyes averted, although he had heard Devlin's warning.

Touchstone slapped his gloves against his open palm, perhaps hinting, appraising his challenger.

The duke's eyes narrowed. "Do not forget with whom you are dealing, Touchstone."

The other man jutted his chin a moment, then bowed, conceding the point.

Making no effort to hurry, Touchstone donned his gloves. When he delayed his departure, Devlin made a growling noise in his throat, as if he were clearing it.

Touchstone's eyes rounded, he wheeled and walked briskly to the door, which Patterson opened with uncharacteristic haste.

Devlin felt better satisfied by the way both Touchstone and Patterson responded to his anger, but as he turned, he came face to face with someone who did not: Jessica.

"You are never to do that again." Her voice rasped with raw emotion.

"Do what?" Devlin asked, pretending innocence.

"Intimidate a caller of mine."

He tried to realign his features to a more docile expression as he moved closer, his arms opening to embrace her. "Now, now, Nightingale. Darling."

She turned a shoulder to him, pivoting to return to the salon. "Do not try to gull me changing faces like that. I have seen your entire repertoire, chameleon. Neither dissembling nor disguise will work on me."

Posting himself between Jessica and the door to the salon, where his mother remained seated, Devlin touched the girl's shoulder.

"Jessica, there is no reason to carry on. Not one man calling here today is worth the snap of your fingers." He snapped his fingers, demonstrating. "Certainly not one of them deserves the dowry I've put behind you."

She rubbed her hands together as she whirled to face him. "Damn you, Devlin Miracle, my regard cannot be reduced to a sum of money, nor am I a horse to be auctioned to the highest bidder. I am a woman, with a heart and a soul."

The unfairness of her statement offended him. "Your welfare is my only interest, dear heart." He looked toward the salon as if conjuring images of the men who had paraded in and out through the morning.

"Which of those do you consider whole cloth from which you might tailor a suitable husband? Enlighten me, for I cannot venture a guess. I guarantee you one thing: if you name at this moment one you deem acceptable, I will have you married to the man before the year is out. Tell me now, which one has won your heart, or even your fancy?"

She looked ready to explode, but something in his face calmed her. She stared at him a long moment. When she spoke, her tone was soft.

"Is your plan to scuttle the interest of any man who finds value in me? Are you determined to protect them from the callous scullery maid you mistakenly took into your home?" She withdrew as he advanced a step toward her. "Do you fear I will corrupt their titles or sacred bloodlines or disturb lives of humdrum tedium, absent any depth of genuine meaning?"

He cleared his throat in an attempt to interrupt, but she was not to be thwarted. "I'll grant I have little knowledge of how society functions, but I have depths neither you nor your kind can plumb."

His face twisted with unbelief. "You cannot be serious. You cannot suppose for a moment that I consider you unworthy of any of these lapdogs. Darling…"

"Don't address me with those empty endearments you use with your friends in that sneering way. I have seen you and your ilk. I understand your contempt for acquaintances you address that way. Do not reduce our…our friendship to that."

"What do you mean my ilk?" His voice contained a warning. Closing the scant distance between them, Devlin caught her arms. Steadying her, his expression softened. He ran his hands to her shoulders and back to her elbows before shifting them to her waist.

"Our friendship? My precious little hen wit, what I feel for you is much more than friendship. You know I adore you. Admit that much, at least."

She struggled in a halfhearted attempt to free herself, but he held her fast.

"Jessica, have you no feminine instincts?" He scanned her face before his gaze settled on her full, pouting mouth. His entire body tensed in remarkable ways—in remarkable places. Surprised, he nearly retreated, but consciously commanded his hands to maintain their hold on her. He tried to rein in his emotions, passion, which, until that moment, he had been only vaguely aware existed.

Reeling, he tried to control his facial expression and his hold on her and, at the same time, examine the reason for his sudden, inexplicable, emotional instability.

Defying his will, one of his hands crept up her arm to her shoulder where it lingered a moment before it rose further to clamp her warm, firm throat.

As if not wanting to challenge his movements, she turned her head and directed her dark, tempestuous gaze to the floor.

Devlin thumbed the point of her pert little chin. Proportionately, it was too short for her face, a face with enormous eyes, the fickle color of which was concealed at the moment by lashes that lay softly on flushed cheeks.

His thoughts darted here and there like a mouse staying beyond the claws of the scullery cat. Of the men pursuing Jessica, Lattimore probably was most promising. In all fairness, however, Devlin wanted to respect Jessica's opinion and she did not favor Lattie. Feeling vaguely satisfied at that random thought, Devlin released a deep, shuddering sigh. Neither he nor Jessica spoke.

His mother opposed Jessica's betrothal to John Lout. That, of course, was a joke. John Lout did not now, nor had he ever, qualified as a mate for their beloved Nightingale.

Then who? Devlin felt genuinely perplexed as he gradually and thoughtfully released her. Dolefully, he watched as she withdrew and fluttered silently up the stairs.

• • •

The dining table was set for one when Devlin went down for supper Saturday evening.

"Where are the ladies?" he asked. Each day he looked forward to meals with his two companions. Lattie was there as often as not.

Patterson presented his usual inscrutable face, but there seemed an unusual twinkle in his eyes. "The lady Jessica requested a tray be brought to her rooms."

"I see." Devlin nodded. "She is sulking, I suppose, angry that I would not allow her to attend Benoits tonight."

Patterson stiffened slightly. "I suppose you are correct, Your Grace."

"What of my mother?"

"She, too, asked for a tray."

"She's not ill, is she?"

Patterson's smile escaped before he could pull it back under control. "No, Your Grace. In fact, she seems in particularly high spirits."

"Then why is she not dining here? With me?"

"She was involved in something and didn't want to set it aside. She even asked that the tray be delayed."

Pacing, Devlin locked his hands behind his back and strolled the length of the room before he finally sat in his lone place at the table that could accommodate as many as thirty.

He did not have much appetite, dawdled over his food, and replayed in his mind his declaration about not allowing Jessica to attend Benoits.

He would make it up to her. Only yesterday he had found a nice, dapple gray gelding to draw the jaunty black cabriolet he had purchased as a surprise for her. Jessica often took his mother out and about—with a driver, of course—in the afternoons on social excursions. He smiled, visualizing Jessica driving them in their airy little conveyance.

Jessica would never have asked for a rig of her own, but he had seen her eying the young matrons who enjoyed the independence of driving themselves, a practice that was the latest rage.

Another thought: Margolin owned a well-behaved black filly that Jessica would enjoy, tall enough to accommodate her long legs, and black, like Sweetness. They would make a handsome, pair, stallion and filly, taking the afternoon air. Devlin scowled, before he allowed a smile of surrender. Jessica had him thinking of Vindicator as Sweetness.

Grinning, he thought of the many differences the girl had brought since she exploded into their staid, well-ordered lives. He had not, of course, realized his life was dull. Now he did not know how they had managed without her.

How might they fare when she was gone? He sobered.

There was no need for her ever to be gone from them again, at least not permanently. Unless she married someone who took her far away…or she chose to return to Welter.

Those random thoughts startled him. How would they get on without her? Without her joy? When he no longer heard the staff laughing and her musical giggling in the far reaches of this house or the keep at Gull's Way?

At first those sounds had been foreign, even annoying. Later on, however, when his study grew too quiet, he would prowl about until he found their little interloper doing those many unexpected—even menial—tasks she enjoyed.

She might be in the stables admiring a new arrival or currying a horse, or digging in a garden of roses or weeding a patch of radishes, ever alert to the occasional fishing worm for a stableman or someone's child. Once he found her wading barefooted at the edge of a pond, squishing mud through her toes. Late one afternoon at Gull's Way, when a prolonged search did not produce his prey, he sought advice from a footman.

She had taken a crude wooden wagon and driven to the home of a cook's assistant to deliver a poultice. It seemed the woman's husband had cut off the tip of his finger while cleaning game.

The footman stammered as he explained that neither he nor the men in the stable felt they had the authority to prevent her going.

"I don't expect you to stop her when she decides to go off like this," Devlin said, scarcely able to control the tumult boiling in his stomach at the thought of her driving a team and rickety wagon on roads that were often little more than footpaths. He didn't finish his thought, uncertain about what he did expect them to do.

He heard chagrin in the man's voice. He himself had dealt with Jessica and not fared any better than the footman. His anger mellowed as the man tried again to explain. "You were not about, Yer Grace, to ask yer leave to abandon our regular duties."

"Yes, well, from this day on, you have my permission to escort young Jessica wherever and whenever she goes. I do not want her traipsing about the countryside alone. Heaven knows what harebrained scheme might take her wandering into trouble." He hesitated. "You must, perhaps, express it as your personal concern for her welfare. It might be better not to tell her you accompany her on my orders."

"Pardon, Yer Grace, but ye're the duke."

Devlin well remembered that his shoulders had slumped at the reminder. "Yes, I am...the duke."

"Every man of us moves at your command."

Devlin offered the footman a sheepish smile. "You know, I don't believe I properly appreciated willing compliance before Miss Blair arrived." Committing the man's voice to memory, he changed the subject. "I don't believe I know your name."

"Dolan, Yer Grace. Michael Dolan."

"How long have you been employed here, Dolan?"

"Goin' on eleven years, Yer Grace."

Devlin nodded. "Does Lady Jessica know your name, Dolan?"

"Aye, she does. She calls me Mike."

"For how long?"

"Pardon?"

"When did she begin calling you by your Christian name?"

Still at that time sightless, the duke had heard a grin in the man's tone. "The second day she was here, Yer Grace." The lightness of his manner dropped to a groan as if the man had been brought up short by something he saw in the duke's expression.

"Oh, it ain't just me. She calls everyone on the place by their given name, from the boys mucking out the barns, to the scullery gels in the kitchen. She knows little things about ever' one of us, just like she knew about Mr. Fagin's finger yesterday, not an hour after it happened." At the duke's glowering silence, Dolan continued. "The one he cut off which was the reason she decided he had need of the poultice."

"I see." The duke made an effort to relax his pinched expression.

Dolan's voice lifted as he seemed to develop sudden insight. "What ye'r asking, Yer Grace, is that we treat her gentle like without telling her ye'r the one ordered it done?"

"I believe that would be best, Dolan. Yes."

"That may not always be easy to do, Yer Grace."

On that day, Devlin had walked away muttering to himself. "An observation worthy of an Oxford man schooled in the humanities."

Distracted by his own thoughts at the otherwise empty dining table, Devlin rose before he finished his second course and went upstairs to dress. Now that he had regained his sight, he could spend the evening, as he did before, at his club. He felt oddly indifferent at the prospect.

By her absence, was Jessica punishing him for forbidding her attendance at Benoits? He didn't consider her a vindictive woman. Pondering that, he hoped in his soul that she was not.

Why had his mother taken her meal in her room as well? Certainly she was not vindictive. Sometimes, however, she tried to enlighten him by making a point with her behavior.

He consoled himself with the thought that the ladies would remain in residence this night, thus, though his method might seem harsh, he had succeeded in foiling the attempt to kidnap his Nightingale.

• • •

Devlin Miracle, the Twelfth Duke of Fornay, received a warm welcome at Dracks that evening. Many of those greeting him with rare enthusiasm quickly managed to guide the topic of conversation to the matter of his ward.

Had he received many offers for her? Had he narrowed the field? When did he think he might announce her betrothal?

He found their eagerness disconcerting and took sanctuary at a table of whist until Marcus Hardwick, Lattie's friend, strolled in shortly after ten.

"Avoiding the tables, Miracle?" Hardwick asked, his tone taunting.

"I find whist more relaxing."

"I am glad your brother has a more adventurous nature, of which I am a regular beneficiary."

Devlin smiled as the game concluded and his partner tallied the score. "Do you and Lattie gamble seriously?"

"Whimsically, Your Grace. On everything, from roaches racing the floor at Malloy's Pub, to which latecomer will order brandy."

"How does he fare?"

"Not well. He pays off regularly. Fry, on the other hand, prefers to accumulate Lattie's vouchers. He holds nearly one thousand pounds of Lattie's markers."

Devlin's light mood darkened. "Why has Fry not demanded payment?"

"He likes having Lattie obligated to him. Here, now, will you join me at the bar? I'll buy you a drink and we can discuss my friend's foibles in greater detail."

Curious, Devlin agreed, but once at the bar, Hardwick promptly opened the conversation by rhapsodizing about…Jessica.

Doubly annoyed, Devlin gulped his brandy. "Good God, man, is every bachelor in London enthralled with one thin eighteen-year-old female?"

"To a man." Hardwick appeared pleased at the question. "You would have seen the nauseating fact with your own eyes if you had been at Benoits tonight when she arrived wearing that…"

"WHAT?" Devlin's bellow drew startled looks from those at the bar and even a couple of curious fellows who glanced in from other rooms. Veins suddenly grew noticeable at his neck and temples. "You have seen her tonight? Out?"

Hardwick looked bewildered as he nodded, and retreated a step. "Yes."

"At Benoits? You are saying you saw her there with your own eyes?"

Hardwick studied his friend's brother curiously. "Yes, but she was well-chaperoned, old man. Your mother was at her side."

"WHAT?"

The amiable man-about-town eased back another pace, but the move proved unnecessary as the duke trembled in what appeared a devilish contest to bring himself under control. Devlin's eyes narrowed, his jaw muscles popped, and his fists clenched until he pivoted and executed a determined march to the exit. The expression on his face made the barman shiver involuntarily. Rumors buzzed as gentlemen asked one another and Hardwick what had prompted the duke's relapse into temper.

Hardwick replayed each word of their conversation. Men pulled writing materials from their pockets and began jotting wagers. Shortly thereafter, Dracks was virtually deserted as occupants, young and old, left for Benoits, whether they had been invited or not.

People in society had commented on how Devlin's fabled temper had mellowed following his temporary blindness. Some speculated that God had struck him blind specifically to bridle that tempestuous side of him. Others suggested it was the lady Jessica's quiet manner that had brought him to heel. There were other theories along the pendulum's swing between those two extremes.

When Lattimore and his company entered Dracks moments after the place emptied, the barkeep stared at the duke's younger brother, prompting the nobleman to interrupt a ribald story being told by one of his party.

"What's going on?" Lattimore asked, glancing through doorways at the nearly empty rooms.

"The duke just raged out of here."

"Devlin?" Lattie's expression sharpened. "What set him off?"

The barkeep stopped wiping a tankard. "The way I understand it, he and the baron, Marcus Hardwick, were discussing the girl."

Lattie nodded. "Jessica," he said, prodding. "What about her?"

"Nothing at all. Hardwick said something about how well she looked when she arrived tonight at Benoits…"

Lattimore Miracle's eyes rounded and he laughed knowingly as he turned and bolted toward the exit scrambling his entourage.

"You've gone and done it again," a straggler said, speaking to the barkeep. As they stared at one another, their faces twisted in puzzlement. Raising his voice the straggler called loudly at Lattimore's back. "Lattie, my boy, where are you going?"

Without missing a step or muffling his rousing good humor, Lattie shouted back, "To prevent a throttling."

The remaining members clustered and their voices rose as they speculated on his meaning.

Mystified, definitely intrigued, more club members moved to the exit, calling to footmen and runners at the door, summoning carriages. Something was about to erupt at Benoits and they wanted to be there to give an accurate account when asked to bear witness later.

Chapter Twenty-One

Jessica enjoyed being the most sought-after young lady in attendance. She was hard-pressed to understand why she felt haunted by a sense of doom.

Her foreboding worsened when Peter Fry stepped up to claim his dance. She went reluctantly to his arms, wondering at his reason for asking Lady Anne for a place on Jessica's card.

"Why did you insist we dance, Mr. Fry?"

"Why not?"

"You know why not. I know about your connection with John Lout and with Martha, the housemaid at Gull's Way who was," she lowered her voice, "murdered by the nobleman whose babe she carried."

"You believe I am that man?"

"Possibly. Yes."

"I am not. You are wrong. Have you voiced those wild assertions to anyone else? If so, I shall charge you with slandering my good name."

"If your name were good before, it might come away from such a hearing tainted indeed."

His fingers bit into her waist and she winced, unable to break free of his hold.

"She was a simple country girl," he said, "not a woman who mattered."

"She mattered to me."

"You, my dear, share her lack of consequence, yet you will soon be wed and beyond my concern."

"I may wed someday, but I shall remain aware of your activities, Mr. Fry."

"Then perhaps I should get rid of you the old-fashioned way."

"Murder me as you did poor, dear Martha? I think not." Her words reflected an assurance she did not feel.

"I have friends, Miss Blair, who would gladly assist should your death become necessary."

"Lattimore might add his own accusations rather than aid in your defense, Mr. Fry."

Fry gave a wicked laugh. "Lattie is in no position to oppose me. I hold his vouchers. One reminder brings him to my side. I can ruin Lattimore Miracle by demanding payment in full of what he owes me, and he is finished."

"Is that why you want Lattimore to have the title? Because you hold his markers and think them enough to control him?"

"You obviously lack proper appreciation for the power of money or the peerage, Miss Blair. You have fooled many who suppose you wiser than you are. In truth, you are more of a nuisance than an obstruction. I have a plan to see you gone."

"Devlin might not deal kindly if you murder me."

"Nothing so dramatic. My plan is underway. When you realize what has transpired, remember to credit me."

"What are you talking about?"

The music ended and Fry turned her toward the terrace displaying tender attention, as if they spoke of pleasant things rather than murder. "It's stuffy in here. Let's take some air."

She yanked hard to pull free of Fry's grasp, determined not to go anywhere with the man, and spun about directly into the arms of Donald Preston, the younger son of one of Lady Anne's close friends. A large, muscular fellow, Mr. Preston decisively pulled her into his possession.

"I believe I have the next set." Preston spoke quietly, but his eyes conveyed another message to Peter Fry, quelling the fellow's plans. Fry shrugged, threw a meaningful glare at Jessica, and stepped aside. She went weak with relief.

In the ladies' retiring room later, Jessica stared at her reflection in the mirror and wondered about her premonition. Something seemed to be charging the air. Possibly it had to do with Peter Fry. If some plan of his truly were in motion, she needed to be vigilant.

Eerily, the candles in the chandelier overhead flickered with the door opening and closing as ladies entered and left the fore chamber and, as they did, an image of Devlin's face spiraled among the reflections. If only he were here. He wouldn't be, of course. Her own presence at Benoits was defiance of his order. He probably had forgotten that ridiculous edict as soon as it was issued and he received benefit of its effect. He was only flexing his manly muscle, demonstrating his domination over women in his household. The declaration was too arbitrary to have been of actual consequence.

In spite of tales shared by the household staff, Jessica had seen little of the duke's infamous temper, certainly nothing she could not quell, if she needed to do so.

Patterson went so far as to say His Grace's close call with death or permanent injury had given him new humility and had made him a gentler man.

Others in the household suggested Devlin had become a dullard in comparison with his earlier, rowdier self. Recently, they said, instead of being the prowling predator of old, he had become as tame as a house cat.

As two women her age, new acquaintances, prepared to leave the withdrawing room, Jessica dismissed her scowl in the mirror, put an errant curl back in place, and joined them.

She was dancing by the time voices in the ballroom heightened with new excitement. Circling the floor in the rather limp embrace of a sweet, elderly contemporary of Lady Anne's, Jessica looked around to determine the cause of the uproar.

All eyes trailed to two tall, rather attractive men. Jessica assumed they were two of the older, sought-after bachelors who usually avoided preseason balls to avoid the sometimes noisy attentions of young ladies anticipating their first season.

Both of the new arrivals were attractive, she supposed, but hardly worth the attention they received. Neither compared with either of the dowager's sons. Jessica sobered as she realized that, in her opinion, both Lattie and Devlin set a high mark other men rarely approached.

The younger swains, like the novice ladies, new to the heady atmosphere of the ton and its social intercourse, lacked the sophistication and practiced boredom of the older gentlemen.

Murmuring swelled with other new arrivals. Jessica didn't bother looking. The additions likely would be surrounded by doting females, fans aflutter, at first. She could join the gawking later.

As the musicians ended the selection and Jessica's partner escorted her back to the dowager, she was aware of people looking at them. She blushed, suddenly self-conscious, as people nearby grew quiet and stared her direction.

Turning, she found herself looking down a human corridor, at the far end of which was a pair of ominous sapphire eyes staring at her from a face she nearly did not recognize. A second look verified: Devlin.

As people greeted him congenially, he glided along the makeshift corridor, looking neither right nor left, never shifting his menacing stare from Jessica's face.

She attempted a smile, but the effort wavered at his unyielding glower. What could possibly be wrong? She reached for the old earl, might have taken his arm, but he had melted into the crowd. Looking at Devlin's face, Jessica wished she might do the same, and vanish among the bystanders.

Men loitering nearby laughed nervously. Ladies pulled fans in front of their faces and giggled. Even the musicians held silent, emphasizing the murmurings of the onlookers.

Seeing no escape, Jessica stood paralyzed as Devlin's jaws tightened and his lips thinned.

When he loomed, towering over her, he stopped, so close she could feel his breath brushing the curls about her face.

"Would you care to dance?" His voice was strained.

"The next is promised to…" She could not look at her card, unable to elude his gaze for even a brief glance.

"He won't mind."

"You are certain?"

He nodded, his countenance grim. "Quite."

To her horror, the musicians struck up a waltz, requiring partners to be close.

Devlin's right hand slipped about her waist, gathering her roughly as his left caught her right too tightly.

"You do not realize your own strength, Your Grace."

"And you, my dear, do not realize your own peril."

As his mother hurried to intervene, other couples moved onto the floor and Devlin swept Jessica into a turn which might have thrust her from him, if he had not held her almost indecently close.

"Mrs. Conifer says it is not seemly, Your Grace, for a man to hold a woman thus."

She could have sworn steam issued from his ears. "Consider yourself fortunate that I am not behaving in an even more unseemly manner, my darling, and wringing your swanlike little neck."

"What?"

"Do you pretend you did not understand my order that you were not to attend this affair?"

Jessica tried to twist out of his grasp, but Devlin pressed their bodies closer in a convincing demonstration of his superior strength and, perhaps, proprietorship.

Her anger piqued, Jessica gritted her teeth and, with the next step, brought an expensive heel down hard on Devlin's foot. His biceps bulged against her breast as he lifted her feet from the floor and put his mouth against her ear. "If it's combat you want, perhaps we should retire to the terrace where there will be more space and fewer witnesses."

Before she could respond, he lowered her feet back to the floor, clamped her arm in a viselike grip, turned and nudged her along ahead of him toward the terrace doors.

As they stepped into the darkness and out of the sight of astonished observers, she yanked her arm from his hold and doubled her fists. "I will not be treated like this." Her voice carried, drawing curious stares from onlookers attempting to follow the couple outside.

Devlin flashed a hard look at bystanders and followers alike, which seemed to quench their interest and encourage them to drift quickly down the steps into the garden or retreat into the ballroom.

"Treated like what?" he asked, his voice a low hiss. "Like a scullery maid? No, I forget myself, you had not achieved that, had you? You were a scullery maid's assistant, were you not?"

She stared at him, cut by his tone as well as the hurtful words. Although she occasionally alluded to her lowly status, he had never before done so.

"At least servants treat one another civilly," she countered. "Common folks see one another clearly, unlike the nobility," she fairly spat the last two words, "who strut about pretending to be superior, as if human beings born without titles are somehow of less value. Even the most devoted servants are invisible to members of the ton."

Devlin looked as if he had been slapped. "At this moment, I wish to heaven you had remained invisible to me."

She glared at him, her blood roiling, angrier than she had ever been in her life. "As I recall, when you and I met, I was quite literally invisible to you, your haughtiness." Her voice took on an ugly, sneering quality. "You were cowering in the leaves and foliage. You did not appear superior then. You didn't bother asking if I were worthy to deliver you. You were happy enough then to welcome a scullery maid's assistant into your life."

For all his raging, arrogant disavowals, Devlin admired her, respected her, particularly as she stood there defying him, a veritable temptress of the first stare, flushing, vibrant, magnificent, swaddled as she was in righteous indignation.

Yet her words knifed into his soul and bled his spirit. When had her opinion of him become so important?

She had entered his life as his eyes and had insidiously attached herself to every vital part until he scarcely wanted to breathe without her near.

Here he stood hurling unforgivable insults at the one person who gave his life meaning.

He dropped his voice to a whisper. "Could you love me, Jessica Blair?"

She couldn't believe he had said those words at the height of their furious exchange. She must have misunderstood. "What?"

"Could you ever bring yourself to love me?"

"Don't be ridiculous."

"Are you saying you could not?" He locked his fists at his back and turned toward the shadowy forms of distant trees.

"No, you…hen wit."

Her using that ridiculous term in addressing him made him turn. Without any warning, he exploded with whoops of bellowing laughter. Hen wit! He had never before heard the term used addressing a man. The insult flew beyond reason all the way to absurd. Looking at her, he shouted noisy guffaws, releasing his rage and sending pent-up emotions into the silent night in raucous, unbounded hilarity. Jessica wore a mischievous, satisfied expression. She had committed the *faux pas* intentionally, of course, a realization that made him laugh all the harder.

Finally, as he blotted tears streaming from his eyes, he sputtered. "Did you say 'No,' meaning you could not love me, or 'No,' you could not *not* love me?"

Scarcely controlling her own hilarity, Jessica stammered as she considered how to answer the convoluted question.

When she found appropriate words and was able to speak, her answer came quietly. "Yes, Your Grace, I could and I do, though saying so defies my own best judgment."

"Love me?"

"Yes."

He started toward her, but she stopped him with an open hand. "Truly, Your Grace, I did not know anyone like you existed in the world. You set me raging one moment, in black, murderous fury. With the next word, you send me to the heights. You have me shaking with laughter in one breath, and dissolved to tears with the next."

In one fluid movement, he stepped up, wrapped his arms about her, and sealed her to his chest.

Finally, feelings incubating all these weeks had escaped, prompting her revelation and clearing the confusion between them. At last, she was where she belonged, with no pretense that this embrace was anything other than a man holding the woman he loved.

Holding her, he noticed a garden gate ajar midway down the fence that paralleled a dark side street. Devlin nudged Jessica's shoulders to turn her around and said, "Look."

Reluctant to disengage, she held fast. He clamped both hands on her shoulders and forced her to pivot until her back was spooned against the front of him. Then he put his mouth to her ear. "Do you see the open gate?"

She peered into the night. "Yes."

"What do you see beyond it?"

"A coachman on his box. The carriage door is open and the outer lanterns alight."

"Yes. That is Steen's carriage. The interior is under full wraps, as if against the weather. As you may observe, this is a fair, perhaps overly warm evening."

She nodded. "Do you wonder why the carriage is enclosed?"

"I know why. It is to muffle a lady's screams and conceal her struggle as she fights her abductors. The coachman is to go as soon as Steen and his hirelings force the man's ill-gotten prize inside."

Jessica turned unbelieving eyes on her companion. "Lord Steen is too decrepit to be a rake or a highwayman, assuming he ever was."

"He has hired help for tonight. He planned to lure you into this very garden, Nightingale."

Her eyes grew large as saucers, but he did not allow her to interrupt.

"He would take you through that gate and into that carriage, whisk you off and hold you overnight. On the morrow, I would have to accept his offer for your hand to save your reputation." Devlin released her. "Or, I could call him out and kill him, which I might be inclined to do. A duel, however, would destroy your reputation as surely as spending a night with the man."

So that's what Fry meant by his threat, and his invitation to walk with him in the garden. She turned wondering eyes to Devlin's face. "You thought to avoid all that by forbidding my attendance here?"

"Precisely."

"Whyever didn't you tell me?"

"I am not accustomed to explaining myself, Nightingale. Normally, my orders are obeyed."

"Yes, well, I'm afraid you have spoiled me to the point I no longer feel bound to obey what appear to be unreasonable commands."

"I see. Are you saying your disregard of my edict was in some way my fault?"

"One might see it that way. Yes."

"What of your declaration of love?"

She gave him an unbelieving look. "Do you think you could demand I say I love you and I would do so, if I did not? I am the same person who defied your lesser command not to attend a ball?"

He grinned. Her reasoning made perplexing sense. "Will you marry me?"

She regarded him skeptically. "Why?"

"So you may continue to live under my protection and in my homes. So you may continue knitting and reading and playing the spinet evenings with Mother and me, and live in peace, without a constant parade of suitors."

"Are those your most compelling reasons why we should wed?"

"They seem adequate. The three of us are compatible. We are comfortable together. You say you love me. You enjoy my family, my homes, the gardens and the stables. As my wife, you will share my title and may have anything money can buy."

Her chin quivered. "I already have access to your family, your homes and your holdings. You already provide all I need or want. I would not marry you for the reasons you have named."

He reached for her hand, but she sallied back. His mercurial mood took a decided turn.

"All that I possess is not enough? You say you love me. Is love not enough?"

She blinked at him and swallowed hard, but did not respond.

"You entertained thoughts of marrying John Lout, whom you did not love, a man who could not give you any of the things I can. Do you deny my suit because I offer you the world?" He looked genuinely perplexed.

Swiping at determined tears, Jessica did not answer. Her chin dimpled. She turned back toward the ballroom. Devlin growled unseemly words as he pivoted to follow her inside.

His frustration became full-blown rage when he met Lord Steen sauntering up the terrace steps from the garden, trying to appear casual as he scanned the area. Devlin's voice was menacing. "I will murder you here with my own two hands if you advance one step more in her direction."

Those within the sound of his words withdrew several paces. The Duke of Fornay's infamous temper obviously was restored to its legendary vehemence and unleashed.

Steen pivoted on the ball of one gouty foot and limped back down the garden steps without casting a glance toward Jessica who stood unmoving in the doorway, looking for all the world like the statue of some beautiful, tragic Greek goddess.

Chapter Twenty-Two

As he roused from a restless sleep the next morning, Devlin nursed the devil of a headache and wondered if he were quite sane. He had run an emotional gauntlet the previous night; from raging fury to delirious joy, and back to ire before being plunged into a debilitating funk which grew worse through the morning.

"You are a duke, Your Grace," Lattimore reminded him solemnly. "You cannot marry an undowered, untitled wench. It is unconscionable."

"It is because I am a duke that I can marry anyone I damn well please." Leaning one arm on the mantle, Devlin propped a careless foot on an andiron that extended from the firebox a little distance onto the hearth. "Jessica is, however, well dowered, admittedly by me. Several of the most important, titled, most eligible bachelors in town have offered for her. Mine will simply be the suit I accept."

Lattie looked as if he might smile, then stanched the grin that almost broke his gloomy facade. "What if she won't have you?"

Devlin gave an astonished shout. "Give me one credible reason why she would not have me?" The duke's anguish indicated his question was one he genuinely wanted someone to answer.

Seeing smoke curl from the sole of his boot, Devlin abruptly lifted his foot from the andiron and stamped the foot on the stone hearth.

Lattie smiled, but sobered quickly not willing to risk Devlin seeing his good humor. "Because, in the practical ways of the world, Jessica is wiser than you. She knows such a union likely will not succeed."

Studying his foot as if trying to decide if he should remove the boot, Devlin said, "I thought she demonstrated great wisdom when she declined your offer, Lattimore. Surely her refusal then is not the basis for your opinion. Are you jealous that I might succeed where you failed?" Devlin peered at his brother's face a moment before turning his attention back to his smoldering shoe.

Both men looked toward the doorway when they heard a feminine sneeze on the staircase. Lattimore slanted his brother a wicked smile. "Why don't we pose your questions to her, Your Grace, and end our speculations."

Devlin scowled before he arched his brows, shrugged, and nodded. He could not reconcile the girl's response to his proposal with her earlier admission that she loved him.

Jessica entered the room, glanced at the brothers, then looked to the wing-backed chair the dowager duchess would have occupied had she been present. Seeing the chair empty, Jessica smiled at both men, then turned back to the corridor.

"A moment, if you please, Jessica." Devlin's words stopped her. She came around slowly. Her eyes were puffy and red, as if she had been crying, but her voice gave no indication anything was amiss.

"Yes, Your Grace. How may I be of service?"

"Take a moment to settle an argument between Lattimore and me."

"All right." She allowed a tolerant smile as she looked from one brother to the other.

Lattie was definitely the prettier of the two, with smooth, rosy cheeks and a delicate—even perky—nose and chin. If a woman were blessed with Lattie's coloring, she would never need rouge. His eyelashes, like his raven hair, were enviable. She had heard ladies lauding his many physical attributes.

Although he was tall enough, Lattimore had a sturdier bone structure than his older brother. His hair was dark, apparently like his father's and his eyes hazel. Taken altogether, he gave a pleasing appearance.

In contrast, Devlin stood taller but more stooped, as if the weight of his title was burdensome. He had the more distinctive, marvelous build. The duke had inherited his mother's thick, fair hair with its curls, and the almost incandescent blue eyes, although the color of his irises darkened dramatically when he was angry, as Jessica had cause to know.

"Please, sit with us a moment," Devlin said, directing Jessica to his mother's wingback near the hearth. Without objection, she sat as directed and arranged her skirts. The duke motioned Lattimore onto a Chesterfield and he, himself, eased into a rather severe ladder-back chair directly across from Jessica.

Even after they were settled, Devlin delayed a moment. "Jessica, have you considered it is time—past time, actually—that you married?"

She regarded him coolly. "You, sir, are the greatest impediment to my marrying."

He cleared his throat, was tempted to look at Lattimore, but dared not let his attention wander.

"I am not referring to your betrothal to John Lout, darling. I was thinking of someone infinitely more suitable to the poised, charming young lady you have become."

Her eyes narrowed and she watched him suspiciously before risking a glance at Lattimore, then back. "You have turned away a dozen suitors who have or eventually might have offered for me, Your Grace."

"What about someone you have known for a while?"

"Lattimore does not love me and, although I admire him, I do not love him either. I do not consider him a fit husband for me."

"I am not talking about Lattie, Jessica, and you know it."

"Then who?" Her voice broke slightly, but noticeably. "Not Mr. Hardwick, Your Grace, or that scoundrel Peter Fry, no matter how impressive their family holdings." Suddenly she pulled to the edge of her chair, preparing to stand and perhaps to flee. "I will not do it, Devlin. Except for the wealth, I see little difference between my selling myself to John Lout or your bartering me to a future baron or even an earl."

To allay her increasing discomfort, Devlin sat back a little in his chair and tried to look at ease. "Actually, Nightingale, as I mentioned last night, I thought you might do well to marry me."

Silence enveloped the room as fog might have enshrouded their images, veiling the innermost workings of their hearts and thoughts from one another.

Jessica frowned hard at Devlin as both men steadied their gazes on her. Slowly a smile lifted the corners of her mouth. "Sir, you are far too old and too grand a match for me. As you so eloquently reminded me last night, you are a duke and I a scullery maid."

"A scullery maid's assistant," he corrected, returning her quiet little smile.

She cut her eyes from his. "Have none of the other gallants, ones closer to my own age, perhaps second sons without hopes of a title, offered for me?"

"They have."

"Do you not see yourself better served by palming me off on one of those?"

He chuckled and glanced at his boots, before raising his eyes to lock with hers. "As usual, you are most perceptive and probably right. Yes, such would definitely be the wiser course." He smiled warmly. "But how could I live with my conscience, having misled one of those callow youths who thought he was acquiring a docile, obedient lady when, in fact, you are neither obedient nor a lady?"

She laughed. "If this your idea of a proper way to woo a wife, Your Grace, it's little wonder you remain unattached. Perhaps you should consult with someone about sweet words spoken by men to women. Mrs. Conifer, my duenna, would consider your methods in need of repair."

He smiled for a moment before his face became grave. "I am serious, Jessica. I want us to discuss this calmly and intelligently. Are you saying you have no desire to be my duchess?"

"That is precisely what I am saying. I have no desire to be anyone's duchess."

He frowned, taken aback and obviously perplexed.

She lowered her voice. "I have never aspired to any title. In truth, Your Grace, as you have reminded on several occasions, I lack the qualifications to be either your duchess or your wife."

His expression softened. "You are mistaken, my dear. You qualify quite nicely. You meet all the requirements. With very little help, you have learned to ride and play the spinet. You make quite a nice appearance. You run this household and handle the servants enviably, as if they were your kin. You show compassion that inspires fierce loyalty among family and friends, including the dowager duchess, a duke's younger brother, and the master himself."

"Fierce loyalty? Is that what I inspire in you?"

A glimmer of understanding niggled at him. "That and much more, Nightingale."

Rather than allow herself to harken back to his demonstrations of prurient interest, she stood abruptly. "Thank you, sir, for the lovely words. I shall remember them always." She ducked her head, but as she bolted for the door, Devlin was on his feet and there ahead of her, catching her upper arm in a viselike grip before she could make good her escape.

"What is it, Jessica? What troubles you? Tell me and I will make amends. I have no idea how I offended you last evening. I obviously have done it again, even now."

Tears stung her eyes, but she fought for control, at least until she could break free and flee to a safe haven. She tried to jerk her arm from his grasp, but he held fast and bent over, trying to see her face, to read her expression. "Dear Nightingale, tell me what is amiss and I will make it right."

Hurried footsteps preceded the dowager duchess in the corridor. Quickly, she appraised the scene before her.

"Devlin, what in heaven's name are you about?" She nudged her way between Devlin and Jessica, forcing him to release her. "What manner of ruffian have you become?" Pulling Jessica close, the duchess wrapped both arms protectively around her protégée and began clucking and petting her like a mother hen preening her chick.

Devlin yielded, casting fleeting, mystified glances from one woman to the other as he watched Jessica being shuttled to the stairs and up.

Returning to stand at the hearth, he glanced at Lattie's face. Instead of the triumphant look he expected, his brother looked thoughtful and maybe concerned. Devlin pursed his mouth. "How do you think it went?"

Lattie hesitated, then his expression lifted with a sympathetic smile. "Probably as well as two men might have expected."

"My proposal made her cry."

"At least she didn't dissolve into those embarrassing, hiccoughing sobs as some women might have done."

Devlin looked toward the empty staircase. "No, she didn't, did she? She exhibited exemplary control." He remained thoughtful a moment. "They both did, actually."

"Perhaps we should be grateful."

"I think Mother is going to have more to offer on the subject."

Lattimore laughed. "She did look rather fierce, didn't she?"

Devlin gave a twisted smile. "Rather."

"Do you think we shall be safe in our beds?"

"You might want to bolt your door."

Both men smiled nervously before Lattimore sobered. "We may have miscalculated."

"In what way?"

"I didn't realize…"

"What?" Devlin looked and sounded sincere.

"That she loves you so terribly."

Devlin turned to look again toward the stairway. "You are not referring to our mother, are you?"

"No, you imbecile. I mean Jessica, of course."

"She said as much last night—that she loved me. Later and again this morning, she seems to have changed her mind."

"No. She definitely adores you."

"How can you tell?"

"Your casual comments cut her too deeply. Obviously your proposal meant more to her than I imagined. I have seen her fend off zealous suitors. She does so in a lighthearted manner, each time the subject of matrimony rears its head, regardless of who is plighting his troth. This time her reaction was entirely different. This time it was important to her."

"Then why did she refuse?"

"It is one of those peculiarities of the feminine mind—one of those idiosyncrasies few men can fathom—that seems to be impeding her."

"How shall I know what troubles if she will not tell me?"

Lattie shook his head and shrugged.

"How shall I to know how to proceed?"

Lattie gave his brother an unbelieving look. "Is this truly the great Devlin Miracle, the man who has left highways and byways strewn with the broken hearts of highborn and lowborn ladies alike, asking advice on love from me?"

Devlin blinked at the flame burning low in the firebox. "Yes, well, the feelings of none of those ladies were as important to me as this one unpretentious little maid."

"I can see that." Lattie looked properly concerned. "Perhaps you should seek guidance from the dowager."

"If she is even speaking to me."

Lattie laughed. "If she is speaking to either of us."

Chapter Twenty-Three

That afternoon, rumors ran rampant through kitchens of the ton. Peter Fry had been shot dead. Lord Robert Steen was being questioned regarding the matter. Members of Steen's household confirmed that the two apparently had been involved in some business transaction that went awry. Fry had come to the earl's home after Benoits' ball to confront him. The two argued loudly in the earl's study before shots were fired and Fry lay dead. Steen insisted his visitor fired first and he was only defending himself and his home from the Fry's vicious attack.

. . .

When the Dowager, both of her sons, and Jessica gathered for supper at the usual time, Devlin and Lattimore Miracle saw no remnant of the emotional upheaval they had witnessed earlier. Rather, Jessica appeared smiling and collected, as did the dowager, although the older woman's smiles and behavior were not quite as convincing.

During supper, they conversed about the usual inconsequential matters—the weather, upcoming balls and theater performances. When Devlin addressed Jessica directly over dessert, he would have sworn the others at the table held their breath.

"Jessica, I have a little gift for you."

"Oh?" She appeared to look through him.

"It is a small necessity I planned to present for your birthday, but that being so distant, I decided to give it to you early."

"How kind of you."

He turned his attention back to his fruit. Jessica exchanged curious glances with the dowager and with Lattie, both of whom shrugged indicating they were not privy to the surprise.

When no one else inquired, Jessica spoke up. "Where is it?"

Devlin looked at her as if puzzled by the question, then his feigned puzzlement turned into a knowing smile. "Nearby."

"When do you plan to give me this bauble?"

He grinned. "Soon. Perhaps in the morning after breakfast, if you are a good girl and eat all your porridge, and…" He stopped, taunting her.

"And what, Your Grace?"

"If you show proper respect toward your betters."

"Have I ever been disrespectful to you, Your Grace?"

He choked on a laugh. "Well, let's see. You were unrepentantly rude at our first meeting and have continued in that attitude off and on throughout our acquaintance. Only yesterday," he paused, "ah, yes, and again this very morning, when I took my heart in my hand and proposed, you hurled my sincerest feelings back in my face. I think my reply should be when have you ever been respectful to me for more than half a day?"

The dowager's eyes rounded and she stuffed a napkin to her mouth, muffling a choking cough.

Devlin looked at his mother. "Are you quite well, madam?"

She nodded but kept her eyes averted, her mouth covered, and declined to speak.

Lattie seemed to be having difficulty with his last mouthful of the compote, using his napkin to blot his mouth also.

Jessica's face hardened. "Your sincerest feelings, sir? You have no feelings where I am concerned. You have bullied me from our beginning. You are a spoiled, demanding aristocrat." She spoke the last as if it were the epitome of insults. After a moment to gather her thoughts, she continued. "You toy with me as if I were not born to feelings as you and other members of the nobility were. It's true, I could not afford luxuries like sensitivity before I met you. You provided me that and now you plague me as a cat plays with a mouse, allowing me no place to run."

"What in heaven's name are you talking about?"

"I mean that having been spoiled and coddled as you have insisted I be spoiled and coddled, I can scarcely go back to my old life in Maxwell's kitchens. Before, I planned to wait until the time my mum didn't need me anymore, pay myself free of John Lout, and make a new life. I planned to earn a respectable living in business or as a teacher or a governess. You have spoiled me even for that. How can I ever be at home anywhere else after having lived with...what I mean to say is...here...in...in...this?"

She sputtered and swiped at a telltale tear seeping from one eye as she awkwardly scrambled to her feet. "How can I teach someone else's children and deprive myself of the joy, of the reward of rearing and of influencing my own children? How can I...?"

As she started for the door, Devlin leaped to his feet. The dowager motioned Lattimore to remain where he was.

This time, however, Jessica flew to the stairs and was halfway to the top before Devlin caught her skirts. She stopped, mopping her face with a tiny lace handkerchief, keeping her back to him. He hesitated a moment to let her compose herself before he gave two tugs at her skirt. Her shoulders shook as she choked on a sob.

Devlin tugged again, moving up a step, placing himself directly behind her.

"Jessica," he whispered. "Darling?" He paused, allowing her another moment, then said, "My own, most precious, Nightingale?"

She whirled and the pain in her face almost shattered his resolve, but he plunged ahead anyway. He had little left to lose. His pride was already in shambles.

"When I proposed earlier, I failed to mention what may be a rather pertinent aspect of the thing. I love you, you know."

Her eyes glistened and her mouth quivered, bowing at the ends. Seeing he had achieved an advantage, he added. "To distraction, actually."

She blinked, trying to clear her eyes. "Oh, Your Grace, whyever didn't you say so?"

She opened her arms and, from a step below her, he slid easily into her clutches, their faces at the same level. Her tears wet the whole side of his face as she crushed hers to his in a violent collision. He looked heavenward and began laughing. Once begun, he couldn't seem to stop the rolling, rumbling hilarity.

He could foresee that in the years ahead, the woman probably truly would drive him to distraction—her word—still, he would rather face every riotous calamity with her at his side than live a single tranquil day without her.

• • •

As the four of them, Devlin, Lattimore, Jessica, and the dowager duchess, sat in the duke's study later, the matriarch smiled at her elder son.

"What is the present you are to bestow in the morning, Devlin?"

"A stylish black filly." He glanced at Jessica who sat by his side on the divan. "I thought Jessica's love of horses would somehow translate to me. I had no idea what prevented her agreeing to marry me."

His mother shook her head. "How could you possibly propose marriage, Devlin, and fail to speak the most important words any bride simply must hear?"

He stretched an arm across Jessica's lap and marveled aloud. "Naturally, I assumed she knew I loved her. Why else would I ask her to be my wife?"

"Why, indeed," the dowager huffed. "After all our discussions about arranged, loveless marriages among the nobility, how could you not know she needed to hear those words above all?"

"Is that what made John Lout's troth superior to mine?" he asked, raising Jessica's face so their gazes met.

She gave him a watery smile. "You often mentioned that though I did not love him, I seriously considered John's suit. You did not ask why."

"The reason being because he loved you?"

"That he declared he loved me, shouting it loudly, embarrassingly, to the world. I concluded long ago that the best thing in this world for any woman is to be married to a man who adores her. I saw with my own parents what happens when a woman loves a man more than he loves her. My mother was shattered, her love flung back in her face time and again. I vowed that would never happen to me. What I did not understand about my mother's situation was the overweening power of love. With you, I was tempted into my mother's trap. It was a constant struggle not to yield to your will in the matter based entirely on my own passion, but I kept pounding into my mind the images of a family abandoned, denied a husband and father's love or support."

"You did not know my feelings for you?"

"You never set them to words. How could I anticipate what you admittedly did not know yourself for a long while?"

"And now?"

"You spoke the words, not only to me, but in front of highly credible witnesses."

"My mother and my brother?"

"Yes."

"You found that more convincing than if I had spoken the words to you privately?"

She gave him a sheepish smile. "In Welter, a man often makes such declarations trying to convince a girl to meet him in a barn after dark or to bake him an apple pie."

Devlin arched his brows. "Sound reasons, indeed."

She and the dowager laughed lightly. "As a man, you naturally would think so, but in the past you have had women eager for clandestine meetings with you at inns or taverns or places of your choosing. That is correct, is it not?"

He flashed an uneasy glance at his mother. "Well, yes, but I have excellent cooks who produce apple pies at my request."

Her expression darkened. "So, exactly why is it you need me?"

He looked deeply into her eyes. "To keep me alert, of course, and, perhaps, eventually," he cast a quick glance at his mother, "to produce a little Miracle or two, or six—heirs to the title and others to share his responsibilities."

Jessica blushed. "If I agree to that, sir, I shall expect your indulgence until we produce at least one little girl. This family could do with another female or two."

"A daughter, eh?" He smiled at the delight in his mother's face. "Perhaps we shall produce several of those. I will have to insist on naming the first little girl after the first woman I ever loved outside my own family."

Jessica looked crestfallen.

He grinned wickedly. "I will name her Nightingale. Nightingale Miracle?"

And Jessica Blair, Devlin Miracle's unrepentant, much adored Nightingale, married the Twelfth Duke of Fornay.

Like the prior Duchess, Jessica was disappointed at first to produce only sons, three in a row. With characteristic determination, she finally gave birth to a daughter, a winsome little girl who bore her mother's dark coiling hair, petite yet captivating chin, and gray eyes. True to his word, her father insisted they christen her, "the lyrical Miracle, Nightingale."

About the Author

Once a newspaper reporter, Sharon Ervin has a degree in journalism from the University of Oklahoma. She now works half days in her husband and son's law office in McAlester, Oklahoma, and spends the balance of her workdays writing novels. Ten of those have now been published.

Ervin's writing stems from observing human behavior. She contends that truth is stranger than fiction because fiction requires some measure of believability, whereas human behavior often defies it.

Ervin is married and has four grown children.

24371447R10192

Made in the USA
Middletown, DE
22 September 2015